Lion Time in Timbuctoo

Robert Silverberg was born in New York in 1935. He sold his first novel while still a student at Columbia University, and has been a full-time writer since graduation. He has published more than fifty novels as well as serious works of history and archaeology, and has been nominated for more awards for his fiction than any other science fiction writer, alive or dead. He and his wife now live in San Francisco.

D1493996

Voyager

The Collected Stories of Robert Silverberg

Volume Six: Lion Time in Timbuctoo

HarperCollins*Publishers*

Voyager
An Imprint of HarperCollins*Publishers*
77-85 Fulham Palace Road,
Hammersmith, London W6 8JB

www.voyager-books.com

A Paperback Original 2000
1 3 5 7 9 8 6 4 2

Copyright © Agberg Ltd 2000
For further copyright details see Acknowledgments

A catalogue record for this book
is available from the British Library

ISBN 0 00 651220 8

Typeset in Times by Palimpsest Book Production Limited,
Polmont, Stirlingshire

Printed and bound in Great Britain by
Caledonian International Book Manufacturing Ltd, Glasgow

For

Kevin Anderson

Greg Bear

Gregory Benford

Janet Berliner

Ellen Datlow

Gardner Dozois

Martin H. Greenberg

Kim Mohan

Byron Preiss

And – of course – Alice K. Turner

Acknowledgments

'Lion Time in Timbuctoo' first appeared in *Isaac Asimov's Science Fiction Magazine*.

'A Tip on a Turtle' first appeared in *Amazing Stories*.

'In the Clone Zone' first appeared in *Playboy*.

'Hunters in the Forest' first appeared in *Omni*.

'A Long Night's Vigil at the Temple' first appeared in *After the King*, edited by Martin H. Greenberg.

'It Comes and Goes' first appeared in *Playboy*.

'Looking for the Fountain' first appeared in *Isaac Asimov's Science Fiction Magazine*.

'The Way to Spook City' first appeared in *Playboy*.

'The Red Blaze is the Morning' first appeared in *New Legends*, edited by Greg Bear.

'Death Do Us Part' first appeared in *Omni On-Line*.

'The Invasion Diaries of Henry James' first appeared in *The War of the Worlds: Global Dispatches*, edited by Kevin J. Anderson.

'Crossing into the Empire' first appeared in *David Copperfield's Beyond Imagination*.

'The Second Shield' first appeared in *Playboy*.

Contents

Introduction

The stories in this volume were written between October of 1989 and February of 1995 – the second half of the fourth decade of my career as a science-fiction writer. I don't think I could have imagined, when I began that career in the early 1950s, that science-fiction publishing would evolve the way it did over the next forty years.

Science fiction was small-time stuff, back there in the first years of President Eisenhower's era. There were forty or fifty writers, maybe, who strove to amuse an audience (largely made up of boys and young men) that could not have amounted to as many as a hundred thousand people. The bulk of the science fiction that was published in those days appeared in magazine form: fifteen or twenty existed at any one time, usually, most of them little scruffy things, printed on cheap paper, with names like *Marvel Science Fiction*, *Dynamic Science Fiction*, *Planet Stories*, and *Thrilling Wonder Stories*. They had garish covers and paid the writers next to nothing, but you could live pretty well on next to nothing then, if you raked in those next-to-nothing checks often enough. It was an era of deft and prolific writers – Philip K. Dick, Robert Sheckley, Poul Anderson, Gordon R. Dickson, Philip Jose Farmer, and many more, including, by 1954, the very young Robert Silverberg.

We all read every magazine and kept up to date on all of our colleagues' work; we knew the editors and their quirks; we all knew each other, too, since most of us were clustered either in the New York area or in and around Los Angeles. Professional science-fictiondom back then was like a small town. (With a small town's proclivity for soap-opera sexuality, too: most of our marriages were tenuous things and the rate of marital breakup and rearrangement was quite extraordinary. X, after divorcing his wife Y so that she could marry Z, would marry B's former wife Q, who also had been formerly married to P, who now was married to C's ex-wife J, and so on and so on around the circle in dizzying fashion. I was just a little too young, then, to have become involved in all that.)

Life would have been considerably less hectic if we could have written a book or two a year instead of having to churn out ten or twenty short stories, but there was no real market for science fiction in book form in the early 1950s. A couple of hardcover publishers and one or two paperback houses did have something like regular science-fiction programs – a book or two a month – but they concentrated mainly on reprinting material by the best-known authors that had previously appeared in the magazines – Bradbury's *Martian Chronicles*, Asimov's *Caves of Steel*, Heinlein's *Puppet Masters*. For most of us, proposing a new novel to a publisher and walking away with a nice contract simply wasn't possible.

Nor did Hollywood have much to offer. Nowadays we see a new hundred-million-dollar-budget science-fiction epic opening every few weeks, but the sf movies of the 50s were few and far between – *Destination Moon*, *When Worlds Collide*, *This Island Earth* – and no vast sums were lavished on them by their makers. Television offered the creaky kiddie show Captain Video and not much else.

How different it all is today, as television bristles with a dozen different sf shows a week, crowds swarm the movie theaters to see the latest futuristic special-effects extravaganza, and hundreds and even thousands of science-fiction and fantasy novels pour from the presses every year (the most successful of them linked to television or movie sources). Books and movies and television have become the essence of the thing; the old-fashioned science-fiction magazine is all but extinct and short story-writing is a marginal activity pursued mainly by beginners, part-time professionals, and sentimental oldsters like me. It's not something that one does for the money, because there's not really any money in it. The rates per word that the sf magazines pay for their material have actually declined over the last forty years, after adjustment for inflation. (In some cases, magazines are paying the *same* word rates in absolute dollars that we were getting back in the fifties!) And although by 1990 magazines like *Playboy* and *Omni* were paying ten and even twenty times as much for short stories as the highest-paying magazines of 1955 were able to offer, they were buying no more than one or two stories a month, hardly enough to keep a population of hungry freelancers in bagels, and not even *Playboy*'s lofty fees were really that much superior to those of the old days, after adjustment for inflation.

But, as I've said in other volumes in this series, money is not the only or even the primary reason why people write science fiction, and I have kept on writing short stories all these years, if only to keep my hand in, a story or two a year, more than that if someone comes to me with a tempting project, some anthology with an interesting theme, perhaps. Some writers – me, for example – are prone to have quite a few story ideas a year, but writing quite a few novels a year is hardly a feasible proposition. (And some good story ideas simply aren't suitable for development to novel length, anyway, though they make lovely short stories.)

Here, then, is the cream of the Silverberg output, 1989-95. I suppose I wrote more short stories in the first six months of 1957 than in that entire six-year period; but so be it. It's a different world today. I look back nostalgically on the small-town atmosphere of the era in which I began my career, and there are times when I'd be glad to 'call back yesterday, bid time return'. As Shakespeare pointed out, though, that can't be done. The one recourse is the one I have chosen, which is to soldier staunchly onward through the years, come what may, writing a story or two here and a book there, while the world changes out of all recognition around me. And so – to leap neatly from the Bard of Avon to F. Scott Fitzgerald – 'so we beat on, boats against the current, borne back ceaselessly into the past.'

– Robert Silverberg
Oakland, California

Lion Time in Timbuctoo

The late 1980s were the golden age of that strange publishing phenomenon, the shared-world anthology. The notion was for one science-fiction or fantasy writer to propose a scenario depicting some concept that he had developed, and for other writers then to set stories in the universe of that scenario.

It wasn't a new concept, writing to a common fictional background. *The Petrified Planet*, a book that appeared back in 1952, made use of an extraterrestial-world scenario devised by Dr John D. Clark that the writers Fletcher Pratt, H. Beam Piper, and Judith Merril developed into separate stories. I edited several such shared-world three-novella books in the early 1970s; Harlan Ellison produced the spectacular Medea anthology a few years later; and Robert Asprin launched the highly successful fantasy series *Thieves' World* not long after that. So popular were the Asprin books that every publisher soon was casting about for an imitative series.

It was hard for any active writer of the time to resist the siren call of the shared world. I involved myself in a number of the new series, and even walked away with two Hugos for my participation, one in 1987 for 'Gilgamesh in the Outback' from the Heroes in Hell series, and one in 1990 for 'Enter a Soldier' from my own Time Gate series. By then I was beginning to tire of the whole idea of working this way, since many of the newer shared-world projects were haphazardly conceived and hazily edited and the results were less than admirable. But before I quit the game I assembled one more shared-world book of my own devising, the anthology *Beyond the Gate of Worlds*, which Tor Books would publish in 1991. I based it on an alternate-history novel I had written nearly thirty years before, *The Gate of Worlds*, the premise of which was that the Black Death of 1348 had wiped out nearly all the population of Western Europe instead of just one fourth, and that the survivors had been unable to resist the westward march of the expansionist Ottoman Turks. All of Europe thus had become Turkish-speaking and Moslem; the Renaissance had never happened; nor had the European conquest of the New World and Africa taken place, and the Aztec and Inca empires had remained intact on into the twentieth century, as had the black kingdoms of Africa.

The Gate of Worlds itself was the story of the adventures of a young British boy in Aztec North America. I had intended it to be the first of a trilogy, with the second volume taking place in Africa and the third in England, but I never did get around to writing the other two books. The basic story situation, though, remained in my mind and continued to tempt me. And so, in October, 1989, I finally did get to tell the African part of the story, by writing the first third of *The Gate of Worlds* shared-world anthology myself – the novella 'Lion Time in Timbuctoo'. (Chelsea Quinn Yarbro and John Brunner did the other two sections of the book.) *Asimov's Science Fiction* published my story in magazine form, and Axolotl Press of Oregon did it as a one-volume limited-edition book, both prior to its publication in the Tor anthology. In all those forms the story is unavailable today, so here it is once more. I admire it for its evocation of place and for what I think is a successful depiction of life in the capital of a powerful African kingdom of a considerably altered twentieth century.

In the dry stifling days of early summer the Emir lay dying, the king, the imam, Big Father of the Songhay, in his cool dark mud-walled palace in the Sankore quarter of Old Timbuctoo. The city seemed frozen, strange though it was to think of freezing in this season of killing heat that fell upon you like a wall of hot iron. There was a vast stasis, as though everything were entombed in ice. The river was low and sluggish, moving almost imperceptibly in its bed with scarcely more vigor than a sick weary crocodile. No one went out of doors, no one moved indoors, everyone sat still, waiting for the old man's death and praying that it would bring the cooling rains.

In his own very much lesser palace alongside the Emir's, Little Father sat still like all the rest, watching and waiting. His time was coming now at last. That was a sobering thought. How long had he been the prince of the realm? Twenty years? Thirty? He had lost count. And now finally to rule, now to be the one who cast the omens and uttered the decrees and welcomed the caravans and took the high seat in the Great Mosque. So much toil, so much responsibility: but the Emir was not yet dead. Not yet. Not quite.

'Little Father, the ambassadors are arriving.'

In the arched doorway stood Ali Pasha, bowing, smiling. The vizier's face, black as ebony, gleamed with sweat, a dark moon shining against the lighter darkness of the vestibule. Despite his name, Ali Pasha was pure Songhay, black as sorrow, blacker by far than Little Father, whose blood was mixed with that of would-be conquerors of years gone by. The aura of the power that soon would be his was glistening and crackling around Ali Pasha's head like midwinter lightning: for Ali Pasha was the future Grand Vizier, no question of it. When Little Father became king, the old Emir's officers would resign and retire. An Emir's ministers did not hold office beyond his reign. In an earlier time they would have been lucky to survive the old Emir's death at all.

Little Father, fanning himself sullenly, looked up to meet his vizier's insolent grin.

'Which ambassadors, Ali Pasha?'

'The special ones, here to attend Big Father's funeral. A Turkish. A Mexican. A Russian. And an English.'

'An English? Why an English?'

'They are a very proud people, now. Since their independence. How could they stay away? This is a very important death, Little Father.'

'Ah. Ah, of course.' Little Father contemplated the fine wooden Moorish grillwork that bedecked the doorway. 'Not a Peruvian?'

'A Peruvian will very likely come on the next riverboat, Little Father. And a Maori one, and they say a Chinese. There will probably be others also. By the end of the week the city will be filled with dignitaries. This is the most important death in some years.'

'A Chinese,' Little Father repeated softly, as though Ali Pasha had said an ambassador from the Moon was coming. A Chinese! But yes, yes, this was a very important death. The Songhay Empire was no minor nation. Songhay controlled the crossroads of Africa; all caravans journeying between desert north and tropical south must pass through Songhay. The Emir of Songhay was one of the grand kings of the world.

Ali Pasha said acidly, 'The Peruvian hopes that Big Father will last until the rains come, I suppose. And so he takes his time getting here. They are people of a high country, these Peruvians. They aren't accustomed to our heat.'

'And if he misses the funeral entirely, waiting for the rains to come?'

Ali Pasha shrugged. 'Then he'll learn what heat really is, eh, Little Father? When he goes home to his mountains and tells the Grand Inca that he didn't get here soon enough, eh?' He made a sound that was something like a laugh, and Little Father, experienced in his vizier's sounds, responded with a gloomy smile.

'Where are these ambassadors now?'

'At Kabara, at the port hostelry. Their riverboat has just come in. We've sent the royal barges to bring them here.'

'Ah. And where will they stay?'

'Each at his country's embassy, Little Father.'

'Of course. Of course. So no action is needed from me at this time concerning these ambassadors, eh, Ali Pasha?'

'None, Little Father.' After a pause the vizier said, 'The Turk has brought his daughter. She is very handsome.' This with a rolling of the eyes, a baring of the teeth. Little Father felt a pang of appetite, as Ali Pasha had surely intended. The vizier knew his prince very well, too. 'Very handsome, Little Father! In a white way, you understand.'

'I understand. The English, did he bring a daughter too?'

'Only the Turk,' said Ali Pasha.

'Do you remember the Englishwoman who came here once?' Little Father asked.

'How could I forget? The hair like strands of fine gold. The breasts like milk. The pale pink nipples. The belly-hair down below, like fine gold also.'

Little Father frowned. He had spoken often enough to Ali Pasha about the Englishwoman's milky breasts and pale pink nipples. But he had no recollection of having described to him or to anyone else the golden hair down below. A rare moment of carelessness, then, on Ali Pasha's part; or else a bit of deliberate malice, perhaps a way of testing Little Father. There were risks in that for Ali Pasha, but surely Ali Pasha knew that. At any rate it was a point Little Father

8

chose not to pursue just now. He sank back into silence, fanning himself more briskly.

Ali Pasha showed no sign of leaving. So there must be other news.

The vizier's glistening eyes narrowed. 'I hear they will be starting the dancing in the marketplace very shortly.'

Little Father blinked. Was there some crisis in the king's condition, then? Which everyone knew about but him?

'The death dance, do you mean?'

'That would be premature, Little Father,' said Ali Pasha unctuously. 'It is the life dance, of course.'

'Of course. I should go to it, in that case.'

'In half an hour. They are only now assembling the formations. You should go to your father, first.'

'Yes. So I should. To the Emir, first, to ask his blessing; and then to the dance.'

Little Father rose.

'The Turkish girl,' he said. 'How old is she, Ali Pasha?'

'She might be eighteen. She might be twenty.'

'And handsome, you say?'

'Oh, yes. Yes, very handsome, Little Father!'

There was an underground passageway connecting Little Father's palace to that of Big Father; but suddenly, whimsically, Little Father chose to go there by the out-of-doors way. He had not been out of doors in two or three days, since the worst of the heat had descended on the city. Now he felt the outside air hit him like the blast of a furnace as he crossed the courtyard and stepped into the open. The whole city was like a smithy these days, and would be for weeks and weeks more, until the rains came. He was used to it, of course, but he had never come to like it. No one ever came to like it except the deranged and the very holy, if indeed there was any difference between the one and the other.

Emerging onto the portico of his palace, Little Father looked out on the skyline of flat mud roofs before him, the labyrinth of alleys and connecting passageways, the towers of the mosques, the walled mansions of the nobility. In the hazy distance rose the huge modern buildings of the New City. It was late afternoon, but that brought no relief from the heat. The air was heavy, stagnant, shimmering. It vibrated like a live thing. All day long the myriad whitewashed walls had been soaking up the heat, and now they were beginning to give it back.

Atop the vibration of the air lay a second and almost tangible vibration, the tinny quivering sound of the musicians tuning up for the dance in the marketplace. The life dance, Ali Pasha had said. Perhaps so; but Little Father would not be surprised to find some of the people dancing the death dance as well, and still others dancing the dance of the changing of the king. There was little linearity of time in Old Timbuctoo; everything tended to happen at once. The death of the old king and the ascent of the new one were simultaneous affairs, after all: they were one event. In some countries, Little Father knew, they used to kill the king when he grew sick and feeble, simply to hurry things along. Not here, though. Here they danced him out, danced the new king in. This was a civilized land. An ancient kingdom, a mighty power in the world. He stood for a time, listening to the music in the marketplace, wondering if his father in his sickbed could hear it, and what he might be thinking, if he could. And he wondered too how it would feel when his own time came to lie abed listening to them tuning up in the market for the death dance. But then Little Father's face wrinkled in annoyance at his own foolishness. He would rule for many years; and when the time came to do the death dance for him out there he would not care at all. He might even be eager for it.

Big Father's palace rose before him like a mountain. Level upon level sprang upward, presenting a dazzling white facade broken only by the dark butts of the wooden beams jutting through the plaster and the occasional grillwork of a window. His own palace was a hut compared with that of the Emir. Implacable blue-veiled Tuareg guards stood in the main doorway. Their eyes and foreheads, all that was visible of their coffee-colored faces, registered surprise as they saw Little Father approaching, alone and on foot, out of the aching sunblink of the afternoon; but they stepped aside. Within, everything was silent and dark. Elderly officials of the almost-late Emir lined the hallways, grieving soundlessly, huddling into their own self-pity. They looked toward Little Father without warmth, without hope, as he moved past them. In a short while he would be king, and they would be nothing. But he wasted no energy on pitying them. It wasn't as though they would be fed to the royal lions in the imperial pleasure-ground, after all, when they stepped down from office. Soft retirements awaited them. They had had their greedy years at the public trough; when the time came for them to go, they would move along to villas in Spain, in Greece, in the south of France, in chilly remote Russia, even, and live comfortably on the fortunes they had embezzled during Big Father's lengthy reign. Whereas he, he, he, he was doomed to spend all his days in this wretched blazing city of mud, scarcely even daring ever to go abroad for fear they would take his throne from him while he was gone.

The Grand Vizier, looking twenty years older than he had seemed when Little Father had last seen him a few days before, greeted him formally at the head of the Stairs of Allah and said, 'The imam your father is resting on the porch, Little Father. Three saints and one of the Tijani are with him.'

'Three saints? He must be very near the end, then!'

'On the contrary. We think he is rallying.'

'Allah let it be so,' said Little Father.

Servants and ministers were everywhere. The place reeked of incense. All the lamps were lit, and they were flickering wildly in the conflicting currents of the air within the palace, heat from outside meeting the cool of the interior in gusting wafts. The old Emir had never cared much for electricity.

Little Father passed through the huge, musty, empty throne room, bedecked with his father's hunting trophies, the 20-foot-long crocodile skin, the superb white oryx head with horns like scimitars, the hippo skulls, the vast puzzled-looking giraffe. The rich gifts from foreign monarchs were arrayed here too, the hideous Aztec idol that King Moctezuma had sent a year or two ago, the brilliant feather cloaks from the Inca Capac Yupanqui of Peru, the immense triple-paneled gilded painting of some stiff-jointed Christian holy men with which the Czar Vladimir had paid his respects during a visit of state a decade back, and the great sphere of ivory from China on which some master craftsman had carved a detailed map of the world, and much more, enough to fill half a storehouse. Little Father wondered if he would be able to clear all this stuff out when he became Emir.

In his lifetime Big Father had always preferred to hold court on his upstairs porch, rather than in this dark, cluttered, and somehow sinister throne room; and now he was doing his dying on the porch as well. It was a broad square platform, open to the skies but hidden from the populace below, for it was at the back of the palace facing toward the distant river and no one in the city could look into it.

The dying king lay swaddled, despite the great heat, in a tangle of brilliant blankets of scarlet and turquoise and lemon-colored silk on a rumpled divan to Little Father's left. He was barely visible, a pale sweaty wizened face and nothing more, amid the rumpled bedclothes. To the right was the royal roof-garden, a mysterious collection of fragrant exotic trees and shrubs planted in huge square porcelain vessels from Japan, another gift of the bountiful Czar. The dark earth that filled those blue-and-white tubs had been carried in panniers by donkeys from the banks of the Niger, and the plants were watered every evening at sunset by prisoners, who had to haul great leather sacks of immense weight to this place and were forbidden by the palace guards to stumble or complain. Between the garden and the divan was the royal viewing-pavilion, a low structure of rare satin-smooth woods upon which the Emir in better days would sit for hours, staring out at the barren sun-hammered sandy plain, the pale tormented sky, the occasional wandering camel or hyena, the gnarled scrubby bush that marked the path of the river, six or seven miles away. The cowrie-studded ebony scepter of high office was lying abandoned on the floor of the pavilion, as though nothing more than a cast-off toy.

Four curious figures stood now at the foot of the Emir's divan. One was the Tijani, a member of the city's chief fraternity of religious laymen. He was a man of marked Arab features, dressed in a long white robe over droopy yellow pantaloons, a red turban, a dozen or so strings of amber beads. Probably he was a well-to-do

12

merchant or shopkeeper in daily life. He was wholly absorbed in his orisons, rocking back and forth in place, crooning indefatigably to his hundred-beaded rosary, working hard to efface the Emir's sins and make him fit for Paradise. His voice was thin as feathers from overuse, a low eroded murmur which scarcely halted even for breath. He acknowledged Little Father's arrival with the merest flick of an eyebrow, without pausing in his toil.

The other three holy men were marabouts, living saints, two black Songhay and a man of mixed blood. They were weighted down with leather packets of grigri charms hanging in thick mounds around their necks and girded by other charms by the dozen around their wrists and hips, and they had the proper crazy glittering saint-look in their eyes, the true holy baraka. It was said that saints could fly, could raise the dead, could make the rains come and the rivers rise. Little Father doubted all of that, but he was one who tended to keep his doubts to himself. In any case the city was full of such miracle-workers, dozens of them, and the tombs of hundreds more were objects of veneration in the poorer districts. Little Father recognized all three of these: he had seen them now and then hovering around the Sankore Mosque or sometimes the other and greater one at Dyingerey Ber, striking saint-poses on one leg or with arms outflung, muttering saint-gibberish, giving passersby the saint-stare. Now they stood lined up in grim silence before the Emir, making cryptic gestures with their fingers. Even before Big Father had fallen ill, these three had gone about declaring that he was doomed shortly to be taken by a vampire, as various recent omens indisputably proved – a flight of owls by day, a flight of vultures by night, the death of a sacred dove that lived on the minaret of the Great Mosque. For them to be in the palace at all was remarkable; for them to be in the presence of the king was astounding. Someone in the royal entourage must be at the point of desperation, Little Father concluded.

He knelt at the bedside.

'Father?'

The Emir's eyes were glassy. Perhaps he was becoming a saint too.

'Father, it's me. They said you were rallying. I know you're going to be all right soon.'

Was that a smile? Was that any sort of reaction at all?

'Father, it'll be cooler in just a few weeks. The rains are already on the way. Everybody's saying so. You'll feel better when the rains come.'

The old man's cheeks were like parchment. His bones were showing through. He was eighty years old and he had been Emir of Songhay for fifty of those years. Electricity hadn't even been invented when he became king, nor the motorcar. Even the railroad had been something new and startling.

There was a claw-like hand suddenly jutting out of the blankets. Little Father touched it. It was like touching a piece of worn leather. By the time the rains had reached Timbuctoo, Big Father would have made the trip by ceremonial barge to the old capital of Gao, two hundred miles down the Niger, to take his place in the royal cemetery of the Kings of Songhay.

Little Father went on murmuring encouragement for another few moments, but it was apparent that the Emir wasn't listening. A stray burst of breeze brought the sound of the marketplace music, growing louder now. Could he hear that? Could he hear anything? Did he care? After a time Little Father rose, and went quickly from the palace.

In the marketplace the dancing had already begun. They had shoved aside the booths of the basket-weavers and the barbers and the slipper-makers and the charm-peddlers, the dealers in salt and fruit and donkeys and rice and tobacco and meat, and a frenetic procession of dancers was weaving swiftly back and forth across the central square from the place of the milk vendors at the south end to the place of the wood vendors at the north when Little Father and Ali Pasha arrived.

'You see?' Ali Pasha asked. 'The life dance. They bring the energy down from the skies to fill your father's veins.'

There was tremendous energy in it, all right. The dancers pounded the sandy earth with their bare feet, they clapped their hands, they shouted quick sharp punctuations of wordless sound, they made butting gestures with their outflung elbows, they shook their heads

14

convulsively and sent rivers of sweat flying through the air. The heat seemed to mean nothing to them. Their skins gleamed. Their eyes were bright as new coins. They made rhythmic grunting noises, oom oom oom, and the whole city seemed to shake beneath their tread.

To Little Father it looked more like the death dance than the dance of life. There was the frenzied stomp of mourning about it. But he was no expert on these things. The people had all sorts of beliefs that were mysteries to him, and which he hoped would melt away like snowflakes during his coming reign. Did they still put pressure on Allah to bring the rains by staking small children out in the blazing sun for days at a time outside the tombs of saints? Did they still practice alchemy on one another, turning wrapping paper into banknotes by means of spells? Did they continue to fret about vampires and djinn? It was all very embarrassing. Songhay was a modern state; and yet there was all this medieval nonsense still going on. Very likely the old Emir had liked it that way. But soon things would change.

The close formation of the dancers opened abruptly, and to his horror Little Father saw a group of foreigners standing in a little knot at the far side of the marketplace. He had only a glimpse of them; then the dance closed again and the foreigners were blocked from view. He touched Ali Pasha's arm.

'Did you see them?'

'Oh, yes. Yes!'

'Who are they, do you think?'

The vizier stared off intently toward the other side of the market-place, as though his eyes were capable of seeing through the knot of dancers.

'Embassy people, Little Father. Some Mexicans, I believe, and perhaps the Turks. And those fair-haired people must be the English.'

Here to gape at the quaint tribal dances, enjoying the fine barbaric show in the extravagant alien heat.

'You said they were coming by barge. How'd they get here so fast?'

Ali Pasha shook his head.

'They must have taken the motorboat instead, I suppose.'

'I can't receive them here, like this. I never would have come here if I had known that they'd be here.'

'Of course not, Little Father.'

'You should have told me!'

'I had no way of knowing,' said Ali Pasha, and for once he sounded sincere, even distressed. 'There will be punishments for this. But come, Little Father. Come: to your palace. As you say, they ought not find you here this way, without a retinue, without your regalia. This evening you can receive them properly.'

Very likely the newly arrived diplomats at the upper end of the marketplace had no idea that they had been for a few moments in the presence of the heir to the throne, the future Emir of Songhay, one of the six or seven most powerful men in Africa. If they had noticed anyone at all across the way, they would simply have seen a slender, supple, just-barely-still-youngish man with Moorish features, wearing a simple white robe and a flat red skullcap, standing beside a tall, powerfully built black man clad in an ornately brocaded robe of purple and yellow. The black man might have seemed more important to them in the Timbuctoo scheme of things than the Moorish-looking one, though they would have been wrong about that.

But probably they hadn't been looking toward Little Father and Ali Pasha at all. Their attention was on the dancers. That was why they had halted here, en route from the river landing to their various embassies.

'How tireless they are!' Prince Itzcoatl said. The Mexican envoy, King Moctezuma's brother. 'Why don't their bones melt in this heat?' He was a compact copper-colored man decked out grandly in an Aztec feather cape, golden anklets and wristlets, a gold headband studded with brilliant feathers, golden ear-plugs and nose-plugs. 'You'd think they were glad their king is dying, seeing them jump around like that.'

'Perhaps they are,' observed the Turk, Ismet Akif.

He laughed in a mild, sad way. Everything about him seemed to be like that, mild and sad: his droopy-lidded melancholic eyes, his fleshy downcurved lips, his sloping shoulders, even the curiously

16

stodgy and inappropriate European-style clothes that he had chosen to wear in this impossible climate, the dark heavy woolen suit, the narrow gray necktie. But wide cheekbones and a broad, authoritative forehead indicated his true strength to those with the ability to see such things. He too was of royal blood, Sultan Osman's third son. There was something about him that managed to be taut and slack both at once, no easy task. His posture, his expression, the tone of his voice, all conveyed the anomalous sense of self that came from being the official delegate of a vast empire which – as all the world knew – had passed the peak of its greatness some time back and was launched on a long irreversible decline. To the diminutive Englishman at his side he said, 'How does it seem to you, Sir Anthony? Are they grieving or celebrating?'

Everyone in the group understood the great cost of the compliment Ismet Akif was paying by amiably addressing his question to the English ambassador, just as if they were equals. It was high courtesy: it was grace in defeat.

Turkey still ruled a domain spanning thousands of miles. England was an insignificant island kingdom. Worse yet, England had been a Turkish province from medieval times onward, until only sixty years before. The exasperated English, weary of hundreds of years of speaking Turkish and bowing to Mecca, finally had chased out their Ottoman masters in the first year of what by English reckoning was the twentieth century, thus becoming the first of all the European peoples to regain their independence. There were no Spaniards here today, no Italians, no Portuguese, and no reason why there should be, for their countries all still were Turkish provinces. Perhaps envoys from those lands would show up later to pay homage to the dead Emir, if only to make some pathetic display of tattered sovereignty; but it would not matter to anyone else, one way or the other. The English, though, were beginning once again to make their way in the world, a little tentatively but nevertheless visibly. And so Ismet Akif had had to accommodate himself to the presence of an English diplomat on the slow journey upriver from the coast to the Songhay capital, and everyone agreed he had managed it very well.

Sir Anthony said, 'Both celebrating and grieving, I'd imagine.'

He was a precise, fastidious little man with icy blue eyes, an angular bony face, a tight cap of red curls beginning to shade now into gray. 'The king is dead, long live the king – that sort of thing.'

'*Almost* dead,' Prince Itzcoatl reminded him.

'Quite. Terribly awkward, our getting here before the fact. Or *are* we here before the fact?' Sir Anthony glanced toward his young chargé d'affaires. 'Have you heard anything, Michael? Is the old Emir still alive, do you know?'

Michael was long-legged, earnest, milky-skinned, very fair. In the merciless Timbuctoo sunlight his golden hair seemed almost white. The first blush of what was likely to be a very bad sunburn was spreading over his cheeks and forehead. He was twenty-four and this was his first notable diplomatic journey.

He indicated the flagpole at the eastern end of the plaza, where the black and red Songhay flag hung like a dead thing high overhead.

'They'd have lowered the flag if he'd died, Sir Anthony.'

'Quite. Quite. They do that sort of thing here, do they?'

'I'd rather expect so, sir.'

'And then what? The whole town plunged into mourning? Drums, chanting? The new Emir paraded in the streets? Everyone would head for the mosques, I suppose.' Sir Anthony glanced at Ismet Akif. 'We would too, eh? Well, I could stand to go into a mosque one more time, I suppose.'

After the Conquest, when London had become New Istanbul, the worship of Allah had been imposed by law. Westminster Abbey had been turned into a mosque, and the high pashas of the occupation forces were buried in it alongside the Plantagenet kings. Later the Turks had built the great golden-domed Mosque of Ali on the Strand, opposite the Grand Palace of Sultan Mahmud. To this day perhaps half the English still embraced Islam, out of force of habit if nothing else, and Turkish was still heard in the streets nearly as much as English. The conquerors had had five hundred years to put their mark on England, and that could not be undone overnight. But Christianity was fashionable again among the English well-to-do, and had never really been relinquished by the poor, who had kept their underground chapels through the worst of the Islamic

persecutions. And it was obligatory for the members of the governing class.

'It would have been better for us all,' said Ismet Akif gravely, 'if
we had not had to set out so early that we would arrive here before
the Emir's death. But of course the distances are so great, and travel
is so very slow –'

'And the situation so explosive,' Prince Itzcoatl said.

Unexpectedly Ismet Akif's bright-eyed daughter Selima, who was
soft-spoken and delicate-looking and was not thought to be particularly forward, said, 'Are you talking about the possibility that King
Suleiyman of Mali might send an invasion force into Songhay when
the old man finally dies?'

Everyone swung about to look at her. Someone gasped and someone else choked back shocked laughter. She was extremely young and
of course she was female, but even so the remark was exceedingly
tactless, exceedingly embarrassing. The girl had not come to Songhay
in any official capacity, merely as her father's traveling companion,
for he was a widower. The whole trip was purely an adventure for
her. All the same, a diplomat's child should have had more sense.
Ismet Akif turned his eyes inward and looked as though he would like
to sink into the earth. But Selima's dark eyes glittered with something
very much like mischief. She seemed to be enjoying herself. She stood
her ground.

'No,' she said. 'We can't pretend it isn't likely. There's Mali, right
next door, controlling the coast. It stands to reason that they'd like to
have the inland territory too, and take total control of West African
trade. King Suleiyman could argue that Songhay would be better off
as part of Mali than it is this way, a landlocked country.'

'My dear –'

'And the prince,' she went on imperturbably, 'is supposed to be
just an idler, isn't he, a silly dissolute playboy who's spent so many
years waiting around to become Emir that he's gone completely to
ruin. Letting him take the throne would be a mistake for everybody.
So this is the best possible time for Mali to move in and consolidate the
two countries. You all see that. That's why we're here, aren't we, to
stare the Malians down and keep them from trying it? Because they'd

19

be too strong for the other powers' comfort if they got together with the Songhayans. And it's all too likely to happen. After all, Mali and Songhay have been consolidated before.'

'Hundreds of years ago,' said Michael gently. He gave her a great soft blue-eyed stare of admiration and despair. 'The principle that the separation of Mali and Songhay is desirable and necessary has been understood internationally since –'

'Please,' Ismet Akif said. 'This is an unfortunate discussion. My dear, we ought not indulge in such speculations in a place of this sort, or anywhere else, let me say. Perhaps it's time to continue on to our lodgings, do you not all agree?'

'A good idea. The dancing is becoming a little repetitious,' Prince Itzcoatl said.

'And the heat –' Sir Anthony said. 'This unthinkable diabolical heat –'

They looked at each other. They shook their heads, and exchanged small smiles.

Prince Itzcoatl said quietly to Sir Anthony, 'An unfortunate discussion, yes.'

'Very unfortunate.'

Then they all moved on, in groups of two and three, their porters trailing a short distance behind bowed under the the great mounds of luggage. Michael stood for a moment or two peering after the retreating form of Selima Akif in an agony of longing and chagrin. Her movements seemed magical. They were as subtle as Oriental music: an exquisite semitonal slither, an enchanting harmonious twang.

The love he felt for her had surprised and mortified him when it had first blossomed on the riverboat as it came interminably up the Niger from the coast, and here in his first hour in Timbuctoo he felt it almost as a crucifixion. There was no worse damage he could do to himself than to fall in love with a Turk. For an Englishman it was virtual treason. His diplomatic career would be ruined before it had barely begun. He would be laughed out of court. He might just as well convert to Islam, paint his face brown, and undertake the pilgrimage to Mecca. And live thereafter as an anchorite in some desert cave, imploring the favor of the Prophet.

'Michael?' Sir Anthony called. 'Is anything wrong?'

'Coming, sir. Coming!'

The reception hall was long and dark and cavernous, lit only by wax tapers that emitted a smoky amber light and a peculiar odor, something like that of leaves decomposing on a forest floor. Along the walls were bowers of interwoven ostrich and peacock plumes, and great elephant tusks set on brass pedestals rose from the earthen floor like obelisks at seemingly random intervals. Songhayans who might have been servants or just as easily high officials of the court moved among the visiting diplomats bearing trays of cool lime-flavored drinks, musty wine, and little delicacies fashioned from a bittersweet red nut.

The prince, in whose name the invitations had gone forth, was nowhere in sight so far as any of the foreigners could tell. The apparent host of the reception was a burly jet-black man of regal bearing clad in a splendid tawny robe that might actually have been made of woven lionskins. He had introduced himself as Ali Pasha, vizier to the prince. The prince, he explained, was at his father's bedside, but would be there shortly. The prince was deeply devoted to his father, said Ali Pasha; he visited the failing Emir constantly.

'I saw that man in the marketplace this afternoon,' Selima said. 'He was wearing a purple and yellow robe then. Down at the far side, beyond the dancers, for just a moment. He was looking at us. I thought he was magnificent, somebody of great importance. And he is.'

A little indignantly Michael said, 'These blacks all look alike to me. How can you be sure that's the one you saw?'

'Because I'm sure. Do all Turks look alike to you too?'

'I didn't mean –'

'All English look alike to us, you know. We can just about distinguish between the red-haired ones and the yellow-haired ones. And that's as far as it goes.'

'You aren't serious, Selima.'

'No. No, I'm not. I actually can tell one of you from another most of the time. At least I can tell the handsome ones from the ugly ones.'

Michael flushed violently, so that his already sunburned face turned flaming scarlet and emanated great waves of heat. Everyone had been telling him how handsome he was since his boyhood. It was as if there was nothing to him at all except regularly formed features and pale flawless skin and long athletic limbs. The notion made him profoundly uncomfortable.

She laughed. 'You should cover your face when you're out in the sun. You're starting to get cooked. Does it hurt very much?'

'Not at all. Can I get you a drink?'

'You know that alcohol is forbidden to –'

'The other kind, I mean. The green soda. It's very good, actually. Boy! Boy!'

'I'd rather have the nut thing,' she said. She stretched forth one hand – her hand was very small, and the fingers were pale and perfect – and made the tiniest of languid gestures. Two of the black men with trays came toward her at once, and, laughing prettily, she scooped a couple of the nut-cakes from the nearer of the trays. She handed one to Michael, who fumbled it and let it fall. Calmly she gave him the other. He looked at it as though she had handed him an asp.

'Are you afraid I've arranged to have you poisoned?' she asked. 'Go on. Eat it! It's good! Oh, you're so absurd, Michael! But I do like you.'

'We aren't supposed to like each other, you know,' he said bleakly.

'I know that. We're enemies, aren't we?'

'Not any more, actually. Not officially.'

'Yes, I know. The Empire recognized English independence a good many years ago.'

The way she said it, it was like a slap. Michael's reddened cheeks blazed fiercely.

In anguish he crammed the nut-cake into his mouth with both hands.

She went on, 'I can remember the time when I was a girl and King Richard came to Istanbul to sign the treaty with the Sultan. There was a parade.'

'Yes. Yes. A great occasion.'

'But there's still bad blood between the Empire and England. We haven't forgiven you for some of the things you did to our people in your country in Sultan Abdul's time, when we were evacuating.'

'*You* haven't forgiven *us* –?'

'When you burned the bazaar. When you bombed that mosque. The broken shopwindows. We were going away voluntarily, you know. You were much more violent toward us than you had any right to be.'

'You speak very directly, don't you?'

'There were atrocities. I studied them in school.'

'And when you people conquered us in 1490? Were you gentle then?' For a moment Michael's eyes were hot with fury, the easily triggered anger of the good Englishman for the bestial Turk. Appalled, he tried to stem the rising surge of patriotic fervor before it ruined everything. He signalled frantically to one of the tray-wielders, as though another round of nut-cakes might serve to get the conversation into a less disagreeable track. 'But never mind all that, Selima. We mustn't be quarreling over ancient history like this.' Somehow he mastered himself, swallowing, breathing deeply, managing an earnest smile. 'You say you like me.'

'Yes. And you like me. I can tell.'

'Is that all right?'

'Of course it is, silly. Although I shouldn't allow it. We don't even think of you English as completely civilized.' Her eyes glowed. He began to tremble, and tried to conceal it from her. She was playing with him, he knew, playing a game whose rules she herself had defined and would not share with him. 'Are you a Christian?' she asked.

'You know I am.'

'Yes, you must be. You used the Christian date for the year of the conquest of England. But your ancestors were Moslem, right?'

'Outwardly, during the time of the occupation. Most of us were. But for all those centuries we secretly continued to maintain our faith in –' She was definitely going to get him going again. Already his head was beginning to pound. Her beauty was unnerving enough; but this roguishness was more than he could take. He wondered how old she was. Eighteen? Nineteen? No more than that, surely. Very likely she had a fiancé back in Istanbul, some swarthy mustachioed fez-wearing

Ottoman princeling, with whom she indulged in unimaginable Oriental perversions and to whom she confessed every little flirtation she undertook while traveling with her father. It was humiliating to think of becoming an item of gossip in some perfumed boudoir on the banks of the Bosporus. A sigh escaped him. She gave him a startled look, as though he had mooed at her. Perhaps he had. Desperately he sought for something, anything, that would rescue him from this increasingly tortured moment of impossible intimacy; and, looking across the room, he was astounded to find his eyes suddenly locked on those of the heir apparent to the throne of Songhay. 'Ah, there he is,' Michael said in vast relief. 'The prince has arrived.'

'Which one? Where?'

'The slender man. The red velvet tunic.'

'Oh. Oh, yes. *Him.* I saw him in the marketplace too, with Ali Pasha. Now I understand. They came to check us out before we knew who they were.' Selima smiled disingenuously. 'He's very attractive, isn't he? Rather like an Arab, I'd say. And not nearly as dissolute-looking as I was led to expect. Is it all right if I go over and say hello to him? Or should I wait for a proper diplomatic introduction? I'll ask my father, I think. Do you see him? Oh, yes, there he is over there, talking to Prince Itzcoatl –' She began to move away without a backward look.

Michael felt a sword probing in his vitals.

'Boy!' he called, and one of the blacks turned to him with a somber grin. 'Some of that wine, if you please!'

On the far side of the room Little Father smiled and signalled for a drink also – not the miserable palm wine, which he abhorred and which as a good Moslem he should abjure anyway, but the clear fiery brandy that the caravans brought him from Tunis, and which to an outsider's eyes would appear to be mere water. His personal cupbearer, who served no one else in the room, poured until he nodded, and slipped back into the shadows to await the prince's next call.

In the first moments of his presence at the reception Little Father had taken in the entire scene, sorting and analyzing and comprehending. The Turkish ambassador's daughter was even more beautiful than Ali

Pasha had led him to think, and there was an agreeable slyness about
her that Little Father was able to detect even at a distance. Lust awoke
in him at once and he allowed himself a little smile as he savored its
familiar throbbing along the insides of his thighs. The Turkish girl
was very fine. The tall fair-haired young man, probably some sort of
subsidiary English official, was obviously and stupidly in love with
her. He should be advised to keep out of the sun. The Aztec prince,
all done up in feathers and gold, was arrogant and brutal and smart,
as Aztecs usually were. The Turk, the girl's father, looked soft and
effete and decadent, which he probably found to be a useful pose. The
older Englishman, the little one with the red hair who most likely was
the official envoy, seemed tough and dangerous. And over there was
another one who hadn't been at the marketplace to see the dancing,
the Russian, no doubt, a big man, strong and haughty, flat face and
flat sea-green eyes and a dense little black beard through which a
glint of gold teeth occasionally showed. He too seemed dangerous,
physically dangerous, a man who might pick things up and smash
them for amusement, but in him all the danger was on the outside,
and with the little Englishman it was the other way around. Little
Father wondered how much trouble these people would manage to
create for him before the funeral was over and done with. It was
every nation's ambition to create trouble in the empires of Africa,
after all: there was too much cheap labor here, too much in the way
of raw materials, for the pale jealous folk of the overseas lands to
ignore, and they were forever dreaming dreams of conquest. But no
one had ever managed it. Africa had kept itself independent of the
great overseas powers. The Pasha of Egypt still held his place by
the Nile, in the far south the Mambo of Zimbabwe maintained his
domain amidst enough gold to make even an Aztec feel envy, and
the Bey of Marrakesh was unchallenged in the north. And the strong
western empires flourished as ever, Ghana, Mali, Kongo, Songhay –
no, no, Africa had never let itself be eaten by Turks or Russians or
even the Moors, though they had all given it a good try. Nor would
it ever. Still, as he wandered among these outlanders Little Father
felt contempt for him and his people drifting through the air about
him like smoke. He wished that he could have made a properly

royal entrance, coming upon the foreigners in style, with drums and trumpets and bugles. Preceded as he entered by musicians carrying gold and silver guitars, and followed by a hundred armed slaves. But those were royal prerogatives, and he was not yet Emir. Besides, this was a solemn time in Songhay, and such pomp was unbefitting. And the foreigners would very likely look upon it as the vulgarity of a barbarian, anyway, or the quaint grandiosity of a primitive.

Little Father downed his brandy in three quick gulps and held out the cup for more. It was beginning to restore his spirit. He felt a sense of deep well-being, of ease and assurance.

But just then came a stir and a hubbub at the north door of the reception hall. In amazement and fury he saw Serene Glory entering, Big Father's main wife, surrounded by her full retinue. Her hair was done up in the elaborate great curving horns of the scorpion style, and she wore astonishing festoons of jewelry, necklaces of gold and amber, bracelets of silver and ebony and beads, rings of stone, earrings of shining ivory.

To Ali Pasha the prince said, hissing, 'What's *she* doing here?'

'You invited her yourself, Little Father.'

Little Father stared into his cup.

'I did?'

'There is no question of that, sir.'

'Yes. Yes, I did.' Little Father shook his head. 'I must have been drunk. What was I thinking of?' Big Father's main wife was young and beautiful, younger, indeed, than Little Father himself; and she was an immense annoyance. Big Father had had six wives in his time, or possibly seven – Little Father was not sure, and he had never dared to ask – of whom all of the earliest ones were now dead, including Little Father's own mother. Of the three that remained, one was an elderly woman who lived in retirement in Gao, and one was a mere child, the old man's final toy; and then there was this one, this witch, this vampire, who placed no bounds on her ambitions. Only six months before, when Big Father had still been more or less healthy, Serene Glory had dared to offer herself to Little Father as they returned together from the Great Mosque. Of course he desired her. Who would not? But the idea was monstrous. Little Father would no more

26

lay a hand on one of Big Father's wives than he would lie down with a crocodile. Clearly this woman, suspecting that the father was approaching his end, had had some dream of beguiling the son. That would not happen. Once Big Father was safely interred in the royal cemetery Serene Glory would go into chaste retirement, however beautiful she might be.

'Get her out of here, fast!' Little Father whispered.

'But she has every right – she is the wife of the Emir –'

'Then keep her away from me, at least. If she comes within five feet of me tonight, you'll be tending camels tomorrow, do you hear? Within *ten* feet. See to it.'

'She will come nowhere near you, Little Father.'

There was an odd look on Ali Pasha's face.

'Why are you smiling?' Little Father asked.

'Smiling? I am not smiling, Little Father.'

'No. No, of course not.'

Little Father made a gesture of dismissal and walked toward the platform of audience. A reception line began to form. The Russian was the first to present his greetings to the prince, and then the Aztec, and then the Englishman. There were ceremonial exchanges of gifts. At last it was the turn of the Turk. He had brought a splendid set of ornate daggers, inlaid with jewels. Little Father received them politely and, as he had with the other ambassadors, he bestowed an elaborately carved segment of ivory tusk upon Ismet Akif. The girl stood shyly to one side.

'May I present also my daughter Selima,' said Ismet Akif.

She was well trained. She made a quick little ceremonial bow, and as she straightened her eyes met Little Father's, only for a moment, and it was enough. Warmth traveled just beneath his skin nearly the entire length of his body, a signal he knew well. He smiled at her. The smile was a communicative one, and was understood and reciprocated. Even in that busy room those smiles had the force of thunderclaps. Everyone had been watching. Quickly Little Father's gaze traversed the reception hall, and in a fraction of an instant he took in the sudden flicker of rage on the face of Serene Glory, the sudden knowing look on Ali Pasha's, the sudden anguished comprehension

27

on that of the tall young Englishman. Only Ismet Akif remained impassive; and yet Little Father had little doubt that he too was in on the transaction. In the wars of love there are rarely any secrets amongst those on the field of combat.

Every day there was dancing in the marketplace. Some days the dancers kept their heads motionless and put everything else into motion; other days they let their heads oscillate like independent creatures, while scarcely moving a limb. There were days of shouting dances and days of silent dances. Sometimes brilliant robes were worn and sometimes the dancers were all but naked.

In the beginning the foreign ambassadors went regularly to watch the show. But as time went on, the Emir continued not to die, and the intensity of the heat grew and grew, going beyond the uncomfortable into the implausible and then beyond that to the unimaginable, they tended to stay within the relative coolness of their own compounds despite the temptations of the daily show in the plaza. New ambassadors arrived daily, from the Maori Confederation, from China, from Peru finally, from lesser lands like Korea and Ind and the Teutonic States, and for a time the newcomers went to see the dancing with the same eagerness as their predecessors. Then they too stopped attending.

The Emir's longevity was becoming an embarrassment. Weeks were going by and the daily bulletins were a monotonous succession of medical ups and downs, with no clear pattern. The special ambassadors, unexpectedly snared in an ungratifying city at a disagreeable time of year, could not leave, but were beginning to find it an agony to stay on. It was evident to everyone now that the news of Big Father's imminent demise had gone forth to the world in a vastly overanticipatory way.

'If only the old bastard would simply get up and step out on his balcony and tell us he's healthy again, and let us all go home,' Sir Anthony said. 'Or succumb at last, one or the other. But this suspension, this indefiniteness –'

'Perhaps the prince will grow weary of the waiting and have him smothered in a pillow,' Prince Itzcoatl suggested.

The Englishman shook his head. 'He'd have done that ten years ago, if he had it in him at all. The time's long past for him to murder his father.'

They were on the covered terrace of the Mexican embassy. In the dreadful heat-stricken silence of the day the foreign dignitaries, as they awaited the intolerably deferred news of the Emir's death, moved in formal rotation from one embassy to another, making ceremonial calls in accordance with strict rules of seniority and precedence.

'His Excellency the Grand Duke Alexander Petrovich,' the Aztec major domo announced.

The foreign embassies were all in the same quarter of New Timbuctoo, along the grand boulevard known as The Street of All Nations. In the old days the foreigners had lived in the center of the Old Town, in fine houses in the best native style, palaces of stone and brick covered with mauve or orange clay. But Big Father had persuaded them one by one to move to the New City. It was undignified and uncomfortable, he insisted, for the representatives of the great overseas powers to live in mud houses with earthen floors.

Having all the foreigners' dwellings lined up in a row along a single street made it much simpler to keep watch over them, and, in case international difficulties should arise, it would be ever so much more easy to round them all up at once under the guise of 'protecting' them. But Big Father had not taken into account that it was also very much easier for the foreigners to mingle with each other, which was not necessarily a good idea. It facilitated conspiracy as well as surveillance.

'We are discussing our impatience,' Prince Itzcoatl told the Russian, who was the cousin of the Czar. 'Sir Anthony is weary of Timbuctoo.'

'Nor am I the only one,' said the Englishman. 'Did you hear that Maori ranting and raving yesterday at the Peruvian party? But what can we do? What can we do?'

'We could to Egypt go while we wait, perhaps,' said the Grand Duke. 'The Pyramids, the Sphinx, the temples of Karkak!'

'Karnak,' Sir Anthony said. 'But what if the old bugger dies while we're gone? We'd never get back in time for the funeral. What a black eye for us!'

'And how troublesome for our plans,' said the Aztec.

'Mansa Suleiyman would never forgive us,' said Sir Anthony.

'Mansa Suleiyman! Mansa Suleiyman!' Alexander Petrovich spat. 'Let the black brigand do his own dirty work, then. Brothers, let us go to Egypt. If the Emir dies while we are away, will not the prince be removed whether or not we happen to be in attendance at the funeral?'

'Should we be speaking of this here?' Prince Itzcoatl asked, plucking in displeasure at his earplugs.

'Why not? There is no danger. These people are like children. They would never suspect –'

'Even so –'

But the Russian would not be deterred. Bull-like, he said, 'It will all go well whether we are here or not. Believe me. It is all arranged, I remind you. So let us go to Egypt, then, before we bake to death. Before we choke on the sand that blows through these miserable streets.'

'Egypt's not a great deal cooler than Songhay right now,' Prince Itzcoatl pointed out. 'And sand is not unknown there either.'

The Grand Duke's massive shoulders moved in a ponderous shrugging gesture.

'To the south, then, to the Great Waterfalls. It is winter in that part of Africa, such winter as they have. Or to the Islands of the Canaries. Anywhere, anywhere at all, to escape from this Timbuctoo. I fry here. I sizzle here. I remind you that I am Russian, my friends. This is no climate for Russians.'

Sir Anthony stared suspiciously into the sea-green eyes. 'Are you the weak link in our little affair, my dear Duke Alexander? Have we made a mistake by asking you to join us?'

'Does it seem so to you? Am I untrustworthy, do you think?'

'The Emir could die at any moment. Probably will. Despite what's been happening, or not happening, it's clear that he can't last very much longer. The removal of the prince on the day of the funeral, as you have just observed, has been arranged. But how can we dare risk being elsewhere on that day? How can we even *think* of such a thing?' Sir Anthony's lean face grew florid; his tight mat of graying red hair began to rise and crackle with inner electricity; his chilly blue eyes became utterly arctic. 'It is *essential* that in the moment of chaos that follows, the great-power triumvirate we represent – the troika, as you say – be on hand here to invite King Suleiyman of Mali to take charge of the country. I repeat, your excellency: *essential*. The time factor is critical. If we are off on holiday in Egypt, or anywhere else – if we are so much as a day too late getting back here –'

Prince Itzcoatl said, 'I think the Grand Duke understands that point, Sir Anthony.'

'Ah, but does he? Does he?'

'I think so.' The Aztec drew in his breath sharply and let his gleaming obsidian eyes meet those of the Russian. 'Certainly he sees that we're all in it too deep to back out, and that therefore he has to abide by the plan as drawn, however inconvenient he may find it personally.'

The Grand Duke, sounding a little nettled, said, 'We are traveling too swiftly here, I think. I tell you, I hate this filthy place, I hate its impossible heat, I hate its blowing sand, I hate its undying Emir, I hate its slippery lecherous prince. I hate the smell of the air, even. It is the smell of camel shit, the smell of old mud. But I am your partner in this undertaking to the end. I will not fail you, believe me.' His great shoulders stirred like boulders rumbling down a slope. 'The consolidation of Mali and Songhay would be displeasing to the Sultan, and therefore it is pleasing to the Czar. I will assist you in making it happen, knowing that such a consolidation has value for your own nations as well, which also is pleasing to my royal cousin. By the Russian Empire from the plan there will be no withdrawal. Of such a possibility let there be no more talk.'

'Of holidays in Egypt let there be no more talk either,' said Prince Itzcoatl. 'Agreed? None of us likes being here, Duke Alexander. But here we have to stay, like it or not, until everything is brought to completion.'

'Agreed. Agreed.' The Russian snapped his fingers. 'I did not come here to bicker. I have hospitality for you, waiting outside. Will you share vodka with me?' An attaché of the Russian Embassy entered, bearing a crystal beaker in a bowl of ice. 'This arrived today, by the riverboat, and I have brought it to offer to my beloved friends of England and Mexico. Unfortunately of caviar there is none, though there should be. This heat! This heat! Caviar, in this heat – impossible!' The Grand Duke laughed. 'To our great countries! To international amity! To a swift and peaceful end to the Emir's terrible sufferings! To your healths, gentlemen! To your healths!'

'To Mansa Suleiyman, King of Mali and Songhay,' Prince Itzcoatl said.

'Mansa Suleiyman, yes.'

'Mansa Suleiyman!'

'What splendid stuff,' said Sir Anthony. He held forth his glass, and the Russian attaché filled it yet again. 'There are other and perhaps more deserving monarchs to toast. To His Majesty King Richard the Fifth!'

'King Richard, yes!'

'And His Imperial Majesty Vladimir the Ninth!'

'Czar Vladimir! Czar Vladimir!'

'Let us not overlook His Highness Moctezuma the Twelfth!'

'King Moctezuma! King Moctezuma!'

'Shall we drink to cooler weather and happier days, gentlemen?'

'Cooler weather! Happier days! – And the Emir of Songhay, may he soon rest in peace at last!'

'And to his eldest son, the prince of the realm. May he also soon be at rest,' said Prince Itzcoatl.

Selima said, 'I hear you have vampires here, and djinn. I want to know all about them.'

Little Father was aghast. She would say anything, anything at all.

'Who's been feeding you nonsense like that? There aren't any vampires. There aren't any djinn either. Those things are purely mythical.'

'There's a tree south of the city where vampires hold meetings at midnight to choose their victims. Isn't that so? The tree is half white and half red. When you first become a vampire you have to bring one of your male cousins to the meeting for the others to feast on.'

'Some of the common people may believe such stuff. But do you think I do? Do you think we're all a bunch of ignorant savages here, girl?'

'There's a charm that can be worn to keep vampires from creeping into your bedroom at night and sucking your blood. I want you to get me one.'

'I tell you, there aren't any vamp –'

'Or there's a special prayer you can say. And while you say it you spit in four directions, and that traps the vampire in your house so he can be arrested. Tell me what it is. And the charm for making the vampire give back the blood he's drunk. I want to know that too.'

They were on the private upstairs porch of Little Father's palace. The night was bright with moonlight, and the air was as hot as wet velvet. Selima was wearing a long silken robe, very sheer. He could see the shadow of her breasts through it when she turned at an angle to the moon.

'Are you always like this?' he asked, beginning to feel a little irritable. 'Or are you just trying to torment me?'

'What's the point of traveling if you don't bother to learn anything about local customs?'

'You do think we're savages.'

'Maybe I do. Africa is the dark continent. Black skins, black souls.'

'My skin isn't black. It's practically as light as yours. But even if it were –'

'You're black *inside*. Your blood is African blood, and Africa is the strangest place in the world. The fierce animals you have, gorillas and hippos running around everywhere, giraffes, tigers – the masks, the nightmare carvings – the witchcraft, the drums, the chanting of the high priests –'

'Please,' Little Father said. 'You're starting to drive me crazy. I'm not responsible for what goes on in the jungles of the tropics. This is Songhay. Do we seem uncivilized to you? We were a great empire when you Ottomans were still herding goats on the steppes. The only giraffe you'll see in this city is the stuffed one in my father's throne room. There aren't any gorillas in Songhay, and tigers come from Asia, and if you see a hippo running, here or anywhere, please tell

33

the newspaper right away.' Then he began to laugh. 'Look, Selima, this is a modern country. We have motorcars here. We have a stock exchange. There's a famous university in Timbuctoo, six hundred years old. I don't bow down to tribal idols. We are an Islamic people, you know.'

It was lunacy to have let her force him onto the defensive like this. But she wouldn't stop her attack.

'Djinn are Islamic. The Koran talks about them. The Arabs believe in djinn.'

Little Father struggled for patience. 'Perhaps they did five hundred years ago, but what's that to us? In any case we aren't Arabs.'

'But there are djinn here, plenty of them. My head porter told me. A djinni will appear as a small black spot on the ground and will grow until he's as big as a house. He might change into a sheep or a dog or a cat, and then he'll disappear. The porter said that one time he was at the edge of town in Kabara, and he was surrounded by giants in white turbans that made a weird sucking noise at him.'

'What is this man's name? He has no right filling your head with this trash. I'll have him fed to the lions.'

'Really?' Her eyes were sparkling. 'Would you? What lions? Where?'

'My father keeps them as pets, in a pit. No one is looking after them these days. They must be getting very hungry.'

'Oh, you *are* a savage! You are!'

Little Father grinned lopsidedly. He was regaining some of the advantage, he felt. 'Lions need to be fed now and then. There's nothing savage about that. *Not* feeding them, that would be savage.'

'But to feed a servant to them –?'

'If he speaks idiotic nonsense to a visitor, yes. Especially when the visitor is an impressionable young girl.'

Her eyes flashed quick lightning, sudden pique. 'You think I'm impressionable? You think I'm silly?'

'I think you are young.'

'And I think you're a savage underneath it all. Even savages can start a stock exchange. But they're still savages.'

'Very well,' Little Father said, putting an ominous throb into his tone. 'I admit it. I am the child of darkness. I am the pagan prince.' He pointed to the moon, full and swollen, hanging just above them like a plummeting polished shield. 'You think that is a dead planet up there? It is alive, it is a land of djinn. And it must be nourished. So when it is full like this, the king of this land must appear beneath its face and make offerings of energy to it.'

'Energy?'

'Sexual energy,' he said portentously. 'Atop the great phallic altar, beneath which we keep the dried umbilicus of each of our dead kings. First there is a procession, the phallic figures carried through the streets. And then –'

'The sacrifice of a virgin?' Selima asked.

'What's wrong with you? We are good Moslems here. We don't countenance murder.'

'But you countenance phallic rites at the full moon?'

He couldn't tell whether she was taking him seriously or not.

'We maintain certain pre-Islamic customs,' he said. 'It is folly to cut oneself off from one's origins.'

'Absolutely. Tell me what you do on the night the moon is full.'

'First, the king coats his entire body in rancid butter –'

'I don't think I like that!'

'Then the chosen bride of the moon is led forth –'

'The fair-skinned bride.'

'Fair-skinned?' he said. She saw it was a game, he realized. She was getting into it. 'Why fair-skinned?'

'Because she'd be more like the moon than a black woman would. Her energy would rise into the sky more easily. So each month a white woman is stolen and brought to the king to take part in the rite.'

Little Father gave her a curious stare. 'What a ferocious child you are!'

'I'm not a child. You do prefer white women, don't you? One thing you regret is that I'm not white enough for you.'

'You seem very white to me,' said Little Father. She was at the edge of the porch now, looking outward over the sleeping city. Idly he watched her shoulderblades moving beneath her sheer gown. Then suddenly the garment began to slide downward, and he realized she

35

had unfastened it at the throat and cast it off. She had worn nothing underneath it. Her waist was very narrow, her hips broad, her buttocks smooth and full, with a pair of deep dimples at the place where they curved outward from her back. His lips were beginning to feel very dry, and he licked them thoughtfully.

She said, 'What you really want is an Englishwoman, with skin like milk, and pink nipples, and golden hair down below.'

Damn Ali Pasha! Was he out of his mind, telling such stuff to her? He'd go to the lions first thing tomorrow!

Amazed, he cried, 'What are you talking about? What sort of madness is this?'

'That is what you want, isn't it? A nice juicy golden-haired one. All of you Africans secretly want one. Some of you not so secretly. I know all about it.'

No, it was inconceivable. Ali Pasha was tricky, but he wasn't insane. This was mere coincidence. 'Have you ever had an English-woman, prince? A true pink-and-gold one?'

Little Father let out a sigh of relief. It was only another of her games, then. The girl was all mischief, and it came bubbling out randomly, spontaneously. Truly, she would say anything to anyone. Anything.

'Once,' he said, a little vindictively. 'She was writing a book on the African empires and she came here to do some research at our university. Our simple barbaric university. One night she interviewed me, on this very porch, a night almost as warm as this one. Her name was – ah – Elizabeth. Elizabeth, yes.' Little Father's gaze continued to rest on Selima's bare back. She seemed much more frail above the waist than below. Below the waist she was solid, splendidly fleshly, a commanding woman, no girl at all. Languidly he said, 'skin like milk, indeed. And rosy nipples. I had never even imagined that nipples could be like that. And her hair –'

Selina turned to face him. 'My nipples are dark.'

'Yes, of course. You're a Turk. But Elizabeth –'

'I don't want to hear any more about Elizabeth. Kiss me.'

Her nipples *were* dark, yes, and very small, almost like a boy's, tiny dusky targets on the roundness of her breasts. Her thighs were surprisingly full. She looked far more voluptuous naked than when she was clothed. He hadn't expected that. The heavy thatch at the base of her belly was jet black.

He said, 'We don't care for kissing in Songhay. It's one of our quaint tribal taboos. The mouth is for eating, not for making love.'

'Every part of the body is for making love. Kiss me.'

'You Europeans!'

'I'm not European. I'm a Turk. You do it in some peculiar way here, don't you? Side by side. Back to back.'

'No,' he said. 'Not back to back. Never like that, not even when we feel like reverting to tribal barbarism.'

Her perfume drifted toward him, falling over him like a veil. Little Father went to her and she rose up out of the night to him, and they laughed. He kissed her. It was a lie, the thing he had told her, that Songhayans did not like to kiss. Songhayans liked to do everything: at least this Songhayan did. She slipped downward to the swirl of silken pillows on the floor, and he joined her there and covered her body with his own. As he embraced her he felt the moonlight on his back like the touch of a goddess' finger-tips, cool, delicate, terrifying.

On the horizon a sharp dawn-line of pale lavender appeared, cutting between the curving grayness above and the flat grayness below. It was like a preliminary announcement by the oboes or the French horns, soon to be transformed into the full overwhelming trumpetblast of morning. Michael, who had been wandering through Old Timbuctoo all night, stared eastward uneasily as if he expected the sky to burst into flame when the sun came into view.

Sleep had been impossible. Only his face and hands were actually sunburned, but his whole body throbbed with discomfort, as though the African sun had reached him even through his clothing. He felt the glow of it behind his knees, in the small of his back, on the soles of his feet.

Nor was there any way to escape the heat, even when the terrible glaring sun had left the sky. The nights were as warm as the days. The motionless air lay on you like burning fur. When you drew a breath you could trace its path all the way down, past your nostrils, past your throat, a trickle of molten lead descending the forking paths into your lungs and spreading out to weigh upon every individual air-sac inside you. Now and then came a breeze, but it only made things worse: it gave you no more comfort than a shower of hot ashes might have afforded. So Michael had risen after a few hours of tossing and turning and gone out unnoticed to wander under the weird and cheerless brilliance of the overhanging moon, down from the posh Embassy district into the Old Town somehow, and then from street to street, from quarter to quarter, no destination in mind, no purpose, seeking only to obliterate the gloom and misery of the night.

He was lost, of course – the Old Town was complex enough to negotiate in daylight, impossible in the dark – but that didn't matter. He was somewhere on the western side of town, that was all he knew. The moon was long gone from the sky, as if it had been devoured, though he had not noticed it setting. Before him the ancient metropolis of mud walls and low square flat-roofed buildings lay humped in the thinning darkness, a gigantic weary beast slowly beginning to stir. The thing was to keep on walking, through the night and into the dawn, distracting himself from the physical discomfort and the other, deeper agony that had wrapped itself like some voracious starfish around his soul.

By the faint light he saw that he had reached a sort of large pond. Its water looked to be a flat metallic green. Around its perimeter crouched a shadowy horde of water-carriers, crouching to scoop the green water into goatskin bags, spooning it in with gourds. Then they straightened, with the full bags – they must have weighed a hundred pounds – balanced on their heads, and went jogging off into the dawn to deliver their merchandise at the homes of the wealthy. Little ragged girls were there too, seven or eight years old, filling jugs and tins to bring to their mothers. Some of them waded right into the pool to get what they wanted. A glowering black man in the uniform of the Emirate sat to one side, jotting down notations on a sheet of yellow paper. So this was probably the Old Town's municipal reservoir. Michael shuddered and turned away, back into the city proper. Into the labyrinth once more.

A gray, sandy light was in the sky now. It showed him narrow dusty thoroughfares, blind walls, curving alleyways leading into dark cul-de-sacs. Entire rows of houses seemed to be crumbling away, though they were obviously still inhabited. Under foot everything was sand, making a treacherous footing. In places the entrances to buildings were half choked by the drifts. Camels, donkeys, horses wandered about on their own. The city's mixed population – veiled Tuaregs, black Sudanese, aloof and lofty Moors, heavy-bearded Syrian traders, the whole West African racial goulash – was coming forth into the day. Who were all these people? Tailors, moneylenders, scribes, camel-breeders, masons, bakers, charm-sellers, weavers – necromancers, sages, warlocks, perhaps a few vampires on their way home from their night's toil – Michael looked around, bewildered, trapped within his skull by the barriers of language and his own disordered mental state. He felt as though he were moving about under the surface of the sea, in a medium where he did not belong and could neither breathe nor think.

'Selima?' he said suddenly, blinking in astonishment.

His voice was voiceless. His lips moved, but no sound had come forth.

Apparition? Hallucination? No, no, she was really there. Selima glowed just across the way like a second sun suddenly rising over the city.

Michael shrank back against an immense buttress of mud brick. She had stepped out of a doorway in a smooth gray wall that surrounded what appeared to be one of the palaces of the nobility. The building, partly visible above the wall, was coated in orange clay and had elaborate Moorish windows of dark wood. He trembled. The girl wore only a flimsy white gown, so thin that he could make out the dark-tipped spheres of her breasts moving beneath it, and the dark triangle at her thighs. He wanted to cry. Had she no shame? No. No. She was indifferent to the display, and to everything around her; she would have walked completely naked through this little plaza just as casually as she strode through in this one thin garment.

'Selima, where have you spent this night? Whose palace is this?'

His words were air. No one heard them. She moved serenely

onward. A motorcar appeared from somewhere, one of the five or six that Michael had seen so far in this city. A black plume of smoke rose from the vent of its coal-burning engine, and its two huge rear wheels slipped and slid about on the sandy track. Selima jumped up onto the open seat behind the driver, and with great booming exhalations the vehicle made its way through an arched passageway and disappeared into the maze of the town.

An embassy car, no doubt. Waiting here for her all night?

His soul ached. He had never felt so young, so foolish, so vulnerable, so wounded.

'Effendi?' a voice asked. 'You wish a camel, effendi?'

'Thank you, no.'

'Nice hotel? Bath? Woman to massage you? Boy to massage you?'

'Please. No.'

'Some charms, maybe? Good grigri. Souvenir of Timbuctoo.'

Michael groaned. He turned away and looked back at the house of infamy from which Selima had emerged.

'That building – what is it?'

'That? Is palace of Little Father. And look, look there, effendi – Little Father himself coming out for a walk.'

The prince himself, yes. Of course. Who else would she have spent the night with, here in the Old Town? Michael was engulfed by loathing and despair. Instantly a swarm of eager citizens had surrounded the prince, clustering about him to beg favors the moment he showed himself. But he seemed to move through them with the sort of divine indifference that Selima, in her all-but-nakedness, had displayed. He appeared to be enclosed in an impenetrable bubble of self-concern. He was frowning, he looked troubled, not at all like a man who had just known the favors of the most desirable woman in five hundred miles. His lean sharp-angled face, which had been so animated at the official reception, now had a curiously stunned, immobile look about it, as though he had been struck on the head from behind a short while before and the impact was gradually sinking in.

Michael flattened himself against the buttress. He could not bear the thought of being seen by the prince now, here, as if he had been haunting the palace all night, spying on Selima. He put his arm across his face in a frantic attempt to hide himself, he whose Western clothes and long legs and white skin made him stand out like a meteor. But the prince wasn't coming toward him. Nodding in an abstracted way, he turned quickly, passed through the throng of chattering petitioners as if they were ghosts, disappeared in a flurry of white fabric.

Michael looked about for his sudden friend, the man who had wanted to sell him camels, massages, souvenirs. What he wanted now was a guide to get him out of the Old Town and back to the residence of the English ambassador. But the man was gone.

'Pardon me –' Michael said to someone who looked almost like the first one. Then he realized that he had spoken in English. Useless. He tried in Turkish and in Arabic. A few people stared at him. They seemed to be laughing. He felt transparent to them. They could see his sorrow, his heartache, his anguish, as easily as his sunburn.

Like the good young diplomat he was, he had learned a little Songhay too, the indigenous language. 'Town talk,' they called it. But the few words he had seemed all to have fled. He stood alone and helpless in the plaza, scuffing angrily at the sand, as the sun broke above the mud rooftops like the sword of an avenging angel and the full blast of morning struck him. Michael felt blisters starting to rise on his cheeks. Agitated flies began to buzz around his eyes. A camel, passing by just then, dropped half a dozen hot green turds right at his feet. He snatched one out of the sand and hurled it with all his strength at the bland blank mud-colored wall of Little Father's palace.

Big Father was sitting up on his divan. His silken blankets were knotted around his waist in chaotic strands, and his bare torso rose above the chaos, gleaming as though it had been oiled. His arms were like sticks and his skin was three shades paler than it once had been and cascades of loose flesh hung like wattles from his neck, but there was the brilliance of black diamonds in his glittering little eyes.

'Not dead yet, you see? You see?' His voice was a cracked wailing screech, but the old authoritative thunder was still somewhere behind it. 'Back from the edge of the grave, boy! Allah walks with me yet!'

Little Father was numb with chagrin. All the joy of his night with Selima had vanished in a moment when word had arrived of his father's miraculous recovery. He had just been getting accustomed to the idea that he soon would be king, too. His first misgivings about the work involved in it had begun to ebb; he rather liked the idea of ruling, now. The crown was descending on him like a splendid gift. And here was Big Father sitting up, grinning, waving his arms around in manic glee. Taking back his gift. Deciding to live after all.

What about the funeral plans? What about the special ambassadors who had traveled so far, in such discomfort, to pay homage to the late venerable Emir of Songhay and strike their various deals with his successor?

Big Father had had his head freshly shaved and his beard had been trimmed. He looked like a gnome, ablaze with demonic energies. Off in the corner of the porch, next to the potted trees, the three marabouts stood in a circle, making sacred gestures at each other with lunatic vigor, each seeking to demonstrate superior fervor.

Hoarsely Little Father said, 'Your majesty, the news astonishes and delights me. When the messenger came, telling of your miraculous recovery, I leaped from my bed and gave thanks to the All-Merciful in a voice so loud you must have heard it here.'

'Was there a woman with you, boy?'

'Father –'

'I hope you bathed before you came here. You come forth without bathing after you've lain with a woman and the djinn will make you die an awful death, do you realize that?'

'Father, I wouldn't think of –'

'Frothing at the mouth, falling down in the street, that's what'll happen to you. Who was she? Some nobleman's wife as usual, I suppose. Well, never mind. As long as she wasn't mine. Come closer to me, boy.'

'Father, you shouldn't tire yourself by talking so much.'

'Closer!'

A wizened claw reached for him. Little Father approached and the claw seized him. There was frightening strength in the old man still.

Big Father said, 'I'll be up and around in two days. I want the Great Mosque made ready for the ceremony of thanksgiving. And I'll sacrifice to all the prophets and saints.' A fit of coughing overcame him for a space, and he pounded his fist furiously against the side of the divan. When he spoke again, his voice seemed weaker, but still determined. 'There was a vampire upon me, boy! Each night she came in here and drank from me.'

'She?'

'With dark hair and pale foreign skin, and eyes that eat you alive. Every night. Stood above me, and laughed, and took my blood. But she's gone now. These three have imprisoned her and carried her off to the Eleventh Hell.' He gestured toward the marabouts. 'My saints. My heroes. I want them rewarded beyond all reckoning.'

'As you say, Father, so will I do.'

The old man nodded. 'You were getting my funeral ready, weren't you?'

'The prognosis was very dark. Certain preparations seemed advisable when we heard –'

'Cancel them!'

'Of course.' Then, uncertainly: 'Father, special envoys have come from many lands. The Czar's cousin is here, and the brother of Moctezuma, and a son of the late Sultan, and also –'

'I'll hold an audience for them all,' said Big Father in great satisfaction. 'They'll have gifts beyond anything they can imagine. Instead of a funeral, boy, we'll have a jubilee! A celebration of life. Moctezuma's brother, you say? And who did the Inca send?' Big Father laughed raucously. 'All of them clustering around to see me put away underground!' He jabbed a finger against Little Father's breast. It felt like a spear of bone. 'And in Mali they're dancing in the streets, aren't they? Can't contain themselves for glee. But they'll dance a different dance now.' Big Father's eyes grew somber. 'You know, boy, when I really do die, whenever that is, they'll try to take you out too, and Mali will invade us. Guard yourself. Guard the nation. Those bastards on the coast hunger to control our caravan routes. They're probably already scheming now with the foreigners to swallow us the instant I'm gone, but you mustn't allow them to – ah – ah –'

43

'Father?'

Abruptly the Emir's shriveled face crumpled in a frenzy of coughing. He hammered against his thighs with clenched fists. An attendant came running, bearing a beaker of water, and Big Father drank until he had drained it all. Then he tossed the beaker aside as though it were nothing. He was shivering. He looked glassy-eyed and confused. His shoulders slumped, his whole posture slackened. Perhaps his 'recovery' had been merely the sudden final upsurge of a dying fire.

'You should rest, majesty,' said a new voice from the doorway to the porch. It was Serene Glory's ringing contralto. 'You over-tax yourself, I think, in the first hours of this miracle.'

Big Father's main wife had arrived, entourage and all. In the warmth of the morning she had outfitted herself in a startling robe of purple satin, over which she wore the finest jewels of the kingdom. Little Father remembered that his own mother had worn some of those necklaces and bracelets.

He was unmoved by Serene Glory's beauty, impressive though it was. How could Serene Glory matter to him with the memory, scarcely two hours old, of Selima's full breasts and agile thighs still glistening in his mind? But he could not fail to detect Serene Glory's anger. It surrounded her like a radiant aura. Tension sparkled in her kohl-bedecked eyes.

Perhaps she was still smoldering over Little Father's deft rejection of her advances as they were riding side by side back from the Great Mosque that day six months earlier. Or perhaps it was Big Father's unexpected return from the brink that annoyed her. Anyone with half a mind realized that Serene Glory dreamed of putting her own insipid brother on the throne in Little Father's place the moment the old Emir was gone, and thus maintaining and even extending her position at the summit of power. Quite likely she, like Little Father, had by now grown accustomed to the idea of Big Father's death and was having difficulty accepting the news that it would be somewhat postponed.

To Little Father she said, 'Our prayers have been answered, all glory to Allah! But you mustn't put a strain on the Emir's energies in this time of recovery. Perhaps you ought to go.'

'I was summoned, lady.'

'Of course. Quite rightly. And now you should go to the mosque and give thanks for what has been granted us all.'

Her gaze was imperious and unanswerable. In one sentence Serene Glory had demoted him from imminent king to wastrel prince once again. He admired her gall. She was three years younger than Little Father, and here she was ordering him out of the royal presence as though he were a child. But of course she had had practice at ordering people around: her father was one of the greatest landlords of the eastern province. She had moved amidst power all her life, albeit power of a provincial sort. Little Father wondered how many noblemen of that province had spent time between the legs of Serene Glory before she had ascended to her present high position.

He said, 'If my royal father grants me leave to go –'

The Emir was coughing again. He looked terrible.

Serene Glory went to him and bent close over him, so the old man could smell the fragrance rising from her breasts, and instantly Big Father relaxed. The coughing ceased and he sat up again, almost as vigorous as before. Little Father admired that maneuver too. Serene Glory was a worthy adversary. Probably her people were already spreading the word in the city that it was the power of her love for the Emir, and not the prayers of the three saints, that had brought him back from the edge of death.

'How cool it is in here,' Big Father said. 'The wind is rising. Will it rain today? The rains are due, aren't they? Let me see the sky. What color is the sky?' He looked upward in an odd straining way, as though the sky had risen to such a height that it could no longer be seen.

'Father,' Little Father said softly.

The old man glared. 'You heard her, didn't you? To the mosque! To the mosque and give thanks! Do you want Allah to think you're an ingrate, boy?' He started coughing once again. Once again he began visibly to descend the curve of his precarious vitality. His withered cheeks began to grow mottled. There was a feeling of impending death in the air.

Servants and ministers and the three marabouts gathered by his side, alarmed.

'Big Father! Big Father!'

And then once more he was all right again, just as abruptly. He gestured fiercely, an unmistakable dismissal. The woman in purple gave Little Father a dark grin of triumph. Little Father nodded to her gallantly: this round was hers. He knelt at the Emir's side, kissed his royal ring. It slipped about loosely on his shrunken finger. Little Father, thinking of nothing but the pressure of Selima's dark, hard little nipples against the palms of his hands two hours before, made the prostration of filial devotion to his father and, with ferocious irony, to his stepmother, and backed quickly away from the royal presence.

Michael said, distraught, 'I couldn't sleep, sir. I went out for a walk.'

'And you walked *the whole night long*?' Sir Anthony asked, in a voice like a flail.

'I didn't really notice the time. I just kept walking, and by and by the sun came up and I realized that the night was gone.'

'It's your mind that's gone, I think.' Sir Anthony, crooking his neck upward to Michael's much greater height, gave him a whip-crack glare. 'What kind of calf are you, anyway? Haven't you any sense at all?'

'Sir Anthony, I don't underst –'

'Are you in *love*? With the Turkish girl?'

Michael clapped his hand over his mouth in dismay.

'You know about that?' he said lamely, after a moment.

'One doesn't have to be a mind-reader to see it, lad. Every camel in Timbuctoo knows it. The pathetic look on your face whenever she comes within fifty feet of you – the clownish way you shuffle your feet around, and hang your head – those occasional little groans of deepest melancholy –' The envoy glowered. He made no attempt to hide his anger, or his contempt. 'By heaven, I'd like to hang your head, and all the rest of you as well. Have you no sense? Have you no sense whatsoever?'

Everything was lost, so what did anything matter? Defiantly Michael said, 'Have you never fallen unexpectedly in love, Sir Anthony?'

'With a *Turk*?'

'Unexpectedly, I said. These things don't necessarily happen with one's political convenience in mind.'

'And she reciprocates your love, I suppose? That's why you were out walking like a moon-calf in this miserable parched mudhole of a city all night long?'

'She spent the night with the crown prince,' Michael blurted in misery.

'Ah. Ah, now it comes out!' Sir Anthony was silent for a while. Then he glanced up sharply, his eyes bright with skepticism. 'But how do you know that?'

'I saw her leaving his palace at dawn, sir.'

'Spying on her, were you?'

'I just happened to be there. I didn't even know it was his palace, until I asked. He came out himself a few minutes later, and went quickly off somewhere. He looked very troubled.'

'He should have looked troubled. He'd just found out that he might not get to be king as quickly as he'd like to be.'

'I don't understand, please, sir.'

'There's word going around town this morning that the Emir has recovered. And has sent for his son to let him know that he wasn't quite as moribund as was generally believed.'

Michael recoiled in surprise.

'Recovered? Is it true?'

Sir Anthony offered him a benign, patronizing smile.

'So they say. But the Emir's doctors assure us that it's nothing more than a brief rally in an inevitable descent. The old wolf will be dead within the week. Still, it's rather a setback for Little Father's immediate plans. The news of the Emir's unanticipated awakening from his coma must rather have spoiled his morning for him.'

'Good,' said Michael vindictively.

Sir Anthony laughed.

'You hate him, do you?'

'I despise him. I loathe him. I have nothing but the greatest detestation for him. He's a cynical amoral voluptuary and nothing more. He doesn't deserve to be a king.'

47

'Well, if it's any comfort to you, lad, he's not going to live long enough to become one.'

'What?'

'His untimely demise has been arranged. His stepmother is going to poison him at the funeral of the old Emir, if the old Emir ever has the good grace to finish dying.'

'What? What?'

Sir Anthony smiled.

'This is quite confidential, you understand. Perhaps I shouldn't be entrusting you with it just yet. But you'd have needed to find out sooner or later. We've organized a little coup d'état.'

'What? What? What?' said Michael helplessly.

'Her Highness the Lady Serene Glory would like to put her brother on the throne instead of the prince. The brother is worthless, of course. So is the prince, of course, but at least he does happen to be the rightful heir. We don't want to see either of them have it, actually. What we'd prefer is to have the Mansa of Mali declare that the unstable conditions in Songhay following the death of the old Emir have created a danger to the security of all of West Africa that can be put to rest only by an amalgamation of the kingdoms of Mali and Songhay under a single ruler. Who would be, of course, the Mansa of Mali, precisely as your young lady so baldly suggested the other day. And that is what we intend to achieve. The Grand Duke and Prince Itzcoatl and I. As representatives of the powers whom we serve.'

Michael stared. He rubbed his cheeks as if to assure himself that this was no dream. He found himself unable to utter a sound.

Sir Anthony went on, clearly and calmly.

'And so Serene Glory gives Little Father the deadly cup, and then the Mansa's troops cross the border, and we, on behalf of our governments, immediately recognize the new combined government. Which makes everyone happy except, I suppose, the Sultan, who has such good trade relationships with Songhay and is on such poor terms with the Mansa of Mali. But we hardly shed tears for the Sultan's distress, do we, boy? Do we? The distress of the Turks is no concern of ours. Quite the contrary, in fact, is that not so?' Sir Anthony clapped his hand to Michael's shoulder. It was an obvious strain for him, reaching so high. The fingers clamping into Michael's tender sunburned skin were agony. 'So let's see no more mooning over this alluring Ottoman goddess of yours, eh, lad? It's inappropriate for a lovely blond English boy like yourself to be lusting after a Turk, as you know very well. She's nothing but a little slut, however she may seem to your infatuated eyes. And you needn't take the trouble to expend any energy loathing the prince, either. His days are numbered. He won't survive his evil old father by so much as a week. It's all arranged.'

Michael's jaw gaped. A glazed look of disbelief appeared in his eyes. His face was burning fiercely, not from the sunburn now, but from the intensity of his confusion.

'But sir – sir –'

'Get yourself some sleep, boy.'

'*Sir!*'

'Shocked, are you? Well, you shouldn't be. There's nothing shocking about assassinating an inconvenient king. What's shocking to me is a grown man with pure English blood in his veins spending the night creeping pitifully around after his dissolute little Turkish inamorata as she makes her way to the bed of her African lover. And then telling me how heartsore and miserable he is. Get yourself some sleep, boy. Get yourself some sleep!'

In the midst of the uncertainty over the Emir's impending death the semi-annual salt caravan from the north arrived in Timbuctoo. It was a great, if somewhat unexpected, spectacle, and all the foreign ambassadors, restless and by now passionately in need of diversion, turned out despite the heat to watch its entry into the city.

There was tremendous clamor. The heavy metal-studded gates of the city were thrown open and the armed escort entered first, a platoon of magnificent black warriors armed both with rifles and with scimitars. Trumpets brayed, drums pounded. A band of fierce-looking hawk-nosed fiery-eyed country chieftains in flamboyant robes came next, marching in phalanx like conquerors. And then came the salt-laden camels, an endless stream of them, a tawny river, strutting absurdly along in grotesque self-important grandeur with their heads held high and their sleepy eyes indifferent to the throngs of excited spectators. Strapped to each camel's back were two or three huge flat slabs of salt, looking much like broad blocks of marble.

'There are said to be seven hundred of the beasts,' murmured the Chinese ambassador, Li Hsiao-ssu.

'One thousand eight hundred,' said the Grand Duke Alexander sternly. He glowered at Li Hsiao-ssu, a small, fastidious-looking man with drooping mustachios and gleaming porcelain skin, who seemed a mere doll beside the bulky Russian. There was little love lost between the Grand Duke and the Chinese envoy. Evidently the Grand Duke thought it was presumptuous that China, as a client state of the Russian Empire, as a mere vassal, in truth, had sent an ambassador at all. 'One thousand eight hundred. That is the number I was told, and it is reliable. I assure you that it is reliable.'

The Chinese shrugged. 'Seven hundred, three thousand, what difference is there? Either way, that's too many camels to have in one place at one time.'

'Yes, what ugly things they are!' said the Peruvian, Manco Roca. 'Such stupid faces, such an ungainly stride! Perhaps we should do these Africans a favor and let them have a few herds of llamas.'

Coolly Prince Itzcoatl said, 'Your llamas, brother, are no more fit for the deserts of this continent than these camels would be in the passes of the Andes. Let them keep their beasts, and be thankful that you have handsomer ones for your own use.'

'Such stupid faces,' the Peruvian said once more.

Timbuctoo was the center of distribution for salt throughout the whole of West Africa. The salt mines were hundreds of miles away, in the center of the Sahara. Twice a year the desert traders made the twelve-day journey to the capital, where they exchanged their salt for the dried fish, grain, rice, and other produce that came up the Niger from the agricultural districts to the south and east. The arrival of the caravan was the occasion for feasting and revelry, a time of wild big-city gaiety for the visitors from such remote and placid rural outposts.

But the Emir of Songhai was dying. This was no time for a festival. The appearance of the caravan at such a moment was evidently a great embarrassment to the city officials, a mark of bad management as well as bad taste.

'They could have sent messengers upcountry to turn them back,' Michael said. 'Why didn't they, I wonder?'

'Blacks,' said Manco Roca morosely. 'What can you expect from blacks.'

'Yes, of course,' Sir Anthony said, giving the Peruvian a disdainful look. 'We understand that they aren't Incas. Yet despite that shortcoming they've somehow managed to keep control of most of this enormous continent for thousands of years.'

'But their colossal administrative incompetence, my dear Sir Anthony – as we see here, letting a circus like this one come into town while their king lies dying –'

'Perhaps it's deliberate,' Ismet Akif suggested. 'A much needed distraction. The city is tense. The Emir's been too long about his dying; it's driving everyone crazy. So they decided to let the caravan come marching in.'

'I think not,' said Li Hsiao-ssu. 'Do you see those municipal officials there? I detect signs of deep humiliation on their faces.'

'And who would be able to detect such things more acutely than you?' asked the Grand Duke.

The Chinese envoy stared at the Russian as though unsure whether he was being praised or mocked. For a moment his elegant face was dusky with blood. The other diplomats gathered close, making ready to defuse the situation. Politeness was ever a necessity in such a group.

Then the envoy from the Teutonic States said, 'Is that not the prince arriving now?'

'Where?' Michael demanded in a tight-strung voice. 'Where is he?'

Sir Anthony's hand shot out to seize Michael's wrist. He squeezed it unsparingly.

In a low tone he said, 'You will cause no difficulties, young sir. Remember that you are English. Your breeding must rule your passions.'

Michael, glaring toward Little Father as the prince approached the city gate, sullenly pulled his arm free of Sir Anthony's grasp and amazed himself by uttering a strange low growling sound, like that of a cat announcing a challenge. Unfamiliar hormones flooded the channels of his body. He could feel the individual bones of his cheeks and forehead moving apart from one another, he was aware of the tensing and coiling of muscles great and small. He wondered if he was losing his mind. Then the moment passed and he let out his breath in a long dismal exhalation.

Little Father wore flowing green pantaloons, a striped robe wide enough to cover his arms, and an intricately deployed white turban with brilliant feathers of some exotic sort jutting from it. An entourage of eight or ten men surrounded him, carrying iron-shafted lances. The prince strode forward so briskly that his bodyguard was hard pressed to keep up with him.

Michael, watching Selima out of the corner of his eye, murmured to Sir Anthony, 'I'm terribly sorry, sir. But if he so much as glances at her you'll have to restrain me.'

'If you so much as flicker a nostril I'll have you billeted in our Siberian consulate for the rest of your career,' Sir Anthony replied, barely moving his lips as he spoke.

But Little Father had no time to flirt with Selima now. He barely acknowledged the presence of the ambassadors at all. A stiff formal nod, and then he moved on, into the midst of the group of caravan leaders. They clustered about him like a convocation of eagles. Among those sun-crisped swarthy upright chieftains the prince seemed soft, frail, overly citified, a dabbler confronting serious men.

Some ritual of greeting seemed to be going on. Little Father touched his forehead, extended his open palm, closed his hand with a snap, presented his palm again with a flourish. The desert men responded with equally stylized maneuvers.

When Little Father spoke, it was in Songhay, a sharp outpouring of liquid incomprehensibilities.

'What was that? What was that?' asked the ambassadors of one another. Turkish was the international language of diplomacy, even in Africa; the native tongues of the dark continent were mysteries to outsiders.

Sir Anthony, though, said softly, 'He's angry. He says the city's closed on account of the Emir's illness and the caravan was supposed to have waited at Kabara for further instructions. They seem surprised. Someone must have missed a signal.'

'You speak Songhay, sir?' Michael asked.

'I was posted in Mali for seven years,' Sir Anthony muttered. 'It was before you were born, boy.'

'So I was right,' cried Manco Roca. 'The caravan should never have been allowed to enter the city at all. Incompetence! Incompetence!'

'Is he telling them to leave?' Ismet Akif wanted to know.

'I can't tell. They're all talking at once. I think they're saying that their camels need fodder. And he's telling them that there's no merchandise for them to buy, that the goods from upriver were held back because of the Emir's illness.'

'What an awful jumble,' Selima said.

It was the first thing she had said all morning. Michael, who had been trying to pay no attention to her, looked toward her now in agitation. She was dressed chastely enough, in a red blouse and flaring black skirt, but in his inflamed mind she stood revealed suddenly nude, with the marks of Little Father's caresses flaring like stigmata on her breasts and thighs. Michael sucked in his breath and held himself stiffly erect, trembling like a drawn bowstring. A sound midway between a sigh and a groan escaped him. Sir Anthony kicked his ankle sharply.

Some sort of negotation appeared to be going on. Little Father gesticulated rapidly, grinned, did the open-close-open gesture with his hand again, tapped his chest and his forehead and his left elbow. The apparent leader of the traders matched him, gesture for gesture. Postures began to change. The tensions were easing. Evidently the caravan would be admitted to the city.

Little Father was smiling, after a fashion. His forehead glistened with sweat; he seemed to have come through a difficult moment well, but he looked tired.

The trumpets sounded again. The camel-drovers regained the attention of their indifferent beasts and nudged them forward.

There was new commotion from the other side of the plaza.

'What's this, now?' Prince Itzcoatl said.

A runner clad only in a loincloth appeared, coming from the direction of the city center, clutching a scroll. He was moving fast, loping in a strange lurching way. In the stupefying heat he seemed to be in peril of imminent collapse. But he staggered up to Little Father and put the scroll in his hand.

Little Father unrolled it quickly and scanned it. He nodded somberly and turned to his vizier, who stood just to his left. They spoke briefly in low whispers. Sir Anthony, straining, was unable to make out a word.

A single chopping gesture from Little Father was enough to halt the resumption of the caravan's advance into the city. The prince beckoned the leaders of the traders to his side and conferred with them a moment or two, this time without ceremonial gesticulations. The desert men exchanged glances with one another. Then they barked rough commands. The whole vast caravan began to reverse itself.

Little Father's motorcar was waiting a hundred paces away. He went to it now, and it headed cityward, emitting belching bursts of black smoke and loud intermittent thunderclaps of inadequate combustion.

The prince's entourage, left behind in the suddenness, milled about aimlessly. The vizier, making shooing gestures, ordered them in some annoyance to follow their master on foot toward town. He himself held his place, watching the departure of the caravaneers.

'Ali Pasha!' Sir Anthony called. 'Can you tell us what's happened? Is there bad news?'

The vizier turned. He seemed radiant with self-importance.

'The Emir has taken a turn for the worse. They think he'll be with Allah within the hour.'

'But he was supposed to be recovering,' Michael protested.

Indifferently, Ali Pasha said, 'That was earlier. This is now.' The vizier seemed not to be deeply moved by the news. If anything his smugness seemed to have been enhanced by it. Perhaps it was something he had been very eager to hear. 'The caravan must camp outside the city walls until after the funeral. There is nothing more to be seen here today. You should all go back to your residences.'

The ambassadors began to look around for their drivers.

Michael, who had come out here with Sir Anthony in the embassy motorcar, was disconcerted to discover that the envoy had already vanished, slipping away in the uproar without waiting for him. Well, it wasn't an impossible walk back to town. He had walked five times as far in his night of no sleep.

'Michael?'

Selima was calling to him. He looked toward her, appalled.

'Walk with me,' she said. 'I have a parasol. You can't let yourself get any more sun on your face.'

'That's very kind of you,' he said mechanically, while lunatic jealousy and anger roiled him within. Searing contemptuous epithets came to his lips and died there, unspoken. To him she was ineluctably soiled by the presumed embraces of that night of shame. How could she have done it? The prince had wiggled his finger at her, and she had run to him without a moment's hesitation. Once more unwanted images surged through his mind: Selima and the prince entwined on a leopardskin rug; the prince mounting Selima in some unthinkable bestial African position of love; Selima, giggling girlishly, instructing the prince afterward in the no doubt equally depraved sexual customs of the land of the Sultan. Michael understood that he was being foolish; that Selima was free to do as she pleased in this loathsome land; that he himself had never staked any claim on her attention more significant than a few callow love-sick stares, so why should she have felt any compunctions about amusing herself with the prince if the prince offered amusement? 'Very kind,' he said. She handed the parasol up to him and he took it from her with a rigid nerveless hand. They began to walk side by side in the direction of town, close together under the narrow, precisely defined shadow of the parasol beneath the unsparing eye of the noonday sun.

She said, 'Poor Michael. I've upset you terribly, haven't I?'

'Upset me? How have you possibly upset me?'

'You know.'

'No. No, really.'

His legs were leaden. The sun was hammering the top of his brain through the parasol, through his wide-brimmed topee, through his skull itself. He could not imagine how he would find the strength to walk all the way back to town with her.

'I've been very mischievous,' she said.

'Have you?'

He wished he were a million miles away.

'By visiting the prince in his palace that night.'

'Please, Selima.'

'I saw you, you know. Early in the morning, when I was leaving. You ducked out of sight, but not quite fast enough.'

'Selima –'

'I couldn't help myself. Going there, I mean. I wanted to see what his palace looked like. I wanted to get to know him a little better. He's very nice, you know. No, nice isn't quite the word. He's shrewd, and part of being shrewd is knowing how to seem nice. I don't really think he's nice at all. He's quite sophisticated – quite subtle.'

She was flaying him, inch by inch. Another word out of her and he'd drop the parasol and run.

'The thing is, Michael, he enjoys pretending to be some sort of a primitive, a barbarian, a jungle prince. But it's only a pretense. And why shouldn't it be? These are ancient kingdoms here in Africa. This isn't any jungle land with tigers sleeping behind every palm tree. They've got laws and culture, they've got courts, they have a university. And they've had centuries to develop a real aristocracy. They're just as complicated and cunning as we are. Maybe more so. I was glad to get to know the man behind the facade, a little. He was fascinating, in his way, but –' She smiled brightly. 'But I have to tell you, Michael: he's not my type at all.'

That startled him, and awakened sudden new hope. Perhaps he never actually touched her, Michael told himself. Perhaps they had simply talked all night. Played little sly verbal games of one-upmanship, teasing each other, vying with each other to be sly and cruel and playful. Showing each other how complicated and cunning they could really be. Demonstrating the virtues of hundreds of years of aristocratic inbreeding. Perhaps they were too well bred to think of doing anything so commonplace as – as –

'What is your type, then?' he asked, willy-nilly.

56

'I prefer men who are a little shy. Men who can sometimes be foolish, even.' There was unanticipated softness in her voice, conveying a sincerity that Michael prayed was real. 'I hate the kind who are always calculating, calculating, calculating. There's something very appealing to me about English men, I have to tell you, precisely because they *don't* seem so dark and devious inside – not that I've met very many of them before this trip, you understand, but – oh, Michael, Michael, you're terribly angry with me, I know, but you shouldn't be! What happened between me and the prince was nothing. Nothing! And now that he'll be preoccupied with the funeral, perhaps there'll be a chance for you and me to get to know each other a little better – to slip off, for a day, let's say, while all the others are busy with the pomp and circumstance –'

She gave him a melting look. He thought for one astounded moment that she actually might mean what she was telling him.

'They're going to assassinate him,' he suddenly heard his own voice saying, 'right at the funeral.'

'What?'

'It's all set up.' The words came rolling from him spontaneously, unstoppably, like the flow of a river. 'His stepmother, the old king's young wife – she's going to slip him a cup of poisoned wine, or something, during one of the funeral rituals. What she wants is to make her stupid brother king in the prince's place, and rule the country as the power behind the throne.'

Selima made a little gasping sound and stepped away from him, out from under the shelter of the parasol. She stood staring at him as though he had been transformed in the last moment or two into a hippopotamus, or a rock, or a tree.

It took her a little while to find her voice.

'Are you serious? How do you know?'

'Sir Anthony told me.'

'Sir Anthony?'

'He's behind it. He and the Russian and Prince Itzcoatl. Once the prince is out of the way, they're going to invite the King of Mali to step in and take over.'

Her gaze grew very hard. Her silence was inscrutable, painfully so.

Then, totally regaining her composure with what must have been an extraordinary act of inner discipline, she said, 'I think this is all very unlikely.'

She might have been responding to a statement that snow would soon begin falling in the streets of Timbuctoo.

'You think so?'

'Why should Sir Anthony support this assassination? England has nothing to gain from destabilizing West Africa. England is a minor power still struggling to establish its plausibility in the world as an independent state. Why should it risk angering a powerful African empire like Songhay by meddling in its internal affairs?'

Michael let the slight to his country pass unchallenged, possibly because it seemed less like a slight to him than a statement of the mere reality. He searched instead for some reason of state that would make what he had asserted seem sensible.

After a moment he said, 'Mali and Songhay together would be far more powerful than either one alone. If England plays an instrumental role in delivering the throne of Songhay up to Mali, England will surely be given a preferential role by the Mansa of Songhay in future West African trade.'

Selima nodded. 'Perhaps.'

'And the Russians – you know how they feel about the Ottoman Empire. Your people are closely allied with Songhay and don't get along well with Mali. A coup d'état here would virtually eliminate Turkey as a commercial force in West Africa.'

'Very likely.'

She was so cool, so terribly calm.

'As for the Aztec role in this –' Michael shook his head. 'God knows. But the Mexicans are always scheming around in things. Maybe they see some way of hurting Peru. There's a lot of sea trade, you know, between Mali and Peru – it's an amazingly short hop across the ocean from West Africa to Peru's eastern provinces in Brazil – and the Mexicans may believe they could divert some of that trade to themselves by winning the Mansa's favor by helping him gain possession of –'

He faltered to a halt. Something was happening. Her expression was starting to change. Her facade of detached skepticism was visibly collapsing, slowly but irreversibly, like a brick wall undermined by a great earthquake.

'Yes. Yes, I see. There are substantial reasons for such a scheme. And so they will kill the prince,' Selima said.

'Have him killed, rather.'

'It's the same thing! The very same thing!'

Her eyes began to glisten. She drew even further back from him and turned her head away, and he realized that she was trying to conceal tears from him. But she couldn't hide the sobs that racked her.

He suspected that she was one who cried very rarely, if at all. Seeing her weep now in this uncontrollable way plunged him into an abyss of dejection.

She was making no attempt to hide her love of the prince from him. That was the only explanation for these tears.

'Selima – please, Selima –'

He felt useless.

He realized, also, that he had destroyed himself.

He had committed this monstrous breach of security, he saw now, purely in the hope of insinuating himself into her confidence, to bind her to him in a union that proceeded from shared possession of an immense secret. He had taken her words at face value when she had told him that the prince was nothing to her.

That had been a serious error. He had thought he was making a declaration of love; but all he had done was to reveal a state secret to England's ancient enemy.

He waited, feeling huge and clumsy and impossibly naive.

Then, abruptly, her sobbing stopped and she looked toward him, a little puffy-eyed now, but otherwise as inscrutable as before.

'I'm not going to say anything about this to anyone.'

'What?'

'Not to him, not to my father, not to anyone.'

He was mystified. As usual.

'But – Selima –'

'I told you. The prince is nothing to me. And this is only a crazy rumor. How do I know it's true? How do you know it's true?'

'Sir Anthony –'

'Sir Anthony! Sir Anthony! For all I know, he's floated this whole thing simply to ensnare my father in some enormous embarrassment. I tell my father there's going to be an assassination and my father tells the prince, as he'd feel obliged to do. And then the prince arrests and expels the ambassadors of England and Russia and Mexico? But where's the proof? There isn't any. It's all a Turkish invention, they say. A scandal. My father is sent home in disgrace. His career is shattered. Songhay breaks off diplomatic relations with the Empire. No, no, don't you see, I can't say a thing.'

'But the prince –'

'His stepmother hates him. If he's idiotic enough to let her hand him a cup of something without having it tested, he deserves to be poisoned. What is is that to me? He's only a savage. Hold the parasol closer, Michael, and let's get back to town. Oh, this heat! This unending heat! Do you think it'll ever rain here?' Her face now showed no sign of tears at all. Wearily Michael lowered the parasol. Selima utterly baffled him. She was an exhausting person. His head was aching. For a shilling he'd be glad to resign his post and take up sheep farming somewhere in the north of England. It was getting very obvious to him and probably to everyone else that he had no serious future in the diplomatic corps.

Little Father, emerging from the tunnel that led from the Emir's palace to his own, found Ali Pasha waiting in the little colonnaded gallery known as the Promenade of Askia Mohammed. The prince was surprised to see a string charm of braided black, red, and yellow cords dangling around the vizier's neck. Ali Pasha had never been one for wearing grigri before; but no doubt the imminent death of the Emir was unsettling everyone, even a piece of tough leather like Ali Pasha.

The vizier offered a grand salaam. 'Your royal father, may Allah embrace him, sir –'

'My royal father is still breathing, thank you. It looks now as if he'll last until morning.' Little Father glanced around, a little wildly, peering into the courtyard of his palace. 'Somehow we've left too much for the last minute. The Lady Serene Glory is arranging for the washing of the body. It's too late to do anything about that, but we can supply the graveclothes, at least. Get the very finest white silks; the royal burial shroud should be something out of the *Thousand and One Nights*; and I want rubies in the turban. Actual rubies, no damned imitations. And after that I want you to set up the procession to the Great Mosque – I'll be one of the pallbearers, of course, and we'll ask the Mansa of Mali to be another – he's arrived by now, hasn't he? – and let's have the King of Benin as the third one, and for the fourth, well, either the Asante of Ghana or the Grand Fon of Dahomey, whichever one shows up here first. The important thing is that all four of the pallbearers should be kings, because Serene Glory wants to push her brother forward to be one, and I can't allow that. She won't be able to argue precedence for him if the pallbearers are all kings, when all he is is a provincial cadi. Behind the bier we'll have the overseas ambassadors marching five abreast – put the Turk and the Russian in the front row, the Maori too, and the Aztec and the Inca on the outside edges to keep them as far apart as we can, and the order of importance after that is up to you, only be sure that little countries like England and the Teutonic States don't wind up too close to the major powers, and that the various vassal nations like China and Korea and Ind are in the back. Now, as far as the decorations on the barge that'll be taking my father downriver to the burial place at Gao –'

'Little Father,' the Vizier said, as the prince paused for breath, 'the Turkish woman is waiting upstairs.'

Little Father gave him a startled look.

'I don't remember asking her to come here.'

'She didn't say you had. But she asked for an urgent audience, and I thought –' Ali Pasha favored Little Father with an obscenely knowing smile. 'It seemed reasonable to admit her.'

'She knows that my father is dying, and that I'm tremendously busy?'

'I told her what was taking place, majesty,' said Ali Pasha unctuously.

'Don't call me "majesty" yet!'

'A thousand pardons, Little Father. But she is aware of the nature of the crisis, no question of that. Nevertheless, she insisted on –'

'Oh, damn. Damn! But I suppose I can give her two or three minutes. Stop smiling like that, damn you! I'll feed you to the lions if you don't! What do you think I am, a mountain of lechery? This is a busy moment. When I say two or three minutes, two or three minutes is what I mean.'

Selima was pacing about on the porch where she and Little Father had spent their night of love. No filmy robes today, no seductively visible breasts bobbing about beneath, this time. She was dressed simply, in European clothes. She seemed all business.

'The Emir is in his last hours,' Little Father said. 'The whole funeral has to be arranged very quickly.'

'I won't take up much of your time, then.' Her tone was cool. There was a distinct edge on it. Perhaps he had been too brusque with her. That night on the porch *had* been a wonderful one, after all. She said, 'I just have one question. Is there some sort of ritual at a royal funeral where you're given a cup of wine to drink?'

'You know that the Koran doesn't permit the drinking of –'

'Yes, yes, I know that. A cup of *something*, then.'

Little Father studied her carefully. 'This is anthropological research? The sort of thing the golden-haired woman from England came here to do? Why does this matter to you, Selima?'

'Never mind that. It matters.'

He sighed. She *seemed* so gentle and retiring, until she opened her mouth.

'There's a cup ceremony, yes. It isn't wine or anything else alcoholic. It's an aromatic potion, brewed from various spices and honeys and such, very disagreeably sweet, my father once told me. Drinking it symbolizes the passage of royal power from one generation to the next.'

'And who is supposed to hand you the cup?'

'May I ask why at this particularly hectic time you need to know these details?'

'Please,' she said.

There was an odd urgency in her voice.

'The former queen, the mother of the heir to the throne, is the one who hands the new Emir the cup.'

'But your mother is dead. Therefore your stepmother Serene Glory will hand it to you.'

'That's correct.' Little Father glanced at his watch. 'Selima, you don't seem to understand. I need to finish working out the funeral arrangements and then get back to my father's bedside before he dies. If you don't mind –'

'There's going to be poison in the cup.'

'This is no time for romantic fantasies.'

'It isn't a fantasy. She's going to slip you a cup of poison, and you won't be able to tell that the poison is there because what you drink is so heavily spiced anyway. And when you keel over in the mosque her brother's going to leap forward in the moment of general shock and tell everyone that he's in charge.'

The day had been one long disorderly swirl. But suddenly now the world stood still, as though there had been an unscheduled eclipse of the sun. For a moment he had difficulty simply seeing her.

'What are you saying, Selima?'

'Do you want me to repeat it all, or is that just something you're saying as a manner of speaking because you're so astonished?'

He could see and think again. He examined her closely. She was unreadable, as she usually was. Now that the first shock of her bland statement was past, this all was starting to seem to him like fantastic nonsense; and yet, and yet, it certainly wasn't beyond Serene Glory's capabilities to have hatched such a scheme.

How, though, could the Turkish girl possibly know anything about it? How did she even know about the ritual of the cup?

'If we were in bed together right now,' he said, 'and you were in my arms and right on the edge of the big moment, and I stopped moving and asked you right then and there what proof you had of this story, I'd probably believe whatever you told me. I think people tend to be honest at such moments. Even you would speak the truth. But we have no time for that now. The kingship will change hands in a few hours, and I'm exceedingly busy. I need you to cast away all of your fondness for manipulative amusements and give me straight answers.'

Her dark eyes flared. 'I should simply have let them poison you.'

'Do you mean that?'

'What you just said was insufferable.'

'If I was too blunt, I ask you to forgive me. I'm under great strain today and if what you've told me is any sort of joke, I don't need it. If this isn't a joke, you damned well can't withhold any of the details.'

'I've given you the details.'

'Not all. Who'd you hear all this from?'

She sighed and placed one wrist across the other.

'Michael. The tall Englishman.'

'That adolescent?'

'He's a little on the innocent side, especially for a diplomat, yes. But I don't think he's as big a fool as he's been letting himself appear lately. He heard it from Sir Anthony.'

'So this is an English plot?'

'English and Russian and Mexican.'

'All three.' Little Father digested that. 'What's the purpose of assassinating me?'

'To make Serene Glory's brother Emir of Songhay.'

'And serve as their puppet, I suppose?'

Selima shook her head. 'Serene Glory and her brother are only the ignorant instruments of their real plan. They'll simply be brushed aside when the time comes. What the plotters are really intending to do, in the confusion following your death, is ask the Mansa of Mali to seize control of Songhay. They'll put the support of their countries behind him.'

'Ah,' Little Father said. And after a moment, again, 'Ah.'

'Mali-Songhay would favor the Czar instead of the Sultan. So the Russians like the idea. What injures the Sultan is good for the English. So they're in on it. As for the Aztecs –'

Little Father shrugged and gestured to her to stop. Already he could taste the poison in his gut, burning through his flesh. Already he could see the green-clad troops of Mali parading in the streets of Timbuctoo and Gao, where kings of Mali had been hailed as supreme monarchs once before, hundreds of years ago.

'Look at me,' he said. 'You swear that you're practicing no deception, Selima?'

'I swear it by – by the things we said to each other the night we lay together.'

He considered that. Had she fallen in love with him in the midst of all her game-playing? So it might seem. Could he trust what she was saying, therefore? He believed he could. Indeed the oath she had just proposed might have more plausibility than any sort of oath she might have sworn on a Koran.

'Come here,' he said.

She approached him. Little Father swept her up against him, holding her tightly, and ran his hands down her back to her buttocks. She pressed her hips forward. He covered her mouth with his and jammed down hard, not a subtle kiss but one that would put to rest forever, if that were needed, the bit of fake anthropology he had given to her earlier, about the supposed distaste of Songhayans for the act of kissing. After a time he released her. Her eyes were a little glazed, her breasts were rising and falling swiftly.

He said, 'I'm grateful for what you've told me. I'll take the appropriate steps, and thank you.'

'I had to let you know. I was going just to sit back and let whatever happened happen. But then I saw I couldn't conceal such a thing from you.'

'Of course not, Selima.'

Her look was a soft and eager one. She was ready to run off to the bedchamber with him, or so it seemed. But not now, not on this day of all days. That would be a singularly bad idea.

'On the other hand,' he said, 'if it turns out that there's no truth to any of this, that it's all some private amusement of your own or some intricate deception being practiced on me by the Sultan for who knows what unfathomable reason, you can be quite certain that I'll avenge myself in a remarkably vindictive way once the excitements of the funeral and the coronation are over.'

The softness vanished at once. The hatred that came into her eyes was extraordinary.

'You black bastard,' she said.

'Only partly black. There is much Moorish blood in the veins of the nobility of Songhay.' He met her seething gaze with tranquility. 'In the old days we believed in absorbing those who attempt to conquer us. These days we still do, something that the Mansa of Mali ought to keep in mind. He's got a fine harem, I understand.'

'Did you *have* to throw cold water on me like that? Everything I told you was the truth.'

'I hope and believe it is. I think there was love between us that night on the porch, and I wouldn't like to think that you'd betray someone you love. The question, I suppose, is whether the Englishman was telling *you* the truth. Which still remains to be seen.' He took her hand and kissed it lightly, in the European manner. 'As I said before, I'm very grateful, Selima. And hope to continue to be. If I may, now –'

She gave him one final glare and took her leave of him. Little Father walked quickly to the edge of the porch, spun about, walked quickly back. For an instant or two he stood in the doorway like his own statue. But his mind was in motion, and moving very swiftly.

He peered down the stairs to the courtyard below.

'Ali Pasha!'

The vizier came running.

'What the woman wanted to tell me,' Little Father said, 'is that there is a plot against my life.'

The look that appeared on the vizier's face was one of total shock and indignation.

'You believe her?'

'Unfortunately I think I do.'

Ali Pasha began to quiver with wrath. His broad glossy cheeks grew congested, his eyes bulged. Little Father thought the man was in danger of exploding.

'Who are the plotters, Little Father? I'll have them rounded up within the hour.'

'The Russian ambassador, apparently. The Aztec one. And the little Englishman, Sir Anthony.'

'To the lions with them! They'll be in the pit before night comes!'

Little Father managed an approximation of a smile.

'Surely you recall the concept of diplomatic immunity, Ali Pasha?'

'But – a conspiracy against your majesty's life –!'

'Not yet my majesty, Ali Pasha.'

'Your pardon.' Ali Pasha struggled with confusion. 'You must take steps to protect yourself, Little Father. Did she tell you what the plan is supposed to be?'

Little Father nodded. 'When Serene Glory hands me the coronation cup at the funeral service, there will be poison in the drink.'

'Poison!'

'Yes. I fall down dead. Serene Glory turns to her miserable brother and offers him the crown on the spot. But no, the three ambassadors have other ideas. They'll ask Mansa Suleiyman to proclaim himself king, in the name of the general safety. In that moment Songhay will come under the rule of Mali.'

'Never! To the lions with Mansa Suleiyman too, majesty!'

'No one goes to the lions, Ali Pasha. And stop calling me majesty. We'll deal with this in a calm and civilized way, is that understood?'

'I am completely at your command, sir. As always.'

Little Father nodded. He felt his strength rising, moment by moment. His mind was wondrously clear. He asked himself if that was what it felt like to be a king. Though he had spent so much time being a prince, he had in fact given too little thought to what the actual sensations and processes of being a king might be, he realized now. His royal father had held the kingdom entirely in his own hands throughout all his long reign. But something must be changing now.

He went unhurriedly to the edge of the porch, and stared out into the distance. To his surprise, there was a dark orange cloud on the horizon, sharply defined against the sky.

'Look there, Ali Pasha. The rains are coming!'

'The first cloud, yes. There it is!' And he began to finger the woven charm that hung about his neck.

It was always startling when the annual change came, after so many months of unbroken hot dry weather. Even after a lifetime of watching the shift occur, no one in Songhay was unmoved by the approach of the first cloud, for it was a powerful omen of transition and culmination, removing a great element of uncertainty and fear from the minds of the citizens; for until the change finally arrived, there was always the chance that it might never come, that this time the summer would last forever and the parched world would burn to a crisp.

Little Father said, 'I should go to my father without any further delay. Certainly this means that his hour has come.'

'Yes. Yes.'

The orange cloud was sweeping toward the city with amazing rapidity. In another few minutes all Timbuctoo would be enveloped in blackness as a whirling veil of fine sand whipped down over it. Little Father felt the air grow moist. There would be a brief spell of intolerable humidity, now, so heavy that breathing itself would be a vast effort. And then, abruptly, the temperature would drop, the chill rain would descend, rivers would run in the sandy streets, the marketplace would become a lake.

He raced indoors, with Ali Pasha following along helter-skelter behind him.

'The plotters, sir –' the vizier gasped.

Little Father smiled. 'I'll invite Serene Glory to share the cup with me. We'll see what she does then. Just be ready to act when I give the orders.'

There was darkness at every window. The sandstorm was at hand. Trillions of tiny particles beat insistently at every surface, setting up a steady drumming that grew and grew and grew in intensity. The air had turned sticky, almost viscous: it was hard work to force oneself forward through it.

Gasping for breath, Little Father moved as quickly as he was able down the subterranean passageway that linked his palace with the much greater one that shortly would be his.

The ministers and functionaries of the royal court were wailing and weeping. The Grand Vizier of the realm, waiting formally at the head of the Stairs of Allah, glared at Little Father as though he were the Angel of Death himself.

'There is not much more time, Little Father.'

'So I understand.'

He rushed out onto his father's porch. There had been no opportunity to bring the Emir indoors. The old man lay amidst his dazzling blankets with his eyes open and one hand upraised. He was in the correct position in which a Moslem should pass from this world to the next, his head to the south, his face turned toward the east.

The sky was black with sand, and it came cascading down with unremitting force. The three saintly marabouts who had attended Big Father throughout his final illness stood above him, shielding the Emir from the shower of tiny abrasive particles with an improvised canopy, an outstretched bolt of satin.

'Father! Father!'

The Emir tried to sit up. He looked a thousand years old. His eyes glittered like lightning-bolts, and he said something, three or four congested syllables. Little Father was unable to understand a thing. The old man was already speaking the language of the dead.

There was a clap of thunder. The Emir fell back against his pillows.

The sky opened and the first rain of the year came down in implacable torrents, in such abundance as had not been seen in a thousand years.

In the three days since the old Emir's death Little Father had lived through this scene three thousand times in his imagination. But now it was actually occurring. They were in the Great Mosque; the mourners, great and simple, were clustered elbow to elbow; the corpse of Big Father, embalmed so that it could endure the slow journey downriver to the royal burial grounds, lay in splendor atop its magnificent bier. Any ordinary citizen of Songhay would have gone from his deathbed to his grave in two hours, or less; but kings were exempt from the ordinary customs.

They were done at last with the chanting of the prayer for the dead. Now they were doing the prayer for the welfare of the kingdom. Little Father held his body rigid, barely troubling to breathe. He saw before him the grand nobles of the realm, the kings of the adjacent countries, the envoys of the overseas lands, all staring, all maintaining a mien of the deepest solemnity, even those who could not comprehend a word of what was being said.

And here was Serene Glory, now, coming forth bearing the cup that would make him Emir of Songhay, Great Imam, master of the nation, successor to all the great lords who had led the empire in grandeur for a thousand years.

She looked magnificent, truly queenly, more beautiful in her simple funeral robe and unadorned hair than she could ever have looked in all her finery. The cup, a stark bowl of lustrous chalcedony, so translucent that the dark liquor that would make him king was plainly visible through its thin walls, was resting lightly on her upturned palms.

He searched her for a sign of tremor and saw none. She was utterly calm. He felt a disturbing moment of doubt.

She handed him the cup, and spoke the words of succession, clearly, unhesitatingly, omitting not the smallest syllable. She was in full control of herself.

When he lifted the cup to his lips, though, he heard the sharp unmistakable sound of her suddenly indrawn breath, and all hesitation went from him.

'Mother,' he said.

The unexpected word reverberated through the whitewashed alcoves of the Great Mosque. They must all be looking at him in bewilderment.

'Mother, in this solemn moment of the passing of the kingship, I beg you share my ascension with me. Drink with me, mother. Drink. Drink.'

He held the untouched cup out toward the woman who had just handed it to him.

Her eyes were bright with horror.

'Drink with me, mother,' he said again.

'No – no –'

She backed a step or two away from him, making sounds like gravel in her throat.

'Mother – lady, dear lady –'

He held the cup out, insistently. He moved closer to her. She seemed frozen. The truth was emblazoned on her face. Rage rose like a fountain in him, and for an instant he thought he was going to hurl the drink in her face; but then he regained his poise. Her hand was pressed against her lips in terror. She moved back, back, back.

And then she was running toward the door of the mosque; and abruptly the Grand Duke Alexander Petrovich, his face erupting with red blotches of panic, was running also, and also Prince Itzcoatl of Mexico.

'No! Fools!' a voice cried out, and the echoes hammered at the ancient walls.

Little Father looked toward the foreign ambassadors. Sir Anthony stood out as though in a spotlight, his cheeks blazing, his eyes popping, his fingers exploring his lips as though he could not believe they had actually uttered that outcry.

There was complete confusion in the mosque. Everyone was rushing about, everyone was bellowing. But Little Father was quite calm. Carefully he set the cup down, untouched, at his feet. Ali Pasha came to his side at once.

'Round them up quickly,' he told the vizier. 'The three ambassadors are *persona non grata*. They're to leave Songhay by the next riverboat. Escort Mansa Suleiyman back to the Embassy of Mali and put armed guards around the building – for purely protective purposes, of course. And also the embassies of Ghana, Dahomey, Benin, and the rest, for good measure – and as window-dressing.'

'It will be done, majesty.'

'Very good.' He indicated the chalcedony cup. 'As for this stuff, give it to a dog to drink, and let's see what happens.'

Ali Pasha nodded and touched his forehead.

'And the lady Serene Glory, and her brother?'

'Take them into custody. If the dog dies, throw them both to the lions.'

'Your majesty –!'

'To the lions, Ali Pasha.'

'But you said –'

'To the lions, Ali Pasha.'

'I hear and obey, majesty.'

'You'd better.' Little Father grinned. He was Little Father no longer, he realized. 'I like the way you say it: *Majesty*. You put just the right amount of awe into it.'

'Yes, majesty. Is there anything else, majesty?'

'I want an escort too, to take me to my palace. Say, fifty men. No, make it a hundred. Just in case there are any surprises waiting for us outside.'

'To your old palace, majesty?'

The question caught him unprepared. 'No,' he said after a moment's reflection. 'Of course not. To my new palace. To the palace of the Emir.'

Selima came hesitantly forward into the throne room, which was one of the largest, most forbidding rooms she had ever entered. Not even the Sultan's treasurehouse at the Topkapi Palace had any chamber to match this one for for sheer dismal mustiness, for clutter, or for the eerie hodgepodge of its contents. She found the new Emir standing beneath a stuffed giraffe, examining an ivory globe twice the size of a man's head that was mounted on an intricately carved spiral pedestal.

'You sent for me, your highness?'

'Yes. Yes, I did. It's all calm outside there, now, I take it?'

'Very calm. *Very* calm.'

'Good. And the weather's still cool?'

'Quite cool, your majesty.'

'But not raining again yet?'

'No, not raining.'

'Good.' Idly he fondled the globe. 'The whole world is here, do you know that? Right under my hand. Here's Africa, here's Europe, here's Russia. This is the Empire, here.' He brushed his hand across the globe from Istanbul to Madrid. 'There's still plenty of it, eh?' He spun the ivory sphere easily on its pedestal. 'And this, the New World. Such emptiness there. The Incas down here in the southern continent, the Aztecs here in the middle, and a lot of nothing up here in the north. I once asked my father, do you know, if I could pay a visit to those empty lands. So cool there, I hear. So green, and almost empty. Just the red-skinned people, and not very many of them. Are they really red, do you think? I've never seen one.' He looked closely at her. 'Have you ever thought of leaving Turkey, I wonder, and taking up a new life for yourself in those wild lands across the ocean?'

'Never, your majesty.'

She was trembling a little.

'You should think of it. We all should. Our countries are all too old. The land is tired. The air is tired. The rivers move slowly. We should go somewhere where things are fresh.' She made no reply. After a moment's silence he said, 'Do you love that tall gawky pink-faced Englishman, Selima?'

'Love?'

'Love, yes. Do you have any kind of fondness for him? Do you care for him at all? If love is too strong a word for you, would you say at least that you enjoy his company, that you see a certain charm in him, that – well, surely you understand what I'm saying.'

She seemed flustered. 'I'm not sure that I do.'

'It appears to me that you feel attracted to him. God knows he feels attracted to you. He can't go back to England, you realize. He's compromised himself fifty different ways. Even after we patch up this conspiracy thing, and we certainly will, one way or another, the fact still remains that he's guilty of treason. He has to go somewhere. He can't stay here – the heat will kill him fast, if his own foolishness doesn't. Are you starting to get my drift, Selima?'

Her eyes rose to meet his. Some of her old self-assurance was returning to them now.

'I think I am. And I think that I like it.'

'Very good,' he said. 'I'll give him to you, then. For a toy, if you like.' He clapped his hands. A functionary poked his head into the room.

'Send in the Englishman.'

Michael entered. He walked with the precarious stride of someone who has been decapitated but thinks there might be some chance

73

of keeping his head on his shoulders if only he moves carefully enough. The only traces of sunburn that remained now were great peeling patches on his cheeks and forehead.

He looked toward the new Emir and murmured a barely audible courtly greeting. He seemed to have trouble looking in Selima's direction.

'Sir?' Michael asked finally.

The Emir smiled warmly. 'Has Sir Anthony left yet?'

'This morning, sir. I didn't speak with him.'

'No. No, I imagine you wouldn't care to. It's a mess, isn't it, Michael? You can't really go home.'

'I understand that, sir.'

'But obviously you can't stay here. This is no climate for the likes of you.'

'I suppose not, sir.'

The Emir nodded. He reached about behind him and lifted a book from a stand. 'During my years as prince I had plenty of leisure to read. This is one of my favorites. Do you happen to know which book it is?'

'No, sir.'

'The collected plays of one of your great English writers, as a matter of fact. The greatest, so I'm told. Shakespeare's his name. You know his work, do you?'

Michael blinked. 'Of course, sir. Everyone knows –'

'Good. And you know his play *Alexius and Khurrem*, naturally?'

'Yes, sir.'

The Emir turned to Selima. 'And do you?'

'Well –'

'It's quite relevant to the case, I assure you. It takes place in Istanbul, not long after the Ottoman Conquest. Khurrem is a beautiful young woman from one of the high Turkish families. Alexius is an exiled Byzantine prince who has slipped back into the capital to try to rescue some of his family's treasures from the grasp of the detested conqueror. He disguises himself as a Turk and meets Khurrem at a banquet, and of course they fall in love. It's an impossible romance – a Turk and a Greek.' He opened the book. 'Let me read a little.

It's amazing that an Englishman could write such eloquent Turkish poetry, isn't it?'

> *From forth the fatal loins of these two foes*
> *A pair of star-cross'd lovers take their life;*
> *Whose misadventur'd piteous overthrows*
> *Do with their death bury their parents' strife –*

The Emir glanced up. '"Star-cross'd lovers." That's what you are, you know.' He laughed. 'It all ends terribly for poor Khurrem and Alexius, but that's because they were such hasty children. With better planning they could have slipped away to the countryside and lived to a ripe old age, but Shakespeare tangles them up in a scheme of sleeping potions and crossed messages and they both die at the end, even though well-intentioned friends were trying to help them. But of course that's drama for you. It's a lovely play. I hope to be able to see it performed some day.'

He put the book aside. They both were staring at him.

To Michael he said, 'I've arranged for you to defect to Turkey. Ismet Akif will give you a writ of political asylum. What happens between you and Selima is of course entirely up to you and Selima, but in the name of Allah I implore you not to make as much of a shambles of it as Khurrem and Alexius did. Istanbul's not such a bad place to live, you know. No, don't look at me like that! If she can put up with a ninny like you, you can manage to get over your prejudices against Turks. You asked for all this, you know. You didn't *have* to fall in love with her.'

'Sir, I – I –'

Michael's voice trailed away.

The Emir said, 'Take him out of here, will you, Selima?'

'Come,' she told the gawking Englishman. 'We need to talk, I think.'

'I – I –'

The Emir gestured impatiently. Selima's hand was on Michael's wrist, now. She tugged, and he followed. The Emir looked after them until they had gone down the stairs.

Then he clapped his hands.

'Ali Pasha!'

The vizier appeared so quickly that there could be no doubt he had been lurking just beyond the ornate doorway.

'Majesty?'

'We have to clear this place out a little,' the Emir said. 'This crocodile – this absurd giraffe – find an appropriate charity and donate them, fast. And these hippo skulls, too. And this, and this, and this –'

'At once, majesty. A clean sweep.'

'A clean sweep, yes.'

A cool wind was blowing through the palace now, after the rains. He felt young, strong, vigorous. Life was just beginning, finally. Later in the day he would visit the lions at their pit.

A Tip on a Turtle

Amazing Stories, the first all-science-fiction magazine ever published, constantly kept reinventing itself in its long history, which covered the years from 1926 to 1995. Its first editor, Hugo Gernsback, wanted to educate people to the wonders of science and technology through the medium of science fiction, and the stories he published were often fattened with lengthy passages of lecture and festooned with footnotes. Then it passed into the hands of the Ziff-Davis pulp-magazine chain, which turned it into a slam-bang action magazine for boys. After fifteen years of that, it evolved into an elegant slick-paper magazine that published thoughtful stories by the likes of Ray Bradbury and Theodore Sturgeon and Robert A. Heinlein, and (when that policy failed to bring in the desired dollars) it reverted to formula fiction once again, about 1955. That was the year I came on the scene as a professional sf writer, and in youthful glee I filled the pages of *Amazing* with pulpy epics with titles like 'Guardian of the Crystal Gate' and 'The Monster Died at Dawn'.

Later editors made periodic attempts at upgrading the quality of *Amazing*'s fiction – notably Cele Goldsmith in 1964 and George Scithers in 1982. I upgraded right with them, and my stories appeared regularly in *Amazing* across the decades. Indeed, Scithers commissioned a story from me, for a higher price than the magazine had been wont to pay, for his first issue. When yet another ambitious new editor, Kim Mohan, took over the once-again-moribund *Amazing Stories* in 1990 and turned it into a gloriously printed large-sized magazine with dazzling interior illustrations in four colors, he too invited me to contribute a short story for the first of the renovated issues. I had just finished 'A Tip on a Turtle' the day he asked, and had sent it off to *Playboy*, where I was a regular contributor. But my old friend Alice Turner, *Playboy*'s acute and demanding fiction editor, had reservations about my use of a female protagonist, *Playboy* being, after all, a men's magazine; she thought the story would be more at home in *Cosmopolitan* or one of its competitors. But when Mohan told me he would pay *Playboy/Cosmopolitan*-level rates for a new short story from me for *Amazing*, I obligingly diverted the piece in his direction. *Playboy*, though, is a mass-circulation publication read mainly by people who would never go near a science-fiction magazine, and so the tone of this one, with its mainstream-reader orientation, is as far removed from 'The Monster Died at Dawn' and my other early *Amazing* contributions as it is possible to be.

The sun was going down in the usual spectacular Caribbean way, disappearing in a welter of purple and red and yellow streaks that lay across the wide sky beyond the hotel's manicured golf course like a magnificent bruise. It was time to head for the turtle pool for the pre-dinner races. They held the races three times a day now, once after lunch, once before dinner, once after dinner. Originally the races had been nothing more than a casual diversion, but by now they had become a major item of entertainment for the guests and a significant profit center for the hotel.

As Denise took her place along the blazing bougainvillea hedge that flanked the racing pool a quiet deep voice just back of her left ear said, 'You might try Number Four in the first race.'

It was the man she had noticed at the beach that afternoon, the tall tanned one with the powerful shoulders and the tiny bald spot. She had been watching him snorkeling along the reef, nothing visible above the surface of the water but his bald spot and the blue strap of his goggles and the black stalk of the snorkel. When he came to shore he walked right past her, seemingly lost in some deep reverie; but for a moment, just for a moment, their eyes had met in a startling way. Then he had gone on, without a word or even a smile. Denise was left with the feeling that there was something tragic about him, something desperate, something haunted. That had caught her attention. Was he down here by himself? So it appeared. She too was vacationing alone. Her marriage had broken up during Christmas, as marriages so often did, and everyone had said she ought to get away for some midwinter sunshine. And, they hadn't needed to add, for some postmarital diversion. She had been here three days so far and there had been plenty of sunshine but none of the other thing, not for lack of interest but simply because after five years of marriage she was out of practice at being seduced, or shy, or simply uneasy. She had been noticed, though. And had done some noticing.

She looked over her shoulder at him and said, 'Are you telling me that the race is fixed?'

'Oh, no. Not at all.'

'I thought you might have gotten some special word from one of the hotel's boys.'

'No,' he said. He was very tall, perhaps too tall for her, with thick, glossy black hair and dark, hooded eyes. Despite the little bald spot he was probably forty at most. He was certainly attractive enough, almost movie-star handsome, and yet she found herself thinking unexpectedly that there was something oddly asexual about him. 'I just have a good feeling about Number Four, that's all. When I have a feeling of that sort it often works out very well.' A musical voice. Was that a faint accent? Or just an affectation?

He was looking at her in a curiously expectant way.

She knew the scenario. He had made the approach; now she should hand him ten Jamaican dollars and ask him to go over to the tote counter and bet them on Number Four for her; when he returned with her ticket they would introduce themselves; after the race, win or lose, they'd have a daiquiri or two together on the patio overlooking the pool, maybe come back to try their luck on the final race, then dinner on the romantic outdoor terrace and a starlight stroll under the palisade of towering palms that lined the beachfront promenade, and eventually they'd get around to settling the big question: his cottage or hers? But even as she ran through it all in her mind she knew she didn't want any of it to happen. That lost, haunted look of his, which had seemed so wonderfully appealing for that one instant on the beach, now struck her as simply silly, melodramatic, overdone. Most likely it was nothing more than his modus operandi: women had been falling for that look of masterfully contained agony at least since Lord Byron's time, probably longer. But not me, Denise told herself.

She gave him a this-leads-nowhere smile and said, 'I dropped a fortune on these damned turtles last night, I'm afraid. I decided I was going to be just a spectator this evening.'

'Yes,' he said. 'Of course.'

It wasn't true. She had won twenty Jamaican dollars the night before and had been looking forward to more good luck now. Gambling of any sort had never interested her until this trip, but there had been a peculiar sort of pleasure last night in watching the big turtles gliding toward the finish line, especially when her choices finished first in three of the seven races. Well, she had committed herself to the sidelines for this evening by her little lie, and so be it. Tomorrow was another day.

The tall man smiled and shrugged and bowed and went away. A few moments later Denise saw him talking to the leggy, freckled woman from Connecticut whose husband had died in some kind of boating accident the summer before. Then they were on their way over to the tote counter and he was buying tickets for them. Denise felt sudden sharp annoyance, a stabbing sense of opportunity lost.

'Place your bets, ladees gemmun, place your bets!' the master of ceremonies called.

Mr Eubanks, the night manager – shining black face, gleaming white teeth, straw hat, red-and-white-striped shirt – sat behind the counter, busily ringing up the changing odds on a little laptop computer. A boy with a chalkboard posted them. Number Three was the favorite, three to two; Number Four was a definite long shot at nine to one. But then there was a little flurry of activity at the counter, and the odds on Four dropped abruptly to five to one. Denise heard people murmuring about that. And then the tote was closed and the turtles were brought forth.

Between races the turtles slept in a shallow, circular concrete-walled holding tank that was supplied with sea water by a conduit running up from the beach. They were big green ones, each with a conspicuous number painted on its upper shell in glowing crimson, and they were so hefty that the brawny hotel boys found it hard going to carry them the distance of twenty feet or so that separated the holding tank from the long, narrow pool where the races were held.

Now the boys stood in a row at the starting line, as though they themselves were going to race, while the glossy-eyed turtles that they were clutching to their chests made sleepy graceless swimming

80

motions in the air with their rough leathery flippers and rolled their spotted green heads slowly from side to side in a sluggish show of annoyance. The master of ceremonies fired a starter's pistol and the boys tossed the turtles into the pool. Graceless no longer, the big turtles were swimming the moment they hit the water, making their way into the blue depths of the pool with serene, powerful strokes.

There were six lanes, separated by bright yellow ribbons, but of course the turtles had no special reason for remaining in them. They roamed about randomly, perhaps imagining that they had been returned to the open sea, while the guests of the hotel roared encouragement: 'Come on, Five! Go for it, One! Move your green ass, Six!'

The first turtle to touch any part of the pool's far wall was the winner. Ordinarily it took four or five minutes for that to happen; as the turtles wandered, they sometimes approached the finish line but didn't necessarily choose to make contact with it, and wild screams would rise from the backers of this one or that as their turtle neared the wall, sniffed it, perhaps, and turned maddeningly away without making contact.

But this time one of the turtles was swimming steadily, almost purposefully, in a straight line from start to finish. Denise saw it moving along the floor of the pool like an Olympic competitor going for the gold. The brilliant crimson number on its back, though blurred and mottled by the water, was unmistakable.

'Four! Four! Four! Look at that bastard go!'

It was all over in moments. Four completed its traversal of the pool, lightly bumped its hooked snout against the far wall with almost contemptuous satisfaction, and swung around again on a return journey to the starting point, as if it had been ordered to swim laps. The other turtles were still moving about amiably in vague circles at mid-pool.

'Numbah Four,' called the master of ceremonies. 'Pays off at five to one for de lucky winnahs, yessah yessah!'

The hotel boys had their nets out, scooping up the heavy turtles for the next race. Denise looked across the way. The leggy young widow from Connecticut was jubilantly waving a handful of gaudy

Jamaican ten-dollar bills in the face of the tall man with the tiny bald spot. She was flushed and radiant; but he looked down at her solemnly from his great height without much sign of excitement, as though the dramatic victory of Number Four had afforded him neither profit nor joy nor any surprise at all.

The short, stocky, balding Chevrolet dealer from Long Island, whose features and coloration looked to be pure Naples but whose name was like something out of *Brideshead Revisited* – Lionel Gregson? Anthony Jenkins? – something like that – materialized at Denise's side and said, 'It don't matter which turtle you bet, really. The trick is to bet the boys who throw them.'

His voice, too, had a hoarse Mediterranean fullness. Denise loved the idea that he had given himself such a fancy name.

'Do you really think so?'

'I know so. I been watching them three days, now. You see the boy in the middle? Hegbert, he's called. Smart as a whip, and damn strong. He reacts faster when the gun goes off. And he don't just throw his turtle quicker, he throws it harder. Look, can I get you a daiquiri? I don't like being the only one drinking.' He grinned. Two gold teeth showed. 'Jeffrey Thompkins, Oyster Bay. I had the privilege of talking with you a couple minutes two days ago on the beach.'

'Of course. I remember. Denise Carpenter. I'm from Clifton, New Jersey, and yes, I'd love a daiquiri.'

He snagged one from a passing tray. Denise thought his Hegbert theory was nonsense – the turtles usually swam in aimless circles for a while after they were thrown in, so why would the thrower's reaction time or strength of toss make any difference? – but Jeffrey Thompkins himself was so agreeably real, so cheerfully blatant, that she found herself liking him tremendously after her brush with the Byronic desperation of the tall man with the little bald spot. The phonied-up name was a nice capping touch, the one grotesque bit of fraudulence that made everything else about him seem more valid. Maybe he needed a name like that where he lived, or where he worked.

Now that she had accepted a drink from him, he moved a half step closer to her, taking on an almost proprietary air. He was about two inches shorter than she was.

'I see that Hegbert's got Number Three in the second race. You want I should buy you a ticket?'

The tall man was covertly watching her, frowning a little. Maybe he was bothered that she had let herself be captured by the burly little car dealer. She hoped so.

But she couldn't let Thompkins get a ticket for her after she had told the tall man she wasn't betting tonight. Not if the other one was watching. She'd have to stick with her original fib.

'Somehow I don't feel like playing the turtles tonight,' she said. 'But you go ahead, if you want.'

'Place your bets, ladies gemmun, place your bets!'

Hegbert did indeed throw Number Three quickly and well, but it was Five that won the race, after some minutes of the customary random noodling around in the pool. Five paid off at three to one. A quick sidewise glance told Denise that the tall man and the leggy Connecticut widow had been winners again.

'Watch what that tall guy does in the next race,' she heard someone say nearby. 'That's what I'm going to do. He's a pro. He's got a sixth sense about these turtles. He just wins and wins and wins.'

But watching what the tall man did in the next race was an option that turned out not to be available. He had disappeared from the pool area somewhere between the second and third races. And so, Denise noted with unexpectedly sharp displeasure, had the woman from Connecticut.

Thompkins, still following his Hegbert system, bet fifty on Number Six in the third race, cashed in at two to one, then dropped his new winnings and fifty more besides backing Number Four in the fourth. Then he invited Denise to have dinner with him on the terrace. What the hell, she thought. Last night she had had dinner alone: very snooty, she must have seemed. It hadn't been fun.

In the uneasy first moments at the table they talked about the tall man. Thompkins had noticed his success with the turtles also.

'Strange guy,' he said. 'Gives me the creeps – something about the look in his eye. But you see how he makes out at the races?'

'He does very well.'

'Well? He cleans up! Can't lose for winning.'

'Some people have unusual luck, I suppose.'

'This ain't luck. My guess is maybe he's got a fix in with the boys – like they tell him what turtle's got the mojo in the upcoming race. Some kind of high sign they give him when they're lining up for the throw-in.'

'How? Turtles are turtles. They just swim around in circles until one of them happens to hit the far wall with his nose.'

'No,' said Thompkins. 'I think he knows something. Or maybe not. But the guy's hot for sure. Tomorrow I'm going to bet the way he does, right down the line, race by race. There are other people here doing it already. That's why the odds go down on the turtle he bets, once they see which one he's backing. If the guy's hot, why not get in on his streak?'

He ordered a white Italian wine with the first course, which was grilled flying fish with brittle orange caviar globules on the side. 'I got to confess,' he said, grinning again, 'Jeffrey Thompkins's not really my name. It's Taormina, Joey Taormina. But that's hard to pronounce out where I live, so I changed it.'

'I did wonder. You look – is it Neapolitan?'

'Worse. Sicilian. Anybody you meet named Taormina, his family's originally Sicilian. Taormina's a city on the east coast of Sicily. Gorgeous place. I'd love to show you around it some day.'

He was moving a little too fast, she thought. A lot too fast.

'I have a confession too,' she said. 'I'm not from Clifton any more. I moved back into the city a month ago after my marriage broke up.'

'That's a damn shame.' He might almost have meant it. 'I'm divorced too. It practically killed my mother when I broke the news. Well, you get married too young, you get surprised later on.' A quick grin: he wasn't all that saddened by what he had learned about her. 'How about some red wine with the main course? They got a good Brunello here.'

A little later he invited her, with surprising subtlety, to spend the night with him. As gently as she could she declined. 'Well, tomorrow's another day,' he said cheerfully. Denise found herself wishing he had looked a little wounded, just a little.

The daytime routine was simple. Sleep late, breakfast on the cottage porch looking out at the sea, then a long ambling walk down the beach, poking in tide pools and watching ghostly gray crabs scutter over the pink sand. Mid-morning, swim out to the reef with snorkel and fins, drift around for half an hour or so staring at the strangely contorted coral heads and the incredibly beautiful reef creatures. It was like another planet, out there on the reef. Gnarled coral rose from the sparkling white sandy ocean floor to form fantastic facades and spires through which a billion brilliant fishes, scarlet and green and turquoise and gold in every imaginable color combination, chased each other around. Every surface was plastered with pastel-hued sponges and algae. Platoons of tiny squids swam in solemn formation. Toothy, malevolent-looking eels peered out of dark caverns. An occasional chasm led through the coral wall to the deep sea beyond, where the water was turbulent instead of calm, a dark blue instead of translucent green, and the ocean floor fell away to invisible depths. But Denise never went to the far side. There was something ominous and threatening about the somber outer face of the reef, whereas here, within, everything was safe, quiet, lovely.

After the snorkeling came a shower, a little time spent reading on the porch, then the outdoor buffet lunch. Afterwards a nap, a stroll in the hotel's flamboyant garden, and by mid-afternoon down to the beach again, not for a swim this time, but just to bake in the blessed tropical sun. She'd worry about the possibility of skin damage some other time: right now what she needed was that warm caress, that torrid all-enfolding embrace. Two hours dozing in the sun, then back to the room, shower again, read, dress for dinner. And off to the turtle races. Denise never bothered with the ones after lunch – they were strictly for the real addicts – but she had gone every evening to the pre-dinner ones.

A calm, mindless schedule. Exactly the ticket, after the grim, exhausting domestic storms of October and November and the sudden

final cataclysm of December. Even though in the end she had been
the one who had forced the breakup, it had still come as a shock
and a jolt: she too getting divorced, just another pathetic casualty
of the marital wars, despite all the high hopes of the beginning,
the grand plans she and Michael had liked to make, the glowing
dreams. Everything dissolving now into property squabbles, bitter
recriminations, horrifying legal fees. How sad: how boring, really.
And how destructive to her peace of mind, her self-esteem, her sense
of order, her this, her that, her everything. For which there was no
cure, she knew, other than to lie here on this placid Caribbean beach
under this perfect winter sky and let the healing slowly happen.

Jeffrey Thompkins had the tact – or the good strategic sense –
to leave her alone during the day. She saw him in the water, not
snorkeling around peering at the reef but simply chugging back and
forth like a blocky little machine, head down, arms windmilling,
swimming parallel to the hotel's enormous ocean frontage until
he had reached the cape just to the north, then coming back the
other way. He was a formidable swimmer with enough energy for
six men. Quite probably he was like that in bed, too, but Denise
had decided somewhere between the white wine and the red at
dinner last night that she didn't intend to find out. She liked him,
yes. And she intended to have an adventure of some sort with
someone while she was down here. But a Chevrolet dealer from
Long Island? Shorter than she was, with thick hairy shoulders?
Somehow she couldn't. She just couldn't, not her first fling after
the separation. He seemed to sense it too, and didn't bother her at
the beach, even had his lunch at the indoor dining room instead of
the buffet terrace. But she suspected she'd encounter him again at
evening turtle-race time.

Yes: there he was. Grinning hopefully at her from the far side of
the turtle pool, but plainly waiting to pick up some sort of affirmative
signal from her before coming toward her.

There was the tall dark-haired man with the tiny bald spot, too.
Without the lady from Connecticut. Denise had seen him snorkeling
on the reef that afternoon, alone, and here he was alone again, which
meant, most likely, that last night had been Mme Connecticut's final

night at the hotel. Denise was startled to realize how much relief that conclusion afforded her.

Carefully not looking in Jeffrey Thompkins's direction, she went unhesitatingly toward the tall man.

He was wearing a dark cotton suit and, despite the warmth, a narrow black tie flecked with gold, and he looked very, very attractive. She couldn't understand how she had come to think of him as sexless the night before: some inexplicable flickering of her own troubled moods, no doubt. Certainly he didn't seem that way now. He smiled down at her. He seemed actually pleased to see her, though she sensed behind the smile a puzzling mixture of other emotions – aloofness, sadness, regret? That curious tragic air of his: not a pose, she began to think, but the external manifestation of some deep and genuine wound.

'I wish I had listened to you last night,' she said. 'You knew what you were talking about when you told me to bet Number Four.'

He shrugged almost imperceptibly. 'I didn't really think that you'd take my advice. But I thought I'd make the gesture all the same.'

'That was very kind of you,' she said, leaning inward and upward toward him. 'I'm sorry I was so skeptical.' She flashed her warmest smile. 'I'm going to be very shameless. I want a second chance. If you've got any tips to offer on tonight's races, please tell me. I promise not to be such a skeptic this time.'

'Number Five in this one,' he replied at once. 'Nicholas Holt, by the way.'

'Denise Carpenter. From Clifton, New Jer –' She cut herself off, reddening. He hadn't told her where he was from. She wasn't from Clifton any longer anyway; and what difference did it make where she might live up north? This island resort was intended as a refuge from all that, a place outside time, outside familiar realities. 'Shall we place our bets?' she said briskly.

Women didn't usually buy tickets themselves here. Men seemed to expect to do that for them. She handed him a fifty, making sure as she did so that her fingers were extended to let him see that she wore no wedding band. But Holt didn't make any attempt to look. His own fingers were just as bare.

She caught sight of Jeffrey Thompkins at a distance, frowning at her but not in any very troubled way; and she realized after a moment that he evidently was undisturbed by her defection to the tall man's side and simply wanted to know which turtle Holt was backing. She held up her hand, five fingers outspread. He nodded and went scurrying to the tote counter.

Number Five won easily. The payoff was at seven to three. Denise looked at Holt with amazement.

'How do you do it?' she asked.

'Concentration,' he said. 'Some people have the knack.'

He seemed very distant, suddenly.

'Are you concentrating on the next race, now?'

'It'll be Number One,' he told her, as though telling her that the weather tomorrow would be warm and fair.

Thompkins stared at her out of the crowd. Denise flashed one finger at him.

She felt suddenly ill at ease. Nicholas Holt's knack, or whatever it was, bothered her. He was too confident, too coolly certain of what was going to happen. There was something annoying and almost intimidating about such confidence. Although she had bet fifty Jamaican dollars on Number One, she found herself wishing perversely that the turtle would lose.

Number One it was, though, all the same. The payoff was trifling; it seemed as if almost everyone in the place had followed Holt's lead, and as a result the odds had been short ones. Since the races, as Denise was coming to see, were truly random – the turtles didn't give a damn and were about equal in speed – the only thing governing the patterns of oddsmaking was the way the guests happened to bet, and that depended entirely on whatever irrational set of theories the bettors had fastened on. But the theory Nicholas Holt was working from didn't appear to be irrational.

'And in the third race?' she said.

'I never bet more than the first two. It gets very dull for me after that. Shall we have dinner?'

He said it as if her acceptance were a foregone conclusion, which would have offended her, except that he was right.

The main course that night was island venison. 'What would you say to a bottle of Merlot?' he asked.

'It's my favorite wine.'

How did he do it? Was everything simply an open book to him?

He let her do most of the talking at dinner. She told him about the gallery where she worked, about her new little apartment in the city, about her marriage, about what had happened to her marriage. A couple of times she felt herself beginning to babble – the wine, she thought, it was the wine – and she reined herself in. But he showed no sign of disapproval, even when she realized she had been going on about Michael much too long. He listened gravely and quietly to everything she said, interjecting a bland comment now and then, essentially just a little prompt to urge her to continue: 'Yes, I see,' or 'Of course,' or 'I quite understand.' He told her practically nothing about himself, only that he lived in New York – where? – and that he did something on Wall Street – unspecified – and that he spent two weeks in the West Indies every February but had never been to Jamaica before. He volunteered no more than that: she had no idea where he had grown up – surely not in New York, from the way he spoke – or whether he had ever been married, or what his interests might be. But she thought it would be gauche to be too inquisitive, and probably unproductive. He was very well defended, polite and calm and remote, the most opaque man she had ever known. He played his part in the dinner conversation with the tranquil, self-possessed air of someone who was following a very familiar script.

After dinner they danced, and it was the same thing there: he anticipated her every move, smoothly sweeping her around the open-air dance floor in a way that soon had everyone watching them. Denise was a good dancer, skilled at the tricky art of leading a man who thought he was leading her; but with Nicholas Holt the feedback was so complex that she had no idea who was leading whom. They danced as though they were one entity, moving with a single accord: the way people dance who have been dancing together for years. She had never known a man who danced like that.

On one swing around the floor she had a quick glimpse of Jeffrey Thompkins, dancing with a robust redhaired woman half a head taller than he was. Thompkins was pushing her about with skill and determination but no grace at all, somewhat in the style of a rhinoceros who has had a thousand hours of instruction at Arthur Murray. As he went thundering past he looked back at Denise and smiled an intricate smile that said a dozen different things. It acknowledged the fact that he was clumsy and his partner was coarse, that Holt was elegant and Denise was beautiful, that men like Holt always were able to take women like Denise away from men like Thompkins. But also the smile seemed to be telling her that Thompkins didn't mind at all, that he accepted what had happened as the natural order of things, had in fact expected it with much the same sort of assurance as Holt had expected Number Five to win tonight's first race. Denise realized that she had felt some guilt about sidestepping Thompkins and offering herself to Holt and that his smile just now had canceled it out; and then she wondered why she had felt the guilt in the first place. She owed nothing to Thompkins, after all. He was simply a stranger who had asked her to dinner last night. They were all strangers down here: nobody owed anything to anyone.

'My cottage is just beyond that little clump of bamboo,' Holt said, after they had had the obligatory beachfront stroll on the palm promenade. He said it as if they had already agreed to spend the night there. She offered no objections. This was what she had come here for, wasn't it? Sunlight and warmth and tropical breezes and this.

As he had on the dance floor, so too in bed was he able to anticipate everything she wanted. She had barely thought of something but he was doing it; sometimes he did it even before she knew she wanted him to. It was so long since she had made love with anyone but Michael that Denise wasn't sure who the last one before him had been; but she knew she had never been to bed with anyone like this. She moved here, he was on his way there already. She did this, he did it too. That and that. Her hand, his hand. Her lips, his lips. It was all extremely weird: very thrilling and yet oddly hollow, like making love to your own reflection.

He must be able to read minds, she thought suddenly, as they lay side by side, resting for a while.

An eerie notion. It made her feel nakeder than naked: bare right down to her soul, utterly vulnerable, defenseless.

But the power to read minds, she realized after a moment, wouldn't allow him to do that trick with the turtle races. That was prediction, not mind-reading. It was second sight.

Can he see into the future? Five minutes, ten minutes, half a day ahead? She thought back. He always seemed so unsurprised at everything. When she had told him she didn't intend to do any betting, that first night, he had simply said, 'Of course.' When his turtle had won the race he had shown no flicker of excitement or pleasure. When she had apologized tonight for not having acted on his tip, he had told her blandly that he hadn't expected her to. The choice of wine – the dinner conversation – the dancing – the lovemaking –

Could he see everything that was about to happen? *Everything?*

On Wall Street, too? Then he must be worth a fortune.

But why did he always look so sad, then? His eyes so bleak and haunted, those little lines of grimness about his lips?

This is all crazy, Denise told herself. Nobody can see the future. The future isn't a place you can look into, the way you can open a door and look into a room. The future doesn't exist until it's become the present.

She turned to him. But he was already opening his arms to her, bringing his head down to graze his lips across her breasts.

She left his cottage long before dawn, not because she really wanted to but because she was unwilling to have the maids and gardeners see her go traipsing back to her place in the morning still wearing her evening clothes, and hung the DO NOT DISTURB sign on her door.

When she woke, the sun was blazing down through the bamboo slats of the cottage porch. She had slept through breakfast and lunch. Her throat felt raspy and there was the sensation of recent lovemaking between her legs, so that she automatically looked around for Michael and was surprised to find herself alone in the big bed; and then she remembered, first that she and Michael were all finished, then that she was here by herself, then that she had spent the night with Nicholas Holt.

Who can see the future. She laughed at her own silliness.

She didn't feel ready to face the outside world, and called room service to bring her tea and a tray of fruit. They sent her mango, jackfruit, three tiny reddish bananas, and a slab of papaya. Later she suited up and went down to the beach. She didn't see Holt anywhere around, neither out by the reef as he usually was in the afternoon, nor on the soft pink sand. A familiar stocky form was churning up the water with cannonball force, doing his laps, down to the cape and back, again, again, again. Thompkins. After a time he came stumping ashore. Not at all coy now, playing no strategic games, he went straight over to her.

'I see that your friend Mr Holt's in trouble with the hotel,' he said, sounding happy about it.

'He is? How so?'

'You weren't at the turtle races after lunch, were you?'

'I never go to the afternoon ones.'

'That's right, you don't. Well, I was there. Holt won the first two races, the way he always does. Everybody bet the way he did. The odds were microscopic, naturally. But everybody won. And then two of the hotel managers – you know, Eubanks, the night man who has that enormous grin all the time, and the other one with the big yellow birthmark on his forehead? – came over to him and said, "Mr Holt, sah, we would prefer dat you forego the pleasure of the turtle racing from this point onward."' The Chevrolet dealer's imitation of the Jamaican accent was surprisingly accurate. '"We recognize dat you must be an authority on turtle habits, sah," they said. "Your insight we find to be exceedingly uncanny. And derefore it strikes us dat it is quite unsporting for you to compete. Quite, sah!"'

'And what did he say?'

'That he doesn't know a goddamned thing about turtles, that he's simply on a roll, that it's not his fault if the other guests are betting the same way he is. They asked him again not to play the turtles – "We implore you, sah, you are causing great losses for dis establishment" – and he kept saying he was a registered guest and entitled to all the privileges of a guest. So they canceled the races.'

'Canceled them?'

'They must have been losing a fucking fortune this week on those races, if you'll excuse the French. You can't run parimutuels where everybody bets the same nag and that nag always wins, you know? Wipes you out after a while. So they didn't have races this afternoon and there won't be any tonight unless he agrees not to play.' Thompkins smirked. 'The guests are pretty pissed off, I got to tell you. The management is trying to talk him into changing hotels, that's what someone just said. But he won't do it. So no turtles. You ask me, I still think he's been fixing it somehow with the hotel boys, and the hotel must think so too, but they don't dare say it. Man with a winning streak like that, there's just no accounting for it any other way, is there?'

'No,' Denise said. 'No accounting for it at all.'

It was cocktail time before she found him: the hour when the guests gathered on the garden patio where the turtle races were held to have a daiquiri or two before the tote counter opened for business. Denise drifted down there automatically, despite what Thompkins had told her about the cancelation of the races. Most of the other guests had done the same. She saw Holt's lanky figure looming up out of a group of them. They had surrounded him, they were gesturing and waving their daiquiris around as they talked. It was easy enough to guess that they were trying to talk him into refraining from playing the turtles so that they could have their daily amusement back.

When she came closer she saw the message chalked across the tote board in an ornate Jamaican hand, all curlicues and flourishes:

Technical Problem
No races today
Your kind indulgence is asked

'Nicholas?' she called, as though they had a prearranged date.

He smiled at her gratefully. 'Excuse me,' he said in his genteel way to the cluster around him, and moved smoothly through them to her side. 'How lovely you look tonight, Denise.'

'I've heard that the hotel's putting pressure on you about the races.'

'Yes. Yes.' He seemed to be speaking to her from another galaxy. 'So they are. They're quite upset, matter of fact. But if there's going to be racing, I have a right to play. If they choose to cancel, that's their business.'

In a low voice she said, 'You aren't involved in any sort of collusion with the hotel boys, are you?'

'You asked me that before. You know that that isn't possible.'

'Then how are you always able to tell which turtle's going to win?'

'I know,' he said sadly. 'I simply do.'

'You always know what's about to happen, don't you? Always.'

'Would you like a daiquiri, Denise?'

'Answer me. Please.'

'I have a knack, yes.'

'It's more than a knack.'

'A gift, then. A special – something.'

'A something, yes.' They were walking as they talked; already they were past the bougainvillea hedge, heading down the steps toward the beachfront promenade, leaving the angry guests and the racing pool and the turtle tank behind.

'A very reliable something,' she said.

'Yes. I suppose it is.'

'You said that you knew, the first night when you offered me that tip, that I wasn't going to take you up on it. Why did you offer it to me, then?'

'I told you. It seemed like a friendly gesture.'

'We weren't friends then. We'd hardly spoken. Why'd you bother?'

'Just because.'

'Because you wanted to test your special something?' she asked him. 'Because you wanted to see whether it was working right?'

He stared at her intently. He looked almost frightened, she thought. She had broken through.

'Perhaps I did,' he said.

'Yes. You check up on it now and then, don't you? You try something that you know won't pan out, like tipping a strange woman to the outcome of the turtle race even though your gift tells you that she won't bet your tip. Just to see whether your guess was on the mark. But what would you have done if I had put a bet down that night, Nicholas?'

'You wouldn't have.'

'You were certain of that.'

'Virtually certain, yes. But you're right: I test it now and then, just to see.'

'And it always turns out the way you expect?'

'Essentially, yes.'

'You're scary, Nicholas. How long have you been able to do stuff like this?'

'Does that matter?' he asked. 'Does it really?'

He asked her to have dinner with him again, but there was something perfunctory about the invitation, as though he were offering it only because the hour was getting toward dinnertime and they happened to be standing next to each other just then. She accepted quickly, perhaps too quickly. But the dining terrace was practically empty when they reached it – they were very early, on account of the cancelation of the races – and the meal was a stiff, uncomfortable affair. He was so obviously bothered by her persistent inquiries about his baffling skill, his special something, that she quickly backed off, but that left little to talk about except the unchanging perfect weather, the beauty of the hotel grounds, the rumors of racial tension elsewhere on the island. He toyed with his food and ate very little. They ordered no wine. It was like sitting across the table from a stranger who was dining with her purely by chance. And yet less than twenty-four hours before she had spent a night in this man's bed.

She didn't understand him at all. He was alien and mysterious and a little frightening. But somehow, strangely, that made him all the more desirable.

As they were sipping their coffee she looked straight at him and sent him a message with her mind:

Ask me to come dancing with you, next. And then let's go to your cottage again, you bastard.

But instead he said abruptly, 'Would you excuse me, Denise?'

She was nonplussed. 'Why – yes – if –'

He looked at his watch. 'I've rented a glass-bottomed boat for eight o'clock. To have a look at the night life out on the reef.'

The night was when the reef came alive. The little coral creatures awoke and unfolded their brilliant little tentacles; phosphorescent organisms began to glow; octopuses and eels came out of their dark crannies to forage for their meals; sharks and rays and other big predators set forth on the hunt. You could take a boat out there that was equipped with bottom-mounted arc lights and watch the show, but very few of the hotel guests actually did. The waters that were so crystalline and inviting by day looked ominous and menacing in the dark, with sinister coral humps rising like black ogres' heads above the lapping wavelets. She had never even thought of going.

But now she heard herself saying, in a desperate attempt at salvaging something out of the evening, 'Can I go with you?'

'I'm sorry. No.'

'I'm really eager to see what the reef looks like at –'

'No,' he said, quietly but with real finality. 'It's something I'd rather do by myself, if you don't mind. Or even if you do mind, I have to tell you. Is that all right, Denise?'

'Will I see you afterward?' she asked, wishing instantly that she hadn't. But he had already risen and given her a gentlemanly little smile of farewell and was striding down the terrace toward the steps that led to the beachfront promenade.

She stared after him, astounded by the swiftness of his disappearance, the unexpectedness of it.

She sat almost without moving, contemplating her bewildering abandonment. Five minutes went by, maybe ten. The waiter unobtrusively brought her another coffee. She held the cup in her hand without drinking from it.

Jeffrey Thompkins materialized from somewhere, hideously cheerful. 'If you're free,' he said, 'how about an after-dinner liqueur?' He was wearing a white dinner jacket, very natty, and sharply pressed black trousers. But his round neckless head and the blaze of sunburn across his bare scalp spoiled the elegant effect. 'A Strega, a Galliano, a nice cognac, maybe?' He pronounced it *coneyac*.

'Something weird's going on,' she said.

'Oh?'

'He went out on the reef in one of those boats, by himself. Holt. Just got up and walked away from the table, said he'd rented a boat for eight o'clock. Poof. Gone.'

'I'm heartbroken to hear it.'

'No, be serious. He was acting really strange. I asked to go with him, and he said no, I absolutely couldn't. He sounded almost like some sort of a machine. You could hear the gears clicking.'

Thompkins said, all flippancy gone from his voice now, 'You think he's going to do something to himself out there?'

'No. Not him. That's one thing I'm sure of.'

'Then what?'

'I don't know.'

'A guy like that, all keyed up all the time and never letting on a thing to anybody –' Thompkins looked at her closely. 'You know him better than I do. You don't have any idea what he might be up to?'

'Maybe he just wants to see the reef. I don't know. But he seemed so peculiar when he left – so rigid, so *focused* –'

'Come on,' Thompkins said. 'Let's get one of those boats and go out there ourselves.'

'But he said he wanted to go alone.'

'Screw what he said. He don't own the reef. We can go for an expedition too, if we want to.'

It took a few minutes to arrange things. 'You want a guided tour, sah?' the boy down at the dock asked, but Thompkins said no, and helped Denise into the boat as easily as though she were made of feathers. The boy shook his head. 'Nobody want a guide tonight. You be careful out there, stay dis side the reef, you hear me, sah?'

Thompkins switched on the lights and took the oars. With quick, powerful strokes he moved away from the dock. Denise looked down. There was nothing visible below but the bright white sand of the shallows, a few long-spined black sea urchins, some starfish. As they approached the reef, a hundred yards or so off shore, the density of marine life increased: schools of brilliant fishes whirled and dived, a somber armada of squids came squirting past.

There was no sign of Holt. 'We ought to be able to see his lights,' Denise said. 'Where can he have gone?'

Thompkins had the boat butting up against the flat side of the reef now. He stood up carefully and stared into the night.

'The crazy son of a bitch,' he muttered. 'He's gone outside the reef! Look, there he is.'

He pointed. Denise, half rising, saw nothing at first; and then there was the reflected glow of the other boat's lights, on the far side of the massive stony clutter and intricacy that was the reef. Holt had found one of the passageways through and was coasting along the reef's outer face, where the deep-water hunters came up at night, the marlins and swordfish and sharks.

'What the hell does he think he's doing?' Thompkins asked. 'Don't he know it's dangerous out there?'

'I don't think that worries him,' said Denise.

'So you do think he's going to do something to himself.'

'Just the opposite. He knows that he'll be all right out there, or he wouldn't be there. He wouldn't have gone if he saw any real risk in it.'

'Unless risk is what he's looking for.'

'He doesn't live in a world of risk,' she said. 'He's got a kind of sixth sense. He always knows what's going to happen next.'

'Huh?'

Words came pouring out of her. 'He sees the future,' she said fiercely, not caring how wild it sounded. 'It's like an open book to him. How do you think he does that trick with the turtles?'

'Huh?' Thompkins said again. 'The future?' He peered at her, shaking his head slowly.

Then he swung sharply around as if in response to some unexpected sound from the sea. He shaded his forehead with his hand, the way he might have done if he were peering into bright sunlight. After a moment he pointed into the darkness beyond the reef and said in a slow awed tone, 'What the fuck! Excuse me. But Jesus, will you look at that?'

She stared past him, toward the suddenly foaming sea.

Something was happening on the reef's outer face. Denise saw it unfolding as if in slow motion. The ocean swelling angrily, rising, climbing high. The single great wave barrelling in as though it had traveled all the way from Alaska for this one purpose. The boat tilting up on end, the man flying upward and outward, soaring gracefully into the air, traveling along a smooth curve like an expert diver and plummeting down into the black depths just beside the reef's outer face. And then the last curling upswing of the wave, the heavy crash as it struck the coral wall.

In here, sheltered by the reef, they felt only a mild swaying, and then everything was still again.

Thompkins clapped his hand over his mouth. His eyes were bulging. 'Jesus,' he said after a moment. 'Jesus! How the fuck am I going to get out there?' He turned toward Denise. 'Can you row this thing back to shore by yourself?'

'I suppose so.'

'Good. Take it in and tell the boat boy what happened. I'm going after your friend.'

He stripped with astonishing speed, the dinner jacket, the sharply creased pants, the shirt and tie, the black patent leather shoes. Denise saw him for a moment outlined against the stars, the fleshy burly body hidden only by absurd bikini pants in flamboyant scarlet silk. Then he was over the side, swimming with all his strength, heading for one of the openings in the reef that gave access to the outer face.

She was waiting among the crowd on the shore when Thompkins brought the body in, carrying it like a broken doll. He had been much too late, of course. One quick glance told her that Holt must have been tossed against the reef again and again, smashed, cut to ribbons by the sharp coral, partly devoured, even, by the creatures of the night.

Thompkins laid him down on the beach. One of the hotel boys put a beach blanket over him; another gave Thompkins a robe. He was scratched and bloody himself, shivering, grim-faced, breathing in windy gusts. Denise went to him. The others backed away, stepping back fifteen or twenty feet, leaving them alone, strangely exposed, beside the blanketed body.

'Looks like you were wrong,' Thompkins said. 'About that sixth sense of his. Or else it wasn't working so good tonight.'

'No,' she said. For the past five minutes she had been struggling to put together the pattern of what had happened, and it seemed to her now that it was beginning to come clear. 'It was working fine. He knew that this would happen.'

'What?'

'He knew. Like I said before, he knew everything ahead of time. Everything. Even this. But he went along with it anyway.'

'But if he knew everything, then why – why –' Thompkins shook his head. 'I don't get it.'

Denise shuddered in the warm night breeze. 'No, you don't. You can't. Neither can I.'

'Miss Carpentah?' a high, strained voice called. 'Mistah Thompkins?'

It was the night manager, Mr Eubanks of the dazzling grin, belatedly making his way down from the hotel. He wasn't grinning now. He looked stricken, panicky, strangely pasty-faced. He came to a halt next to them, knelt, picked up one corner of the beach blanket, stared at the body beneath it as though it were some bizarre monster that had washed ashore. A guest had died on his watch, and it was going to cost him, he was sure of that, and his fear showed in his eyes.

Thompkins, paying no attention to the Jamaican, said angrily to Denise, 'If he knew what was going to happen, if he could see the fucking future, why in the name of Christ didn't he simply not take the boat out, then? Or if he did, why fool around outside the reef where it's so dangerous? For that matter why didn't he just stay the hell away from Jamaica in the first place?'

'That's what I mean when I tell you that we can't understand,' she said. 'He didn't think the way we do. He wasn't like us. Not at all. Not in the slightest.'

'Mistah Tompkins – Miss Carpentah – if you would do me de courtesy of speaking with me for a time – of letting me have de details of dis awful tragedy –'

Thompkins brushed Eubanks away as if he were a gnat.

'I don't know what the fuck you're saying,' he told Denise.

Eubanks said, exasperated, 'If de lady and gemmun will give me deir kind attention, *please* –'

He looked imploringly toward Denise. She shook him off. She was still groping, still reaching for the answer.

Then, for an instant, just for an instant, everything that was going on seemed terribly familiar to her. As if it had all happened before. The warm, breezy night air. The blanket on the beach. The round, jowly, baffled face of Jeffrey Thompkins hovering in front of hers. Mr Eubanks, pale with dismay. An odd little moment of déjà vu. It appeared to go on and on. Now Eubanks will lose his cool and try to take me by the arm, she thought; now I will pull back and slip on the sand; now Jeffrey will catch me and steady me. Yes. Yes. And here it comes. 'Please, you may not ignore me dis way! You must tell me what has befallen dis unfortunate gemmun!' That was Eubanks, eyes popping, forehead shiny with sweat. Making a pouncing movement toward her, grabbing for her wrist. She backed hastily away from him. Her legs felt suddenly wobbly. She started to sway and slip, and looked toward Thompkins. But he was already coming forward, reaching out toward her to take hold of her before she fell. Weird, she thought. Weird.

Then the weirdness passed, and everything was normal again, and she knew the answer.

That was how it had been for him, she thought in wonder. Every hour, every day, his whole goddamned life.

'He came to this place and he did what he did,' she said to Thompkins, 'because he knew that there wasn't any choice for him. Once he had seen it in his mind it was certain to happen. So he just came down here and played things through to the end.'

'Even though he'd *die*?' Thompkins asked. He looked at Denise stolidly, uncomprehendingly.

'If you lived your whole life as if it had already happened,

101

without surprise, without excitement, without the slightest unpredictable event, not once, not ever, would you give a damn whether you lived or died? Would you? He knew he'd die here, yes. So he came here to die, and that's the whole story. And now he has.'

'Jesus,' Thompkins said. 'The poor son of a bitch!'

'You understand now? What it must have been like for him?'

'Yeah,' he said, his arm still tight around her as though he didn't ever mean to let go. 'Yeah. The poor son of a bitch.'

'I got to tell you,' said Mr Eubanks, 'dis discourtesy is completely improper. A mahn have died here tragically tonight, and you be de only witnesses, and I ask you to tell me what befell, and you –'

Denise closed her eyes a moment. Then she looked at Eubanks.

'What's there to say, Mr Eubanks? He took his boat into a dangerous place and it was struck by a sudden wave and overturned. An accident. A terrible accident. What else is there to say?' She began to shiver. Thompkins held her. In a low voice she said to him, 'I want to go back to my cottage.'

'Right,' he said. 'Sure. You wanted a statement, Mr Eubanks? There's your statement. Okay? Okay?'

He held her close against him and slowly they started up the ramp toward the hotel together.

In the Clone Zone

In the years when I was writing the stories that are collected here, I routinely sent one every summer to Alice Turner of *Playboy*, and generally she bought it, although most of the time we went through an elaborate duel over the length and structure of the story before one or the other of us gave up. Since 'Tip on a Turtle' had wound up at *Amazing Stories* instead, I felt obliged to come up with something else for Alice that year. So, a month or so after 'Turtle', I spent some time pondering various dramatic (and *melo*-dramatic) aspects of cloning human beings, and came up with this sinister little item, seven years ahead of the headlines about the cloned sheep Dolly. Alice thought it needed a little trimming, of course. (She almost always does.) But she bought it and ran it in the March, 1991 *Playboy*. Every now and then I get a movie nibble on it; and the nibbles will come harder and faster now, I suspect, with the controversy over cloning rapidly moving out of science fiction and into the real-world political arena.

The airport was very new. It had a bright, shiny, majorworld-capital feel, and for a moment Mondschein thought the plane had landed in Rio or Buenos Aires by mistake. But then he noticed the subtle signs of deception, the tackiness around the edges, the spongy junk behind the gleaming facades, and knew that he must indeed be in Tierra Alvarado.

'Senor Mondschein?' a deep male voice said, while he was still marching down the corridors that led to the immigration lounge. He turned and saw a short, wide-shouldered man in a beribboned green-and-red comic-opera uniform which he remembered after a moment was that of the Guardia de la Patria, the Maximum Leader's elite security corps. 'I am Colonel Aristegui,' he said. 'You may come with me, please. It was a good journey? You are not overly fatigued?'

Aristegui didn't bother with passport formalities. He led Mondschein through a steel doorway marked SEGURIDAD, INGRESO PROHIBIDO which admitted them to a series of bewildering passageways and catwalks and spiral staircases. There was no veneer back here: everything was severely functional, gunmetal-gray walls, exposed rivets and struts, harsh unshielded light-fixtures that looked a century old. Here it comes, Mondschein thought: this man will take me to some deserted corner of the airstrip and touch his laser pistol to my temple and they will bury me in an unmarked grave, and that will be that, five minutes back in the country and I am out of the way forever.

The final visa approval had come through only the day before, the fifth of June, and just hours later Mondschein had boarded the Aero Alvarado flight that would take him in a single soaring supersonic arc nonstop from Zurich to his long-lost homeland on the west coast of South America. Mondschein hadn't set foot there in twenty-five years, not since the Maximum Leader had expelled him for life as a sort of upside-down reward for his extraordinary technological achievements: for it was Mondschein, at the turn of the century, who had turned his impoverished little country into the unchallenged world leader in the field of human cloning.

In those days it had been called the Republic of the Central Andes. The Maximum Leader had put it together out of parts of the shattered nations which in an earlier time, when things were very different in the world, had been known as Peru, Chile, and Bolivia. During his years of exile in Europe Mondschein had always preferred to speak of himself as a Peruvian, whenever he spoke of himself at all. But now the name of the country was Tierra Alvarado and its airline was Aero Alvarado and its capital was Ciudad Alvarado, Alvarado this and Alvarado that wherever you looked. That was all right, a fine old South American tradition. You expected a Maximum Leader to clap his own name on everything, to hang his portrait everywhere, to glorify himself in every imaginable way.

Alvarado had carried things a little further than most, though, by having two dozen living replicas of himself created, the better to serve his people. That had been Mondschein's final task as a citizen of the Republic, the supreme accomplishment of his art: to produce two dozen AAA Class clones of the Maximum Leader. which could function as doubles for Alvarado at the dreary meetings of the Popular Assembly, stand in for him at the interminable National Day of Liberation parades, and keep would-be assassins in a constant state of befuddlement. They were masterpieces, those two dozen Alvarados – all but indistinguishable from the original, the only AAA Class clones ever made. With their aid the Maximum Leader was able to maintain unblinking vigilance over the citizens of Tierra Alvarado – twenty-four hours a day.

But Mondschein didn't care how many Alvarados he might be coming home to. Twenty, fifty, a hundred, what did that matter? Singular or plural, Alvarado still held the entire country in his pocket, as he had for the past generation and a half. That was the essential situation. Everything else was beside the point, a mere detail. To Mondschein the clones made no real difference at all.

In fact there was very little that did make a difference to Mondschein these days. He was getting old and slept badly most of the time and his days were an agony of acute homesickness. He wanted to speak his native language again, Spanish as it had been spoken in Peru and not the furry Spanish of Spain, and he wanted to breathe the sharp air of the high mountains and eat *papas a la huancaina* and *anticuchos* and a proper *ceviche* and maybe see the ancient walls of Cuzco once more and the clear dark water of Lake Titicaca. It didn't seem likely to him that Alvarado had granted him a pardon after all this time simply for the sake of luring him back to face a firing squad. The safe conduct, which Mondschein hadn't in any way solicited but had been overjoyed to receive, was probably sincere: a sign that the old tyrant had mellowed at last. And if not, well, at least he would die on his native soil, which somehow seemed better than dying in Bern, Toulon, Madrid, Stockholm, Prague, wherever, any of the innumerable cities in which he had lived during his long years of exile.

They emerged from the building into a bleak, deserted rear yard where empty baggage carts were strewn around like the fossil carcasses of ancient beasts, a perfect place for a quiet execution. The dry cool wind of early winter was sweeping a dark line of dust across the bare pavement. But to Mondschein's astonishment an immense sleek black limousine materialized from somewhere almost at once and two more Guardia men hopped out, saluting madly. Aristegui beckoned him into the rear of the vast car. 'Your villa has been prepared for you, Dr Mondschein. You are the guest of the nation, you understand. When you are refreshed the Minister of Scientific Development requests your attendance at the Palace of Government, perhaps this afternoon.' He flicked a finger and a mahogany panel swung open, revealing a well-stocked bar. 'You will have a cognac? It is the rare old. Or champagne, perhaps? A whiskey? Everything imported, the best quality.'

'I don't drink,' said Mondschein.

'Ah,' said Aristegui uncertainly, as though that were a fact that should have been on his prep-sheet and unaccountably hadn't been. Or perhaps he had simply been looking forward to nipping into the rare old himself, which now would be inappropriate. 'Well, then. You are comfortable? Not too warm, not too cool?' Mondschein nodded and peered out the window. They were on an imposing-looking highway now, with a city of pastel-hued high-rise buildings visible off to the side. He didn't recognize a thing. Alvarado had built this city from scratch in the empty highland plains midway between the coast and the lake and it had been only a few years old when Mondschein had last seen it, a place of raw gouged hillsides and open culverts and half-paved avenues with stacks of girders and sewer pipes and cable reels piled up everywhere. From a distance, at least, it looked quite splendid now. But as they left the beautifully landscaped road that had carried them from the airport to the city and turned off into the urban residential district he saw that the splendor was, unsurprisingly, a fraud of the usual Alvarado kind: the avenues had been paved, all right, but they were reverting to nature again, cracking and upheaving as the swelling roots of the bombacho trees and the candelero palms that had been planted down the central dividers ripped them apart. The grand houses of pink and green and azure stucco were weather-stained and crumbling, and Mondschein observed ugly random outcroppings of tin-roofed squatter-shacks sprouting like mushrooms in the open fields behind them, where elegant gardens briefly had been. And this was the place he had longed so desperately to behold one last time before he died. He thought of his comfortable little apartment in Bern and felt a pang.

But then the car swung off onto a different road, into the hills to the east which even in the city's earliest days had been the magnificently appointed enclave of the privileged and powerful. Here there was no sign of decay. The gardens were impeccable, the villas spacious and well kept. Mondschein remembered this district well. He had lived in it himself before Alvarado had found it expedient to give him a one-way ticket abroad. Names he hadn't thought of in decades came to the surface of his mind: this was the Avenida de las Flores, this was Calle del Sol, this was Camino de los Toros, this was Calle de los Indios, and this – this –

He gasped. 'Your villa has been prepared for you,' Aristegui had told him at the airport. Guest of the nation, yes. But Mondschein hadn't thought to interpret Aristegui's words literally. They'd be giving him *a* villa, *some* villa. But the handsome two-story building with the white facade and the red tile roof in front of which the limousine had halted was in fact his villa, the actual and literal and much-beloved one he had lived in long ago, until the night when the swarthy little frog-faced officer of the Guardia had come to him to tell him that he was expelled from the country. He had had to leave everything behind then, his books, his collection of ancient scientific instruments, his pre-Columbian ceramics, his rack of Italian-made suits and fine vicuna coats, his pipes, his cello, his family albums, his greenhouse full of orchids, even his dogs. One small suitcase was all they had let him take with him on the morning flight to Madrid, and from that day on he had never permitted himself to acquire possessions, but had lived in a simple way, staying easily within the very modest allowance that the Maximum Leader in his great kindness sent him each month wherever he might be. And now they had given him back his actual villa. Mondschein wondered who had been evicted, on how much notice and for what trumped-up cause, to make this building available to him again after all this time.

All that he had wanted, certainly all that he had expected, was some ordinary little flat in the center of the city. The thought of returning to the old villa sickened him. There would be too many ghosts roaming in it. For the first time he wondered whether his impulsive decision to accept Alvarado's astonishing invitation to return to the country had been a mistake.

'You recognize this house?' Aristegui asked. 'You are surprised, are you not? You are amazed with joy?'

They had made no attempt to restore his lost possessions or to undo the changes that had come to the house since he had lived there. Perhaps such a refinement of cruelty was beyond the Maximum Leader's imagination, or, more probably, no one had any recollection of what had become of his things after so many years. It was just as well. He had long since managed to put his collections of antiquities out of his mind and he had no interest in playing the cello any more, or in smoking pipes. The villa now was furnished in standard upper-class Peruvian-style comfort of the early years of the century, everything very safe, very unexceptionable, very familiar, very dull. He was provided with a staff of four, a housekeeper, a cook, a driver, a gardener. Wandering through the airy rambling house, he felt less pain than he had anticipated. His spirit was long gone from it; it was just a house. There were caged parrots in the garden and a white-and-gray cat was slinking about outside as if it belonged there; perhaps it was the cat of the former resident and had found its way back in the night.

He bathed and rested and had a light lunch. In the afternoon the driver came to him and said, 'May I take you to the Palace of Government now, Senor Dr Mondschein? The Minister is eager.' The driver must be a Guardia man also, Mondschein realized. But that was all right. All of it was all right, whatever they did now.

The Palace of Government hadn't been finished in Mondschein's time. It was a huge sprawling thing made of blocks of black stone, fitted together dry-wall fashion to give it a massive pseudo-Inca look, and it was big enough to have housed the entire bureaucracy of the Roman Empire at its peak. Relays of functionaries, some in

Guardia uniform, some not, led him through gloomy high-vaulted corridors, across walled courtyards, and up grand and ponderous stone staircases until at last an officious florid-faced aide-de-camp conducted him into the wing that was the domain of the Ministry of Scientific Development. Here he passed through a procession of outer offices and finally was admitted to a brightly lit reception hall lined with somber portraits in oils. He recognized Einstein and Leonardo da Vinci and guessed that the others were Aristotle, Darwin, Galileo, perhaps Isaac Newton. And in the place of honor, of course, a grand representation of the Maximum Leader himself, looking down with brooding intensity.

'His Excellency the Minister,' said the florid aide-de-camp, waving him into an office paneled with dark exotic woods at the far end of the reception hall. A tall man in an ornately brocaded costume worthy of a bullfighter rose from a glistening desk to greet him. And unexpectedly Mondschein found himself staring yet again at the unforgettable face of Diego Alvarado.

One of the clones, Mondschein thought. It had to be.

All the same it felt like being clubbed in the teeth. The Minister of Scientific Development had Alvarado's hard icy blue eyes, his thin lips, his broad brow, his jutting cleft chin. His smile was Alvarado's cold smile, his teeth were Alvarado's perfect glistening teeth. He had the coarse curling bangs – graying now – that gave the Maximum Leader the look of a youthful indomitable Caesar. His lanky body was lean and gaunt, a dancer's body, and his movements were a dancer's movements, graceful and precise. Seeing him awoke long-forgotten terrors in Mondschein. And yet he knew that this must be one of the clones. After that first shock of recognition, something told Mondschein subliminally that he was looking at an example of his own fine handiwork.

'President Alvarado asks me to convey his warmest greetings,' the clone said. It was Alvarado's voice, cool and dry. 'He will welcome you personally when his schedule permits, but he wishes you to know that he is honored in the deepest way by your decision to accept his hospitality.'

The aging had worked very well, Mondschein thought. Alvarado would be about seventy now, still vigorous, still in his prime. There were lines on this man's face in the right places, changes in the lines of his cheekbones and jaw, exactly as should have happened in twenty-five years.

'It wasn't any decision at all,' Mondschein said. He tried to sound casual. 'I was ready and eager to come back. Your homeland, your native soil, the place where your ancestors lived and died for three hundred years – as you get older you realize that nothing can ever take its place.'

'I quite understand,' said the clone.

Do you? Mondschein wondered. Your only ancestor is a scrap of cellular material. You were born in a tissue-culture vat. And yet you quite understand.

I made you, Mondschein thought. I made you.

He said, 'Of course the invitation to return came as an immense surprise.'

'Yes. No doubt it did. But the Maximum Leader is a man of great compassion. He felt you had suffered in exile long enough. One day he said, We have done a great injustice to that man, and now it must be remedied. So long as Rafael Mondschein y Gonzalez dwells in foreign lands, our soul can never rest. And so the word went forth to you that all is forgiven, that you were pardoned.'

'Only a man of true greatness could have done such a thing,' said Mondschein.

'Indeed. Indeed.'

Mondschein's crime had been the crime of over-achievement. He had built Alvarado's cloning laboratories to such a level of technical skill that they were the envy of all the world; and when eventually the anti-cloning zealots in North America and Europe had grown so strident that there was talk of trade sanctions and the laboratories had to be shut down, Mondschein had become the scapegoat. Alvarado had proposed to find him guilty of creating vile unnatural abominations, but Mondschein had not been willing to let them hang such an absurdity around his neck, and in the end he had allowed them to manufacture supposed embezzlements in his name instead. In return for a waiver of trial he accepted exile for life. Of course the laboratories had reopened after a while, this time secretly and illicitly, and before long ten or eleven other countries had started to turn out A and even AA Class clones also and the industry had become too important to the world economy to allow zealotry to interfere with it any longer; but Mondschein remained overseas, rotting in oblivion, purposelessly wandering like a wraith from Madrid to Prague, from Prague to Stockholm, from Stockholm to Marseilles. And now at last the Maximum Leader in his great compassion had relented.

The Minister said, 'You know we have made vast strides in the biological sciences since you last were here. Once you have had some time to settle in, we will want you to visit our laboratories, which as you may be aware are once again in legal operation.'

Mondschein was aware of that, yes. Throughout the world Tierra Alvarado was known informally as the Clone Zone, the place where anyone could go to have a reasonable facsimile manufactured at a reasonable price. But that was no longer any concern of his.

'I'm afraid that I have very little interest in cloning technology these days,' he said.

The Minister's chilly Alvarado-eyes blazed with sudden heat. 'A visit to our laboratories may serve to reawaken that interest, Dr Mondschein.'

'I doubt that very much.'

The Minister looked unhappy. 'We had hoped quite strongly that you would be willing to share the benefits of your scientific wisdom with us, doctor. Your response greatly disappoints us.'

Ah. It was all very clear, now, and very obvious. Strange that he hadn't foreseen it.

'I have no scientific wisdom, really,' said Mondschein evenly. 'None that would be of any use. I haven't kept up with the state of the art.'

'There are those who would be pleased to refresh your –'

'I'd much rather prefer to remain in retirement. I'm too old to make any worthwhile contributions.'

Now the thin lips were quirking. 'The national interest is in jeopardy, Dr Mondschein. For the first time we are challenged by competition from other countries. Genetic technology, you understand, is our primary source of hard currency. We are not a prosperous land, doctor. Our cloning industry is our one great asset, which you created for us virtually singlehandedly. Now that it faces these new threats, surely we may speak to your sense of patriotism, if not your one-time passion for scientific achievement, in asking you –'

The Minister broke off abruptly, as though seeing his answer in Mondschein's expression. In a different tone he said, 'No doubt you are tired after your long journey, doctor. I should have allowed you more time to rest. We'll continue these discussions at a later date, perhaps.'

He turned away. The florid aide-de-camp appeared as though from the air and showed Mondschein out. His driver was waiting in the courtyard.

Mondschein spent most of the night trying to sleep, but it was difficult for him, as it usually was. And there was a special problem this night, for his mind was still on Swiss time, and what was the night in Tierra Alvarado was in Switzerland the beginning of a new day. His thoughts went ticking ceaselessly on, hour after hour. Sleep finally took him toward dawn, like a curtain falling, like the blade of a guillotine.

Colonel Aristegui of the Guardia de la Patria came to him, phoning first for an appointment, saying the matter was urgent. Mondschein assumed that this would be the next attempt to put pressure on him to take charge of the cloning labs, but that did not appear to be what was on Aristegui's mind. The wide-shouldered little man looked remarkably ill at ease; he paced, he fidgeted, he mopped his sweating forehead with a lace handkerchief. Then he said, as if forcing the words out, 'This is extremely delicate.'

'Is it?'

Aristegui studied him with care. 'You control yourself extremely well, doctor. In particular I mark your restraint in regard to the President. You speak of your gratitude to him for allowing you to return. But inwardly you must hate him very much.'

'No,' Mondschein said. 'It's all ancient history. I'm an old man now. What does any of it matter any more?'

'He took away the scientific work that was your life. He forced you to leave the land of your birth.'

'If you think you're going to get me to launch into an attack on him, you're totally mistaken. What's past is past and I'm happy to be home again and that's all there is to it.'

Aristegui stared at his brilliantly gleaming patent-leather shoes. Then he sighed and raised his head like a diver coming up to the surface and said, 'The country is dying, doctor.'

'Is it?'

'Of the Latin American disease. The strong man comes, he sees the evils and injustices and remedies them, and then he stays and stays and stays until he is the evils and the injustices. President Alvarado has ruled here for thirty-five years. He drains the treasury for his palaces; he ignores what must be done to preserve and sustain. He is our great burden, our great curse. It is time for him to step aside. Or else be thrust aside.'

Mondschein's eyes widened. 'You're trying to draw me into some sort of conspiracy? You must be out of your mind.'

'I risk my life telling you this.'

'Yes. You do. And I risk my life listening.'

'You are essential to our success. *Essential*. You must help us.'

'Look,' said Mondschein, 'if Alvarado simply wants to do away with me, he doesn't have to bother with anything as elaborate as this. Nobody in the world cares whether I live or die. It isn't necessary to inveigle me into a fantastic nonexistent plot on his life. He can just have me shot. All right? All right?'

'This is not a trap. As God is my witness, I am not here as part of a scheme to ensnare you. I beg for your assistance. If you wish, report me to the authorities, and I will be tortured and the truth will come out and I will be executed, and then you will know that I was honest with you.'

Wearily Mondschein said, 'What is all this about?'

'You possess the ability to distinguish between the brothers of Alvarado and Alvarado himself.'

'The brothers?'

'The clones. There is a secret method, known only to you, that allows you to tell the true Alvarado from the false.'

'Don't be silly.'

'It is so. You need not pretend. I have access to very high sources.'

Mondschein shrugged. 'For the sake of argument let's say that it's so. What then?'

'When we aim our blow at Alvarado, we want to be certain we are assassinating the real one.'

'Yes. Of course you do.'

'You can guide our hand. He often appears in public, but no one knows whether it is really he, or one of the brothers. And if we strike down one of the brothers, thinking we have killed the true Alvarado –'

'Yes,' Mondschein said. 'I see the problem. But assuming that I'm able to tell the difference, and I'm not conceding that I can, what makes you think I'd want to get mixed up in your plot? What do I stand to gain from it, other than useless revenge on a man who did me harm a very long time ago? Will his death give me back my life? No, I simply want to live out my last few years in peace. Kill Alvarado without me, if you want to kill him. If you're not sure whether you're killing the right one, kill them all. Kill them one by one until there are none at all left.'

'I *could* kill you,' Aristegui said. 'Right now. I should. After what I have told you, you own my life.'

Again Mondschein shrugged. 'Then kill me. For whatever good it'll do you. I'm not going to inform on you.'

'Nor cooperate with me.'

'Neither one nor the other.'

'All you want is to live in peace,' said Aristegui savagely. 'But how do you know you will? Alvarado has asked you to work for him again, and you have refused.' He held up a hand. 'Yes, yes, I know that. I will not kill you, though I should. But he might, though he has no reason to. Think about that, Senor Doctor.'

114

He rose and glared at Mondschein a moment, and left without another word.

Mondschein's body clock had caught up with Tierra Alvarado time by this time. But that night, once again, he lay until dawn in utterly lucid wakefulness before exhaustion at last brought him some rest. It was as though sleep were a concept he had never quite managed to understand.

The next summons came from Alvarado himself.

The Presidential Palace, which Mondschein remembered as a compact, somewhat austere building in vaguely Roman style, had expanded in the course of a quarter of a century into an incomprehensible mazelike edifice that seemed consciously intended to rival Versailles in ostentatious grandeur. The Hall of Audience was a good sixty meters long, with rich burgundy draperies along the walls and thick blood-red carpeting. There was a marble dais at the far end where the Maximum Leader sat enthroned like an emperor. Dazzling sunlight flooded down on him through a dome of shimmering glass set in the ceiling. Mondschein wondered if he was supposed to offer a genuflection.

There were no guards in the room, only the two of them. But security screens in the floor created an invisible air-wall around the dais. Mondschein found himself forced to halt by subtle pressure when he was still at least fifteen meters short of the throne. Alvarado came stiffly to his feet and they stood facing each other in silence for a long moment.

It seemed anticlimactic, this confrontation at last. Mondschein was surprised to discover that he felt none of the teeth-on-edge uneasiness that the man had always been able to engender in him. Perhaps having seen the clone-Alvarado earlier had taken the edge off the impact.

Alvarado said, 'You have found all the arrangements satisfactory so far, I hope, doctor?'

'In the old days you called me Rafael.'

'Rafael, yes. It was so long ago. How good it is to see you again, Rafael. You look well.'

'As do you.'

'Yes. Thank you. Your villa is satisfactory, Rafael?'

'Quite satisfactory,' said Mondschein. 'I look forward to a few last years of quiet retirement in my native country.'

'So I am told,' Alvarado said.

He seemed overly formal, weirdly remote, hardly even human. In the huge hall his crisp, cool voice had a buzzing androidal undertone that Mondschein found unfamiliar. Possibly that was an atmospheric diffraction effect caused by the security screens. But then it occurred to Mondschein that this too might be one of the clones. He stared hard, trying to tell, trying to call on the intuitive sense that once had made it possible for him to tell quite easily, even without running the alpha-wave test. The AAA Class clones had been intended to be indistinguishable from the original to nine decimal places, but nevertheless when you collapsed the first twenty or thirty years of a man's life into the three-year accelerated-development period of the cloning process you inevitably lost something, and Mondschein had always been able to detect the difference purely subjectively, at a single glance. Now, though, he wasn't sure. It had been simple enough to see that the Alvarado who had greeted him in the Ministry of Scientific Development was a replica, but here, at this distance, in this room that resonated with the presence of the Maximum Leader, there were too many ambiguities and uncertainties.

He said, 'The Minister explained to me that the national genetic laboratories are facing heavy competition from abroad, that you want me to step in and pull things together. But I can't do it. My technical knowledge is hopelessly out of date. I'm simply not familiar with current work in the field. If I had known ahead of time that the reason you had decided to let me come home was that you wanted me to go back into the labs, I never would have –'

'Forget about the labs,' Alvarado said. 'That isn't why I invited you to return.'

'But the Minister of Scientific Development said –'

'Let the Minister of Scientific Development say anything he wishes. The Minister has his agenda and I have mine, doctor.' He had dropped the first-name talk, Mondschein noticed. 'Is it true that there is a method of determining whether a given individual is an authentic human or merely a highly accurate clone?'

Mondschein hesitated. Something was definitely wrong here.

'Yes,' he said finally. 'There is. You know that there is.'

'You are too certain of what I know and what I do not know. Tell me about this method, doctor.'

He was more and more certain that he was talking to one of the clones. Alvarado must be staging one of his elaborate charades.

'It involves matching brain rhythms. When I created the AAA Class Alvarado clones, I built a recognition key into them that would enable me, using a simple EEG hookup, to distinguish their brain-wave patterns from yours. I did this at your request, so that in the case of a possible coup d'état attempt by one of the clones you'd be able to unmask the pretender. The method uses my own brain-waves as the baseline. If you jack my EEG output into a comparator circuit and overlay it with yours, the two patterns will conflict, the way any two patterns from different human beings will. But if my EEG gets matched against one of your clones, the pattern will drop immediately into alpha rhythms, as if we're both under deep hypnosis. It amazes me that you've forgotten this.' He paused. 'Unless, of course, you're not Alvarado at all, but simply one of his – what's the word? – one of his brothers.'

'Very good, doctor.'

'Am I right?'

'Come closer and see for yourself.'

'I can't. The security screens –'

'I have switched them off.'

Mondschein approached. There was no air resistance. When he was five meters away he felt the unmistakable click of recognition.

'Yes, I am right. Even without an EEG test. You're a clone, aren't you?'

'That is so.'

'Is the real Alvarado too busy for me today, or is it that he doesn't have the courage to look me in the eye?'

'I will tell you something very strange, which is a great secret,' said the clone. 'The real Alvarado is no longer in command here.

For the past several months I have run the government of Tierra Alvarado. No one here is aware of this, no one at all. No one except you, now.'

For a moment Mondschein was unable to speak.

'You seriously expect me to believe that?' he said at last.

The clone managed a glacial smile. 'During the years of your absence there have been several internal upheavals in Tierra Alvarado. On three occasions assassination plots resulted in the deaths of Alvarado clones who were playing the role of the Maximum Leader at public ceremonies. Each time, the death of the clone was successfully covered up. The conspirators were apprehended and things continued as if nothing had occurred. On the fourth such occasion, an implosion grenade was thrown toward the Maximum Leader's car while he was en route to Iquique for a ceremony of rededication. I happened to be accompanying him on that journey so that I could double for him in the riskier parts of the ceremony, when the general public would be present. The impact of the grenade was tremendous. There were many fatalities and serious injuries. In the confusion afterward I was mistaken for the true Maximum Leader. I quickly understood the situation and began to act accordingly. And so it has been ever since.'

Mondschein realized that he was trembling.

'So Alvarado's dead?'

The clone looked smug. 'His reign is over. His time is finished.'

What a strange concept that was. Alvarado dead! His old enemy was really dead! Mondschein felt a flash of satisfaction and surprise – and then a curious sense of loss.

'Why are you telling me all this?' he asked, after a moment. 'Assuming that it's true, and not just some game that your master is playing with me, why do you want to take chances this way? What if I tried to expose you and bring the whole crazy system down?'

'You would not do that,' said the clone.

'Why not?'

'You have said it yourself: you want only to live out your remaining years in peaceful retirement. If you denounced me, who would believe you? And even if you were believed, would things be better in Tierra

118

Alvarado in the wake of my overthrow? No, doctor, the status quo is your only hope. And I am the status quo.'

Mondschein nodded. 'Even so, why confide in me at all?'

'So that you may protect me.'

'How could I do that?'

'You hold the key to identification, this alpha-rhythm thing. I did know that you had such a thing, though not the details of it. Others know it also. Your possession of it gives you great power here. If there were a challenge to my legitimacy, you would be the only arbiter of the truth, do you see?'

'Yes,' said Mondschein. 'Yes, I do.'

'There are twenty-one other surviving clones. One of them might take it into his head to overthrow me, thinking that he could rule the country at least as well. It is quite a comfortable existence, being a clone of the Maximum Leader, but it is not pleasant to serve as his double, exposed to all the risks of public appearances. It is a much better life, believe me, to be Maximum Leader and have others double for you, than to be a double yourself, never knowing when the bullet will come. Besides which, there is the wielding of authority for its own sake. That is a highly desirable thing, if you are of the sort who desires such things, and we are. After all, we are all of us Alvarados to the core, as you know better than anyone else.'

'So you think that if one of your vat-brothers suddenly tries to say that he's the real Alvarado, not you, then I'd be willing to come forward and test him and expose him as a clone for you?'

'So I hope and trust.'

'Why would I want to take the side of one clone against another? It's of no importance to me which one of you calls himself President here.'

'But I am the one who calls himself President just now. I might kill you if you didn't cooperate.'

'And if I don't care whether I live or die?'

'You probably care *how* you die,' the Alvarado-clone said. 'You would not die in an easy or a gentle way, that I could promise you. On the other hand, if you pledge that you will aid me, when and if the need arises, I will see to it that you live out the remaining years of

119

your life in the most complete happiness that I can make available. It seems to me a very reasonable offer.'

'It is,' Mondschein said. 'I see that it is.'

'You protect me, and I will protect you. Do we have a deal?'

'If I say no, what are my chances of leaving this building alive today?'

The clone smiled. It was the pure Alvarado-smile. 'They would be quite poor.'

'Then we have a deal,' Mondschein said.

The weeks went by. June gave way to July and the year descended toward its winter depths. Often there was fog; some nights there was frost; always the dry harsh wind blew from the west. Mondschein slept poorly. He heard nothing from the Maximum Leader or any of his minions. Evidently all was tranquil in the ruling circles.

He rarely left the villa. His meals were prepared for him according to his wishes, which were uncomplicated. He had a few books. No one came to see him. Sometimes during the day he went out with his driver to explore the city. It was larger than he expected, spreading long, thin tentacles of slum toward the north and south – as in any impoverished country, everyone from the villages was moving to the capital, God only knew what for – and very shoddy everywhere except in its grand governmental district.

On two of these excursions Mondschein was granted a glimpse of the supposed President Alvarado. The first time, his car was halted at a police roadblock and he waited for half an hour in an immense tie-up until at last the President passed by in a motorcade coming from the airport, with the Director-General of the Republic of the Orinoco, here on a state visit, riding beside him in the armored bubble-roof car while the spectators who lined the boulevard offered sullen acclaim. On the second occasion, far in the outskirts, Mondschein stumbled upon the ceremonial dedication of what he was told was the Grand Sanitation Facility of the Northeast, and there was the familiar figure of the Maximum Leader on high in the reviewing stand, surrounded by fierce-eyed, heavily armed bodyguards and orating bravely into the biting wind.

At other times while traversing the city Mondschein caught sight of various of the clones going about some business of their own. It was not at all unusual to encounter one. Doubtless the populace was quite used to it. Wherever you looked you could find one or two of the Maximum Leader's 'brothers'. Five or six of them headed government ministries – a meeting of the Cabinet must have been like a hall of mirrors – and the others, apparently, simply stood by to serve as presidential doubles when needed, and lived as private citizens the rest of the time. The real Alvarado, if there still was one, could probably have passed in the streets without causing a stir, everyone assuming he was just a clone: a fine kind of shell game that could keep the whole population fooled all the time.

Colonel Aristegui came to the villa again, eventually.

'We are ready to make our move, doctor.'

'Move, then. I don't want to know anything about it.'

Aristegui looked tense, grim, right at the breaking point. 'We need very little from you. Station yourself in the crowd, and when our man asks you, is this one the real one, simply nod or shake your head. We want no more from you than that. Later, when he is dead, we'll ask you to examine the body and confirm that it is the body of the dictator and not one of the imitations. A small service, and you will live forever in the hearts of your countrymen.'

'There's no way I can give you the kind of information you want just by looking at him from a distance.'

'It can be done, and you are the one who can do it. This much I know.'

'No,' Mondschein said. 'What you think you know is wrong. I can't help you. And in any case I don't want to. I told you that before, Colonel. I'm not interested in joining your conspiracy. It isn't any affair of mine.'

'It is an affair of every loyal citizen of this country.'

Mondschein looked at him sadly. He could at least warn Aristegui, he thought, that there was no real Alvarado there to shoot, that they were *all* clones. But would the Colonel believe him? In any case what Aristegui was trying to do was fundamentally futile. Kill one Alvarado, another would move into his place and announce that he was the authentic article. Aristegui could bring down one or two, maybe, but he couldn't get them all. This country was going to be ruled by Alvarados for a long time to come.

'They took my citizenship away twenty-five years ago,' Mondschein said, after a pause. 'I'm here now purely as a guest of the nation, remember? Good guests don't conspire against their hosts. Please go away, Colonel. I haven't heard a thing you've said to me today. I'm already beginning to forget even that you were here.'

Aristegui glowered at him in a way that seemed to mingle anguish and fury. For a moment Mondschein thought the man was going to strike him. But then, with a visible effort, the Colonel brought himself under control.

'I thank you for your continued silence, at least,' said Aristegui bitterly. 'Good day, Senor Doctor Mondschein.'

Late that afternoon Mondschein heard loud voices from below, shouts and outcries in the servants' quarters. He rang up on the housekeeper's intercom and said, 'What's going on?'

'There has been an attack on the President, Senor Doctor. At the Palace of Government. We have just seen it on the television.'

So Aristegui had been telling the truth, it seemed, when he said that they were ready to make their move. Or else they had decided it was too risky to wait any longer, now that Mondschein had been told that an assassination attempt was impending.

'And?' Mondschein said.

'By the mercy of the Virgin he is safe, senor. Order has been restored and the criminals have been captured. One of the others was slain, one of the brothers, but the President was not harmed.'

He thanked her and switched on his television set.

They were in the midst of showing a replay of it now. The President arriving at the Palace of Government for the regular midweek meeting of the ministers; the adoring populace obediently waiting behind the barricades to hail him as he emerged from his car; the sudden scuffle in the crowd, evidently a deliberate distraction, and then the shot, the screams, the slim long-legged figure beginning to sag into the arms of his bodyguards, the policemen rushing forward.

And then a cut to the Hall of Audience, the grim-faced Maximum Leader addressing the nation from his throne in broken phrases, in a voice choked with emotion: 'This despicable act . . . This bestial attempt to overrule the will of the people as expressed through their chosen President . . . We must root out the forces of chaos that are loose among us . . . We proclaim a week of national mourning for our fallen brother . . .'

Followed by an explanation from a sleek, unruffled-looking official spokesman. The Guardia de la Patria, he said, had received advance word of a possible plot. One of the President's 'brothers' had cour-ageously agreed to bear the risk of entering the Palace of Government in the usual way; the Maximum Leader himself had gone into the building through a secret entrance. The identity of the main con-spirators was known; arrests had already been made; others would follow. Return to your homes, remain calm, all is well.

All is well.

The executions took place a few weeks later. They were shown on huge television screens set up before great throngs of spectators in the main plazas of the city, and relayed to home viewers everywhere. Mondschein, despite earlier resolutions to the contrary, watched along with everyone else in a kind of horrified fascination as Colonel Aristegui and five other officers of the elite guard, along with three other men and four women, all of them members of the Popular Assembly, were led to the wall one by one, faces expressionless, bodies rigid. They were not offered the opportunity to utter last words, even of carefully rehearsed contrition. Their names were spoken and they were blindfolded and shot, and the body taken away, and the next conspirator brought forth.

Mondschein felt an obscure sense of guilt, as though he had been the one who had informed on them. But of course he had said nothing to anyone. The country was full of governmental agents and spies and provocateurs; the Maximum Leader had not needed Mondschein's help in protecting himself against Colonel Aristegui. The guilt that he felt, Mondschein realized, was that of having let Aristegui go to his death without trying to make him see that he was attempting something impossible, that there was no way, with or without Mondschein's help, that Aristegui could ever rid the country of Alvarado. But the Colonel wouldn't have listened to him in any case, Mondschein told himself.

The days went by. The season brightened toward spring. Mondschein's driver took him up the mountain roads to see Lake Titicaca, and north from there to Cuzco and its grand old Inca relics, and up beyond that to the splendors of Machu Picchu. On another journey he went down to the fogswept coast, to Nazca where it never rains, where in a landscape as barren as the Moon's he inspected the huge drawings of monkeys and birds and geometrical figures that prehistoric artists had inscribed in the bone-dry soil of the plateaus.

On a brilliant September day that felt like midsummer a car bearing the insignia of the Guardia came to his villa and a brisk young officer with thick hair that was like spun gold told him that he was requested to go at once to the Palace of Justice.

'Have I done something wrong?' Mondschein asked mildly.

'It is by order of the President,' said the blond young officer, and that was all the explanation he gave.

Mondschein had been in the Palace of Justice only once before, during the weeks just prior to the agreement that led to his being exiled, when they had briefly imprisoned him on the supposed charge of creating abominations and monsters. Like most of the other governmental buildings it was a massive, brutal-looking stone structure, two long parallel wings with a smaller one set between them at their head, so that it crouched on its plaza like a ponderous sphinx. There were courtrooms in the upper levels of the two large wings, prison cells below; the small central wing was the headquarters of the Supreme Court, whose chief justice, Mondschein had recently discovered, was another of the clones.

His Guardia escort led him into the building on the lower level, and they descended even below that, to the dreaded high-security area in the basement. Was he to be interrogated, then? For what?

The Maximum Leader, in full uniform and decorations, was waiting for him in a cold, clammy-walled interrogation cell, under a single bare incandescent bulb of a kind that Mondschein thought had been obsolete for a hundred years. He offered Mondschein a benign smile, as benign as that sharp-edged face was capable of showing.

'Our second meeting is in rather less grand surroundings than the first, eh, doctor?'

Mondschein peered closely. This seemed to be the same clone who had spoken with him in the Hall of Audience. He felt quite sure of that. Only intuition, of course. But he trusted it.

'You remember the agreement we reached that day?' the clone asked.

'Of course.'

'Today I need to invoke it. Your special expertise is now essential to the stability of the nation.'

The clone gestured to an aide-de-camp, who signalled to a figure in the shadows behind him that Mondschein had not noticed before. A door opened at the rear of the cell and a gurney bearing electronic equipment was wheeled in. Mondschein recognized the familiar intricacies of an electroencephalograph.

'This is the proper machinery for your brain-wave test, is it not?' the Alvarado clone asked.

Mondschein nodded.

'Good,' the clone said. 'Bring in the prisoner.'

The door opened again and two guards dragged in the ragged, disheveled-looking figure of an Alvarado. His hands were shackled behind his back. His face was bruised and sweaty and smeared with dirt. His clothes, rough peasant clothes, were torn. His eyes were blazing with fury of astonishing intensity. Mondschein felt a tremor of the old fear at the sight of him.

The prisoner shot a fiery look at the Alvarado clone and said, 'You bastard, let me out of here right now. You know who I am. You know who you are, too. *What* you are.'

Mondschein turned to the clone. 'But you told me he was dead!' he said.

'Dead? Who? What do you mean?' the Alvarado clone said calmly. 'This clone was gravely injured in an attempt on my life and has hovered close to death for many weeks, despite the finest care we could give him. Now that he has begun to recover he is exhibiting delusional behavior. He insists that he is the true Maximum Leader and I am nothing but an artificial genetic duplicate. I ask you to test the authenticity of his claim, Senor Doctor.'

'*Mondschein!* Rafael Mondschein!' the ragged Alvarado cried. A convulsive quiver of amazement ran through his shoulders and chest. 'You here? They've brought you back?'

Mondschein said nothing. He stared at the ragged man.

The prisoner's eyes gleamed. 'All right, go on! Test me, Rafael. Do your mumbo-jumbo and tell this fraud who I am! And then we'll see if he dares keep up the masquerade. Go on, Rafael! Plug in your damned machine! Stick the electrodes on me!'

'Go ahead, Senor Doctor,' the Alvarado clone said.

Mondschein stepped forward and began the preparations for the test, wondering whether he would remember the procedure after so many years.

The prisoner looked toward the Alvarado clone and said, 'He'll prove that I am who I say I am. And you won't have the guts to carry the pretense any further, will you, you test-tube fraud? Because half the staff in the hospital knows the real story already, and somehow the truth will get out. Somehow, no matter how you try to suppress it. And it'll bring you down. Once the country finds out that you're a fake, that you simply seized power when the motorcade bomb went off. Once word gets around that I didn't die, that you've had me hidden away in the hospital all this time with people thinking I was you and you were me, what do you think will happen to your regime? Will anyone want to take orders from a clone?'

'You mustn't speak now,' Mondschein told him. 'It'll distort the test results.'

'All right. Yes. Listen, Rafael, no matter what you tell him he'll say that you identified me as a clone, but you know that it's a lie. When you get back outside, you tell people the true story. You hear me? And afterward I'll see to it that you get whatever you want. Anything. No reward would be too great. Money, women, country estates, your own laboratory, whatever.'

'Please,' Mondschein said. 'I ask you not to speak.'

He attached the electrodes to himself. He touched the dials.

He remembered, now. The whole technique. He had written these personality-organization algorithms himself. He closed his eyes and felt the data come flooding in. The prisoner's brain-waves met his own – collided – clashed – clashed violently –

To the Alvarado clone Mondschein said, 'The alpha match is perfect, Senor Presidente. What we have here is a clone.'

'No, Rafael!' the prisoner roared. 'You filthy lying bastard, no! You know it isn't so!'

'Take him away,' the Alvarado clone said.

'No. You won't do anything to me. I'm the only legitimate President of Tierra Alvarado.'

'You are nothing,' the clone told him. 'You are a mere creature. We have scientific proof that you are simply one of the artificial brothers. Dr Mondschein has just demonstrated that.'

'Balls,' the prisoner said. 'Listen, Mondschein, I know he has you intimidated. But when you get out of here, spread the word. Tell everyone what your real reading was. That there's a usurper in the presidential palace, that he must be overthrown. You'll be a national hero, you'll be rewarded beyond your wildest dreams –'

Mondschein smiled. 'Ah, but I already have everything that I want.'

He looked toward the Alvarado clone. 'I'll prepare a formal report and sign it, Senor Presidente. And I will be willing to attest to it at the public trial.'

'This has been the trial, doctor,' the clone said smoothly, indicating an opening in the ceiling of the cell, where Mondschein now saw an opening through which the snout of a television camera protruded. 'All the information that we need has been recorded. But I am grateful for your offer. You have been extremely helpful. Extremely helpful, Senor Doctor.'

That night, in the safety and comfort of his beloved villa, Mondschein slept soundly for the first time since his return to Tierra Alvarado – more soundly than he had slept in years.

Hunters in the Forest

One pleasant aspect of being a writer who dabbles in editing is that every once in a while you get to sell a story to yourself. Of course, I have to sell every story I write to myself before I can sell it to anyone else – if I don't think much of it, after all, how can I offer it to someone for publication with a straight face? – but when I'm simultaneously both writer and editor I don't have to worry, at least, about all those silly little editorial quibbles that other editors often insist on inflicting on me before they'll publish something of mine.

In this case, the well-known book packager Byron Preiss was assembling a majestic coffee-table volume called *The Ultimate Dinosaur*, a large-size volume offering a mixture of scientific essays, short stories, and color plates, and I was serving as fiction editor for the book. I assembled a team of top-level science-fictionists (Poul Anderson, L. Sprague de Camp, Gregory Benford, etc.) to write the stories, each of which was matched in theme to one of the essays. And I grabbed the theme of 'Dinosaur Predators' for myself and illustrated it with this nasty little item, in which, as often happens in my fiction, the most dangerous beast turns out to be something other than the obvious one.

I wrote the story in November, 1990. *Omni* published it in magazine form in its October, 1991 issue and *The Ultimate Dinosaur* appeared the following year.

Twenty minutes into the voyage nothing more startling than a dragon-fly the size of a hawk has come into view, fluttering for an eyeblink moment in front of the timemobile window and darting away, and Mallory decides it's time to exercise Option Two: abandon the secure cozy comforts of the timemobile capsule, take his chances on foot out there in the steamy mists, a futuristic pygmy roaming virtually unprotected among the dinosaurs of this fragrant Late Cretaceous forest. That has been his plan all along – to offer himself up to the available dangers of this place, to experience the thrill of the hunt without ever quite being sure whether he was the hunter or the hunted.

Option One is to sit tight inside the timemobile capsule for the full duration of the trip – he has signed up for twelve hours – and watch the passing show, if any, through the invulnerable window. Very safe, yes. But self-defeating, also, if you have come here for the sake of tasting a little excitement for once in your life. Option Three, the one nobody ever talks about except in whispers and which perhaps despite all rumors to the contrary no one has actually ever elected, is self-defeating in a different way: simply walk off into the forest and never look back. After a prearranged period, usually twelve hours, never more than twenty-four, the capsule will return to its starting point in the 23rd century whether or not you're aboard. But Mallory isn't out to do himself in, not really. All he wants is a little endocrine action, a hit of adrenaline to rev things up, the unfamiliar sensation of honest fear contracting his auricles and chilling his bowels: all that good old chancy stuff, damned well unattainable down the line in the modern era where risk is just about extinct. Back here in the Mesozoic, risk aplenty is available enough for those who can put up the price of admission. All he has to do is go outside and look for it. And so it's Option Two for him, then, a lively little walkabout, and then back to the capsule in plenty of time for the return trip.

With him he carries a laser rifle, a backpack medical kit, and lunch. He jacks a thinko into his waistband and clips a drinko to his shoulder. But no helmet, no potted air supply. He'll boldly expose his naked nostrils to the Cretaceous atmosphere. Nor does he avail himself of the one-size-fits-all body armor that the capsule is willing to provide. That's the true spirit of Option Two, all right: go forth unshielded into the Mesozoic dawn.

Open the hatch, now. Down the steps, hop skip jump. Booted feet bouncing on the spongy primordial forest floor.

There's a hovering dankness but a surprisingly pleasant breeze is blowing. Things feel tropical but not uncomfortably torrid. The air has an unusual smell. The mix of nitrogen and carbon dioxide is different from what he's accustomed to, he suspects, and certainly none of the impurities that six centuries of industrial development have poured into the atmosphere are present. There's something else, too, a strange subtext of an odor that seems both sweet and pungent: it must be the aroma of dinosaur farts, Mallory decides. Uncountable hordes of stupendous beasts simultaneously releasing vast roaring boomers for a hundred million years surely will have filled the prehistoric air with complex hydrocarbons that won't break down until the Oligocene at the earliest.

Scaly treetrunks thick as the columns of the Parthenon shoot heavenward all around him. At their summits, far overhead, whorls of stiff long leaves jut tensely outward. Smaller trees that look like palms, but probably aren't, fill in the spaces between them, and at ground level there are dense growths of awkward angular bushes. Some of them are in bloom, small furry pale-yellowish blossoms, very diffident-looking, as though they were so newly evolved that they were embarrassed to find themselves on display like this. All the vegetation big and little has a battered, shopworn look, trunks leaning this way and that, huge leaf-stalks bent and dangling, gnawed boughs hanging like broken arms. It is as though an army of enormous tanks passes through this forest every few days. In fact that isn't far from the truth, Mallory realizes.

But where are they? Twenty-five minutes gone already and he still hasn't seen a single dinosaur, and he's ready for some.

'All right,' Mallory calls out. 'Where are you, you big dopes?'

As though on cue the forest hurls a symphony of sounds back at him: strident honks and rumbling snorts and a myriad blatting snuffling wheezing skreeing noises. It's like a chorus of crocodiles getting warmed up for Handel's Messiah.

Mallory laughs. 'Yes, I hear you, I hear you!'

He cocks his laser rifle. Steps forward, looking eagerly to right and left. This period is supposed to be the golden age of dinosaurs, the grand tumultuous climactic epoch just before the end, when bizarre new species popped out constantly with glorious evolutionary profligacy, and all manner of grotesque goliaths roamed the earth. The thinko has shown him pictures of them, spectacularly decadent in size and appearance, long-snouted duckbilled monsters as big as a house and huge lumbering ceratopsians with frilly baroque bony crests and toothy things with knobby horns on their elongated skulls and others with rows of bristling spikes along their high-ridged backs. He aches to see them. He wants them to scare him practically to death. Let them loom; let them glower; let their great jaws yawn. Through all his untroubled days in the orderly and carefully regulated world of the 23rd century Mallory has never shivered with fear as much as once, never known a moment of terror or even real uneasiness, is not even sure he understands the concept; and he has paid a small fortune for the privilege of experiencing it now.

Forward. Forward.

Come on, you oversized bastards, get your asses out of the swamp and show yourselves!

There. Oh, yes, yes, *there*!

He sees the little spheroid of a head first, rising above the treetops like a grinning football attached to a long thick hose. Behind it is an enormous humped back, unthinkably high. He hears the piledriver sound of the behemoth's footfall and the crackle of huge treetrunks breaking as it smashes its way serenely toward him.

He doesn't need the murmured prompting of his thinko to know that this is a giant sauropod making its majestic passage through the forest – 'one of the titanosaurs or perhaps an ultrasaur,' the quiet voice says, admitting with just a hint of chagrin in its tone that it can't identify the particular species – but Mallory isn't really concerned with detail on that level. He is after the thrill of size. And he's getting size, all right. The thing is implausibly colossal. It emerges into the clearing where he stands and he is given the full view, and gasps. He can't even guess how big it is. Twenty meters high? Thirty? Its ponderous corrugated legs are thick as sequoias. Giraffes on tiptoe could go skittering between them without grazing the underside of its massive belly. Elephants would look like housecats beside it. Its tail, held out stiffly to the rear, decapitates sturdy trees with its slow steady lashing. A hundred million years of saurian evolution have produced this thing, Darwinianism gone crazy, excess building remorselessly

131

on excess, irrepressible chromosomes gleefully reprogramming themselves through the millennia to engender thicker bones, longer legs, ever bulkier bodies, and the end result is this walking mountain, this absurdly overstated monument to reptilian hyperbole.

'Hey!' Mallory cries. 'Look here! Can you see this far down? There's a human down here. *Homo sapiens.* I'm a mammal. Do you know what a mammal is? Do you know what my ancestors are going to do to your descendants?' He is practically alongside it, no more than a hundred meters away. Its musky stink makes him choke and cough. Its ancient leathery brown hide, as rigid as cast iron, is pocked with parasitic growths, scarlet and yellow and ultramarine, and crisscrossed with the gulleys and ravines of century-old wounds deep enough for him to hide in. With each step it takes Mallory feels an earthquake. He is nothing next to it, a flea, a gnat. It could crush him with a casual stride and never even know.

And yet he feels no fear. The sauropod is so big he can't make sense out of it, let alone be threatened by it.

Can you fear the Amazon River? The planet Jupiter? The pyramid of Cheops? No, what he feels is anger, not terror. The sheer preposterous bulk of the monster infuriates him. The pointless superabundance of it inspires him with wrath.

'My name is Mallory,' he yells. 'I've come from the 23rd century to bring you your doom, you great stupid mass of meat. I'm personally going to make you extinct, do you hear me?'

He raises the laser rifle and centers its sight on the distant tiny head. The rifle hums its computations and modifications and the rainbow beam jumps skyward. For an instant the sauropod's head is engulfed in a dazzling fluorescent nimbus. Then the light dies away, and the animal moves on as though nothing has happened.

No brain up there? Mallory wonders.

Too dumb to die?

He moves up closer and fires again, carving a bright track along one hypertrophied haunch. Again, no effect. The sauropod moves along untroubled, munching on treetops as it goes. A third shot, too hasty, goes astray and cuts off the crown of a tree in the forest canopy. A fourth zings into the sauropod's gut but the dinosaur doesn't seem to care. Mallory is furious now at the unkillability of the thing. His thinko quietly reminds him that these giants supposedly had had their main nerve-centers at the base of their spines. Mallory runs around behind the creature and stares up at the galactic expanse of its rump, wondering where best to place his shot. Just then the great tail swings upward and to the left and a torrent of immense steaming green turds as big as boulders comes cascading down, striking the ground all around Mallory with thunderous impact. He leaps out of the way barely in time to keep from being entombed, and goes scrambling frantically away to avoid the choking fetor that rises from the sauropod's vast mound of excreta. In his haste he stumbles over a vine, loses his footing in the slippery mud, falls to hands and knees. Something that looks like a small blue dog with a scaly skin and a ring of sharp spines around its neck jumps up out of the muck, bouncing up and down and hissing and screeching and snapping at him. Its teeth are deadly-looking yellow fangs. There isn't room to fire the laser rifle. Mallory desperately rolls to one side and bashes the thing with the butt instead, hard, and it runs away growling. When he has a chance finally to catch his breath and look up again, he sees the great sauropod vanishing in the distance.

He gets up and takes a few limping steps further away from the reeking pile of ordure.

He has learned at last what it's like to have a brush with death. Two brushes, in fact, within the span of ten seconds. But where's the vaunted thrill of danger narrowly averted, the hot satisfaction of the *frisson*? He feels no pleasure, none of the hoped-for rush of keen endocrine delight.

Of course not. A pile of falling turds, a yapping little lizard with big teeth: what humiliating perils! During the frantic moments when he was defending himself against them he was too busy to notice what he was feeling, and now, muddy all over, his knee aching, his dignity dented, he is left merely with a residue of annoyance, frustration, and perhaps a little ironic self-deprecation, when what he had wanted was the white ecstasy of genuine terror followed by the post-orgasmic delight of successful escape recollected in tranquility.

Well, he still has plenty of time. He goes onward, deeper into the forest.

Now he is no longer able to see the timemobile capsule. That feels good, that sudden new sense of being cut off from the one zone of safety he has in this fierce environment. He tries to divert himself with fantasies of jeopardy. It isn't easy. His mind doesn't work that way; nobody's does, really, in the nice, tidy, menace-free society he lives in. But he works at it. Suppose, he thinks, I lose my way in the forest and can't get back to – no, no hope of that, the capsule sends out constant directional pulses that his thinko picks up by microwave transmission. What if the thinko breaks down, then? But they never do. If I take it off and toss it into a swamp? That's Option Three, though, selfdamaging behavior designed to maroon him here. He doesn't do such things. He can barely even fantasize them.

Well, then, the sauropod comes back and steps on the capsule, crushing it beyond use –

Impossible. The capsule is strong enough to withstand submersion to 30-atmosphere pressures.

The sauropod pushes it into quicksand, and it sinks out of sight?

Mallory is pleased with himself for coming up with that one. It's good for a moment or two of interesting uneasiness. He imagines himself standing at the edge of some swamp, staring down forlornly as the final minutes tick away and the timemobile, functional as ever even though it's fifty fathoms down in gunk, sets out for home without him. But no, no good: the capsule moves just as effectively through space as through time, and it would simply activate its powerful engine and climb up onto terra firma again in plenty of time for his return trip.

What if, he thinks, a band of malevolent *intelligent* dinosaurs appears on the scene and forcibly prevents me from getting back into the capsule?

That's more like it. A little shiver that time. Good! Cut off, stranded in the Mesozoic! Living by his wits, eating God knows what, exposing himself to extinct bacteria. Getting sick, blazing with fever, groaning in unfamiliar pain. Yes! Yes! He piles it on. It becomes easier as he gets into the swing of it. He will lead a life of constant menace.

He imagines himself taking out his own appendix. Setting a broken leg. And the unending hazards, day and night. Toothy enemies lurking behind every bush. Baleful eyes glowing in the darkness. A life spent forever on the run, never a moment's ease. Cowering under fern-fronds as the giant carnivores go lalloping by. Scorpions, snakes, gigantic venomous toads. Insects that sting. Everything that has been eliminated from life in the civilized world pursuing him here: and he flitting from one transitory hiding place to another, haggard, unshaven, bloodshot, brow shining with sweat, struggling unceasingly to survive, living a gallant life of desperate heroism in this nightmare world –

'Hello,' he says suddenly. 'Who the hell are you?'

In the midst of his imaginings a genuine horror has presented itself, emerging suddenly out of a grove of tree ferns. It is a towering bipedal creature with the powerful thighs and small dangling forearms of the familiar tyrannosaurus, but this one has an enormous bony crest like a warrior's helmet rising from its skull, with five diabolical horns radiating outward behind it and two horrendous incisors as long as tusks jutting from its cavernous mouth, and its huge lashing tail is equipped with a set of great spikes at the tip. Its mottled and furrowed skin is a bilious yellow and the huge crest on its head is fiery scarlet. It is everybody's bad dream of the reptilian killer-monster of the primeval dawn, the ghastly overspecialized end-product of the long saurian reign, shouting its own lethality from every bony excrescence, every razor-keen weapon on its long body.

The thinko scans it and tells him that it is a representative of an unknown species belonging to the saurischian order and it is almost certainly predatory.

'Thank you very much,' Mallory replies.

He is astonished to discover that even now, facing this embodiment of death, he is not at all afraid. Fascinated, yes, by the sheer deadliness of the creature, by its excessive horrificality. Amused, almost, by its grotesqueries of form. And coolly aware that in three bounds and a swipe of its little dangling paw it could end his life, depriving him of the sure century of minimum expectancy that remains to him. Despite that threat he remains calm. If he dies, he dies; but he can't actually bring himself to believe that he will. He is beginning to see that the capacity for fear, for any sort of significant psychological distress, has been bred out of him. He is simply too stable. It is an unexpected drawback of the perfection of human society.

The saurischian predator of unknown species slavers and roars and glares. Its narrow yellow eyes are like beacons. Mallory unslings his laser rifle and gets into firing position. Perhaps this one will be easier to kill than the colossal sauropod.

Then a woman walks out of the jungle behind it and says, 'You aren't going to try to shoot it, are you?'

Mallory stares at her. She is young, only fifty or so unless she's on her second or third retread, attractive, smiling. Long sleek legs, a fluffy burst of golden hair. She wears a stylish hunting outfit of black sprayon and carries no rifle, only a tiny laser pistol. A space of no more than a dozen meters separates her from the dinosaur's spiked tail, but that doesn't seem to trouble her.

He gestures with the rifle. 'Step out of the way, will you?'

She doesn't move. 'Shooting it isn't a smart idea.'

'We're here to do a little hunting, aren't we?'

'Be sensible,' she says. 'This one's a real son of a bitch. You'll only annoy it if you try anything, and then we'll both be in a mess.' She walks casually around the monster, which is standing quite still, studying them both in an odd perplexed way as though it actually wonders what they might be. Mallory has aimed the rifle now at the thing's left eye, but the woman coolly puts her hand to the barrel and pushes it aside.

'Let it be,' she says. 'It's just had its meal and now it's sleepy. I watched it gobble up something the size of a hippopotamus and then eat half of another one for dessert. You start sticking it with your little laser and you'll wake it up, and then it'll get nasty again. Mean-looking bastard, isn't it?' she says admiringly.

'Who are you?' Mallory asks in wonder. 'What are you doing here?'

'Same thing as you, I figure. Cretaceous Tours?'

'Yes. They said I wouldn't run into any other –'

'They told me that too. Well, it sometimes happens. Jayne Hyland. New Chicago, 2281.'

'Tom Mallory. New Chicago also. And also 2281.'

'Small geological epoch, isn't it? What month did you leave from?'

'August.'

'I'm September.'

'Imagine that.'

The dinosaur, far above them, utters a soft snorting sound and begins to drift away.

'We're boring it,' she says.

'And it's boring us, too. Isn't that the truth? These enormous terrifying monsters crashing through the forest all around us and we're as blasé as if we're home watching the whole thing on the polyvid.' Mallory raises his rifle again. The scarlet-frilled killer is almost out of sight. 'I'm tempted to take a shot at it just to get some excitement going.'

'Don't,' she says. 'Unless you're feeling suicidal. Are you?'

'Not at all.'

'Then don't annoy it, okay? – I know where there's a bunch of ankylosaurs wallowing around. That's one really weird critter, believe me. Are you interested in having a peek?'

'Sure,' says Mallory.

He finds himself very much taken by her brisk no-nonsense manner, her confident air. When we get back to New Chicago, he thinks, maybe I'll look her up. The September tour, she said. So he'll have to wait a while after his own return. I'll give her a call around the end of the month, he tells himself.

She leads the way unhesitatingly, through the tree-fern grove and around a stand of giant horsetails and across a swampy meadow of small plastic-looking plants with ugly little mud-colored daisyish flowers. On the far side they zig around a great pile of bloodied bones and zag around a treacherous bog with a sinisterly quivering surface. A couple of giant dragonflies whiz by, droning like airborne missiles. A crimson frog as big as a rabbit grins at them from a pond. They have been walking for close to an hour now and Mallory no longer has any idea where he is in relation to his timemobile capsule. But the thinko will find the way back for him eventually, he assumes.

'The ankylosaurs are only about a hundred meters further on,' she says, as if reading his mind. She looks back and gives him a bright smile. 'I saw a pack of troodons the day before yesterday out this way. You know what they are? Little agile guys, no bigger than you or me, smart as whips. Teeth like sawblades, funny knobs on their heads. I thought for a minute they were going to attack, but I stood my ground and finally they backed off. You want to shoot something, shoot one of those.'

'The day before yesterday?' Mallory asks, after a moment. 'How long have you been here?'

'About a week. Maybe two. I've lost count, really. Look, there are those ankylosaurs I was telling you about.'

He ignores her pointing hand. 'Wait a second. The longest available time tour lasts only –'

'I'm Option Three,' she says.

He gapes at her as though she has just sprouted a scarlet bony crust with five spikes behind it.

'Are you serious?' he asks.

'As serious as anybody you ever met in the middle of the Cretaceous forest. I'm here for keeps, friend. I stood right next to my capsule when the twelve hours were up and watched it go sailing off into the ineffable future. And I've been having the time of my life ever since.'

A tingle of awe spreads through him. It is the strongest emotion he has ever felt, he realizes.

She is actually living that gallant life of desperate heroism that he had fantasized. Avoiding the myriad menaces of this incomprehensible place for a whole week or possibly even two, managing to stay fed and healthy, in fact looking as trim and elegant as if she had just stepped out of her capsule a couple of hours ago. And never to go back to the nice safe orderly world of 2281. Never. Never. She will remain here until she dies – a month from now, a year, five years, whenever. Must remain. Must. By her own choice. An incredible adventure.

Her face is very close to his. Her breath is sweet and warm. Her eyes are bright, penetrating, ferocious. 'I was sick of it all,' she tells him. 'Weren't you? The perfection of everything. The absolute predictability. You can't even stub your toe because there's some clever sensor watching out for you. The biomonitors. The automedics. The guides and proctors. I hated it.'

'Yes. Of course.'

Her intensity is frightening. For one foolish moment, Mallory realizes, he was actually thinking of offering to *rescue* her from the consequences of her rashness. Inviting her to come back with him in his own capsule when his twelve hours are up. They could probably both fit inside, if they stand very close to each other. A reprieve from Option Three, a new lease on life for her. But that isn't really possible, he knows. The mass has to balance in both directions of the trip within a very narrow tolerance; they are warned not to bring back even a twig, even a pebble, nothing aboard the capsule that wasn't aboard it before. And in any case being rescued is surely the last thing she wants. She'll simply laugh at him. Nothing could make her go back. She loves it here. She feels truly alive for the first time in her life. In a universe of security-craving dullards she's a woman running wild. And her wildness is contagious. Mallory trembles with sudden new excitement at the sheer proximity of her.

She sees it, too. Her glowing eyes flash with invitation.

'Stay here with me!' she says. 'Let your capsule go home without you, the way I did.'

'But the dangers –' he hears himself blurting inanely.

'Don't worry about them. I'm doing all right so far, aren't I? We can manage. We'll build a cabin. Plant fruits and vegetables. Catch lizards in traps. Hunt the dinos. They're so dumb they just stand there and let you shoot them. The laser charges won't ever run out. You and me, me and you, all alone in the Mesozoic! Like Adam and Eve, we'll be. The Adam and Eve of the Late Cretaceous. And they can all go to hell back there in 2281.'

His fingers are tingling. His throat is dry. His cheeks blaze with savage adrenal fires. His breath is coming in ragged gasps. He has never felt anything like this before in his life.

He moistens his lips.

'Well –'

She smiles gently. The pressure eases. 'It's a big decision, I know. Think about it,' she says. Her voice is soft now. The wild zeal of a moment before is gone from it. 'How soon before your capsule leaves?'

He glances at his wrist. 'Eight, nine more hours.'

'Plenty of time to make up your mind.'

'Yes. Yes.'

Relief washes over him. She has dizzied him with the overpowering force of her revelation and the passionate frenzy of her invitation to join her in her escape from the world they have left behind. He isn't used to such things. He needs time now, time to absorb, to digest, to ponder. To decide. That he would even consider such a thing astonishes him. He has known her how long – an hour, an hour and a half? – and here he is thinking of giving up everything for her. Unbelievable. Unbelievable.

Shakily he turns away from her and stares at the ankylosaurs wallowing in the mudhole just in front of them.

Strange, strange, strange. Gigantic low-slung tubby things, squat as tanks, covered everywhere by armor. Vaguely triangular, expanding vastly toward the rear, terminating in armored tails with massive bony excrescences at the tips, like deadly clubs. Slowly snuffling forward in the muck, tiny heads down, busily grubbing away at soft green weeds. Jayne jumps down among them and dances across their armored backs, leaping from one to another. They don't even seem to notice. She laughs and calls to him. 'Come on,' she says, prancing like a she-devil.

They dance among the ankylosaurs until the game grows stale. Then she takes him by the hand and they run onward, through a field of scarlet mosses, down to a small clear lake fed by a swift-flowing stream. They strip and plunge in, heedless of risk. Afterward they embrace on the grassy bank. Some vast creature passes by, momentarily darkening the sky. Mallory doesn't bother even to look up.

Then it is on, on to spy on something with a long neck and a comic knobby head, and then to watch a pair of angry ceratopsians butting heads in slow motion, and then to applaud the elegant migration of a herd of towering duckbills across the horizon. There are dinosaurs everywhere, everywhere, everywhere, an astounding zoo of them. And the time ticks away.

It's fantastic beyond all comprehension. But even so –

Give up everything for this? he wonders.

The chalet in Gstaad, the weekend retreat aboard the L5 satellite, the hunting lodge in the veldt? The island home in the Seychelles, the plantation in New Caledonia, the *pied-à-terre* in the shadow of the Eiffel Tower?

For this? For a forest full of nightmare monsters, and a life of daily peril?

Yes. Yes. Yes. Yes.

He glances toward her. She knows what's on his mind, and she gives him a sizzling look. *Come live with me and be my love, and we will all the pleasures prove.* Yes. Yes. Yes. Yes.

A beeper goes off on his wrist and his thinko says, 'It is time to return to the capsule. Shall I guide you?'

And suddenly it all collapses into a pile of ashes, the whole shimmering fantasy perishing in an instant.

'Where are you going?' she calls.

'Back,' he says. He whispers the word hoarsely – croaks it, in fact.

'Tom!'

'Please. Please.'

He can't bear to look at her. His defeat is total; his shame is cosmic. But he isn't going to stay here. He isn't. He isn't. He simply isn't. He slinks away, feeling her burning contemptuous glare drilling holes in his shoulderblades. The quiet voice of the thinko steadily instructs him, leading him around pitfalls and obstacles. After a time he looks back and can no longer see her.

On the way back to the capsule he passes a pair of sauropods mating, a tyrannosaur in full slather, another thing with talons like scythes, and half a dozen others. The thinko obligingly provides him with their names, but Mallory doesn't even give them a glance. The brutal fact of his own inescapable cowardice is the only thing that occupies his mind. *She* has had the courage to turn her back on the stagnant overperfect world where they live, regardless of all danger, whereas he – he –

'There is the capsule, sir,' the thinko says triumphantly.

Last chance, Mallory.

No. No. No. He can't do it.

He climbs in. Waits. Something ghastly appears outside, all teeth and claws, and peers balefully at him through the window. Mallory peers back at it, nose to nose, hardly caring what happens to him now. The creature takes an experimental nibble at the capsule. The impervious metal resists. The dinosaur shrugs and waddles away.

A chime goes off. The Late Cretaceous turns blurry and disappears.

In mid-October, seven weeks after his return, he is telling the somewhat edited version of his adventure at a party for the fifteenth time that month when a woman to his left says, 'There's someone in the other room who's just came back from the dinosaur tour too.'

'Really,' says Mallory, without enthusiasm.

'You and she would love to compare notes, I'll bet. Wait, and I'll get her. Jayne! Jayne, come in here for a moment!'

Mallory gasps. Color floods his face. His mind swirls in bewilderment and chagrin. Her eyes are as sparkling and alert as ever, her hair is a golden cloud.

'But you told me –'

'Yes,' she says. 'I did, didn't I?'

'Your capsule – you said it had gone back –'

'It was just on the far side of the ankylosaurs, behind the horsetails. I got to the Cretaceous about eight hours before you did. I had signed up for a 24-hour tour.'

'And you let me believe –'

'Yes. So I did.' She grins at him and says softly, 'It was a lovely fantasy, don't you think?'

He comes close to her and gives her a cold, hard stare. 'What would you have done if I had let my capsule go back without me and stranded myself there for the sake of your lovely fantasy? Or didn't you stop to think about that?'

'I don't know,' she tells him. 'I just don't know.' And she laughs.

A Long Night's Vigil
at the Temple

The rainy season in California, where I live, usually begins in late October
and runs to March or early April, and since it takes me five or six months
to write a novel and I generally write one every year, it is my custom to
write my annual novel during our annual spate of wet months. But in 1990,
as it happened, the novel that I began at the usual autumn date was the
collaboration with Isaac Asimov that is known as *Child of Time* in England
and *The Ugly Little Boy* in the United States, and – with Isaac's existing
novella already in hand to give me a tremendous boost into the story – the
job took me about half the usual time. I was done with the book before
the rains had fairly begun to fall, which left me with an entire winter free. I
could spend it standing at the window watching the raindrops fall, or I could
write a bunch of short stories; and it was the latter course that I chose.

It was just at that time that the formidably productive anthologist Martin
H. Greenberg, with whom I've enjoyed a congenial friendship and a close
professional relationship for some twenty years, invited me to do a story
for a book he was compiling to mark the hundredth birthday of the great
fantasist J.R.R. Tolkien. I confessed that I would be under a certain handicap
here: although I had read Tolkien's children's book *The Hobbit* somewhere
in the vicinity of my eighth birthday, and some of his philological essays at a
rather more recent date, I have never managed to read his celebrated trilogy.
I did, I told Marty Greenberg, have a fair idea of what the thing was about,
as who could not, after enduring thirty years of Tolkien imitations. I knew it
involved a bunch of furry folk going off on a quest for some ring or wand or
sword or other mcguffin that would save the world from Utter Evil. I knew
approximately who Gandalf was, and Gollum, and Frodo, and even Aragorn.
But I had never quite brought myself to embark on the first of the three fat
volumes and was not in any way a member of the Fellowship of the Ring.
Marty urged me to give the story a try anyway. And so I did, in December

144

of 1990, drawing not on my tenuous knowledge of *The Lord of the Rings* but on my awareness that Tolkien's intellectual interests had been focused on such things as the origin of religion, the nature of medieval society, and the uses of archaeology in interpreting the past. And thus I came up with what may very well be the only science-fiction story ever written as an homage to J.R.R. Tolkien, and certainly the only one written by someone who has no first-hand knowledge of the famous trilogy.

The moment of total darkness was about to arrive. The Warder Diriente stepped forward onto the portico of the temple, as he had done every night for the past thirty years, to perform the evening invocation. He was wearing, as always, his bright crimson warder's cassock and the tall double-peaked hat of his office, which had seemed so comical to him when he had first seen his father wearing it long ago, but which he now regarded, when he thought of it at all, as simply an article of clothing. There was a bronze thurible in his left hand and in the right he held a tapering, narrow-necked green vessel, sleek and satisfying to the touch, the fine celadon ware that only the craftsmen of Murrha Island were capable of producing.

The night was clear and mild, a gentle summer evening, with the high, sharp sound of tree-frogs in the air and the occasional bright flash of golden light from the lantern of a glitterfly. Far below, in the valley where the sprawling imperial city of Citherione lay, the myriad lights of the far-off residential districts were starting to come on, and they looked like glitterfly gleams also, wavering and winking, an illusion born of great distance.

It was half an hour's journey by groundwagon from the closest districts of the city to the temple. The Warder had not been down there in months. Once he had gone there more frequently, but now that he was old the city had become an alien place to him, dirty, strange-smelling, discordant. The big stone temple, massive and solid in its niche on the hillside, with the great tawny mountain wall rising steeply behind it, was all that he needed these days: the daily round of prayer and observance and study, the company of good friends, a little work in the garden, a decent bottle of wine with dinner, perhaps some quiet music late at night. A comfortable, amiably reclusive life, untroubled by anguished questions of philosophy or urgent challenges of professional struggle.

His profession had been decided for him before his birth: the post of temple warder was hereditary. It had been in his family for twelve generations. He was the eldest son; his elevation to the wardership was a certainty throughout all his childhood, and Diriente had prepared himself unquestioningly for the post from the first. Of course, somewhere along the way he had lost whatever faith he might once have had in the tenets of the creed he served, and that had been a problem for him for a time, but he had come to terms with that a long while back.

The temple portico was a broad marble slab running the entire length of the building along its western face, the face that looked toward the city. Below the portico's high rim, extending outward from it like a fan, was a sloping lawn thick as green velvet – a hundred centuries of dedicated gardeners had tended it with love – bordered by groves of ornamental flowering shrubs. Along the north side of the temple garden was a stream that sprang from some point high up on the mountain and flowed swiftly downward into the far-off valley. There were service areas just alongside and behind the temple – a garbage dump, a little cemetery, cottages for the temple staff – and back of those lay a tangle of wilderness forming a transitional zone between the open sloping flank of the mountain on which the temple had been constructed and the high wall of rock that rose to the rear of the site.

Warders were supposed to be in some semblance of a state of grace, that receptivity to the infinite which irreverent novices speak of as 'cosmic connection', when they performed the evening invocation. Diriente doubted that he really did achieve the full degree of rapport, or even that such rapport was possible; but he did manage a certain degree of concentration that seemed acceptable enough to him. His technique for attaining it was to focus his attention on the ancient scarred face of the moon, if it was a night when the moon is visible, and otherwise to look toward the Pole Star. Moon or stars, either would do: the essential thing was to turn his spirit outward toward the realm where the great powers of the Upper World resided. It usually took him only a moment or two to attune himself properly for the rite. He had had plenty of practice, after all.

This night as he looked starward – there was no moon – and began to feel the familiar, faintly prickly sensation of contact awakening in him, the giddy feeling that he was climbing his own spinal column and gliding through his forehead into space, he was startled by an unusual interruption. A husky figure came jogging up out of the garden toward the temple and planted itself right below him at the portico's edge.

'Diriente?' he called. 'Listen, Diriente, you have to come and look at something that I've found.'

It was Mericalis, the temple custodian. The Warder, his concentration shattered, felt a sharp jolt of anger and surprise. Mericalis should have had more sense than that.

Testily the Warder indicated the thurible and the celadon vessel.

'Oh,' Mericalis said, sounding unrepentant. 'You aren't finished yet, then?'

'No, I'm not. I was only just starting, as a matter of fact. And you shouldn't be bothering me just this minute.'

'Yes, yes, I know that. But this is important. Look, I'm sorry I broke in on you, but I had a damned good reason for it. Get your ceremony done with quickly, will you, Diriente? And then I want you to come with me. Right away.'

Mericalis offered no other explanation. The Warder demanded none. It would only be a further distraction, and he was distracted enough as it was.

He attempted with no more than partial success to regain some measure of calmness.

'I'll finish as soon as you let me,' he told the custodian irritably.

'Yes. Do. I'll wait for you down here.'

The Warder nodded brusquely. Mericalis disappeared back into the shadows below the portico.

So. Then. Starting over from the beginning. The Warder drew his breath in deeply and closed his eyes a moment and waited until the effects of the intrusion had begun to ebb. After a time the jangling in his mind eased. Then once more he turned his attention to his task, looking up, finding the Pole Star with practiced ease and fixing his eyes upon it. From that direction, ten thousand years ago, the three Visitants had come to Earth to rescue mankind from great peril; or so the Scriptures maintained. Perhaps it actually had happened. There was no reason to think that it hadn't and some to think that it had.

He focused the entire intensity of his being on the Upper World, casting his soul skyward into the dark terrible gulfs between the galaxies. It was a willed feat of the imagination for him: with conscious effort he pictured himself roving the stars, a disembodied attenuated intelligence gliding like a bright needle through the black airless infinities.

The Warder often felt as though there once had been a time when making that leap had not required an effort of will: that in the days when he was new to his priestly office he had simply stepped forth and looked upward, and everything else had followed as a matter of course. The light of the Pole Star had penetrated his soul and he had gone out easily, effortlessly, on a direct course toward the star of the Three. Was it so? He couldn't remember. He had been Warder so long. He had performed the evening invocation some ten thousand times at least. Everything was formula and rote by now. It was difficult now to believe that his mind had ever been capable of ascending in one joyous bound into those blazing depths of endless night, or that he had ever seriously thought that looking at the stars and dumping good wine into a stone channel might have some real and undeniable redemptive power. The best he could hope for these days was some flicker – some quivering little stab – of the old ecstasy, while he stood each night beneath the heavens in all their glory. And even that flicker, that tiny stab, was suspect, a probable counterfeit, an act of wilful self-delusion.

The stars were beautiful, at any rate. He was grateful for that one blessing. His faith in the literal existence of the Visitants and their one-time presence on the Earth might be gone, but not his awareness of the immensity of the universe, the smallness of Man, the majesty of the great vault of night.

Standing poised and steady, head thrust back, face turned toward the heavens, he began to swing the thurible, sending a cloud of pungent incense swirling into the sky. He elevated the sleek green porcelain vessel, offering it to the three cardinal points, east and west and zenith. The reflexes of his professionalism had hold of him now: he was fully into the ceremony, as deeply as his skepticism would allow him ever to get. In the grasp of the moment he would let no doubts intrude. They would come back to him quickly enough, just afterward.

Solemnly now he spoke the Holy Names:

'Oberith . . . Aulimiath . . . Vonubius.'

He allowed himself to believe that he had made contact.

He summoned up the image of the Three before him, the angular alien figures shimmering with spectral light. He told them, as he had told them so many times before, how grateful the world was for all that they had done for the people of Earth long ago, and how eager Earth was for their swift return from their present sojourn in the distant heavens.

For the moment the Warder's mind actually did seem free of all questions of belief and unbelief. Had the Three in fact existed? Had they truly come to Earth in its time of need? Did they rise up to the stars again in a fiery chariot when their work was done, vowing to return someday and gather up all the peoples of the world in their great benevolence? The Warder had no idea. When he was young he believed every word of the Scriptures, like everyone else; then, he was not sure exactly when, he stopped believing. But that made no conspicuous difference to the daily conduct of his life. He was the Warder of the high temple; he had certain functions to perform; he was a servant of the people. That was all that mattered.

The ritual was the same every evening. According to generally accepted belief it hadn't changed in thousands of years, going back to the very night of the Visitants' departure from Earth, though the Warder was privately skeptical of that, as he was of so many other matters. Things change with time; distortions enter any system of belief; of that he was certain. Even so, he outwardly maintained the fiction that there had been no alterations in any aspect of the liturgy, because he was aware that the people preferred to think that that was the case. The people were profoundly conservative in their ways; and he was here to serve the people. That was the family tradition: We are Warders, and that means we serve.

The invocation was at its climax, the moment of the offering. Softly the Warder spoke the prayer of the Second Advent, the point of the entire exercise, expressing the hope that the Three would not long delay their return to the world. The words rolled from him quickly, perfunctorily, as though they were syllables in some lost language, holding no meaning for him. Then he called the Names a second time, with the same theatrical solemnity as before. He lifted the porcelain vessel high, inverted it, and allowed the golden wine that it contained to pour into the stone channel that ran down the hill toward the temple pond. That was the last of it, the finale of the rite. Behind him, at that moment, the temple's hydraulus-player, a thin hatchet-faced man sitting patiently in the darkness beside the stream, struck from his instrument the three great thunderous chords that concluded the service.

At this point any worshippers who had happened to have remained at the temple this late would have fallen to their knees and cried out in joy and hope while making the sign of the Second Advent. But there were no worshippers on hand this evening, only a few members of the temple staff, who, like the Warder, were going about the business of shutting the place down for the night. In the moment of the breaking of the contact the Warder stood by himself, very much conscious of the solitude of his spirit and the futility of his profession as he felt the crashing wave of his unbelief come sweeping back in upon him. The pain lasted only an instant; and then he was himself again.

Out of the shadows then came Mericalis once more, broad-shouldered, insistent, rising before the Warder like a spectre he had conjured up himself.

'You're done? Ready to go?'

The Warder glared at him. 'Why are you in such a hurry? Do you mind if I put the sacred implements away first?'

'Go right ahead,' the custodian said, shrugging. 'Take all the time you want, Diriente.' There was an unfamiliar edge on his voice.

The Warder chose to ignore it. He re-entered the temple and placed the thurible and the porcelain wine-vessel in their niche just within the door. He closed the wrought-iron grillwork cover of the niche and locked it, and quickly muttered the prayer that ended his day's duties. He put aside his tall hat and hung his cassock on its peg. Underneath it he wore a simple linen surplice, belted with a worn strip of leather.

He stepped back outside. The members of the temple staff were drifting off into the night, heading down by torchlight to their cottages along the temple's northern side. Their laughter rose on the soft air. The Warder envied them their youth, their gaiety, their assurance that the world was as they thought it was.

Mericalis, still waiting for him beside a flowering bayerno bush just below the thick marble rim of the portico, beckoned to him.

'Where are we going?' the Warder asked, as they set out briskly together across the lawn.

'You'll see.'

'You're being very damned mysterious.'

'Yes. I suppose I am.'

Mericalis was leading him around the temple's northwestern corner to the back of the building, where the rough road began that by a series of steep switchbacks ascended the face of the hill against which the temple had been built. He carried a small automatic torch, a mere wand of amber light. On this moonless evening the torch seemed more powerful than it really was.

As they went past the garbage dump Mericalis said, 'I really am sorry I broke in on you just as you were about to do the invocation. I did actually think you were done with it already.'

'That doesn't make any difference now.'

'I felt bad, though. I know how important that rite is to you.'

'Do you?' the Warder said, not knowing what to make of the custodian's remark.

The Warder had never discussed his loss of faith with anyone, not even Mericalis, who over the years had become perhaps his closest friend, closer to him than any of the temple's priests. But he doubted that it was much of a secret. Faith shines in a man's face like the full moon breaking through the mists on a winter night. The Warder was able to see it in others, that special glow. He suspected that they were unable to see it in him.

The custodian was a purely secular man. His task was to maintain the structural integrity of the temple, which, after all, had been in constant service for ten thousand years and by now was perpetually in precarious condition, massive and sturdy though it was. Mericalis knew all the weak places in the wall, the subtle flaws in the buttresses, the shifting slabs in the floor, the defects of the drains. He was something of an archaeologist as well, and could discourse learnedly on the various stages of the ancient building's complex history, the details of the different reconstructions, the stratigraphic boundaries marking one configuration of the temple off from another, showing how it had been built and rebuilt over the centuries. Of religious feeling Mericalis seemed to have none at all: it was the temple that he loved, not the creed that it served.

They were well beyond the garbage dump now, moving along the narrow unpaved road that ran up toward the summit of the mountain. The Warder found his breath coming short as the grade grew more steep.

He had rarely had occasion to use this road. There were old altars higher up on the mountain, remnants of a primitive fire-rite that had become obsolete many hundreds of years before, during the Samtharid Interregnum. But they held no interest for him. Mericalis, pursuing his antiquarian studies, probably went up there frequently, the Warder supposed, and now he must have made some startling discovery amidst the charred ancient stones, something bizarre and troublesome enough to justify breaking in on him during the invocation. A scene of human sacrifice? The tomb of some prehistoric king? This mountain had been holy land a long time, going back, so it was said, even into the days before the old civilization of machines and miracles had collapsed. What strangeness had Mericalis found?

But their goal didn't seem to lie above them on the mountain. Instead of continuing to ascend, the custodian turned abruptly off the road when they were still only a fairly short distance behind the temple and began pushing his way vigorously into a tangle of underbrush. The Warder, frowning, followed. By this time he knew better than to waste his breath asking questions. He stumbled onward, devoting all his energy to the job of maintaining his footing. In the deep darkness of the night, with Mericalis's little torch the only illumination, he was hard pressed to keep from tripping over hidden roots or vines.

After about twenty paces of tough going they came to a place where a second road – a crude little path, really – unexpectedly presented itself. This one, to the Warder's surprise, curved back down the slope in the direction of the temple, but instead of returning them to the service area on the northern side it carried them around toward the opposite end of the building, into a zone which the Warder long had thought was inaccessible because of the thickness of the vegetation. They were behind the temple's southeastern corner now, perhaps a hundred paces from the rear wall of the building itself. In all his years here the Warder had never seen the temple from this angle. Its great oblong bulk reared up against the sky, black on black, a zone of intense starless darkness against a star-speckled black backdrop.

There was a clearing here in the scrub. A roughly circular pit lay in the center of it, about as wide across as the length of a man's arm. It seemed recently dug, from the fresh look of the mound of tailings behind it.

Mericalis walked over to the opening and poked the head of his torch into it. The Warder, coming up alongside him, stared downward. Despite the inadequacy of the light he was able to see that the pit was actually the mouth of a subterranean passage-way which sloped off at a sharp angle, heading toward the temple.

'What's all this?' the Warder asked.

'An unauthorized excavation. Some treasure-hunters have been at work back here.'

The Warder's eyes opened wide. 'Trying to tunnel into the temple, you mean?'

'Apparently so,' said Mericalis. 'Looking for a back way into the vaults.' He stepped down a little way into the pit, paused, and looked back, beckoning impatiently to the Warder. 'Come on, Diriente. You need to see what's here.'

The Warder stayed where he was.

'You seriously want me to go down there? The two of us crawling around in an underground tunnel in the dark?'

'Yes. Absolutely.'

'I'm an old man, Mericalis.'

'Not all that old. And it's a very capably built little passageway. You can manage it.'

Still the Warder held back. 'And what if the men who dug it come back and find us while we're in there?'

'They won't,' said Mericalis. 'I promise you that.'

'How can you be so sure?'

'Trust me, Diriente.'

'I'd feel better if we had a couple of the younger priests with us, all the same.'

The custodian shook his head. 'Once you've seen what I'm going to show you, you'll be glad that there's no one here but you and me to see it. Come on, now. Are you going to follow me or aren't you?'

Uneasily the Warder entered the opening. The newly broken ground was soft and moist beneath his sandaled feet. The smell of the earth rose to his nostrils, rich, loamy, powerful. Mericalis was five or six paces ahead of him and moving quickly along without glancing back. The Warder found that he had to crouch and shuffle to keep from hitting his head on the narrow tunnel's low roof. And yet the tunnel was well made, just as the custodian had said. It descended at a sharp angle until it was perhaps twice the the height of a man below the ground, and then leveled out. It was nicely squared off at the sides and bolstered every ten paces by timbers. Months of painstaking work must have been required for all this. The Warder felt a sickly sense of violation. To think that thieves had managed to work back here undisturbed all this time! And had they reached the vaults? The temple wasn't actually a single building, but many, of different eras, each built upon the foundation of its predecessor. Layer beneath layer of inaccessible chambers, some of them thousands of years old, were believed to occupy the area underneath the main ceremonial hall of the present-day temple. The temple possessed considerable treasure, precious stones, ingots of rare metals, works of art: gifts of forgotten monarchs, hidden away down there in those old vaults long ago and scarcely if ever looked at since. It was believed that there were tombs in the building's depths, too, the burial places of ancient kings, priests, heroes. But no one ever tried to explore the deeper vaults. The stairs leading down to them were hopelessly blocked with debris, so that not even Mericalis could distinguish between what might once have been a staircase and what was part of the building's foundation. Getting down to the lower strata would be impossible without ripping up the present-day floors and driving broad shafts through the upper basements, and no one dared to try that: such excavation might weaken the entire structure and bring the building crashing down. As for tunneling into the deep levels from outside – well, no one in the Warder's memory had ever proposed doing that, either, and he doubted that the Grand Assize of the Temple would permit such a project to be carried out even if application were made. There was no imaginable spiritual benefit to be gained from rooting about in the foundations of the holy building, and not much scientific value in it either, considering how many other relics of Earth's former civilizations, still unexcavated after all this time, were on hand everywhere to keep the archaeologists busy.

But if the diggers had been thieves, not archaeologists –

No wonder Mericalis had come running up to him in the midst of the invocation!

'How did you find this?' the Warder asked, as they moved farther in. The air here was dank and close, and the going was very slow.

'It was one of the priests that found it, actually. One of the younger ones, and no, I won't tell you his name, Diriente. He came around back here a few days ago with a certain young priestess to enjoy a little moment or two of privacy and they practically fell right into it. They explored it to a point about as far as we are now and realized it was something highly suspicious, and they came and told me about it.'

'But you didn't tell me.'

'No,' Mericalis said. 'I didn't. It seemed purely a custodial affair then. There was no need to get you involved in it. Someone had been digging around behind the temple, yes. Very likely for quite some time. Coming in by night, maybe, working very, very patiently, hauling away the tailings and dumping them in the woods, pushing closer and closer to the wall of the building, no doubt with the intent of smashing through into one of the deep chambers and carrying off the vast wealth that's supposedly stored down there. My plan was to investigate the tunnel myself, find out just what had been going on here, and then to bring the city police in to deal with it. You would have been notified at that point, of course.'

'So you haven't taken it to the police yet, then?'

'No,' said Mericalis. 'I haven't.'

'But why not?'

'I don't think there's anyone for them to arrest, that's why. Look here, Diriente.'

He took the Warder by the arm and tugged him forward so that the Warder was standing in front of him. Then he reached his arm under the Warder's and flashed the torch into the passageway just ahead of them.

The Warder gasped.

Two men in rough work clothes were sprawled on the tunnel floor, half buried beneath debris that had fallen from overhead. The Warder could see shovels and picks jutting out from the mound of fallen earth beside them. A third man – no, this one was a woman – lay a short distance away. A sickening odor of decay rose from the scene.

'Are they dead?' the Warder asked quietly.

'Do you need to ask?'

'Killed by a rockfall, you think?'

'That's how it looks, doesn't it? These two were the diggers. The girl was their lookout, I suspect, posted at the mouth of the tunnel. She's armed: you see? Two guns and a dagger. They must have called her in here to see something unusual, and just then the roof fell in on them all.' Mericalis stepped over the slender body and picked his way through the rubble beyond it, going a few paces deeper into the passageway. 'Come over here and I'll show you what I think happened.'

'What if the roof collapses again?'

'I don't think it will,' Mericalis said.

'If it can collapse once, it can collapse again,' said the Warder, shivering a little now despite the muggy warmth of the tunnel. 'Right on our heads. Shouldn't we get out of here while we can?'

The custodian ignored him. 'Look here, now: what do you make of this?' He aimed the torch to one side, holding it at a ninety-degree angle to the direction of the tunnel. The Warder squinted into the darkness. He saw what looked like a thick stone lintel which had fallen from the tunnel vault and was lying tipped up on end. There were inscriptions of another era carved in it, runes of some sort. Behind it was an opening, a gaping oval of darkness in the darkness, that appeared to be the mouth of a second tunnel running crosswise to the one they were in. Mericalis leaned over the fallen lintel and flashed his beam beyond it. A tunnel, yes. But constructed in a manner very different from that of the one they had been following. The walls were of narrow stone blocks, carefully laid edge to edge; the roof of the tunnel was a long stone vault, supported by pointed arches. The craftsmanship was very fine. The joints had an archaic look.

'How old is this?' the Warder asked.

'Old. Do you recognize those runes on the lintel? They're protero-historic stuff. This tunnel's as ancient as the temple itself, most likely. Part of the original sacred complex. The thieves couldn't have known it was here. As they were digging their way toward the temple they intersected it by accident. They yelled for the girl to come in and look – or maybe they wanted her to help them pull the lintel loose. Which they proceeded to do, and the weak place where the two tunnels met gave way, and the roof of their own tunnel came crashing down on them. For which I for one feel no great sorrow, I have to admit.'

'Do you have any idea where this other tunnel goes?'

'To the temple,' said Mericalis. 'Or under it, rather, into the earliest foundation. It leads straight toward the deepest vaults.'

'Are you sure?'

'I've been inside already. Come.'

There was no question now of retreating. The Warder, following close along behind Mericalis, stared at the finely crafted masonry of the tunnel in awe. Now and again he saw runic inscriptions, unreadable, mysterious, carved in the stone floor. When they had gone about twenty paces yet another stone-vaulted passageway presented itself, forking off to the left. The custodian went past it without a glance. 'There are all sorts of tunnels down here,' Mericalis said. 'But this is the one we want. So far as I've been able to determine at this point, it's the only one that enters the temple.' The Warder saw that Mericalis had left a marker that glowed by the reflected light of his torch, high up on the wall of the passage they were following, and he supposed that there were other markers farther on to serve as guides for them. 'We're in a processional hypogeum,' the custodian explained. 'Probably it was just about at ground level, ten thousand years ago, but over the centuries it was buried by construction debris from the later temples, and other trash of various sorts. There was a whole maze of other stone-walled processional chambers around it, leading originally to sacrificial sites and open-air altars. The tunnel we just passed was one of them. It's blocked a little way onward. I spent two days in here going down one false trail after another. Until I came through this way, and – behold, Diriente!'

Mericalis waved his torch grandly about. By the pale splash of light that came from its tip the Warder saw that the sides of the tunnel expanded outward here, spreading to the right and the left to form a great looming wall of superbly dressed stone, with one small dark aperture down at the lower left side. They had reached the rear face of the temple. The Warder trembled. He had an oppressive sense of the thickness of the soil above him, the vast weight pressing down, the temple itself rising in all its intricacy of strata above him. He was at the foundation of foundations. Once all this had been in the open: ten thousand years ago, when the Visitants still walked the Earth.

'You've been inside?' the Warder asked hoarsely.

'Of course,' said Mericalis. 'You have to crawl the first part of the way. Take care to breathe shallowly: there's plenty of dust.'

The air here was hot and musty and dry, ancient air, lifeless air. The Warder choked and gagged on it. On hands and knees, head down, he crept along behind Mericalis. Several times, overcome by he knew not what, he closed his eyes and waited until a spasm of dizziness had passed.

'You can stand now,' the custodian told him.

They were in a large square stone chamber. The walls were rough-hewn and totally without ornament. The room was empty except for three long, narrow coffers of unpolished white marble side by side at the far end.

'Steady yourself, old friend,' Mericalis said. 'And then come and see who we have here.'

They crossed the room. The coffers were covered with a thick sheet of some transparent yellowish material that looked much like glass, but in fact was some other substance that the Warder could not identify.

An icy shiver ran through the Warder as he peered through the coverings.

There was a skeleton in each coffer, lying face upward: the glistening fleshless bones of some strange long-shanked creature, man-like in size and general outline, but different in every detail. Their heads bore curving bony crests; their shoulders were crested also; their knees were double ones; they had spike-like protrusions at their ankles. Ribs, pelvises, fingers, toes – everything strange, everything unfamiliar. These were the bodies of starfolk, not those of people of this world.

Mericalis said, 'My guess is that the very tall one in the center is Vonubius. That's probably Aulimiath on the right and the other one has to be Oberith, then.'

The Warder looked up at him sharply. 'What are you saying?'

'This is obviously a sepulcher. Those are sarcophagi. These are three skeletons of starfolk that we're looking at here. They've been very carefully preserved and buried in a large and obviously significant chamber on the deepest and therefore oldest level of the Temple of the Visitants, in a room that once was reached by a grand processional passageway. Who else do you think they would be?'

'The Visitants went up into the heavens when their work on Earth was done,' said the Warder hollowly. 'They ascended on a ship of fire and returned to their star.'

'You believe that?' Mericalis asked, chuckling.

'It says so in the Scriptures.'

'I know that it does. Do you believe it, though?'

'What does it matter what I believe?' The Warder stared again at the three elongated alien skeletons. 'The historical outlines aren't questioned by anybody. The world was in a crisis – in collapse. There was war everywhere. In the midst of it all, three ambassadors from another solar system arrived and saw what was going on, and they used their superior abilities to put things to rights. Once a stable new world order had emerged, they took off for the stars again. The story turns up in approximately the same form in every society's myths and folk-tales, all over the Earth. There's got to be some truth to it.'

'I don't doubt that there is,' said Mericalis. 'And there they are, the three wise men from afar. The Scriptures have the story a little garbled, apparently. Instead of going back to their native star, promising to return and redeem us at some new time of trouble, they died while still on Earth and were buried underneath the temple of the cult that sprang up around them. So there isn't going to be any Second Advent, I'd tend to think. And if there ever is, it may not be a friendly one. They didn't die natural deaths, you'll notice. If you'll take a careful look you'll see that the heads of all three were severed violently from their trunks.'

'What?'

'Look closely,' Mericalis said.

'There's a break in the vertebrae, yes. But that could have been –'

'It's the same sort of break in all three. I've seen the skeletons of executed men before, Diriente. We've dug up dozens of them around the old gibbet down the hill. These three were decapitated. Believe me.'

'No.'

'They were martyrs. They were put to death by their loving admirers and devoted worshippers, the citizens of Earth.'

'No. No. No. No.'

'Why are you so stunned, Diriente? Does it shock you, that such a dreadful thing could have happened on our lovely green planet? Have you been squirreled up in your nest on this hillside so long that you've forgotten everything you once knew about human nature? Or is it the unfortunate evidence that the Scriptural story is wrong that bothers you? You don't believe in the Second Advent anyway, do you?'

'How do you know I don't?'

'Please, Diriente.'

The Warder was silent. His mind was aswirl with confusions.

After a time he said, 'These could be any three starfolk at all.'

'Yes. I suppose they could. But we know of only three beings from space that ever came to this planet: the ones who we call the Visitants. This is the temple of the faith that sprang up around them. Somebody went to great trouble to bury these three underneath it. I have difficulty believing that these would be three different starfolk.'

Stubbornly the Warder said, 'How do you know that these things are genuine skeletons? They might be idols of some sort.'

'Idols in the form of skeletons? Decapitated skeletons, at that?' Mericalis laughed. 'I suppose we could test them chemically to see if they're real, if you like. But they look real enough to me.'

'The Visitants were like gods. They *were* gods, compared with us. Certainly they were regarded as divine – or at least as the ministers and ambassadors of the Divine Being – when they were here. Why would they have been killed? Who would have dared to lay a hand on them?'

'Who can say? Maybe they didn't seem as divine as all that in the days when they walked among us,' Mericalis suggested.

'But the Scriptures say –'

'The Scriptures, yes. Written how long after the fact? The Visitants may not have been so readily recognized as holy beings originally. They might simply have seemed threatening, maybe – dangerous – tyrannical. A menace to free will, to man's innate right to make trouble for himself. It was a time of anarchy, remember. Maybe there were those who didn't *want* order restored. I don't know. Even if they *were* seen as godly, Diriente: remember that there's an ancient tradition on this planet of killing one's gods. It goes back a long, long way. Study your prehistoric cults. You dig down deep enough, you find a murdered god somewhere at the bottom of almost all of them.'

The Warder fell into silence again. He was unable to take his eyes from those bony-crested skulls, those strange-angled empty eye-sockets.

'Well,' Mericalis said, 'there you have them, at any rate: three skeletons of what appear to be beings from another world that somebody just happened to bury underneath your temple a very long time ago. I thought you ought to know about them.'

'Yes. Thank you.'

'You have to decide what to do about them, now.'

'Yes,' the Warder said. 'I know that.'

'We could always seal the passageway up again, I suppose, and not say a word about this to anyone. Which would avoid all sorts of uncomfortable complications, wouldn't it? It strikes me as a real crime against knowledge, doing something like that, but if you thought that we should –'

'Who knows about this so far?'

'You. Me. No one else.'

'What about the priest and priestess who found the excavation pit?'

'They came right to me and told me about it. They hadn't gone very far inside, no more than five or six paces. Why should they have gone any farther?'

'They might have,' the Warder said.

'They didn't. They had no torch and they had their minds on other things. All they did was look a little way in, just far enough to see that something unusual was going on. They hadn't even gone far enough to find the thieves. But they didn't say a thing about dead bodies in the tunnel. They'd certainly have told me about them, if they had come upon them. And they'd have looked a whole lot shakier, too.'

'The thieves didn't come in here either?'

'It doesn't seem that way to me. I don't think they got any farther than the place where they pulled that lintel out of the passage wall. They're dead, in any case.'

'But what if they did get this far? And what if there was someone else with them, someone who managed to escape when the tunnel caved in? Someone who might be out there right now telling all his friends what he saw in this room?'

Mericalis shook his head. 'There's no reason to think that. And I could see, when I first came down this passage and into the sepulchral chamber, that nobody had been through here in more years than we can imagine. There'd have been tracks in the dust, and there weren't any. This place has gone undisturbed a very long time. Long enough for the whole story of how the Visitants died to be forgotten and covered over with a nice pretty myth about their ascent into the heavens on a pillar of fire.'

The Warder considered that for a moment.

'All right,' he said finally. 'Go back outside, Mericalis.'

'And leave you here alone?'

'Leave me here alone, yes.'

Uneasily Mericalis said, 'What are you up to, Diriente?'

'I want to sit here all by myself and think and pray, that's all.'

'Do I have to believe that?'

'Yes. You do.'

'If you go wandering around down here you'll end up trapped in some unknown passageway and most likely we'll never be able to find you again.'

'I'm not going to wander around anywhere. I told you what I'm going to do. I'm going to sit right here, in this very room. You've brought me face to face with the dead bodies of the murdered gods of the religion that I'm supposed to serve, and I need to think about what that means. That's all. Go away, Mericalis. This is something I have to do all by myself. You'll only be a distraction. Come back for me at dawn and I promise you that you'll find me sitting exactly where I am now.'

'There's only one torch. I'll need it if I'm going to be able to find my way out of the tunnel. And that means I have to leave you in the dark.'

'I realize that, Mericalis.'

'But –'

'Go,' the Warder said. 'Don't worry about me. I can stand a few hours of darkness. I'm not a child. Go,' he said again. 'Just go, will you? Now.'

*   *   *

He couldn't deny that he was frightened. He was well along in years; by temperament he was a sedentary man; it was totally against his nature to be spending a night in a place like this, far beneath the ground, where the air managed to seem both dusty-dry and sticky-moist at the same time, and the sharp, pungent odor of immense antiquity jabbed painfully at his nostrils. How different it was from his pleasant little room, surrounded by his books, his jug of wine, his familiar furnishings! In the total darkness he was free to imagine the presence of all manner of disagreeable creatures of the depths creeping about him, white eyeless toads and fleshless chittering lizards and slow, contemplative spiders lowering themselves silently on thick silken cords from invisible recesses of the stone ceiling. He stood in the center of the room and it seemed to him that he saw a sleek fat serpent, pallid and gleaming, with blind blue eyes bright as sapphires, issue from a pit in the floor and rise up before him, hissing and bobbing and swaying as it made ready to strike. But the Warder knew that it was only a trick of the darkness. There was no pit; there was no serpent.

He perspired freely. His light robe was drenched and clung to him like a shroud. With every breath it seemed to him that he was pulling clusters of cobwebs into his lungs. The darkness was so intense it hammered at his fixed, rigidly staring eyes until he was forced to shut them. He heard inexplicable sounds coming from the walls, a grinding hum and a steady unhurried ticking and a trickling sound, as of sand tumbling through hidden inner spaces. There were menacing vibrations and tremors, and strange twanging hums, making him fear that the temple itself, angered by this intrusion into its bowels, was preparing to bring itself down upon him. *What I hear is only the echoes of Mericalis's footfalls*, the Warder told himself. *The sounds that he makes as he retraces his way down the tunnel toward the exit.*

After a time he arose and felt his way across the room toward the coffers in the corner, clinging to the rough stones of the wall to guide himself. Somehow he missed his direction, for the corner was empty when he reached it, and as he continued past it his inquiring fingers found themselves pressing into what surely was the opening that led to the tunnel. He stood quietly for a moment in the utter darkness, trying to remember the layout of the funeral chamber, certain that the coffers must have been in the corner he had gone to and unable to understand why he had not found them. He thought of doubling back his path and looking again. But perhaps he was disoriented; perhaps he had gone in precisely the opposite direction from the one he supposed he had taken. He kept going, past the opening, along the wall on the other side. To the other corner. No coffers here. He turned right, still clinging to the wall. A step at a time, imagining yawning pits opening beneath his feet. His knee bumped into something. He had reached the coffers, yes.

He knelt. Grasped the rim of the nearest one, leaned forward, looked down into it.

To his surprise he was able to see a little now, to make out the harsh, angular lines of the skeleton it contained. How was that possible? Perhaps his eyes were growing accustomed to the darkness. No, that wasn't it. A nimbus of light seemed to surround the coffer. A faint reddish glow had begun to rise from it and with the aid of that unexpected illumination he could actually see the outlines of the elongated shape within.

An illusion? Probably. Hallucination, even. This was the strangest moment of his life, and anything was to be expected, anything at all. There is magic here, the Warder found himself thinking, and then he caught himself up in amazement and wonder that he should have so quickly tumbled into the abyss of the irrational. He was a prosaic man. He had no belief in magic. And yet – and yet –

The glow grew more intense. The skeleton blazed in the darkness. With eerie clarity he saw the alien crests and spines, the gnarled alien vertebrae, everything sending up a strange crimson fire to make its aspect plain to him. The empty eye sockets seemed alive with fierce intelligence.

'Who are you?' the Warder asked, almost belligerently. 'Where did you come from? Why did you ever poke your noses into our affairs? Did you even *have* noses?' He felt strangely giddy. The closeness of the air, perhaps. Not enough oxygen. He laughed, too loudly, too long. 'Oberith, is that who you are? Aulimiath? And that's Vonubius in the center box, yes? The tallest one, the leader of the mission.'

His body shook with sudden anguish. Waves of fear and bewilderment swept over him. His own crude joking had frightened him. He began to sob.

The thought that he might be in the presence of the actual remains of the actual Three filled him with confusion and dismay. He had come over the years to think of the tale of the Advent as no more than a myth – the gods who came from the stars – and now he was stunned by this evidence that they had been real, that they once were tangible creatures who had walked and eaten and breathed and made water – and had been capable of dying, of being killed. He had reached a point long ago of not believing that. This discovery required him to reevaluate everything. Did it trivialize the religion he served into mere history? No – no, he thought; the existence here in this room of these bones elevated history into miracle, into myth. They truly had come. And had served, and had departed: not to the stars, but to the realm, of death. From which they would return in the due course of time, and in their resurrection would bring the redemption that had been promised, the forgiveness for the crime that had been committed against them.

Was that it? Was that the proper way to interpret the things this room held?

He didn't know. He realized that he knew nothing at all.

The Warder shivered and trembled. He wrapped his arms around himself and held himself tight.

He fought to regain some measure of control over himself.

'No,' he said sternly. 'It can't be. You aren't them. I don't believe that those are your names.'

From the coffers no answer came.

'You could be any three starfolk at all,' the Warder told them fiercely. 'Who just happened to come to Earth, just dropped in one afternoon to see what might be here. And lived to regret it. Am I right?'

Still silence. The Warder, crouching down against the nearest coffer with his cheek pressed against the dry cold stone, shivered and trembled.

'Speak to me,' he begged. 'What do I have to do to get you to speak to me? Do you want me to pray? All right, then, I'll pray, if that's what you want.'

In the special voice that he used for the evening invocation he intoned the three Holy Names:

'Oberith . . . Aulimiath . . . Vonubius.'

There was no reply.

Bitterly he said, 'You don't know your names, do you? Or are you just too stubborn to answer to them?'

He glowered into the darkness.

'Why are you here?' he asked them, furious now. 'Why did Mericalis have to discover you? Oh, damn him, why did he ever have to tell me about you?'

Again there was no answer; but now he felt a strange thing beginning to occur. Serpentine columns of light were rising from the three coffers. They flickered and danced like tongues of cold fire before him, commanding him to be still and pay heed. The Warder pressed his hands against his forehead and bowed his head and let everything drain from his mind, so that he was no more than an empty shell crouching in the darkness of the room. And as he knelt there things began to change around him, the walls of the chamber melted and dropped away, and he found himself transported upward and outward until he was standing outside, in the clear sweet air, under the golden warmth of the sun.

The day was bright, warm, springlike, a splendid day, a day to cherish. But there were ugly dissonances. The Warder heard shouts to his right, to his left – harsh voices everywhere, angry outcries.

'There they are! Get them! Get them!'

Three slender grotesque figures came into view, half again as tall as a man, big-eyed, long-limbed, strange of shape, moving swiftly but with somber dignity, as though they were floating rather than striding, keeping just ahead of their pursuers. The Warder understood that these were the Three in their final moments, that they have been harried and hunted all this lovely day across the sweet meadows of this lush green valley. Now there was nowhere further for them to go, they are trapped in a cul-de-sac against the flank of the mountain, the army of their enemies is closing in and all hope of escape is impossible.

Now the Warder heard savage triumphant screams. Saw reddened, swollen, wrathful faces. Weapons bristling in the air, clubs, truncheons, pitchforks, hatchets. Wild eyes, distended lips, clenched fists furiously shaken.

And on a little mound facing their attackers are the Three, standing close together, offering no resistance, seemingly at peace. They appear perplexed by what is happening, perhaps, or perhaps not – how can he tell? What do their alien expressions mean? But almost certainly they are not angry. Anger is not an emotion that can pertain to them in any way. They have a look about them that seems to indicate that they had expected this. *Forgive them, for they know not what they do.* A moment of hesitation: the mob suddenly uneasy at the last, frightened, even, uncertain of the risks in what they are doing. Then the hesitation overcome, the people surging forward like a single berserk creature, the flash of steel in the sunlight –

The vision abruptly ended. He was within the stone chamber again. The light was gone. The air about him was dry and stale, not sweet and mild. The tomb was dark and empty.

The Warder felt stunned by what he had seen, and shamed. A sense of almost suicidal guilt overwhelmed him. Blindly he rushed back and forth across the dark room, frenzied, manic, buffeting himself against the unseen walls. Then, exhausted, he paused for a moment to gasp for breath and stared into the darkness at the place where he thought the coffers were situated. He would break through those transparent coverings, he told himself, and snatch up the three strange skulls and carry them out into the bright light of day, and he would call the people together and show them what he had brought forth from the depths of the Earth, brandishing the skulls in their faces, and he would cry out to them, 'Here are your gods. This is what you did to them. All your beliefs were founded on a lie.' And then he would hurl himself from the mountain.

No.

He will not. How can he crush their hopes that way? And having done it, what good would his death achieve?

And yet – to allow the lie to endure and persist –

'What am I going to do about you?' the Warder asked the skeletons in their coffers. 'What am I going to tell the people?' His voice rose to a wild screech. It echoed and reechoed from the stone walls of the room, reverberating in his throbbing skull. 'The *people*! The *people*! The *people*!'

'Speak to me!' the Warder cried. 'Tell me what I'm supposed to do!'

Silence. Silence. Silence. They would give him no answers.

He laughed at his own helplessness. Then he wept for a time, until his eyes were raw and his throat ached from his sobbing. He fell to his knees once more beside one of the coffers. 'Who are you?' he asked, in nothing more than a whisper. 'Can you really be Vonubius?'

And this time imagines that he hears a mocking answer: *I am who I am. Go in peace, my son.*

Peace? Where? How?

At last, a long while later, he began to grow calm once more, and thought that this time he might be able to remain that way. He saw that he was being ridiculous – the old Warder, running to and fro in a stone chamber underground, crying out like a lunatic, praying to gods in whom he didn't believe, holding conversations with skeletons. Gradually his churning soul moved away from the desperate turbulence into which it had fallen, the manic frenzy, the childish anger. There was no reddish glow, no. His overwrought mind had conjured up some tormented fantasy for him. Darkness still prevailed in the chamber. He was unable to see a thing. Before him, he knew, were three ancient stone boxes containing age-old dry bones, the earthly remains of unearthly creatures long dead.

He was calm, yes. But there seemed no way even now to hide from his despair. These relics, he knew, called his whole life into question. The whole ugly truth of it stood unanswerably revealed. He had served a false creed, knowingly offering people the empty hope that they would be redeemed by benevolent gods. Night after night standing up there on the portico, invoking the Three, praying for their swift return to this troubled planet. Whereas in truth they had never left Earth at all. Had perished, in fact, at the hands of the very people they had come here – so he supposed – to redeem.

What now? the Warder asked himself. Reveal the truth? Display the bodies of the Three to the dismayed, astounded faithful, as he had imagined himself doing just a short time ago? Would he do any such thing? Could he? *Your beliefs were founded on a lie*, he pictured himself telling them. How could he do that? But it was the truth. Small wonder that I lost my own faith long ago, he thought. He had known the truth before he ever knew he knew it. It was the truth that he had sworn to serve, first and always. Was that not so? But there was so much that he did not understand – could not understand, perhaps.

He looked in the direction of the skeletons, and a host of new questions formed in his mind.

'Why did you want to come to us?' he asked, not angrily now, but in a curious tranquility of spirit. 'Why did you choose to serve us as you did? Why did you allow us to destroy you, since surely it was in your power to prevent it?'

Powerful questions. The Warder had no answers to them. But yet who knew what miracles might grow from the asking of them. Yes. Yes. Miracles! True faiths can arise from the ruined fragments of false ones, was that not so?

He was so very tired. It had been such a long night.

Gradually he slipped downward until he was lying completely prone, face pillowed in his arms. It seemed to him that the gentle light of morning was entering the chamber, that the long vigil was over at last. How could that be, light reaching him underground? He chose not to pursue the question. He lay quietly, waiting. And then he heard footsteps. Mericalis was returning. The night was over indeed.

'Diriente? Diriente, are you all right?'

'Help me up,' the Warder says. 'I'm not accustomed to spending my nights lying on stone floors.'

The custodian flashes his torch around the room as if he expects it to have changed in some fashion since he last saw it.

'Well?' he says, finally.

'Let's get out of here, shall we?'

170

'You're all right?'

'Yes, yes, I'm all right!'

'I was very worried. I know you said you wanted to be alone, but I couldn't help thinking –'

'Thinking can be very dangerous,' says the Warder coolly. 'I don't recommend it.'

'I want to tell you, Diriente, that I've decided that what I suggested last night is the best idea. The evidence in this room could blow the Church to pieces. We ought to seal the place up and forget we ever were in here.'

'No,' says the Warder.

'We aren't required to reveal what we've found to anybody. My job is simply to keep the temple building from falling down. Yours is to perform the rituals of the faith.'

'And if the faith is a false one, Mericalis?'

'We don't know that it is.'

'We have our suspicions, don't we?'

'To say that the Three never returned safely to the stars is heresy, isn't it, Diriente? Do you want to be responsible for spreading heresy?'

'My responsibility is to promote the truth,' says the Warder. 'It always has been.'

'Poor Diriente. What have I done to you?'

'Don't waste your pity on me, Mericalis. I don't need it. Just help me find my way out of here, all right? All right?'

'Yes,' the custodian says. 'Whatever you say.'

The passageway is much shorter and less intricate on the way out than it seemed to be when they entered. Neither of them speaks a word as they traverse it. Mericalis trudges quickly forward, never once looking back. The Warder, following briskly along behind, moves with a vigor he hasn't felt in years. His mind is hard at work: he occupies himself with what he will say later in the day, first to the temple staff, then to the worshippers who come that day, and then, perhaps, to the emperor and all his court, down in the great city below the mountain. His words will fall upon their ears like the crack of thunder at the mountaintop; and then let whatever happen that may. *Brothers and sisters, I announce unto you a great joy*, is how he intends to begin. *The Second Advent is upon us. For behold, I can show you the Three themselves. They are with us now, nor have they ever left us –*

It Comes and Goes

The rainy season of 1990-91 went on and on; and I, having finished my allotted rainy-season novel far ahead of schedule, trudged onward into the new year still writing short fiction. First came a novella, *Thebes of the Hundred Gates*, an outgrowth of a trip to Egypt that I had made the previous year; and then, late in January, 1991, this odd little story, occupying the hazy borderline between science-fiction and fantasy, that went to *Playboy*.

And involved me, for the only time in my long career, in an artistic crisis stemming from a magazine's advertising policy. My protagonist in 'It Comes and Goes' is an alcoholic. *Playboy*, unlike science-fiction magazines, depends substantially on advertising for its income, and no little fraction of that comes from ads for liquor. In some embarrassment, the powers that be at *Playboy* let me know that it would be awkward for the magazine to run a story about an alcoholic in an issue that was going to have an advertisement for whiskey on its back cover. But *Playboy* does not run ads for cocaine or marijuana. Would I, I was asked, mind making my character a drug addict instead?

For ten agonizing seconds I debated whether my artistic integrity would be compromised by that. But for story purposes all that mattered, really, was that my character be recovering from some substance-abuse problem that had caused him to suffer from hallucinations; and a drug habit would do that at least as efficiently as alcohol, perhaps better. So I made a few small modifications in my text and the story ran in the January, 1992 *Playboy*, which, as a Christmas issue, was loaded with liquor ads.

On the other hand, I've chosen to reprint my original version of the story here, not as some ultimate gesture of defiance, but simply because it happens that the version of the text that I happened to store in my computer is the one in which Tom was a boozer instead of a druggie. On such casual, even random events are founded the textual issues which literary scholars debate with great passion for centuries.

173

The house comes and goes, comes and goes, and no one seems to know or to care. It's that kind of neighborhood. You keep your head down; you take notice only of the things that are relevant to your own personal welfare; you screen everything else out as irrelevant or meaningless or potentially threatening.

It's a very ordinary house, thirty or forty years old, a cheap one-story white-stucco job on a corner lot, maybe six rooms: green shutters on the windows, a scruffy lawn, a narrow, badly paved path running from the street to the front steps. There's a screen door in front of the regular one. To the right and left of the doorway is some unkempt shrubbery with odds and ends of rusting junk scattered among it – a garbage can, an old barbecue outfit, stuff like that.

All the houses around here look much the same way: there isn't a lot of architectural variety in this neighborhood. Just rows of ordinary little houses adding up to a really ordinary kind of place, neither a slum nor anything desirable, aging houses inhabited by stranded people who can't move upward and who are settled enough so that they've stopped slipping down. Even the street-names are stereotyped small-town standards, instantly forgettable: Maple, Oak, Spruce, Pine. It's hard to tell one street from another, and usually there's no reason why you should. You're able to recognize your own, and the others, except for Walnut Street where the shops are, are just filler. I know how to get to the white house with the screen door from my place – turn right, down to the corner and right again, diagonal left across the street – but even now I couldn't tell you whether it's on Spruce corner of Oak or Pine corner of Maple. I just know how to get there.

The house will stay here for five or six days at a time and then one morning I'll come out and the lot will be vacant, and so it remains for ten days or two weeks. And then there it is again. You'd think people would notice that, you'd think they'd talk; but they're all keeping their heads down, I guess. I keep my head down too but I can't help noticing things. In that sense I don't belong in this part of town. In most other senses I guess I do, because, after all, this is where I am.

The first time I saw the house was on a drizzly Monday morning on the cusp of winter and spring. I remember that it was a Monday because people were going to work and I wasn't, and that was still a new concept for me. I remember that it was on the cusp of winter and spring because there were still some curling trails of dirty snow on the north-facing side of the street, left over from an early-March storm, but the forsythias and crocuses were blooming in the gardens on the south-facing side. I was walking down to the grocery on Walnut Street to pick up the morning paper. Daily walking, rain or shine, is very important to me; it's part of my recovery regime; and I was going for the paper because I was still into studying the help-wanted ads at that time. As I made my way down Spruce Street (or maybe it was Pine Street) some movement in a doorway across the way caught my eye and I glanced up and over.

A flash of flesh, it was.

A woman, turning in the open doorway.

A *naked* woman, so it seemed. I had just a quick side glimpse, fuzzed and blurred by the screen door and the gray light of the cloudy morning, but I was sure I saw gleaming golden flesh: a bare shoulder, a sinuous hip, a long stretch of haunch and thigh and butt and calf, maybe a bit of bright pubic fleece also. And then she was gone, leaving incandescent tracks on my mind.

I stopped right on a dime and stood staring toward the darkness of the doorway, waiting to see if she'd reappear. Hoping that she would. Praying that she would, actually. It wasn't because I was in such desperate need of a free show but because I wanted her to have been real. Not simply an hallucination. I was sober that morning and had been for a month and a half, ever since the seventh of February, and I didn't want to think that I was still having hallucinations.

The doorway stayed dark. She didn't reappear.

Of course not. She couldn't reappear because she had never been there in the first place. What I had seen was an illusion. How could she possibly have been real? Real women around here don't flash their bare butts in front doorways at nine in the morning on cold drizzly days, and they don't have hips and thighs and legs like that.

But I let myself off the hook. After all, I was sober. Why borrow trouble? It had been a trick of the light, I told myself. Or maybe,

maybe a curious fluke of my weary, overwrought mind. An odd mental prank. But in any case nothing to take seriously, nothing symptomatic of significant cerebral decline and collapse.

I went on down to the Walnut Street Grocery and bought that morning's *Post-Star* and looked through the classified ads for the one that said, *If you are an intelligent, capable, hard-working human being who has gone through a bad time but is now in recovery and looking to make a comeback in the great game of life, we have just the job for you.* It wasn't there. Somehow it never was.

On my way home I thought I'd give the white house on the corner lot a second glance, just in case something else of interest was showing. The house wasn't there either.

My name is Tom and I am an alcoholic.

My name is Tom and I am an alcoholic.

My name is Tom and I am an alcoholic.

I tell you that three times because what I tell you three times is true. If anything at all is true about me, that much is. It is also true that I am forty years old, that I have had successful careers in advertising, public relations, mail-order promotion, and several other word-oriented professions. Each of those successful careers came to an unsuccessful end. I have written three novels and a bunch of short stories, too. And between the ages of sixteen and thirty-nine I consumed a quantity of brandy, scotch, bourbon, sherry, rum, and beer – and so on down to Cherry Kijafa, Triple Sec, and gin fizzes – that normal people would find very hard to believe. I suppose I would have gone on to rubbing alcohol and antifreeze if nothing else had been available. On my fortieth birthday I finally took the necessary step, which was to admit that alcohol was a monster too strong for me to grapple with and my life had become unmanageable as a result. And that I was willing to turn to a Power that is stronger than I am, stronger even than the booze monster, and humbly ask that Power to restore me to sanity and help me defend myself against my enemy.

I live now in a small furnished room in a small town so dull you can't remember the names of the streets. I belong to the Program and

I go to meetings three or four times a week and I tell people whose surnames I don't know about my faults, which I freely admit, and my virtues, which I do have, and about my one great weakness. And then they tell me about theirs.

My name is Tom and I am an alcoholic.

I've been doing pretty well since the seventh of February.

Hallucinations were one thing I didn't need in this time of recovery. I had already had my share.

I didn't realize at that point that the house had vanished. People don't customarily think in terms of houses vanishing, not if their heads are screwed on right, and as I have just pointed out I had a vested interest in believing that as of the seventh of February my head was screwed on right and it was going to stay that way.

No, what I thought was simply that I must have gone to the grocery by way of one street and come home by way of another. Since I was sober and had been for a month and a half, there was no other rational explanation.

I went home and made some phone calls to potential employers, with the usual result. I watched some television. If you've never stayed home on a weekday morning you can't imagine what television is like at that time of day, most of it. After a while I found myself tuning to the home shopping channel for the sheer excitement of it.

I thought about the flash of flesh in the screen doorway.

I thought about the color of the label on a bottle of Johnny Walker, too. You don't ever stop thinking about things like that, the look of labels and bottlecaps and the shape of bottles and the taste of what's inside and the effect that it has. You may stop using the product but you don't banish it from your mind, quite the contrary, and when you aren't thinking about the flavor or the effect you're thinking about weird peripheral things like the look of the label. Believe me, you are.

It rained for three or four days, miserable non-stop rain, and I didn't do much of anything. Then finally I went outdoors again, a right and a right and look across to the left, and there was the white house, very bright in the spring sunshine. Very casually I glanced over at it. No flashes of flesh this time.

I saw something much stranger, though. A rolled-up copy of the morning paper was lying on the lawn of a house with brown shingles next door. A dog was sniffing around it, a goofy-faced nondescript white mutt with long legs and a black head. Abruptly the dog scooped the paper up in its jaws, as dogs will do, and turned and trotted around to the front of the white house.

The screen door opened a little way. I didn't see anybody opening it. It remained ajar. The wooden door behind it seemed to be open also.

The dog stood there, looking around, shaking its head from side to side. It seemed bewildered. As I watched, it dropped the paper and began to pant, its tongue hanging out as if this were the middle of July and not the end of March. Then it picked the paper up again, bending for it in an oddly rigid, robotic way. It raised its head and turned and stared right at me, almost as though it was asking me to help it. Its eyes were glassy and its ears were standing up and twitching. Its back was arched like a cat's. Its tail rose straight up behind it. I heard low rusty-sounding growls.

Then, abruptly, it visibly relaxed. It lowered its ears and a look of something like relief came into its eyes and its posture became a good old droopy dog-posture again. It wriggled its shoulders almost playfully. Wagged its tail. And went galloping through the open screen door, bounding and prancing in that dumb doggy way that they have, holding the newspaper high. The door closed behind it.

I stayed around for a little while. The door stayed closed. The dog didn't come out.

I wondered which I would rather believe: that I had seen a door open itself and let a dog in, or that I had *imagined* I had seen a door open itself and let a dog in?

Then there was the cat event. This was a day or two later.

The cat was a lop-eared ginger tom. I had seen it around before. I like cats. I liked this one especially. He was a survivor, a street-smart guy. I hoped to learn a thing or two from him.

He was on the lawn of the white house. The screen door was ajar again. The cat was staring toward it and he looked absolutely *outraged*.

His fur was standing out half a mile and his tail was lashing like a whip and his ears were flattened back against his head. He was hissing and growling at the same time, and the growl was that eerie banshee moan that reminds you what jungle creatures cats still are. He was quivering as if he had electrodes in him. I saw muscles violently rippling along his flanks and great convulsive shivers running the length of his spine.

'Hey, easy does it, fellow!' I told him. 'What's the matter? What's the matter, guy?'

What the matter was was that his legs seemed to want to move toward the house and his brain didn't. He was struggling every step of the way. The house was *calling* him, I thought suddenly, astonishing myself with the idea. As it had called the dog. You call a dog long enough and eventually his dog instincts take command and he comes, whether he feels like it or not. But you can't make a cat do a fucking thing against its will, not without a struggle. There was a struggle going on now. I stood there and watched it and I felt real uneasiness.

The cat lost.

He fought with truly desperate fury, but he kept moving closer to the door all the same. He managed to hold back for a moment just as he reached the first step, and I thought he was going to succeed in breaking loose from whatever was pulling him. But then his muscles stopped quivering and his fur went back where it belonged and his whole body perceptibly slackened; and he crept across the threshold in a pathetically beaten-looking way.

At my meeting that night I wanted to ask the others whether they knew anything about the white house with the screen door. They had all grown up in this place; I had lived here only a couple of months. Maybe the white house had a reputation for weirdness. But I wasn't sure which street it was on and a round-faced man named Eddie had had a close escape from the bottle after an ugly fight with his wife and needed to talk about that, and when that was over we all sat

179

around the table and discussed the high school basketball playoffs. High school basketball is a very big thing in this part of the state. Somehow I couldn't bring myself to say, 'Do you mind if I change the subject, fellows? Because I saw a house a few blocks from here gobble up a dog and then a cat like it was a roach motel.' They'd just think I had gone back on the sauce and they'd rally round like crazy to help me get steady again.

I went back there a few days later and couldn't find the house. Just an empty lot, grizzled brown late-winter grass, no paved pathway, no steps, no garbage cans, nothing. This time I knew I hadn't accidentally gone up some other street. The house next door to the white house was still there, the brown-shingled one where the dog had found the newspaper. But the white house was gone.

What the hell? A house that comes and goes?

Sweat came flooding out all over me. Was it possible to be having hallucinations in such convincing detail when I had been sober for a couple of months? First I was frightened and then I was angry. I didn't deserve this. If the house wasn't a hallucination, and I didn't seriously think it was, then what was it? I was working hard at putting my life back together and I was entitled to have reality stay real around me.

Easy, I thought. Easy. You're not entitled to anything, fellow. But you'll be okay as long as you recognize that nobody requires you to be able to explain mysteries that are beyond your understanding. Just go easy, take things as they come, and stay cool, stay cool, stay cool.

The house came back four days later.

I still couldn't bring myself to talk about it at meetings, even though that probably would have been a good idea. I had no problem at all with admitting publicly that I was an alcoholic, far from it. But standing up and telling everyone that I was crazy was something else entirely.

Things got even more bizarre. One afternoon I was out in front of the house and a kid's tricycle came rolling down the street all by itself, as though on an invisible cord. It rolled right past me and turned the corner and I watched it traverse the path and *go up the steps* of the white house and disappear inside. Some sort of magnetic pull? Radio waves?

Half a minute later the owner of the tricycle came huffing along, a chubby boy of about five in blue leggings. 'My bike!' he was yelling. 'My bike!' I imagined him running up the path and disappearing into the house too, like the dog, the cat, and the tricycle. I couldn't let that happen. But I couldn't just grab him up and hold him, either, not in an era when if a grown man simply smiles at a kid in the street he's likely to get booked. So I did the next best thing and planted myself at the head of the path leading across the white house's lawn. The kid banged into my shins and fell down. I looked up the block and saw a woman coming, his aunt, maybe, or his grandmother. It seemed safe to help the kid up, so I did. Then I smiled at her and said, 'He really ought to look where he's going.'

'My bike!' the boy wailed. 'Where's my *bike*?'

The woman looked at me and said, 'Did you see someone take the child's tricycle?'

'Afraid I can't say, ma'am,' I replied, shrugging my most amiable shrug. 'I was coming around the corner, and there was the boy running full tilt into me. But I didn't see any tricycles.' What else was I going to tell her? *I saw it go up the steps by itself and into the house?*

She gave me a troubled glance. But obviously I didn't have the tricycle in my coat pocket and I guess I don't look like the sort of man who specializes in stealing things from little children.

A dog. A cat. A tricycle.

I turned and walked away. Up Maple to Juniper, and down Juniper to Beech, and left on Beech onto Chestnut. Or maybe it was up Oak to Sycamore and then on to Locust and Hickory. Maple, Oak, Chestnut, Hickory: what difference did it make? They were all alike.

I doubled back eventually and got to the house just in time to see a boy of about fourteen wearing a green-and-yellow jersey come trotting down the street, tossing a football from hand to hand. As he went past the white house the screen door swung open and the inner door swung back and the kid halted, turned, and very neatly threw the football through, a nice high tight arc.

The doors closed.

The kid stood stock-still in the street, staring at his hand as though he had never seen it before. He looked stunned.

Then after a moment he broke out of his stasis and started up the path to the house. I wanted to call out to him to keep away, but I couldn't get any sound out; and I wasn't sure what I could say to him, anyway.

He rang the doorbell. Waited.

I held my breath.

The door started to open again. Trying to warn him, I managed to make a scratchy little choking sort of sound.

But the kid didn't go in. He stood for a moment peering inside and then he turned and began to run, across the lawn, over the hedges, down the street.

What had he seen?

I ran after him. 'Hey, kid! Kid, wait!'

He was going so fast I couldn't believe it. I was a pretty good runner in my time, too. But my time was some time ago.

Instead of going to the meeting that night, I went to scout out the house. Under cover of darkness I crept around it in the shrubbery like your basic peeping-tom, trying to peer through the windows.

Was I scared? Utterly shitless, yes. Wouldn't you be?

Did I want a drink? Don't be naive. I *always* want a drink, and not just one. I certainly wanted a good jolt of the stuff now. Three fingers of Jim Beam and I'd have had the unshakeable savoir-faire of Sherlock Holmes himself. But I wouldn't have stopped at three fingers. My name is Tom and I am an alcoholic.

What did I see? I saw a woman, very likely the same one I had had that quick glimpse of in the doorway that first drizzly Monday morning. I got only quick glimpses now. She was moving around from room to room so that I didn't have a chance to see her clearly, but what I saw was plenty impressive. Tall, blonde, sleek, that much was certain. She wore a floor-length red robe made of some glossy metallic fabric that fell about her in a kind of liquid shimmer. Her movements were graceful and elegant. There didn't seem to be anything in the way of furniture inside, just some cartons and crates, which she was carrying back and forth. Stranger and stranger. I didn't see the cat or the dog or the bicycle.

I scrabbled around from window to window for maybe half an hour, hoping for a good look at her. I was moving with what I thought was real skill, keeping low, staying down behind the lilacs or whatever, rising cautiously toward windowsill level for each quick peek. I suppose I might have been visible from the street, but the night was moonless and people don't generally go out strolling around here after dark.

There didn't appear to be anyone else in the house. And for about fifteen minutes I didn't see her either. Maybe she was in the shower; maybe she had gone to bed. I was tempted to ring the bell. But what for? What would I say to her if she answered? What was I doing here in the first place?

I crept backward through the shrubbery, thinking it was time to leave. And then there she was, framed in a window, looking straight out at me.

Smiling. Beckoning.

Come hither, Tommy-boy.

I thought about the cat. I thought about the dog. I began to shake.

Like the kid with the football, I turned and ran, desperately loping through the quiet streets in an overwhelming access of unreasoning terror.

I was getting to the point where I thought it might be calming to have a drink. In the old days the first drink always settled me down. It lifted the burden; it soothed the pain; it answered the questions. It made taking the second drink very easy. The second suggested the third; the third required the fourth; the fourth demanded the fifth; and so on without hindrance, right on to insomnia, vomiting, falling hair, bloody gums, raw eyes, exploding capillaries, nightmares, hallucinations, impotence, the shakes, the shivers, the queebles, the collywobbles, and all the rest.

I didn't take the drink. I went to a meeting instead, jittery and perplexed. I said I was wrestling with a mystery. I didn't say what it was. Let them fill in the blanks, anything they felt like. Even without the details, they'd know something of what I was going through. They too were wrestling with mysteries. Otherwise what were they doing there?

The house was gone for two weeks. I checked for it every day. Spring had arrived in full force before it returned. Trees turned green, plants were blooming, the air grew warm and soft.

The woman was back too, the blonde. I never failed to see her now, every time I went by, and I went by every day. It was as if she knew I was coming. Sometimes she was at the window, but more usually she was standing just inside the screen door. Some days she dressed in the red slinky robe, some days in a green one. She had a few other outfits too, all of them classy but somewhat oddly designed, shoulders too wide, the cut too narrow. Once – incredibly, unforgettably – she came to the door in nothing at all but a pair of stockings, and stood for a long moment on splendid display, framed perfectly in the doorway, sunlight glinting off her lush lovely body.

She was always smiling. She must have known I was the one who had been peeping that night and it didn't seem to bother her. The look on her face said, *Let's get to know each other a little better shall we?* Always that warm, beckoning smile. Sometimes she'd give me a little come-on-in flick of her fingertips.

Not on your life, sister. Not on your life.

But I couldn't stop coming by. The house, the woman, the mystery, all pulled me like a magnet.

By now I had two theories. The simple one was that she was lonely, horny, bored, looking for distraction. Maybe it excited her to be playing these games with me. In this quiet little town where the chief cause of death surely must be boredom, she liked to live dangerously.

Too simple, much too simple. Why would a woman who looked like that be living a lonely, horny life? Why would she be in this kind of town in the first place? What was more important, the theory didn't account for the comings and goings of the house. Or for what I had seen happen to the cat, the dog, the tricycle, the boy with the football. The dog had returned – he was sitting crosslegged on the steps just below the screen door the day I was given the full frontal show – but he never went more than a couple of yards from the house and he moved in a weird lobotomized way. There had't been any further sign of the cat or the tricycle.

Which led to my other theory, the roach-motel theory.

The house comes from the future, I told myself. They're studying the late twentieth century and they want to collect artifacts. So every now and then they send this time machine disguised as a little white-stucco house here and it scoops up toys, pets, newspapers, whatever it can grab. Most likely they aren't really looking for cats or dogs, but they takes what they gets. And now they're trying to catch an actual live twentieth-century man. Trolling for him the way you'd troll for catfish, using a beautiful woman – sometimes naked – as the bait.

A crazy idea? Sure. But I couldn't come up with a saner one.

Ten days into springtime and the house was gone again. When it came back, about a week later, the woman didn't seem to be with it. They were giving her some time off, maybe. But they still seemed interested in luring me inside. I'd come by and take up my position by the curb and the door would quietly swing open, though no one was visible inside. And would stay open, waiting for me to traipse up the walk and go in.

It was a temptation. I felt it pulling on me harder and harder every day, as my own here-and-now real-life everyday options looked bleaker and bleaker. I wasn't finding a new job. I wasn't making useful contacts. My money, not much to begin with, was running out. All I had was the Program and the people who were part of it here, and though they were fine enough people they weren't the kind I could get really close to in any way not having to do with the Program.

So why not go up that path and into the house? Even if they swept me up and took me off to the year 2999 and I was never heard from again, what did I have to lose? A drab life in a furnished room in a nowhere town, living on the last of my dwindling savings while I dreamed of fifths of Johnny Walker and went to meetings at which a bunch of victims of the same miserable malady struggled constantly to keep their leaky boats from sinking? Wherever I went would be better than that. Perhaps incredibly better.

But of course I didn't *know* that the shining visitors from the future would sweep me off to an astounding new existence in the year 2999. That was only my own nutty guess, my wild fantasy. Anything at all might happen to me if I passed through that doorway. Anything. It was a kind of Russian roulette and I didn't even know the odds against me.

One day I taped a piece of paper to a rubber ball from the five-and-dime and tossed it through the door when it opened for me. On it I had written these questions:

WHO ARE YOU?

WHERE ARE YOU FROM?

WHAT ARE YOU LOOKING FOR?

DO YOU WANT ME?

WHAT'S IN IT FOR ME?

WILL YOU HARM ME?

And I waited for an answering note to come bouncing out. But none ever did.

The house went away. The house came back. The woman still wasn't there. Nobody else seemed to be, either. But the door swung expectantly open for me, seemingly of its own accord. I would stand and stare, making no move, and after a time it would close again.

I bought another rubber ball and threw another message inside.

SEND ME THE GIRL AGAIN. THE BLONDE ONE.

I WANT TO TALK TO HER.

The house went away again and stayed away a long while, nearly a month this time, so that I began to think it would never come back and then that it had never actually been here at all. There were days when I didn't even bother to walk past the vacant lot where I had seen it.

Then I did, and it was there, and the woman was in the doorway smiling, and she said, 'Come on in and visit me, sailor?'

She was wearing something gauzy and she was leaning against the door-frame with her hand on her hip. Her voice was a soft throaty contralto. It all felt like a scene out of a 1940s movie. Maybe it was; maybe they'd been studying up.

'First you tell me who you are, all right? And where you come from.'

'Don't you want to have a good time with me, pal?'

Damn right I do. I felt it in my groin, my pounding chest, my knees.

I moistened my lips. I thought of the way the house had reeled in that angry snarling cat. How it had pulled that tricycle up the stairs. I felt it pulling on me. But I must have more ability to fight back than a cat. Or a tricycle.

I said, 'There's a lot I need to know, first.'

'Come on in and I'll tell you everything.' Softly. Huskily. Irresistibly. *Almost* irresistibly.

'Tell me first. Come out here and talk to me.'

She winked and shook her head. 'Here's looking at *you*, kid.' Studying old movies, all right. She closed the door in my face.

What they hammer into you in the Program is that you may think you're pretty tough but in fact when you've added up all the debits and credits the truth is you aren't as strong as you like to pretend you are. You're too weak not to take the next drink, and it's only after you admit how weak you are and turn Elsewhere for help that you can begin to find the strength you need.

I had found that strength. I hadn't had a drink on the seventh of February, or on the eighth, or on the ninth. One day at a time I wasn't having any drinks and by now that one day at a time had added up to four months and eleven days and when tomorrow came around I would add another day to the string, and I was beginning to feel fairly confident that I could keep going that way for the rest of my life.

But the house was something else again. I was starting to see it as a magic gateway to God knows where, just as booze had once been for me. It came and went and the woman smiled and beckoned and offered throaty invitations, and I recognized that I had let myself become obsessed with it and couldn't keep away from it, and the next time the house came back there was a good chance that I'd go sauntering up the path and through the door.

Which was crazy.

I hadn't put myself through this whole ordeal of recovery just for the sake of waltzing through a different magic gateway, had I? Especially when I didn't have the slightest idea of what might lie on the far side.

I thought about it and thought about it and thought about it and decided that the safest and smartest thing to do was to get out of here: I would move to some other town that didn't have houses that came and went, or languid naked blondes standing in doorways inviting me to step inside for a good time. So one drowsy July morning I bought a bus ticket to a town forty miles from the one where I'd been living. It was about the same size and had a similar name and looked just about as dull; and on the street behind the lone movie theater I found a house with a FURNISHED ROOM sign stuck in its lawn and rented a place very much like the one I had, except that the rent was ten dollars more a month. Then I went around to the local AA headquarters – I had already checked with my own to make sure they had one here, you can bet on that – and picked up the schedule of meeting hours.

Done. Safe. A clean break.

I'd never see that white house again.

I'd never see *her* again.

I'd never face that mysterious doorway and never feel the pull that it exerted.

And as I told myself all that, the pain of irrevocable loss rose up inside me and hit me from within, and I thought I was going to fall down.

I was in the bus depot then, waiting to catch the bus going back, so I could pack my suitcase and settle things with my landlady and say goodbye to my friends, such as they were, in the Program back there. I looked around and there she was, standing stark naked in the doorway of the baggage room, smiling at me in that beckoning way of hers.

Not really. It was a different woman, and she wasn't blonde, and she was wearing a bus company uniform, and she wasn't even looking at me.

I knew that, actually. I wasn't hallucinating. But I had *wanted* her to be the other one so badly that I imagined that I saw her. And I realized how deep the obsession had become.

I must have seen her fifty times during the ride back. Waving at me from the head of a country lane as the bus flashed by. Smiling at me from a bicycle going the other way. Riding in the back of a pickup truck bouncing along in front of us. Standing by the side of the road trying to get a hitch. Her image haunted me wherever I looked. I sat there shivering and sweating, seeing her beckoning in the doorway and watching that door closing and closing and closing again in my mind.

It was evening by the time the bus reached town. The wise thing would have been to take a shower and go to a meeting, but I went to the house instead, and there was someone standing outside, staring at the screen door.

I had never before encountered anyone else, in all my visits to the house.

He was about my age, a short guy with a good gut and touseled reddish hair just beginning to fade into gray. He looked vaguely familiar. I wondered if I had seen him at a meeting once or twice, perhaps. As I came by, he threw me an uneasy, guilty glance, as if he was up to something. His eyes were a pale blue, very bloodshot.

I went past him about ten paces, paused there, turned around.

189

'You waiting for someone?' I asked.

'I might be.'

'Someone who lives in there?'

'What's that to you?'

'I was just wondering,' I said. 'If you could tell me who lives in that house.'

He shrugged as if he hadn't quite heard me. The blue eyes turned chilly. I wanted to pick him up and throw him into the next county. The way he was looking at me, he probably felt the same way about me.

I said, 'A woman lives there, right?'

'Fuck off, will you?'

'A blonde woman?'

'Fuck off, I said.'

Neither of us moved.

'Sometimes I come by here and I see a blonde woman in the window, or standing in the doorway,' I went on. 'I wonder if you've seen her sometimes too.'

He didn't say anything. His eyes flickered almost involuntarily toward the house.

I followed the motion and there she was, visible through the window with the green shutters to the right of the door. She was wearing one of her misty wraps and her hair was shining like spun gold. She smiled. Gestured with a quick movement of her head.

Come on inside, why don't you?

I almost did. Another five seconds, another three, and I would have trotted down that little narrow paved pathway as obediently as the dog who had had the newspaper in his mouth. But I didn't. I was still afraid of what might lie beyond. I froze in my tracks; and then the redheaded man started to move. He went past me and up the path. Like a sleepwalker; like a zombie.

'Hey – wait –'

I caught him by the arm. He swung around, furious, and we struggled for a moment and then he broke loose and clamped both his hands on my shoulders and pushed me with tremendous force into the shrubbery. I tripped over one of the pieces of odd metal junk that were always lying around near the door and went sprawling on my face, and when I got myself disentangled it was just in time to see the redheaded man wrench the screen door open and run inside.

I heard the inner door slam.

And then the house disappeared.

It vanished like a pricked bubble, taking the shrubbery with it, the garbage cans and other junk as well, and I found myself kneeling on weeds in the midst of a vacant lot, trembling as if I had just had a stroke. After a moment or two I got shakily to my feet and walked over to the place where the house had been. Nothing. Nothing. No trace. Gone as though it had never been there at all.

A couple of days later I moved back to my old place. There didn't seem much risk any more, and I missed the place, the town, the guys at the meetings. It's been months now, and no house. I rarely skip a day, going by the lot, but it remains empty. The memory of it, of her, haunts me. I look for the house in other parts of town, even in other towns. I look for the redheaded man too, but I've never seen him. I described him once at a meeting and someone said, 'Yeah, sounds like Ricky. He used to live around here.' Where was he now? Nobody had any idea. Neither do I.

Another time I got brave enough to ask some of them if they had ever heard about a little white house that, well, sort of comes and goes. 'Comes and goes?' they said. 'What the hell does that mean?' I let the question drop.

I have a feeling that it was all some kind of a test, and I may have flunked it. I don't mean that I've missed out on a terrific woman. She was only the bait; I know better than to think that she was real or that she ever could have been available for me if she was. But that sense of a new start – of another life, however weird, beyond the horizon, forever lost to me now – that's what I'm talking about. And the pain runs deep.

But there's always a second chance, isn't there? They tell you that in the Program, and I believe it. I have to. From time to time I've left notes in the empty lot:

WHEN YOU COME BACK NEXT TIME,
DON'T LEAVE WITHOUT ME.

I'M READY NOW. I'M SURE OF IT.

Maybe they will. The house comes and goes, that I know. It's gone now, but it'll come again. I'm here. I'm watching. I'm waiting.

Looking for the Fountain

We are still in the early months of 1991; and I am still writing short stories and waiting for the coming of the long California summer.

This one was commissioned by another friend, Gregory Benford, who in conjunction with the redoubtable Marty Greenberg was editing a series of alternative-history anthologies under the title, *What Might Have Been*. I had already done stories ('To the Promised Land' and 'A Sleep and a Forgetting') for the first two volumes of the series, a couple of years earlier. Somehow I missed Volume Three, but now a fourth was being assembled – stories of Alternate Americas – and, calling on my knowledge of the exploration narratives of the Spanish conquistadores in the New World and throwing in a speculation about a vagrant band of Crusaders, I came up with this one, which saw print first in the May, 1992 issue of *Isaac Asimov's Science Fiction Magazine* before making its way into the anthology for which it was written.

My name is Francisco de Ortega and by the grace of God I am 89 years old and I have seen many a strange thing in my time, but nothing so strange as the Indian folk of the island called Florida, whose great dream it is to free the Holy Land from the Saracen conquerors that profane it.

It was fifty years ago that I encountered these marvelous people, when I sailed with his excellency the illustrious Don Juan Ponce de Leon on his famous and disastrous voyage in quest of what is wrongly called the Fountain of Youth. It was not a Fountain of Youth at all that he sought, but a Fountain of Manly Strength, which is somewhat a different thing. Trust me: I was there, I saw and heard everything, I was by Don Juan Ponce's side when his fate overtook him. I know the complete truth of this endeavor and I mean to set it all down now

193

so there will be no doubt; for I alone survive to tell the tale, and as God is my witness I will tell it truthfully now, here in my ninetieth year, all praises be to Him and to the Mother who bore Him.

The matter of the Fountain, first.

Commonly, I know, it is called the Fountain of Youth. You will read that in many places, such as in the book about the New World which that Italian wrote who lived at Seville, Peter Martyr of Anghiera, where he says, 'The governor of the Island of Boriquena, Juan Ponce de Leon, sent forth two caravels to seek the Islands of Boyuca in which the Indians affirmed there to be a fountain or spring whose water is of such marvelous virtue, that when it is drunk it makes old men young again.'

This is true, so far as it goes. But when Peter Martyr talks of 'making old men young again', his words must be interpreted in a poetic way.

Perhaps long life is truly what that Fountain really provides, along with its other and more special virtue – who knows? For I have tasted of that Fountain's waters myself, and here I am nearly 90 years of age and still full of vigor, I who was born in the year of our Lord 1473, and how many others are still alive today who came into the world then, when Castile and Aragon still were separate kingdoms? But I tell you that what Don Juan Ponce was seeking was not strictly speaking a Fountain of Youth at all, but rather a Fountain that offered a benefit of a very much more intimate kind. For I was there, I saw and heard everything. And they have cowardly tongues, those who say it was a Fountain of Youth, for it would seem that out of shame they choose not to speak honestly of the actual nature of the powers that the Fountain which we sought was supposed to confer.

It was when we were in the island of Hispaniola that we first heard of this wonderful Fountain, Don Juan Ponce and I. This was, I think, in the year 1504. Don Juan Ponce, a true nobleman and a man of high and elegant thoughts, was governor then in the province of Higuey of that island, which was ruled at that time by Don Nicolas de Ovando, successor to the great Admiral Cristobal Colon. There was in Higuey then a certain Indian cacique or chieftain of remarkable strength and force, who was reputed to keep seven wives and to satisfy each and every one of them each night of the week. Don Juan Ponce was curious about the great virility of this cacique, and one day he sent a certain Aurelio Herrera to visit him in his village.

'He does indeed have many wives,' said Herrera, 'though whether there were five or seven or fifty-nine I could not say, for there were women surrounding me all the time I was there, coming and going in such multitudes that I was unable to make a clear count, and swarms of children also, and from the looks of it the women were his wives and the children were his children.'

'And what sort of manner of man is this cacique?' asked Don Juan Ponce.

'Why,' said Herrera, 'he is a very ordinary man, narrow of shoulders and shallow of chest, whom you would never think capable of such marvels of manhood, and he is past middle age besides. I remarked on this to him, and he said that when he was young he was easily exhausted and found the manly exercises a heavy burden. But then he journeyed to Boyuca, which is an island to the north of Cuba that is also called Bimini, and there he drank of a spring that cures the debility of sex. Since then, he asserts, he has been able to give pleasure to any number of women in a night without the slightest fatigue.'

I was there. I saw and heard everything. *El enflaquecimiento del sexo* was the phrase that Aurelio Herrera used, 'the debility of sex'. The eyes of Don Juan Ponce de Leon opened wide at this tale, and he turned to me and said, 'We must go in search of this miraculous fountain some day, Francisco, for there will be great profit in the selling of its waters.'

Do you see? Not a word had been spoken about long life, but only about the curing of *el enflaquecimiento del sexo*. Nor was Don Juan Ponce in need of any such cure for himself, I assure you, for in the year 1504 he was just thirty years old, a lusty and aggressive man of fiery and restless spirit, and red-haired as well, and you know what is said about the virility of red-haired men. As for me, I will not boast, but I will say only that since the age of thirteen I have rarely gone a single night without a woman's company, and have been married four times, on the fourth occasion to a woman fifty years younger than myself. And if you find yourself in the province of Valladolid where I live and come to pay a call on me I can show you young Diego Antonio de Ortega whom you would think was my great-grandson, and little Juana Maria de Ortega who could be my great-granddaughter, for the boy is seven and the girl is five, but in truth they are my own children, conceived when I was past eighty years of age; and I have had many other sons and daughters too, some of whom are old people now and some are dead.

So it was not to heal our own debilities that Don Juan Ponce and I longed to find this wonderful Fountain, for of such shameful debilities we had none at all, he and I. No, we yearned for the Fountain purely for the sake of the riches we might derive from it: for each year saw hundreds or perhaps thousands of men come from Spain to the New World to seek their fortunes, and some of these were older men who no doubt suffered from a certain *enflaquecimiento*. In Spain I understand they use the powdered horn of the unicorn to cure this malady, or the crushed shells of a certain insect, though I have never had need of such things myself. But those commodities are not to be found in the New World, and it was Don Juan Ponce's hope that great profit might be made by taking possession of Bimini and selling the waters of the Fountain to those who had need of such a remedy. This is the truth, whatever others may claim.

But the pursuit of gold comes before everything, even the pursuit of miraculous Fountains of Manly Strength. We did not go at once in search of the Fountain because word came to Don Juan Ponce in Hispaniola that the neighboring island of Borinquen was rich in gold, and thereupon he applied to Governor Ovando for permission to go there and conquer it. Don Juan Ponce already somewhat knew that island, having seen its western coast briefly in 1493 when he was a gentleman volunteer in the fleet of Cristobal Colon, and its beauty had so moved him that he had resolved someday to return and make himself master of the place.

With one hundred men, he sailed over to this Borinquen in a small caravel, landing there on Midsummer Day, 1506, at the same bay he had visited earlier aboard the ship of the great Admiral. Seeing us arrive with such force, the cacique of the region was wise enough to yield to the inevitable and we took possession with very little fighting.

So rich did the island prove to be that we put the marvelous Fountain of which we had previously heard completely out of our minds. Don Juan Ponce was made governor of Borinquen by royal appointment and for several years the natives remained peaceful and we were able to obtain a great quantity of gold indeed. This is the same island that Cristobal Colon called San Juan Bautista and which people today call Puerto Rico.

All would have been well for us there but for the stupidity of a certain captain of our forces, Cristobal de Sotomayor, who treated the natives so badly that they rose in rebellion against us. This was in the year of our Lord 1511. So we found ourselves at war; and Don Juan Ponce fought with all the great valor for which he was renowned, doing tremendous destruction against our pagan enemies. We had among us at that time a certain dog, called Bercerillo, of red pelt and black eyes, who could tell simply by smell alone whether an Indian was friendly to us or hostile, and could understand the native speech as well; and the Indians were more afraid of ten Spaniards with this dog, than of one hundred without him. Don Juan Ponce rewarded Bercerillo's bravery and cleverness by giving the dog a full share of all the gold and slaves we captured, as though he were a crossbowman; but in the end the Indians killed him. I understand that a valiant pup of this Bercerillo, Leoncillo by name, went with Nunez de Balboa when he crossed the Isthmus of Panama and discovered the great ocean beyond.

During this time of our difficulties with the savages of Puerto Rico, Don Diego Colon, the son of the great Admiral, was able to take advantage of the trouble and make himself governor of the island in the place of Don Juan Ponce. Don Juan Ponce thereupon returned to Spain and presented himself before King Ferdinand, and told him the tale of the fabulous Fountain that restores manly power. King Ferdinand, who was greatly impressed by Don Juan Ponce's lordly bearing and noble appearance, at once granted him a royal permit to seek and conquer the isle of Bimini where this Fountain was said to be.

Whether this signifies that His Most Catholic Majesty was troubled by debilities of a sexual sort, I would not dare to say. But the king was at that time a man of sixty years and it would not be unimaginable that some difficulty of that kind had begun to perplex him.

Swiftly Don Juan Ponce returned to Puerto Rico with the good news of his royal appointment, and on the third day of March of the year of our Lord 1513 we set forth from the Port of San German in three caravels to search for Bimini and its extraordinary Fountain.

I should say at this point that it was a matter of course that Don Juan Ponce should have asked me to take part in the quest for this Fountain. I am a man of Tervas de San Campos in the province of Valladolid, where Don Juan Ponce de Leon also was born less than one year after I was, and he and I played together as children and were friends all through our youth. As I have said, he first went to the New World in 1493, when he was nineteen years of age, as a gentleman aboard the ship of Admiral Cristobal Colon, and after settling in Hispaniola he wrote to me and told me of the great wealth of the New World and urged me to join him there. Which I did forthwith; and we were rarely separated from then until the day of his death.

Our flagship was the *Santiago*, with Diego Bermudez as its master – the brother to the man who discovered the isle of Bermuda – and the famous Anton de Alaminos as its pilot. We had two Indian pilots too, who knew the islands of that sea. Our second ship was the *Santa Maria de Consolacion*, with Juan Bono de Quexo as its captain, and the third was the *San Cristobal*. All of these vessels were purchased by Don Juan Ponce himself out of the riches he had laid by in the time when he was governor of Puerto Rico.

I have to tell you that there was not one priest in our company, not that we were ungodly men but only that it was not our commander's purpose on this voyage to bring the word of Jesus to the natives of Bimini. We did have some few women among us, including my own wife Beatriz, who had come out from Spain to be with me, and grateful I was to have her by my side; and my wife's young sister Juana was aboard the ship also, that I could better look after her among these rough Spaniards of the New World.

Northward we went. After ten days we halted at the isle of San Salvador to scrape weeds from the bottom of one of our ships. Then we journeyed west-northwest, passing the isle of Ciguateo on Easter Sunday, and, continuing onward into waters that ran ever shallower, we caught sight on the second day of April of a large delightful island of great and surpassing beauty, all blooming and burgeoning with a great host of wildflowers whose delectable odors came wafting to us on the warm gentle breeze. We named this isle La Florida, because Easter is the season when things flower and so we call that time of year in our language *Pascua Florida*. And we said to one another at once, seeing so beautiful a place, that this island of Florida must surely be the home of the wondrous Fountain that restores men to their fleshly powers and grants all their carnal desires to the fullest.

Of the loveliness of Florida I could speak for a day and a night and a night and a day, and not exhaust its marvels. The shallowing green waters give way to white crests of foam that fall upon beaches paved hard with tiny shells; and when you look beyond the beach you see dunes and marshes, and beyond those a land altogether level, not so much as a hillock upon it, where glistening sluggish lagoons bordered brilliantly with rushes and sedges show the way to the mysterious forests of the interior.

Those forests! Palms and pines, and gnarled gray trees whose names are known only to God! Trees covered with snowy beards! Trees whose leaves are like swords! Flowers everywhere, dizzying us with their perfume! We were stunned by the fragrance of jasmine and honeyflower. We heard the enchanting songs of a myriad of birds. We stared in wonder at the bright blooms. We doffed our helmets and dropped to our knees to give thanks to God for having led us to this most beautiful of shores.

Don Juan Ponce was the first of us to make his way to land, carrying with him the banner of Castile and Leon. He thrust the royal standard into the soft sandy soil and in the name of God and Spain took possession of the place. This was at the mouth of a river which he named in honor of his patron, the blessed San Juan. Then, since there were no Indians thereabouts who might lead us to the

Fountain, we returned to our vessels and continued along the coast of that place.

Though the sea looked gentle we found the currents unexpectedly strong, carrying us northward so swiftly that we feared we would never see Puerto Rico again. Therefore did Don Juan Ponce give orders for us to turn south; but although we had a fair following wind the current was so strong against us that we could make no headway, and at last we were compelled to anchor in a cove. Here we spent some days, with the ships straining against their cables; and during that time the little *San Cristobal* was swept out to sea and we lost sight of her altogether, though the day was bright and the weather fair. But within two days by God's grace she returned to us.

At this time we saw our first Indians, but they were far from friendly. Indeed they set upon us at once and two of our men were wounded by their little darts and arrows, which were tipped with sharp points made of bone. When night came we were able to withdraw and sail on to another place that we called the Rio de la Cruz, where we collected wood and water; and here we were attacked again, by sixty Indians, but they were driven off. And so we continued for many days, until in latitude 28 degrees 15 minutes we did round a cape, which we called Cabo de los Corrientes on account of the powerful currents, which were stronger than the wind.

Here it was that we had the strangest part of our voyage, indeed the strangest thing I have ever seen in all my ninety years. Which is to say that we encountered at this time in this remote and hitherto unknown land the defenders of the Christian Faith, the sworn foes of the Saracens, the last sons of the Crusades, whose great dream it was, even now, to wrest the Holy Land of our Savior's birth from those infidel followers of Muhammad who seized it long ago and rule it today.

We suspected nothing of any of what awaited us when we dropped our anchors near an Indian town on the far side of Cabo de los Corrientes. Cautiously, for we had received such a hostile reception farther up the coast, we made our landfall a little way below the village and set about the task of filling our water casks and cutting firewood. While this work was being carried out we became aware that the Indians had left their village and had set out down the shore to encounter us, for we heard them singing and chanting even before we could see them; and we halted in our labors and made ourselves ready to deal with another attack.

After a short while the Indians appeared, still singing as they approached. Wonder of wonders, they were clothed, though all the previous natives that we had seen were naked, or nearly so, as these savages usually are. Even more marvelous was the nature of their clothing, which was of a kind not very different from that which Christians wear, jerkins and doublets and tunics, and such things. And – marvel of marvel – every man of them wore upon his chest a white garment that bore the holy cross of Jesus painted brightly in red! We could not believe our eyes. But if we had any doubt that these were Christian men, it was eradicated altogether when we saw that in the midst of the procession came certain men wearing the dark robes of priests, who carried great wooden crosses held high aloft.

Were these indeed Indians? Surely not! Surely they must be Spaniards like ourselves! We might almost have been in Toledo, or Madrid, or Seville, and not on the shore of some strange land of the Indies! But indeed we saw without doubt now that the marchers were men of the sort that is native to the New World, with the ruddy skins and black hair and sharp features of their kind, Christian though they might be in dress, and carrying the cross itself in their midst.

When they were close enough so that we could hear distinctly the words of their song, it sounded to some of us that they might be Latin words, though Latin of a somewhat barbarous kind. Could that be possible? We doubted the evidence of our ears. But then Pedro de Plasencia, who had studied for the priesthood before entering the military, crossed himself most vigorously and said to us in wonder, 'Do you hear that? They are singing the *Gloria in excelsis Deo*!' And in truth we could tell that hymn was what they sang, now that Pedro de Plasencia had picked out the words of it for us. Does that sound strange to you, that Indians of an unknown isle should be singing in Latin? Yes, it is strange indeed. But doubt me at your peril. I was there; I saw and heard everything myself.

'Surely,' said Diego Bermudez, 'there must have been Spaniards here before us, who have instructed these people in the way of God.'

'That cannot be,' said our pilot, Anton de Alaminos. 'For I was with Cristobal Colon on his second voyage and have been on every voyage since of any note that has been made in these waters, and I can tell you that no white man has set foot on this shore before us.'

'Then how came these Indians by their crosses and their holy hymns?' asked Diego Bermudez. 'Is it a pure miracle of the saints, do you think?'

'Perhaps it is,' said Don Juan Ponce de Leon, with some heat, for it looked as if there might be a quarrel between the master and the pilot. 'Who can say? Be thankful that these folk are our Christian friends and not our enemy, and leave off your useless speculations.'

And in the courageous way that was his nature, Don Juan Ponce went forward and raised his arms to the Indians, and made the sign of the cross in the air, and called out to them, saying, 'I am Don Juan Ponce de Leon of Valladolid in the land of Spain, and I greet you in the name of the Father, and of the Son, and of the Holy Ghost.' All of which he said clearly and loudly in his fine and beautiful Castilian, which he spoke with the greatest purity. But the Indians, who by now had halted in a straight line before us, showed no understanding in their eyes. Don Juan Ponce spoke again, once more in Spanish, saying that he greeted them also in the name of His Most Catholic Majesty King Ferdinand of Aragon and Castile. This too produced no sign that it had been understood.

One of the Indians then spoke. He was a man of great presence and bearing, who wore chains of gold about his chest and carried a sword of strange design at his side, the first sword I had ever seen a native of these islands to have. From these indications it was apparent that he was the cacique.

He spoke long and eloquently in a language that I suppose was his own, for none of us had ever heard it before, not even the two Indian pilots we had brought with us. Then he said a few words that had the sound and the ring of French or perhaps Catalan, though we had a few men of Barcelona among us who leaned close toward him and put their hands to their ears and even they could make no sense out of what they heard.

But then finally this grand cacique spoke words which we all could understand plainly, garbled and thick-tongued though his speaking of them was: for what he said was, and there could be no doubt of it however barbarous his accent, '*In nomine Patris, et Filii, et Spiritus Sancti,*' and he made the sign of the cross over his chest as any good Christian man would do. To which Don Juan replied, '*Amen. Dominus vobiscum.*' Whereupon the cacique, exclaiming, '*Et cum spiritu tuo,*' went forthrightly to the side of Don Juan Ponce, and they embraced with great love, likewise as any Christian men might do, here on this remote beach in this strange and lovely land of Florida.

They brought us then to their village and offered a great feast for us, with roasted fish and the meat of tortoises and sweet fruits of many mysterious kinds, and made us presents of the skins of animals. For our part we gave them such trinkets as we had carried with us, beads and bracelets and little copper daggers and the like, but of all the things we gave them they were most eager to receive the simple figurines of Jesus on the cross that we offered them, and passed them around amongst themselves in wonder, showing such love for them as if they were made of the finest gold and studded with emeralds and rubies. And we said privately to each other that we must be dreaming, to have met with Indians in this land who were of such great devotion to the faith.

We tried to speak with them again in Spanish, but it was useless, and so too was speaking in any of the native tongues of Hispaniola or Puerto Rico that we knew. In their turn they addressed us in their own language, which might just as well have been the language of the people of the Moon for all we comprehended it, and also in that tantalizing other tongue which seemed almost to be French or Catalan. We could not make anything of that, try though we did. But Pedro de Plasencia, who was the only one of us who could speak Latin out loud like a priest, sat down with the cacique after the meal and addressed him in that language. I mean not simply saying things like the Pater Noster and the Ave Maria, which any child can say, but speaking to him as if Latin was a real language with words and sentences of common meaning, the way it was long ago. To which the cacique answered, though he seemed to be framing his words with much difficulty; and Pedro answered him again, just as hesitatingly; and so they went on, talking to each other in a slow and halting way, far into the night, nodding and smiling most jubilantly whenever one of them reached some understanding of the other's words, while we looked on in astonishment, unable to fathom a word of what they were saying.

At last Pedro rose, looking pale and exhausted like a man who has carried a bull on his back for half a league, and came over to us where we were sitting in a circle.

'Well?' Don Juan Ponce demanded at once.

Pedro de Plasencia shook his head wearily. 'It was all nonsense, what the cacique said. I understood nothing. Nothing at all! It was mere incomprehensible babble and no more than that.' And he picked up a leather sack of wine that lay near his feet and drank from it as though he had a thirst that no amount of drinking ever could quench.

'You appeared to comprehend, at times,' said Don Juan Ponce. 'Or so it seemed to me as I watched you.'

'Nothing. Not a word. Let me sleep on it, and perhaps it will come clear to me in the morning.'

I thought Don Juan Ponce would pursue him on the matter. But Don Juan Ponce, though he was an impatient and high-tempered man, was also a man of great sagacity, and he knew better than to press Pedro further at a time when he seemed so troubled and fatigued. So he dismissed the company and we settled down in the huts that the Indians had given us for lodging, all except those of us who were posted as sentries during the night to guard against treachery.

I rose before dawn. But I saw that Don Juan Ponce and Pedro de Plasencia were already awake and had drawn apart from the rest of us and were talking most earnestly. After a time they returned, and Don Juan Ponce beckoned to me.

'Pedro has told me something of his conversation with the cacique,' he said.

'And what is it that you have learned?'

'That these Indians are indeed Christians.'

'Yes, that seems to be the plain truth, strange though it seems,'
I said. 'For they do carry the cross about, and sing the *Gloria*, and
honor the Father and the Son.'

'There is more.'

I waited.

He continued, 'Unless Pedro much mistook what the cacique told
him, the greatest hope in which these people live is that of wresting
the Holy Land from the Saracen, and restoring it to good Christian
pilgrims.'

At that I burst out into such hearty laughter that Don Juan Ponce, for
all his love of me, looked at me with eyes flashing with reproof. Yet
I could not withhold my mirth, which poured from me like a river.

I said at last, when I had mastered myself, 'But tell me, Don Juan,
what would these savages know of the Holy Land, or of Saracens, or
any such thing? The Holy Land is thousands of leagues away, and
has never been spoken of so much as once in this New World by
any man, I think; nor does anyone speak of the Crusade any longer
in this age, neither here nor at home.'

'It is very strange, I agree,' replied Don Juan Ponce. 'Nevertheless,
so Pedro swears, the cacique spoke to him of *Terra Sancta*, *Terra
Sancta*, and of infidels, and the liberation of the city of Jerusalem.'

'And how does it come to pass,' I asked, 'that they can know of
such things, in this remote isle, where no white man has ever visited
before?'

'Ah,' said Don Juan Ponce, 'that is the great mystery, is it not?'

In time we came to understand the solution to this mystery, though the
tale was muddled and confused, and emerged only after much travail,
and long discussions between Pedro de Plasencia and the cacique of
the Indians. I will tell you the essence of it, which was this:

Some three hundred years ago, or perhaps it was four hundred,
while much of our beloved Spain still lay under the Moorish hand,
a shipload of Frankish warriors set sail from the port of Genoa, or
perhaps it was Marseilles, or some other city along the coast of

Provence. This was in the time when men still went crusading, to make war for Jesus' sake in the Holy Land against the followers of Muhammad who occupied that place.

But the voyage of these Crusaders miscarried; for when they entered the great Mar Mediterraneo, thinking to go east they were forced west by terrible storms and contrary winds, and swept helpless past our Spanish shores, past Almeria and Malaga and Tarifa, and through the narrow waist of the Estrecho de Gibraltar and out into the vastness of the Ocean Sea.

Here, having no sound knowledge as we in our time do of the size and shape of the African continent, they thought to turn south and then east below Egypt and make their voyage yet to the Holy Land. Of course this would be impossible, except by rounding the Buena Fortuna cape and traveling up past Arabia, a journey almost beyond our means to this day. But being unaware of that, these bold but hapless men made the attempt, coasting southerly and southerly and southerly, and the land of course not only not ending but indeed carrying them farther and farther outward into the Ocean Sea, until at last, no doubt weary and half dead of famine, they realized that they had traveled so far to the west that there was no hope of returning eastward again, nor of turning north and making their way back into the Mediterraneo. So they yielded to the westerly winds that prevail near the Canary Isles, and allowed themselves to be blown clear across the sea to the Indies. And so after long arduous voyaging they made landfall in this isle we call Florida. Thus these men of three hundred years ago were the first discoverers of the New World, although I doubt very greatly that they comprehended what it was that they had achieved.

You must understand that we received few of these details from our Indian hosts: only the tale that men bound to Terra Sancta departing from a land in the east were blown off course some hundreds of years previous and were brought after arduous sailing to the isle of Florida and to this very village where our three caravels had made their landfall. All the rest did we conclude for ourselves, that they were Crusaders and so forth, after much discussing of the matter and recourse to the scholarship that the finest men among us possessed.

And what befell these men of the Crusade, when they came to this Florida? Why, they offered themselves to the mercies of the villagers, who greeted them right honorably and took them to dwell amongst them, and married them to their daughters! And for their part the seafarers offered the word of Jesus to the people of the village and thereby gave them hope of Heaven; and taught these kindly savages the Latin tongue so well that it remained with them after a fashion hundreds of years afterward, and also some vestiges of the common speech that the seafaring men had had in their own native land.

But most of all did the strangers from the sea imbue in the villagers the holy desire to rid the birthplace of Jesus of the dread hand of the Mussulman; and ever, in years after, did the Christian Indians of this Florida village long to put to sea, and cross the great ocean, and wield their bows and spears valiantly amidst the paynim enemy in the defense of the True Faith. Truly, how strange are the workings of God Almighty, how far beyond our comprehension, that He should make Crusaders out of the naked Indians in this far-off place!

You may ask what became of those European men who landed there, and whether we saw anyone who plainly might mark his descent from them. And I will tell you that those ancient Crusaders, who intermarried with the native women since they had brought none of their own, were wholly swallowed up by such intermarrying and were engulfed by the fullness of time. For they were only forty or fifty men among hundreds, and the passing centuries so diluted the strain of their race that not the least trace of it remained, and we saw no pale skin or fair hair or blue eyes or other marks of European men here. But the ideas that they had fetched to this place did survive, that is, the practicing of the Catholic faith and the speaking of a debased and corrupt sort of Latin and the wearing of a kind of European clothes, and such. And I tell you it was passing strange to see these red savages in their surplices and cassocks, and in their white tunics bearing the great emblem of our creed, and other such ancient marks of our civilization, and to hear them chanting the *Kyrie eleison* and the *Confiteor* and the *Sanctus, Sanctus, Sanctus Dominus Deus Sabaoth* in that curious garbled way of theirs, like words spoken in a dream.

Nay, I have spoken untruthfully, for the men of that lost voyage did leave other remnants of themselves among the villagers beside our holy faith, which I have neglected to mention here, but which I will tell you of now.

For after we had been in that village several days, the cacique led us through the close humid forest along a tangled trail to a clearing nearby just to the north of the village, and here we saw certain tangible remains of the voyagers: a graveyard with grave markers of white limestone, and the rotting ribs and strakes and some of the keel of a seafaring vessel of an ancient design, and the foundation walls of a little wooden church. All of which things were as sad a sight as could be imagined, for the gravestones were so weathered and worn that although we could see the faint marks of names we could not read the names themselves, and the vessel was but a mere sorry remnant, a few miserable decaying timbers, and the church was only a pitiful fragment of a thing.

We stood amidst these sorry ruins and our hearts were struck into pieces by pity and grief for these brave men, so far from home and lonely, who in this strange place had nevertheless contrived to plant the sacred tree of Christianity. And the noble Don Juan Ponce de Leon went down on his knees before the church and bowed his head and said, 'Let us pray, my friends, for the souls of these men, as we hope that someday people will pray for ours.'

We spent some days amongst these people in feasting and prayer, and replenishing our stock of firewood and water. And then Don Juan Ponce gave new thought to the primary purpose of our voyage, which was, to find the miraculous Fountain that renews a man's energies. He called Pedro de Plasencia to his side and said, 'Ask of the cacique, whether he knows such a Fountain.'

'It will not be easy, describing such things in my poor Latin,' answered Pedro. 'I had my Latin from the Church, Don Juan, and what I learned there is of little use here, and it was all so very long ago.'

'You must try, my friend. For only you of all our company has the power to speak with him and be understood.'

Whereupon Pedro went to the cacique; but I could see even at a distance that he was having great difficulties. For he would speak a few halting words, and then he would act out his meaning with gestures, like a clown upon a stage, and then he would speak again. There would be silence; and then the cacique would reply, and I would see Pedro leaning forward most intently, trying to catch the meaning of the curious Latin that the cacique spoke. They did draw pictures for each other also in the sand, and point to the sky and sweep their arms to and fro, and do many another thing to convey to each other the sense of their words, and so it went, hour after hour.

At length Pedro de Plasencia returned to where we stood, and said, 'There does appear to be a source of precious water that they cherish on this island, which they call the Blue Spring.'

'And is this Blue Spring the Fountain for which we search?' Don Juan Ponce asked, all eagerness.

'Ah, of that I am not certain.'

'Did you tell him that the water of it would allow a man to take his pleasure with women all day and all night, and never tire of it?'

'So I attempted to say.'

'With many women, one after another?'

'These are Christian folk, Don Juan!'

'Yes, so they are. But they are Indians also. They would understand such a thing, just as any man of Estramadura or Galicia or Andalusia would understand such a thing, Christian though he be.'

Pedro de Plasencia nodded. 'I told him what I could, about the nature of the Fountain for which we search. And he listened very close, and he said, Yes, yes, you are speaking of the Blue Spring.'

'So he understood you, then?'

'He understood something of what I said, Don Juan, so I do firmly believe. But whether he understood it all, that is only for God to know.'

I saw the color rise in Don Juan Ponce's face, and I knew that that restless choleric nature of his was coming to the fore, which had always been his great driving force and also his most perilous failing.

He said to Pedro de Plasencia, 'And will he take us to this Blue Spring of his, do you think?'

'I think he will,' said Pedro. 'But first he wishes to enact a treaty with us, as the price of transporting us thither.'

'A treaty.'

'A treaty, yes. He wants our aid and assistance.'

'Ah,' said Don Juan Ponce. 'And how can we be of help to these people, do you think?'

'They want us to show them how to build seafaring ships,' said Pedro. 'So that they can sail across the Ocean Sea, and go to the rescue of the Holy Land, and free it from the paynim hordes.'

There was much more of back and forth, and forth and back, in these negotiations, until Pedro de Plasencia grew weary indeed, and there was not enough wine in our sacks to give him the rest he needed, so that we had to send a boat out to fetch more from one of our ships at anchor in the harbor. For it was a great burden upon him to conduct these conversations, he remembering only little patches of Church Latin from his boyhood, and the cacique speaking a language that could be called Latin only by great courtesy. I sat with them as they talked, on several occasions, and not for all my soul could I understand a thing that they said to each other. From time to time Pedro would lose his patience and speak out in Spanish, or the cacique would begin to speak in his savage tongue or else in that other language, somewhat like Provencal, which must have been what the seafaring Crusaders spoke amongst themselves. But none of that added to the understanding between the two men, which I think was a very poor understanding indeed.

It became apparent after a time that Pedro had misheard the cacique's terms of treaty: what he wished us to do was not to teach them how to build ships but to give them one of ours in which to undertake their Crusade.

'It cannot be,' replied Don Juan Ponce, when he had heard. 'But tell him this, that I will undertake to purchase ships for him with my own funds, in Spain. Which I will surely do, after we have received the proceeds from the sale of the water from the Fountain.'

'He wishes to know how many ships you will provide,' said Pedro de Plasencia, after another conference.

'Two,' said Don Juan Ponce. 'No: three. Three fine caravels.'

Which Pedro duly told the cacique; but his way of telling him was to point to our three ships in the harbor, which led the cacique into thinking that Don Juan Ponce meant to give him those three actual ships then and now, and that required more hours of conferring to repair. But at length all was agreed on both sides, and our journey toward the Blue Spring was begun.

The cacique himself accompanied us, and the three priests of the tribe, carrying the heavy wooden crosses that were their staffs of office, and perhaps two dozen of the young men and girls of the village. In our party there were ten men, Don Juan Ponce and Pedro and I, and seven ordinary seamen carrying barrels in which we meant to store the waters of the Fountain. My wife Beatriz and her sister Juana accompanied us also, for I never would let them be far from me.

Some of the ordinary seamen among us were rough men of Estramadura, who spoke jestingly and with great licentiousness of how often they would embrace the girls of the native village after they had drunk of the Fountain. I had to silence them, reminding them that my wife and her sister could overhear their words. Yet I wondered privately what effects the waters would have on my own manhood: not that it had ever been lacking in any aspect, but I could not help asking myself if I would find it enhanced beyond its usual virtue, for such curiosity is but a natural thing to any man, as you must know.

We journeyed for two days, through hot close terrain where insects of great size buzzed among the flowers and birds of a thousand colors astounded our eyes. And at last we came to a place of bare white stone, flat like all other places in this isle of Florida, where clear cool blue water gushed up out of the ground with wondrous force.

The cacique gestured grandly, with a great sweep of his arms.

'It is the Blue Spring,' said Pedro de Plasencia.

Our men would have rushed forward at once to lap up its waters like greedy dogs at a pond; but the cacique cried out, and Don Juan Ponce also in that moment ordered them to halt. There would be no unseemly haste here, he said. And it was just as well he did, for we very soon came to see that this spring was a holy place to the people of the village, and it would have been profaned by such an assault on it, to our possible detriment and peril.

The cacique came forward, with his priests beside him, and gestured to Don Juan Ponce to kneel and remove his helmet. Don Juan Ponce obeyed; and the cacique took his helmet from him, and passed it to one of the priests, who filled it with water from the spring and poured it down over Don Juan Ponce's face and neck, so that Don Juan Ponce laughed out loud. The which laughter seemed to offend the Indians, for they showed looks of disapproval, and Don Juan Ponce at once grew silent.

The Indians spoke words which might almost have been Latin words, and there was much elevating of their crosses as the water was poured down over Don Juan Ponce, after which he was given the order to rise.

And then one by one we stepped forth, and the Indians did the same to each of us.

'It is very like a rite of holy baptism, is it not?' said Aurelio Herrera to me.

'Yes, very much like a baptism,' I said to him.

And I began to wonder: How well have we been understood here? Is it a new access of manly strength that these Indians are conferring upon us, or rather the embrace of the Church? For surely there is nothing about this rite that speaks of anything else than a religious enterprise. But I kept silent, since it was not my place to speak.

When the villagers were done dousing us with water, and speaking words over us and elevating their crosses, which made me more sure than ever that we were being taken into the congregation of their faith, we were allowed to drink of the spring – they did the same – and to fill our barrels. Don Juan Ponce turned to me after we had drunk, and winked at me and said, 'Well, old friend, this will serve us well in later years, will it not? For though we have no need of such invigoration now, you and I, nevertheless time will have its work with us as it does with all men.'

'If it does,' I said, 'why, then, we are fortified against it now indeed.'

But in truth I felt no change within. The water was pure and cool and good, but it had seemed merely to be water to me, with no great magical qualities about it; and when I turned and looked upon my wife Beatriz, she seemed pleasing to me as she always had, but no more than that. Well, so be it, I thought; this may be the true Fountain or maybe it is not, and only time will tell; and we began our return to the village, carrying the casks of water with us; and the day of our return, Pedro de Plasencia drew up a grand treaty on a piece of bark from a tree, in which we pledged our sacred honor and our souls to do all in our power to supply this village with good Spanish ships so that the villagers would be able to fulfill their pledge to liberate the Holy Land.

'Which we will surely do for them,' said Don Juan Ponce with great conviction. 'For I mean to come back to this place as soon as I am able, with many ships of our own as well as the vessels I have promised them from Spain; and we will fill our holds with cask upon cask of this virtuous water from the Fountain, and replenish our fortunes anew by selling that water to those who need its miraculous power. Moreover we ourselves will benefit from its use in our declining days. And also we will bring this cacique some priests, who will correct him in his manner of practicing our faith, and guide him in his journey to Jerusalem. All of which I will swear by a great oath upon the Cross itself, in the presence of the cacique, so that he may have no doubt whatsover of our kindly Christian purposes.'

And so we departed, filled with great joy and no little wonder at all that we had seen and heard.

Well, and none of the brave intentions of Don Juan Ponce were fulfilled, as you surely must know, inasmuch as the valiant Don Juan Ponce de Leon never saw Spain again, nor did he live to enjoy the rejuvenations of his body that he hoped the water of the Fountain would bring him in his later years. For when we left the village of the Indian Crusaders, we continued on our way along the coast of the isle of Florida a little further in a southerly direction, seeking to catch favorable winds and currents that would carry us swiftly back to Puerto Rico; and on the 23rd of May we halted in a pleasing bay to gather wood and water – for we would not touch the water of our casks from the Fountain! – and to careen the *San Cristobal*, the hull of which was fouled with barnacles. And as we did our work there, a party of Indians came forth out of the woods.

'Hail, brothers in Christ!' Don Juan Ponce called to them with great cheer, for the cacique had told him that his people had done wonderful things in bringing their neighbors into the embrace of Jesus, and he thought now that surely all the Indians of this isle had been converted to the True Faith by those Crusading men of long ago.

But he was wrong in that; for these Indians were no Christians at all, but only pagan savages like most of their kind, and they replied instantly to Don Juan Ponce's halloos with a volley of darts and arrows that struck five of us dead then and there before we were able to drive them off. And among those who took his mortal wound that day was the valiant and noble Don Juan Ponce de Leon of Valladolid, in the thirty-ninth year of his life.

I knelt beside him on the beach in his last moments, and said the last words with him. And he looked up at me and smiled – for death had never been frightening to him – and he said to me, almost with his last breath, 'There is only one thing that I regret, Francisco. And that is that I will never know, now, what powers the water of that Fountain would have conferred upon me, when I was old and greatly stricken with the frailty of my years.' With that he perished.

What more can I say? We made our doleful way back to Puerto Rico, and told our tale of Crusaders and Indians and cool blue waters. But we were met with laughter, and there were no purchasers for the contents of our casks, and our fortunes were greatly depleted. All praise be to God, I survived that dark time and went on afterward to join the magnificent Hernando Cortes in his conquest of the land of Mexico, which today is called New Spain, and in the fullness of time I returned to my native province of Valladolid with much gold in my possession, and here I live in health and vigor to this day.

Often do I think of the isle of Florida and those Christian Indians we found there. It is fifty years since that time. In those fifty years the cacique and his people have rendered most of Florida into Christians by now, as we now know, and I tell you what is not generally known, that this expansion of their nation was brought about the better to support their Crusade against the Mussulman once the ships that Don Juan Ponce promised them had arrived.

So there is a great warlike Christian kingdom in Florida today, filling all that land and spreading over into adjacent isles, against which we men of Spain so far have struggled in vain as we attempt to extend our sway to those regions. I think it was poor Don Juan Ponce de Leon, in his innocent quest for a miraculous Fountain, who without intending it caused them to become so fierce, by making them a promise which he could not fulfill, and leaving them thinking that they had been betrayed by false Christians. Better that they had remained forever in the isolation in which they lived when we found them, singing the *Gloria* and the *Credo* and the *Sanctus*, and waiting with Christian patience for the promised ships that are to take them to the reconquest of the Holy Land. But those ships did not come; and they see us now as traitors and enemies.

I often think also of the valiant Don Juan Ponce, and his quest for the wondrous Fountain. Was the Blue Spring indeed the Fountain of legend? I am not sure of that. It may be that those Indians misunderstood what Pedro de Plasencia was requesting of them, and that they were simply offering us baptism – us, good Christians all our lives! – when what we sought was something quite different from that.

But if the Fountain was truly the one we sought, I feel great sorrow and pity for Don Juan Ponce. For though he drank of its waters, he died too soon to know of its effects. Whereas here I am, soon to be ninety years old, and the father of a boy of seven and a girl of five.

Was it the Fountain's virtue that has given me so long and robust a life, or have I simply enjoyed the favor of God? How can I say? Whichever it is, I am grateful; and if ever there is peace between us and the people of the isle of Florida, and you should find yourself in the vicinity of that place, you could do worse, I think, than to drink of that Blue Spring, which will do you no harm and may perhaps bring you great benefit. If by chance you go to that place, seek out the Indians of the village nearby, and tell them that old Francisco de Ortega remembers them, and cherishes the memory, and more than once has said a Mass in their praise despite all the troubles they have caused his countrymen, for he knows that they are the last defenders of the Holy Land against the paynim infidels.

This is my story, and the story of Don Juan Ponce de Leon and the miraculous Fountain, which the ignorant call the Fountain of Youth, and of the Christian Indians of Florida who yearn to free the Holy Land. You may wonder about the veracity of these things, but I beg you, have no doubt on that score. All that I have told you is true. For I was there. I saw and heard everything.

The Way to Spook City

Here's a case where the author experienced more thrills and chills than his own protagonist in the course of writing one simple 18,000-word story.

The saga begins in the hot, dry summer of 1991, when – looking forward to the autumn writing season – I proposed to the editors of *Playboy* that I write a story of double the usual story length for them. I was having increasing difficulty confining my *Playboy* stories to the top limit of 7500 words or so. Long ago, I pointed out, the magazine had regularly run novellas, such stories as George Langelaan's 'The Fly', Arthur C. Clarke's 'A Meeting with Medusa', and Ray Bradbury's 'The Lost City of Mars'. What about reviving that custom and letting me write a long one now?

The powers that be mulled the idea and gave me a qualified go-ahead; I submitted an outline; on September 10, 1991, we came to an agreement on the deal. Two days later the printer of my venerable computer, which I had been using for nearly a decade, declined to print a document upon receiving the usual command. Somehow I jollied it into going back to work, and, although the rainy season was nowhere in sight yet, I blithely got started on the story that was to become 'The Way to Spook City' a day or two later, thinking to have the piece behind me before settling down to the upcoming winter novel. I promised to deliver it by mid-October so that it could be used in a space being reserved for it in the August, 1992 issue.

But the printer trouble returned, and worsened, and on September 27 – when I was forty pages into the story – the printer died entirely and permanently. I was trying to print out my forty pages at the time, but what came out was this:

'*Everyone had been astonished when Nick announced he was going* LIa kciN disiruprus oo, that he should be setting himself up for such a crazy LKthguoht eh nruter ot *brawny young man Tom had become but of the soft-eyed LJs'kciN fo lla nehgt dna ,n'* and then silence, not another garbled word.

No problem, you say. Get a new printer, hook it up, do the printout. But there *was* a problem. I had been something of a pioneer, as writers go, in the use of a computer for word-processing, and the computer I had been using all those years was now obsolete. The company that had made it was out of business, and no one now alive knew how to connect a modern printer to it. I did, of course, have a backup of my forty pages on a floppy disk; but my computer was a pre-MS-DOS model and its operating system did not happen to be compatible with that of any machine now in use. Whatever texts were on my computer were trapped in it forever, all my business records and the first half of 'Spook City' among them. They could be brought up on screen but they were inaccessible for purposes of printing.

I would need to buy one of the newfangled MS-DOS computers and learn how to use it. But now I contemplated the gloomy prospect of having to type 'Spook City' and hundreds of other documents onto the new computer, one word at a time. It would take forever. What about my mid-October deadline?

At this point, though, the technician who had been servicing my old computer discovered that he still had one of that model in working order (more or less) in his San Francisco office. I gave him my backup disk; he printed out the forty pages of 'Spook City' and faxed them to me that day; and later in the day I began keying the story into the only working computer in the house, which belonged to my wife Karen and was a perfectly standard DOS-based job. I also went out and bought a new computer myself, compatible with hers.

For the next ten days or so, while waiting for the new computer to arrive, I continued writing 'Spook City' using my prehistoric manual typewriter, which had served me nobly circa 1968 but which certainly seemed quaint now, and entering each day's work on Karen's computer after her work-day was over. By October 4 I had fifty-nine pages on disk. By then, though, I saw the need for all sorts of revisions in the early pages, revisions that would be too complicated to make with a typewriter (how did we ever manage to write stories on the things?) and I decided on Sunday, October 6, to print out the 59 pages and halt further work until my own new machine was here.

Karen's computer wouldn't print it. I don't know why. The text looked fine on screen, but when I gave the familiar print command I was told that the document was 'corrupted' and couldn't be sent on to the printer.

Again? Was there a curse on this story?

The backup disk was corrupted too. It began to look as though I had lost the nineteen pages I had written since the first computer glitch plus all the rewriting I had done on the original forty that the computer pro had rescued.

'I'm pretty much in shellshock now,' I wrote Alice Turner of *Playboy*, 'but what I suppose I'll do is wait for the new computer to arrive, maybe Wednesday, and then start putting the whole damn thing in once more, trying to reconstruct (though you never really can) the stuff I had been doing all this past week. I can see that I'm going to wind up earning about five cents an hour on this project even if everything goes perfectly the third time, which is by no means assured.

'The one consolation I have is that I didn't write the final scene yet, and so I didn't lose the final scene. The rest of it exists in my head and in all sorts of fragmentary drafts, which I suppose I can piece together, but the problem is that the second time around I had tidied up all the problems that I had created in the first draft, and I will never be confident in the next version that I've rewritten the dialog properly. Hurts too much to laugh, said Adlai Stevenson, but I'm too old to cry, so I guess I'll have a couple of drinks instead. Tomorrow, as Tolstoy said, is another day.'

Enter a second savior that grim Sunday evening, though: our friend and neighbor Carol Carr, who showed up equipped with some program that allowed us to bring up on screen, page by page, the whole corrupted document, and print it from the screen. What came out, alas, was mostly babble: was a Martian mix, miscellaneous random consonants (not vowels!) and numbers and keyboard symbols with an occasional intelligible phrase glaring out of the welter of nonsense. But that was better than nothing. The next day I told Alice Turner what Carol had achieved: 'She spent hours waving magic wands in front of Karen's computer and was able to coax out pages and pages of gibberish printout, which I am now reassembling, jigsaw-puzzle fashion, by locating recognizable passages, putting them into the proper order, and transcribing them by hand onto the old first draft that the last bunch of computer wizards coaxed out of my old computer last week. So far I've reached page 28 of the original 40-page draft and have pretty much reconstructed all the revisions. Unfortunately a lot of the really good stuff in the climactic scenes didn't emerge yesterday, but at least I have typed rough drafts of that and I ought to be able to put them back together in something approximating the level of yesterday's destroyed version.'

New computer came, finally. I learned how to use it by entering poor

219

garbled 'Spook City' in something like proper form. I rewrote as I went, and cautiously produced a new printout every afternoon. On Friday, October 18, I finally finished what looked like a complete draft of the story, though it still needed some trimming and polishing. Two days later – a furiously hot summer day – my part of California caught fire and three thousand houses all about me were destroyed. It looked as though our house might go as well. Karen and I were forced to flee, taking with us our cats, a handful of household treasures, and a backup disk of the accursed 'Spook City'. Whatever else happened, I didn't want to have to write that thing a third time.

We were able to return home after eighteen hours. The fire had stopped a mile north of us. (Carol Carr had had an even closer singe; all the houses across the street from hers were burned, but hers went unharmed.) After a couple of shaky days I got back to work and on October 25, only two weeks beyond deadline, I sent it to *Playboy*, telling Alice:

'Here, thank God, is the goddamned story, and what a weird experience it has been. Written on four different machines – my old computer, Karen's computer, my ancient manual typewriter, and my jazzy new computer – and lost twice by computers and both times recovered with the aid of technical wizardry, and typed over and over from one machine to the other, and interrupted by a natural disaster that makes our earthquake of a few years ago seem trivial – I feel as though I've been writing it forever. I wake up mumbling it to myself. I never dreamed I was embarking on such an epic struggle when I proposed the story; I thought it would simply be a few weeks of the usual tough work, a nice payday, and on to the next job . . . Anyway, here's the story. I hope you like it. You must be starting to feel as though you've been writing it forever too.'

And, with some trepidation, I will herewith instruct my computer to copy its text from my 1991 story file into this present collection. If you don't find it here, you'll know why.

The air was shining up ahead, a cold white pulsing glow bursting imperiously out of the hard blue desert sky. That sudden chilly dazzle told Demeris that he was at the border, that he was finally getting his first glimpse of the place where human territory ended and the alien-held lands began.

He halted and stood staring for a moment, half expecting to see monsters flying around overhead on the far side of the line; and right on cue something weird went flapping by, a blotch of darkness against the brilliant icy sheen that was lighting everything up over there in the Occupied Zone. It was a heavy thing the size of a hawk and a half, with a lumpy greenish body and narrow wings like sawblades and a long snaky back that had a little globular purple head at the end of it. The creature was so awkward that Demeris had to laugh. He couldn't see how it stayed airborne. The bird, if that was what it was, flew on past, heading north, dropping a line of bright turquoise turds behind it. A little burst of flame sprang up in the dry grass where each one fell.

'Thank you kindly for that pretty welcome,' Demeris called out after it, sounding jauntier than he felt.

He went a little closer to the barrier. It sprang straight up out of the ground like an actual wall, but one that was intangible and more or less transparent: he could make out vague outlines of what lay beyond that dizzying shield of light, a blurry landscape that should have been basically the same on the Spook side of the line as it was over here, low sandy hills, gray splotches of sagebrush, sprawling clumps of prickly pear, but which was in fact mysteriously touched by strangeness – unfamiliar serrated buttes, angular chasms with metallic blue-green walls, black-trunked leafless trees with rigid branches jutting out like horizontal crossbars. Everything was veiled, though, by the glow of the barrier that separated the Occupied Zone from the fragment of the former United States that lay to the west of it, and he couldn't be sure how much he was actually seeing and how much was simply the product of his expectant imagination.

A shiver of distaste ran through him. Demeris's father, who was dead now, had always regarded the Spooks as his personal enemy, and that had carried over to him. 'They're just biding their time, Nick,' his father would say. 'One of these days they'll come across the line and grab our land the way they grabbed what they've got already. And there won't be a goddamned thing we can do about it.' Demeris had dedicated himself ever since to maintaining the order and prosperity of the little ranch near the eastern border of Free Country that was his family heritage, and he loathed the Spooks, not just for what they

221

had done but simply because they were hateful – unknown, strange, unimaginable, alien. Not-us. Others were able to take the aliens and the regime they had imposed on the old USA for granted: all that had happened long ago, ancient history. In any case there had never been a hint that the elder Demeris's fears were likely to be realized. The Spooks kept to themselves inside the Occupied Zone. In a hundred fifty years they had shown no sign of interest in expanding beyond the territory they had seized right at the beginning.

He took another step forward, and another, and waited for things to come into better focus. But they didn't.

Demeris had made the first part of the journey from Albuquerque to Spook Land on muleback, with his brother Bud accompanying him as far as the west bank of the Pecos. But when they reached the river Demeris had sent Bud back with the mules. Bud was five years younger than Demeris, but he had three kids already. Men who had kids had no business going into Spook territory. You were supposed to go across when you were a kid yourself, for a lark, for a stunt.

Demeris had had no time for larks and stunts when he was younger. His parents had died when he was a boy, leaving him to raise his two small sisters and three younger brothers. By the time they were grown he was too old to be very interested in adventures in the Occupied Zone. But then this last June his youngest brother Tom, who had just turned eighteen, an unpredictable kid whose head seemed stuffed with all sorts of incomprehensible fantasies and incoherent yearnings, had gone off to make his Entrada. That was what New Mexicans called someone's first crossing of the border – a sort of rite of passage, the thing you did to show that you had become an adult. Demeris had never seen what was particularly adult about going to Spook Land, but he saw such things differently from most people. So Tom had gone in.

He hadn't come out, though.

The traditional length of time for an Entrada was thirty days. Tom had been gone three months now. Worry over Tom nagged at Demeris like an aching tooth. Tom was his reckless baby. Always had been, always would be. And so Demeris had decided to go in after him. Someone had to fetch Tom out of that place, and Demeris, the head of the family, the one who had always seemed to seek out responsibilities the way other people looked for shade on a sunny day, had appointed himself the one to do it. His father would have expected that of him. And Demeris was the only member of the family besides Tom himself who had never married, who had no kids, who could afford to take a risk.

What you do, Bud had said, is walk right up to the barrier and keep on going no matter what you may see or feel or think you want to do. 'They'll throw all sorts of stuff at you,' Bud had told him. 'Don't pay it any mind. Just keep on going.'

And now he was there, at the barrier zone itself.

You walk right up to it and keep on going, that was what you had to do. No matter what it did, what it threw at you.

Okay. Demeris walked right up to it. He kept on going.

The moment he stepped through the fringes of the field he felt it starting to attack him. It came on in undulating waves, the way he imagined an earthquake would, shaking him unrelentingly and making him slip and slide and struggle to stay upright. The air around him turned thick and yellow and he couldn't see more than a couple of yards in any direction. Just in front of him was a shimmering blood-hued blur that abruptly resolved itself into an army of scarlet caterpillars looping swiftly toward him over the ground, millions of them, a blazing carpet. They spread out all around him. Little teeth were gnashing in their pop-eyed heads and they made angry, muttering sounds as they approached. There was no avoiding them. He walked in among them and it was like walking on a sea of slime. A kind of growling thunder rose from them as he crushed them under foot. 'Bad dreams,' Bud was saying, in his ear, in his brain. 'All they are is a bunch of bad dreams.' Sure. Demeris forged onward. How deep was the boundary strip, anyway? Twenty yards? Fifty? He ached in a dozen places, his eyes were stinging, his teeth seemed to be coming loose. Beyond the caterpillars he found himself at the edge of an abyss of pale quivering jelly, but there was no turning back. He compelled himself into it and its substance rose up around him like a soft blanket, and a wave of pain swept upward through him from the scrotum to the back of his neck: to avoid it he pivoted and twisted, and he felt his backbone bending as if it was going to pop out of his flesh the way the fishbone comes away from the filleted meat. Stinking rain swept horizontally over him, and then hot sleet that raked his forehead and drew howls of rage from him. No wonder you couldn't get a mule to cross this barrier, he thought. Head down, gasping for breath, he pushed himself forward another few steps. Something like a crab with wings came fluttering up out of a steaming mudhole and seized his arm, biting it just below the elbow on the inside. A stream of black blood spurted out. He yelled and flapped his arm until he shook the thing off. The pain lit a track of fire all along his arm, up to the shoulder and doubling back to his twitching fingers. He stared at his hand and saw just a knob of raw meat with blackened sticks jutting from it. Then it flickered and looked whole again.

He felt tears on his cheeks, and that amazed him: the last time he had wept was when his father died, years ago. Suddenly the urge arose in him to give up and turn back while he still could. That surprised him too. It had always been his way to go plugging ahead, doing what needed to be done, even when others were telling him, Demeris, don't be an asshole, Demeris, don't push yourself so hard, Demeris, let someone else do it for once. He had only shrugged. Let others slough off if they liked: he just didn't have the knack of it. Now, here, in this place, when he absolutely could not slough off, he felt the temptation to yield and go back. But he knew it was only the barrier playing devil-tricks with him. So he encapsulated the desire to turn back into a hard little shell and hurled it from him and watched it burn up in a puff of flame. And went onward.

Three suns were blazing overhead, a red one, a green one, a blue. The air seemed to be melting. He heard incomprehensible chattering voices coming out of it like demonic static, and then disembodied faces were hovering all around him suddenly, jittering and shimmering in the soupy murk, the faces of people he knew, his sisters Ellie and Netta, his nieces and nephews, his friends. He cried out to them. But everyone was horridly distorted, blobby-cheeked and bug-eyed, grotesque fun-house images. They were pointing at him and laughing. Then he saw his father and mother pointing and laughing too, which had to be impossible, and he understood. Bud was right: these were nothing but illusions or maybe delusions. The images he was seeing were things that he carried within him. Part of him. Harmless.

He began to run, plunging on through a tangle of slippery threads, a kind of soft, spongy curtain. It yielded as he ripped at it and he fell face down onto a bank of dry sandy soil that was unremarkable in every way: mere desert dirt, real-world stuff, no fancy colors, no crazy textures. More trickery? No. No, this was real. The extra suns were gone and the one that remained was the yellow one he had always known. A fresh wind blew against his face. He was across. He had made it.

He lay still for a minute or two, catching his breath.

Hot stabs of pain were coming from his arm, and when he looked down at it he saw a jagged bloody cut high up near the inside of the elbow, where he had imagined the crab-thing had bitten him. But the crab-thing had been only a dream, only an illusion. Can an illusion bite? he wondered. The pain, at any rate, was no illusion. Demeris felt it all the way up through the back of his throat, his nostrils, his forehead. A nasty pulsation was running through the whole arm, making his hand quiver rhythmically in time with it. The cut was maybe two inches long, and deep enough to see into. Fresh blood came dribbling from it every time his heart pumped. Fine, he thought, I'll bleed to death from an imaginary cut before I'm ten feet inside the Occupied Zone. But after a moment the wound began to clot over and the bleeding stopped, though the pain remained.

Shakily he stood up and glanced about.

Behind him was the vertical column of the barrier field, looking no more menacing than a searchlight beam from this side. Dimly he saw the desert flatlands of Free Country beyond it, the scrubby ordinary place from which he had just come.

On this side, though, everything was a realm of magic and mysteries.

He was able more or less to make out the basic raw material of the landscape, the underlying barren dry New Mexico/Texas nowheresville that he had spent his entire life in. But here on the far side of the barrier the invaders had done some serious screwing around with the look of the land. The jag-edged buttes and blue-green arroyos that Demeris had glimpsed through the barrier field from the other side were no illusions; somebody had taken the trouble to come out here and redesign the empty terrain, sticking in all sorts of bizarre structures and features. He saw strange zones of oddly colored soil, occasional ramshackle metal towers, entire deformed geological formations – twisted cones and spiky spires and uplifted layers – that made his eyes hurt. He saw groves of unknown wire-leaved trees and arroyos crisscrossed by sinister glossy black threads like stitches across a wound. Everything was solid and real, none of it wiggling and shifting about the way things did inside the barrier field. Wherever he looked there was evidence of how the conquerors had put their mark on the land. Some of it was actually almost beautiful, he thought; and then he recoiled, astonished at his own reaction. But there *was* a strange sort of beauty in the alien landscape. It disgusted him and moved him all at once, a response so complex that he scarcely knew how to handle it.

They must have been trying to make the landscape look like the place they had originally come from, he told himself. The idea of a whole world looking that way practically nauseated him. What they had done was a downright affront. Land was something to live on and to use productively, not to turn into a toy. They didn't have any right to take part of ours and make it look like theirs, he thought, and anger rose in him again.

He thought of his ranch, the horses, the turkeys, the barns, the ten acres of good russet soil, the rows of crops ripening in the autumn sun, the fencing that he had made with his own hands running on beyond the line of virtually identical fencing his father had made. All that was a real kind of reality, ordinary, familiar, solid – something he could not only understand but love. It was home, family, good clean hard work, sanity itself. This, though, this – this lunacy, this horror –

He tore a strip of cloth from one of the shirts in his backpack and tied it around the cut on his arm. And started walking east, toward the place where he hoped his brother Tom would be, toward the big settlement midway between the former site of Amarillo and the former site of Lubbock that was known as Spook City.

He kept alert for alien wildlife, constantly scanning to front and rear, sniffing, watching for tracks. The Spooks had brought a bunch of their jungle beasts from their home world and turned them loose in the desert. 'It's like Africa out there,' Bud had said. 'You never know what's going to come up and try to gobble you.' Once a year, Demeris knew, the aliens held a tremendous hunt on the outskirts of Spook City, a huge apocalyptic round-up where they surrounded and killed the strange beasts by the thousands and the streets ran blue and green with rivers of their blood. The rest of the time the animals roamed free in the hinterlands. Some of them occasionally strayed across the border barrier and went wandering around on the Free Country side: while he was preparing himself for his journey Demeris had visited a ranch near Bernalillo where a dozen or so of them were kept on display as a sort of zoo of nightmares, grisly things with red scaly necks and bird-beaks and ears like rubber batwings and tentacles on their heads, huge ferocious animals that seemed to have been put together randomly out of a stock of miscellaneous parts. But so far out here he had encountered nothing more threatening-looking than jackrabbits and lizards. Now and again a bird that was not a bird passed overhead – one of the big snake-necked things he had seen earlier, and another the size of an eagle with four transparent veined wings like a dragonfly's but a thick moth-like furry body between them, and a third one that had half a dozen writhing prehensile rat-tails dangling behind it for eight or ten feet, trolling for food. He watched it snatch a shrieking bluejay out of the air as though it were a bug.

When he was about three hours into the Occupied Zone he came to a cluster of bedraggled little adobe houses at the bottom of a bowl-shaped depression that had the look of a dry lake. A thin fringe of scrubby plant growth surrounded the place, ordinary things, creosote bush and mesquite and yucca. Demeris saw some horses standing at a trough, a couple of scrawny black and white cows munching on prickly pears, a few half-naked children running circles in the dust. There was nothing alien about them, or about the buildings or the wagons and storage bins that were scattered all around. Everyone knew that Spooks were shapeshifters, that they could take on human form when the whim suited them, that when the advance guard of infiltrators had first entered the United States to prepare the way for the invasion they were all wearing human guise. But more likely this was a village of genuine humans. Bud had said there were a few little towns between the border and Spook City, inhabited by the descendants of those who had chosen to remain in the Occupied Zone after the conquest. Most people with any sense had moved out when the invaders came, even though the aliens hadn't formally asked anyone to leave. But some had stayed.

The afternoon was well along and the first chill of evening was beginning to creep into the clear dry air. The cut on his arm was still throbbing and he didn't feel much like camping in the open if he didn't have to. Perhaps these people would let him crash for the night.

When he was halfway to the bottom of the dirt road a gnomish little leathery-skinned man who looked to be about ninety years old stepped slowly out from behind a gnarled mesquite bush and took up a watchful position in the middle of the path. A moment later a boy of about sixteen, short and stocky in torn denim pants and a frayed undershirt, emerged from the same place. The boy was carrying what might have been a gun, which at a gesture from the older man he raised and aimed. It was a shiny tube a foot and a half long with a nozzle at one end and a squeeze-bulb at the other. The nozzle pointed squarely at the middle of Demeris's chest. Demeris stopped short and put his hands in the air.

The old man said something in a language that was full of grunts and clicks, and some whistling snorts. The denim boy nodded and replied in the same language.

To Demeris the boy said, 'You traveling by yourself?' He was dark-haired, dark-eyed, mostly Indian or Mexican, probably. A ragged red scar ran up along his cheek to his forehead.

Demeris kept his hands up. 'By myself, yes. I'm from the other side.'

'Well, sure you are. Fool could see that.' The boy's tone was thick, his accent unfamiliar, the end of each word clipped off in an odd way.

Demeris had to work to understand him. 'You making your Entrada? You a little old for that sort of thing, maybe.' Laughter sparkled in the boy's eyes, but not anywhere else on his face.

'This is my first time across,' Demeris said. 'But it isn't exactly an Entrada.'

'Your first time, that's an Entrada.' The boy spoke again to the old man and got a long reply. Demeris waited patiently. Finally the boy turned back to him and said, 'Okay. Remigio here says we should make it easy for you. You want to stay here your thirty days, we let you do it. You work as a field hand, that's all. We even sell you some Spook things you can take back and show off like all you people do. Okay?'

Demeris's face grew hot. 'I told you, this isn't any Entrada. Entradas are fun and games for kids. I'm not a kid.'

'Then what are you doing here?'

'Trying to find my brother.'

The boy frowned and spat into the dusty ground, not quite in Demeris's direction. 'You think we got your brother here?'

'He's in Spook City, I think.'

'Spook City. Yeah. I bet that's where he is. They all go there. For the hunt, they go.' He put his finger to his head and moved it in a circle. 'You do that, you got to be a little crazy, you know? Going there for the hunt. Sheesh! What dumb crazy fuckers.' He laughed and said, 'Well, come on, I'll show you where you can stay.'

The place where they put him up was a tottering weatherbeaten shack made of wooden slats with big stripes of sky showing through, off at the edge of town, a hundred yards or so from the nearest building. There was nothing in it but a mildewed bundle of rags tied together for sleeping on. Some of the rags bore faded inscriptions in the curvilinear Spook script, impenetrable to Demeris. A ditch out back served as a latrine. A little stream, hardly more than a rivulet, ran nearby. Demeris crouched over it and washed out his wound, which was still pulsing unpleasantly but didn't look as bad as it had at first. The water seemed reasonably safe. He took a long drink and filled his canteens. Then he sat quietly in the open doorway of the shack for a time, not thinking of anything at all, simply unwinding from his long day's march and the border crossing.

As darkness fell the boy reappeared and led him to the communal eating hall. Fifty or sixty people were sitting at long benches in family groups. A few had an Anglo look, most seemed mixed Mexican and Indian. There was little conversation, and what there was was in the local language, all clicks and snorts and whistles. Almost nobody paid any attention to him. It was as if he was invisible; but a few did stare at him now and then and he could feel the force of their hostility, an almost intangible thing.

He ate quickly and went back to his shack. But sleep was a tough proposition. He lay awake for hours, listening to the wind blowing in out of Texas and wishing he was home, on his own ten acres, in his familiar adobe house, with the houses of his brothers and sisters around him. For a while there was singing – chanting, really – coming up from the village. It was harsh and guttural and choppy, a barrage of stiff angular sounds that didn't follow any musical scale he knew. Listening to it, he felt a powerful sense of the strangeness of these people who had lived under Spook rule for so long, tainted by Spook ways, governed by Spook ideas. How had they survived? How had they been able to stand it, the changes, the sense of being owned? But somehow they had adapted, by turning themselves into something beyond his understanding.

Later, other sounds drifted to him, the night sounds of the desert, hoots and whines and screeches that might have been coming from owls and coyotes, but probably weren't. He thought he heard noise just outside his shack, people moving around doing something, but he was too groggy to get up and see what was going on. At last he fell into a sort of stupor and lay floating in it until dawn. Just before morning he dreamed he was a boy again, with his mother and father still alive and Dave and Bud and the girls just babies and Tom not yet even born. He and his dad were out on the plains hunting Spooks, vast swarms of gleaming vaporous Spooks that were drifting overhead as thick as mosquitoes, two brave men walking side by side, the big one and the smaller one, killing the thronging aliens with dart guns that popped them like balloons.

When they died they gave off a screeching sound like metal on metal and released a smell like rotting eggs and plummeted to the ground, covering it with a glassy scum that quickly melted away and left a scorched and flaking surface behind. It was a very satisfying dream. Then a flood of morning light broke through the slats and woke him.

Emerging from the shack, he discovered a small tent pitched about twenty yards away that hadn't been there the night before. A huge mottled yellow animal was tethered nearby, grazing on weeds; something that might have been a camel except there weren't any camels the size of elephants, camels with three shallow humps and great goggling green eyes the size of saucers, or knees on the backs of their legs as well as in front. As he gaped at it a woman wearing tight khaki slacks and a shirt buttoned up to the collar came out of the tent and said, 'Never seen one of those before?'

'You bet I haven't. This is my first time across.'

'Is it, now?' she said. She had an accent too. It wasn't as strange to Demeris as the village boy's but there was some other kind of spin to it, a sound like that of a tolling bell beneath the patterns of the words themselves.

She was youngish, slender, not bad-looking: long straight brown hair, high cheekbones, tanned Anglo face. It was hard to guess her age. Somewhere between twenty-five and thirty-five was the best he could figure. She had very dark eyes, bright, almost glossy, oddly defiant. It seemed to him that there was a kind of aura around her, a puzzling crackle of simultaneous attraction and repulsion.

She told him what the camel-thing was called. The word was an intricate slurred sound midway between a whistle and a drone, rising sharply at the end. 'You do it now,' she said. Demeris looked at her blankly. The sound was impossible to imitate. 'Go on. Do it.'

'I don't speak Spook.'

'It's not all that hard.' She made the sound again. Her eyes flashed with amusement.

'Never mind. I can't do it.'

'You just need some practice.'

Her gaze was focused right on his, strong, direct, almost aggressive.

231

At home he didn't know many women who looked at you like that. He was accustomed to having women depend on him, to draw strength or whatever else they needed from him until they were ready to go on their way and let him go on his.

'My name's Jill,' she said. 'I live in Spook City. I've been in Texas a few weeks and now I'm on my way back.'

'Nick Demeris. From Albuquerque. Traveling up that way too.'

'What a coincidence.'

'I suppose,' he said.

A sudden hot fantasy sprang up just then out of nowhere within him: instant sexual chemistry had stricken her like a thunderbolt and she was going to invite him to travel with her, that they'd ride right off into the desert together, that when they made camp that evening she would turn to him with parted lips and shining eyes and open her arms and beckon him toward her –

The urgency and intensity of the idea surprised him as much as its adolescent foolishness. Had he really let himself get as horny as that? She didn't even seem that interesting to him.

In any case he knew it wasn't going to happen. She looked cool, self-sufficient, self-contained. She wouldn't have any need for his companionship on her trip home and probably not for anything else he might have to offer.

'What brings you over here?' she asked him.

He told her about his missing brother. Her eyes narrowed thoughtfully as he spoke. She was taking a good long look, studying his face with great care, staring at him as though peering right through his skull into his brain. Turning her head this way and that, checking him out.

'I think I may know him, your brother,' she said calmly, after a time.

He blinked. 'You do? Seriously?'

'Not as tall as you and stockier, right? But otherwise he looks pretty much like you, only younger. Face a lot like yours, broader, but the same cheekbones, the same high forehead, the same color eyes, the same blond hair, but his is longer. The same very serious expression all the time, tight as a drum.'

'Yes,' Demeris said, with growing wonder. 'That's him. It has to be.'

'Don, that was his name. No, Tom. Don, Tom, one of those short little names.'

'Tom.'

'Tom, right.'

He was amazed. 'How do you know him?' he asked.

'Turned up in Spook City a couple of months back. June, July, somewhere back then. It isn't such a big place that you don't notice new people when they come in. Had that Free Country look about him, you know. Kind of big-eyed, raw-boned, can't stop gawking at things. But he seemed a little different from most of the other Entrada kids, like there was something coiled up inside him that was likely to pop out any minute, that this trip wasn't just a thing he was doing for the hell of it but that it had some other meaning for him, something deeper that only he could understand. Peculiar sort of guy, actually.'

'That was Tom, yes.' The side of Demeris's face was starting to twitch. 'You think he might still be there?'

'Could be. More likely than not. He was talking about staying quite a while, at least until fall, until hunt time.'

'And when is that?'

'It starts late next week.'

'Maybe I can still find him, then. If I can get there in time.'

'I'm leaving here this afternoon. You can ride with me to Spook City if you want.'

'With you?' Demeris said. He was astonished. The good old instant chemistry after all? His whole little adolescent fantasy coming to life? It seemed too neat, too slick. The world didn't work like this. And yet – yet –

'Sure. Plenty of room on those humps. Take you at least a week if you walk there, if you're a good walker. Maybe longer. Riding, it'll be just a couple of days.'

What the hell, he thought.

It would be dumb to turn her down. That Spook-mauled landscape was an evil place when you were on your own.

233

'Sure,' he said, after a bit. 'Sure, I'd be glad to. If you really mean it.'

'Why would I say it if I didn't mean it?'

Abruptly the notion came to him that this woman and Tom might have had something going for a while in Spook City. Of course. Of course. Why else would she remember in such detail some unknown kid who had wandered into her town months before? There had to be something else there. She must have met Tom in some Spook City bar, a couple of drinks, some chatter, a night or two of lively bed games, maybe even a romance lasting a couple of weeks. Tom wouldn't hesitate, even with a woman ten, fifteen years older than he was. And so she was offering him this ride now as a courtesy to a member of the family, so to speak. It wasn't his tremendous masculine appeal that had done it, it was mere politeness. Or curiosity about what Tom's older brother might be like.

Into his long confused silence she said, 'The critter here needs a little more time to feed itself up. Then we can take off. Around two o'clock, okay?'

After breakfast the boy went over to him in the dining hall and said, 'You meet the woman who come in during the night?'

Demeris nodded. 'She's offering me a ride to Spook City.'

Something that might have been scorn flickered across the boy's face. 'That nice. You take it?'

'Better than walking there, isn't it?'

A quick knowing glance. 'You crazy if you go with her, man.'

Demeris said, frowning, 'Why is that?'

The boy put his hand over his mouth and muffled a laugh. 'That woman, she a Spook, man. You mean you don't see that? Only a damn fool go traveling around with a Spook.'

Demeris was stunned for a moment, and then angry. 'Don't play around with me,' he said, irritated.

'Yeah, man. I'm playing. It's a joke. Just a joke.' The boy's voice was flat, chilly, bearing its own built-in contradiction. The contempt in his dark hard eyes was unmistakable now. 'Look, you go ride with her if you like. Let her do whatever she wants with you once she

234

got you out there in the desert. Isn't none of my goddamn business. Fucking Free Country guys, you all got shit for brains.'

Demeris squinted at him, shaken now, not sure what to believe. The kid's cold-eyed certainty carried tremendous force. But it made no sense to him that this Jill could be an alien. Her voice, her bearing, everything about her, were too convincingly real. The Spooks couldn't imitate humans that well, could they?

Had they?

'You know this thing for a fact?' Demeris asked.

'For a fact I don't know shit,' the boy said. 'I never see her before, not that I can say. She come around and she wants us to put her up for the night, that's okay. We put her up. We don't care what she is if she can pay the price. But anybody with any sense, he can smell Spook on her. That's all I tell you. You do whatever you fucking like, man.'

The boy strolled away. Demeris stared after him, shaking his head. He felt a tremor of bewilderment and shock, as though he had abruptly found himself looking over the edge of an abyss.

Then came another jolt of anger. Jill a Spook? It couldn't be. Everything about her seemed human.

But why would the boy make up something like that? He had no reason for it. And maybe the kid *could* tell. Over on the other side, really paranoid people carried witch-charms around with them to detect Spooks who might be roaming Free Country in disguise, little gadgets that were supposed to sound an alarm when aliens came near you, but Demeris had never taken such things seriously. It stood to reason, though, that people living out here in Spook Land would be sensitive to the presence of a Spook among them, however well disguised it might be. They wouldn't need any witch-charms to tell them. They had had a hundred fifty years to get used to being around Spooks. They'd know the smell of them by now.

The more Demeris thought about it, the more uneasy he got.

He needed to talk to her again.

He found her a little way upstream from his shack, rubbing down the shaggy yellow flanks of her elephantine pack-animal with a rough sponge. Demeris halted a short distance away and studied her, trying to see her as an alien being in disguise, searching for some clue to otherworldly origin, some gleam of Spookness showing through her human appearance.

He couldn't see it. He couldn't see it at all. But that didn't necessarily mean she was real.

After a moment she noticed him. 'You ready to go?' she asked, over her shoulder.

'I'm not sure.'

'What?'

He was still staring.

If she *is* a Spook, he thought, why would she want to pretend she was human? What would a Spook have to gain by inveigling a human off into the desert with her?

On the other hand, what motive did the kid have for lying to him?

Suddenly it seemed to him that the simplest and safest thing was to opt out of the entire arrangement and get to Spook City on his own, as he had originally planned. The kid might just be telling the truth. The possibility of traveling with a Spook, of being close to one, of sharing a campsite and a tent with one, sickened and repelled him. And there might be danger in it as well. He had heard wild tales of Spooks who were soul-eaters, who were energy vampires, even worse things. Why take chances?

He drew a deep breath. 'Listen, I've changed my mind, okay? I think I'd just as soon travel by myself.'

She turned and gave him a startled look. 'You serious?'

'Yep.'

'You really want to walk all the way to Spook City by yourself rather than ride with me?'

'Yep. That's what I prefer to do.'

'Jesus Christ. What the hell *for*?'

Demeris could detect nothing in the least unhuman in her exasperated tone or in the annoyed expression on her face. He began to think he was making a big, big mistake. But it was too late to back off. Uncomfortably he said, 'Just the way I am, I guess. I sort of like to go my own way, I guess, and –'

'Bullshit. I know what's really going on in your head.'

Demeris shifted about uneasily and remained silent. He wished he had never become entangled with her in the first place.

Angrily she said, 'Somebody's been talking to you, right? Telling you a lot of garbage?'

'Well –'

'All right,' she said. 'You dumb bastard. You want to test me, is that it?'

'Test?'

'With a witch-charm.'

'No,' he said. 'I'm not carrying any charms. I don't have faith in them. Those things aren't worth a damn.'

'They'll tell you if I'm a Spook or not.'

'They don't work, is what I hear.'

'Some do, some don't.' She reached into a saddlepack lying near her on the ground and pulled out a small device, wires and black cords intricately wound around and around each other. 'Here,' she said harshly. 'This is one. You point it and push the button and it emits a red glow if you're pointing it at a Spook. Take it. A gift from me to you. Use it to check out the next woman you happen to meet.'

She tossed the little gadget toward him. Demeris grabbed it out of the air by reflex and stood watching helplessly as she slapped the elephant-camel's flank to spur it into motion and started off downstream toward her tent.

Shit, he thought.

He felt like six kinds of idiot. The sound of her voice, tingling with contempt for him and his petty little suspicions, still echoed in his ears.

Baffled and annoyed – with her, with himself, with the boy for starting all this up – he flipped the witch-charm into the stream. There was a hissing and a bubbling around it for a moment and then the thing sank out of sight. Then he turned and walked back to his shack to pack up.

She had already begun to take down her tent. She didn't so much as glance at him. But the elephant-camel thing peered somberly around, extended its long purple lower lip, and gave him a sardonic toothy smirk. Demeris glared at the great beast and made a devil-sign with his upraised fingers. From you, at least, I don't have to take any crap, he thought.

He hoisted his pack to his shoulders and started up the steep trail out of town.

He was somewhere along the old boundary between New Mexico and Texas, he figured, probably just barely on the New Mexico side of the line. The aliens hadn't respected state boundaries when they had carved out their domain in the middle of the United States halfway through the 21st century, and some of New Mexico had landed in alien territory and some hadn't. Spook Land was roughly triangular, running from Montana to the Great Lakes along the Canadian border and tapering southward through what had been Wyoming, Nebraska, and Iowa down to Texas and Louisiana, but they had taken a little piece of eastern New Mexico too. Demeris had learned all that in school long ago. They made you study the map of the United States that once had been: so you wouldn't forget the past, they said, because some day the old United States was going to rise again.

Fat chance. The Spooks had cut the heart right out of the country, both literally and figuratively. They had taken over with scarcely a struggle and every attempt at a counterattack had been brushed aside with astonishing ease: America's weapons had been neutralized, its communications networks were silenced, its army of liberation had disappeared into the Occupied Zone like raindrops into a lake. Now there was not one United States of America but two: the western one, which ran from Washington State and Idaho down to the Mexican border and liked to call itself Free Country, and the other one in the east, along the coast and inland as far as the Mississippi, which still insisted on using the old formal name. Between the two lay the Occupied Zone, and nobody in either United States had much knowledge of what went on in there. Nor did anyone Demeris knew take the notion of a reunited United States very seriously. If America hadn't been able to cope with the aliens at the time of the invasion, it was if anything less capable of defeating them now, with much of its technical capacity eroded away and great chunks of the country having reverted to a pastoral, pre-industrial condition.

What he had to do, he calculated, was keep heading more or less easterly until he saw indications of Spook presence. Right now, though, the country was pretty empty, just barren sandy wastes with a covering of mesquite and sage. He saw more places where the aliens had indulged in their weird remodeling of the landscape, and now and again he was able to make out the traces of some little ancient abandoned human town, a couple of rusty signs or a few crumbling walls. But mainly there was nothing at all.

He was about an hour and a half beyond the village when what looked like a squadron of airborne snakes came by, a dozen of them flying in close formation. Then the sky turned heavy and purplish-yellow, like bruised fruit getting ready to rot, and three immense things with shining red scales and sail-like three-cornered fleshy wings passed overhead, emitting bursts of green gas that had the rank smell of old wet straw. They were almost like dragons. A dozen more of the snake-things followed them. Demeris scowled and waved a clenched fist at them. The air had a tangible pressure. Something bad was about to happen. He waited to see what was coming next. But then, magically, all the ominous effects cleared away and he was in the familiar old Southwest again, untouched by strangers from the far stars, the good old land of dry ravines and big sky that he had lived in all his life. He relaxed a little, but only a little.

Almost at once he heard a familiar snorting sound behind him. He turned and saw the ponderous yellow form of the elephant-camel looming up, with Jill sitting astride it just back of the front hump.

She leaned down and said, 'You change your mind yet about wanting that ride?'

'I thought you were sore at me.'

'I am. Was. But it still seems crazy for you to be doing this on foot when I've got room up here for you.'

He stared up at her. You don't often get second chances in this life, he told himself. But he wasn't sure what to do.

'Oh, Christ,' she said, as he hesitated. 'Do you want a ride or don't you?'

Still he remained silent.

She shot him a quick wicked grin. 'Still worried that I'm a Spook? You can check me out if you like.'

'I threw your gadget in the stream. I don't like to have witch-things around me.'

'Well, that's all right.' She laughed. 'It wasn't a charm at all, just an old power core, and a worn out one at that. It wouldn't have told you anything.'

'What's a power core?'

'Spook stuff. You could have taken it back with you to prove you were over here. Look, do you want a ride or not?'

It seemed ridiculous to turn her down again.

'What the hell,' Demeris said. 'Sure.'

Jill spoke to the animal in what he took to be Spook language, a hiccuping wheeze and a long indrawn whistling sound, and it knelt for him. Demeris took her hand and she drew him on top of the beast with surprising ease. An openwork construction made of loosely woven cord, half poncho and half saddle, lay across the creature's broad back, with the three humps jutting through. Her tent and other possessions were fastened to it at the rear. 'Tie your pack to one of those dangling strings,' she said. 'You can ride right behind me.'

He fitted himself into the valley between the second and third humps and got a secure hold on the weaving, fingers digging down deep into it. She whistled another command and the animal began to move forward.

Its motion was a rolling, thumping, sliding kind of thing, very hard to take. The sway was both lateral and vertical and with every step the ground seemed to rise and plunge around him in lunatic lunges. Demeris had never seen the ocean or any other large body of water, but he had heard about seasickness, and this was what he imagined it was like. He gulped, clamped his mouth shut, gripped the saddle even more tightly.

Jill called back to him, 'How are you doing?'

'Fine. Fine.'

'Takes some getting used to, huh?'

'Some,' he said.

His buttocks didn't have much padding on them. He could feel the vast bones of the elephant-camel grinding beneath him like the pistons of some giant machine. He held on tight and dug his heels in as hard as he could.

'You see those delta-winged things go by a little while ago?' she asked, after a while.

'The big dragons that were giving off the green smoke?'

'Right. Herders is what they are. On their way to Spook City for the hunt. They'll be used to drive the game toward the killing grounds. Every year this time they get brought in to help in the round-up.'

'And the flying snakes?'

'They herd the herders. Herders aren't very smart. About like dogs, maybe. The snake guys are a lot brighter. The snakes tell the herders where to go and the herders make the game animals go there too.'

Demeris thought about that. Level upon level of intelligence among these creatures that the Spooks had transported to the planet they had partly conquered. If the herders were as smart as dogs, he wondered how smart the snakes were. Dogs were pretty smart. He wondered how smart the Spooks were, for that matter.

'What's the hunt all about? Why do they do it?'

'For fun,' Jill said. 'Spook fun.'

'Herding thousands of exotic wild animals together and butchering them all at once, so the blood runs deep enough to swim through? That's their idea of fun?'

'Wait and see,' she said.

They saw more and more transformation of the landscape: whorls and loops of dazzling fire, great opaque spheres floating just above ground level, silvery blades revolving in the air. Demeris glared and glowered. All that strangeness made him feel vulnerable and out of place, and he spat and murmured bitterly at each intrusive wonder.

'Why are you so angry?' she asked.

'I hate this weird shit that they've strewn all over the place. I hate what they did to our country.'

'It was a long time ago. And it wasn't your country they did it to, it was your great-great-grandfather's.'

241

'Even so.'

'Your country is over there. It wasn't touched at all.'

'Even so,' he said again, and spat.

When it was still well before dark they came to a place where bright yellow outcroppings of sulphur, like foamy stone pillows, marked the site of a spring. Jill gave the command to make her beast kneel and hopped deftly to the ground. Demeris got off more warily, feeling the pain in his thighs and butt from his ride.

'Give me a hand with the tent,' she said.

It wasn't like any tent he had ever seen. The centerpost was nothing more than a little rod that seemed to be made of white wax, but at the touch of a hand it tripled in height and an elaborate strutwork sprang out from it in five directions to provide support for the tent fabric. A Spook tent, he supposed. The tent pegs were made of the same waxy material, and all you had to do was position them where you wanted them around the perimeter of the tent and they burrowed into the ground on their own. Faint pinging sounds came from them as they dug themselves in.

'What's that?' he asked.

'Security check. The pegs are setting up a defensive zone for a hundred yards around us. Don't try to go through it in the night.'

'I'm not going anywhere,' Demeris said.

The tent was just about big enough for two. He wondered whether she was going to invite him to sleep inside it.

Together they gathered mesquite brush and built a fire, and she produced some packets of powdered vegetables and a slab of dried meat for their dinner. While they waited for things to cook Jill went to the spring, which despite the sulphurous outcroppings gave fresh, pure water, and crouched by it, stripping to the waist to wash herself. Seeing her like that was unsettling. He flicked a quick glance at her as she bathed, but she didn't seem to care, or even to notice. That was unsettling too. Was she being deliberately provocative? Or did she just not give a damn?

He washed himself also, splashing handfuls of the cold water into his face and over his sweaty shoulders. 'Dinner's ready,' she said a few minutes later.

Darkness descended swiftly. The sky went from deep blue to utter black in minutes. In the clear desert air the stars began quickly to emerge, sharp and bright and unflickering. He looked up at them, trying to guess which of them might be the home star of the Spooks. They had never troubled to reveal that. They had never revealed very much of anything about themselves.

As they ate he asked her whether she made this trip often. 'Often enough,' she said. 'I do a lot of courier work for my father, out to Texas, Louisiana, sometimes Oklahoma.' She paused a moment. 'I'm Ben Gorton's daughter,' she said, as though she expected him to recognize the name.

'Sorry. Who?'

'Ben Gorton. The mayor of Spook City, actually.'

'Spook City's got a human mayor?'

'The human part of it does. The Spooks have their administration and we have ours.'

'Ah,' Demeris said. 'I'm honored, then. The boss's daughter. You should have told me before.'

'It didn't seem important,' she said.

They were done with their meal. She moved efficiently around the campsite, gathering utensils, burying trash. Demeris was sure now that the village boy had simply been playing with his head. He told himself that if Jill was really a Spook he'd have sensed it somehow by this time.

When the cleanup work was done she lifted the tent flap and stepped halfway inside. He held back, unsure of the right move. 'Well?' she asked. 'It's okay to come in. Or would you rather sleep out there?'

Demeris went in. Though the temperature outside was plunging steeply with the onset of night, it was pleasantly warm inside. There was a single bedroll, just barely big enough for two if they didn't mind sleeping very close together. He heard the sounds she made as she undressed, and tried in the absolute darkness to guess how much she was taking off. It wasn't easy to tell. He removed his own shirt and hesitated with his jeans; but then she opened the flap again to call something out to the elephant-camel, which she had tethered just outside, and by starlight he caught a flashing glimpse of bare thigh,

243

bare buttock. He pulled off his trousers and slipped into the bedroll. She joined him a moment later. He lay awkwardly, trying to avoid rubbing up against her. For a time there was a tense expectant silence. Then her hand reached out in the darkness and grazed his shoulder, lightly but clearly not accidentally. Demeris didn't need a second hint. He had never taken any vows of chastity. He reached for her, found the hollow of her clavicle, trailed his hand downward until he was cupping a small, cool breast, resilient and firm. When he ran his thumb lightly across the nipples she made a little purring sound, and he felt the flesh quickly hardening. As was his. She turned to him. Demeris had some difficulty locating her mouth in the darkness, and she had to guide him, chuckling a little, but when his lips met hers he felt the immediate flicker of her tongue coming forth to greet him.

And then almost as though he was willing his own downfall he found himself perversely wondering if he might be embracing a Spook after all; and a wave of nausea swept through him, making him wobble and soften. But she was pressing tight against him, rubbing her breasts from side to side on him, uttering small eager murmuring sounds, and he got himself quickly back on track, losing himself in her fragrance and warmth and banishing completely from his thoughts anything but the sensations of the moment. After that one attack of doubt everything was easy. He located her long smooth thighs with no problem whatever, and when he glided into her he needed no guidance there either, and though their movements together had the usual first-time clumsiness her hot gusts of breath against his shoulder and her soft sharp outcries told him that all was going well.

He lay awake for a time when it was over, listening to the reassuring pinging of the tent pegs and the occasional far-off cry of some desert creature. He imagined he could hear the heavy snuffling breathing of the elephant-camel too, like a huge recirculating device just outside the tent. Jill had curled up against him as if they were old friends and was lost in sleep.

She said out of the blue, after they had been riding a long while in silence the following morning, 'You ever been married, Nick?'

The incongruity of the question startled him. Until a moment ago she had seemed to be a million miles away. His attempt to make love to her a second time at dawn had been met with indifference and she had been pure business, remote and cool, all during the job of breaking camp and getting on the road.

'No,' he said. 'You?'

'Hasn't been on my program,' she said. 'But I thought everybody in Free Country got married. Nice normal people who settle down early and raise big families.' The elephant-camel swayed and bumped beneath them. They were following a wide dirt track festooned on both sides with glittering strands of what looked like clear jelly, hundreds of feet long, mounted on spiny black poles that seemed to be sprouting like saplings from the ground.

'I raised a big family,' he said. 'My brothers and sisters. Dad got killed in a hunting accident when I was ten. Possibly got mixed up with a Spook animal that was on the wrong side of the line: nobody could quite figure it out. Then my mother came down with Blue Fever. I was fifteen then and five brothers and sisters to look after. Didn't leave me a lot of time to think about finding a wife.'

'Blue Fever?'

'Don't you know what that is? Infectious disease. Kills you in three days, no hope at all. Supposed to be something the Spooks brought.'

'We don't have it over here,' she said. 'Not that I ever heard.'

'Spooks brought it, I guess they must know how to cure it. We aren't that lucky. Anyway, there were all these little kids to look after. Of course, they're grown by now.'

'But you still look after them. Coming over here to try to track down your brother.'

'Somebody has to.'

'What if he doesn't want to be tracked down, though?'

Demeris felt a tremor of alarm. He knew Tom was restless and troubled, but he didn't think he was actually disturbed. 'Have you any reason to think Tom would want to stay over here for good?'

'I didn't say I did. But he might just prefer not to be found. A lot of boys come across and stay across, you know.'

'I didn't know. Nobody I ever heard of did that. Why would someone from Free Country want to live on the Spook side?'

'For the excitement?' she suggested. 'To run with the Spooks? To play their games? To hunt their animals? There's all sorts of minglings going on these days.'

'Is that so,' he said uneasily. He stared at the back of her head. She was so damned odd, he thought, such a fucking mystery.

She said, sounding very far away, 'I wonder about marrying.' Back to that again. 'What it's like, waking up next to the same person every day, day after day. Sharing your life, year after year. It sounds very beautiful. But also kind of strange. It isn't easy for me to imagine what it might be like.'

'Don't they have marriage in Spook City?'

'Not really. Not the way you people do.'

'Well, why don't you try it and see? You don't like it, there are ways to get out of it. Nobody I know thinks that being married is any way strange. Christ, I bet whatever the Spooks do is five hundred times as strange, and you probably think that it's the most normal thing in the world.'

'Spooks don't marry. They don't even have sex, really. What I hear, it's more like the way fishes do it, no direct contact at all.'

'That sounds terrifically appealing. I'd really love to try something like that. All I need is a cute Spook to try it with.' He attempted to keep it light. But she glanced around at him.

'Still suspicious, Nick?'

He let that go by. 'Listen, you could always take a fling at getting married for a while, couldn't you?' he said. 'If you're all that curious about finding out what it's like.'

'Is that an offer, Nick?'

'No,' he said. 'Hardly. Just a suggestion.'

An hour after they set out that morning they passed a site where there was a peculiar purple depression about a hundred yards across at its thickest point. It was vaguely turtle-shaped, a long oval with four stubby projections at the corners and one at each end. 'What the devil is that?' Demeris asked. 'A Spook graveyard?'

'It's new,' she said. 'I've never seen it before.'

Some vagrant curiosity impelled him. 'Can we look?'

She halted the elephant-camel and they jumped down. The site might almost have been a lake, deep-hued and dense against the sandy earth, but there was nothing liquid about it: it was like a stain that ran several yards deep into the ground. Together they walked to the edge. Demeris saw something moving beneath the surface out near the middle, a kind of corkscrew effect, and was about to call it to her attention when abruptly the margin of the site started to quiver and a narrow rubbery arm rose up out of the purpleness and wrapped itself around her left leg. It started to pull her forward. She shrieked and made an odd hissing sound.

Demeris yanked his knife from the scabbard at his belt and sliced through the thing that had seized her. There was a momentary twanging sound and he felt a hot zing go up his arm to the shoulder. The energy of it ricocheted around inside his shirt collar briefly; then it ceased and he staggered back a little way. The part of the ropy arm that had been wrapped around Jill fell away; the rest writhed convulsively before them. He caught her by one wrist and pulled her back.

'It's got to be some kind of trap for game,' he said. 'Or for passing travelers stupid enough to go close. Let's get the hell out of here.'

She was pale and shaky. 'Thanks,' she said simply, as they ran toward the elephant-camel.

Not much of a show of gratitude, he thought.

But at least the incident told him something about her that he needed to know. A Spook trap wouldn't have gone after one of their own, would it?

Would it?

At midday they stopped for lunch in a cottonwood grove that the Spooks had redecorated with huge crystalline mushroom-shaped things. The elephant-camel munched on one and seemed to enjoy it, but Demeris and Jill left them alone. There was a brackish little stream running through the trees, and once again she stripped and cleaned herself. Bathing seemed very important to her and she had no self-consciousness about her nudity. He watched her with cool pleasure from the bank.

Once in a while, during the long hours of the ride, she would break the silence with a quirky sort of question: 'What do people like to do at night in Free Country?' or 'Are men closer friends with men than women are with women?' or 'Have you ever wished you were someone else?' He gave the best answers he could. She was a strange, unpredictable kind of woman, but he was fascinated by the quick darting movements of her mind, so different from that of anyone he knew in Albuquerque. Of course he dealt mainly with ranchers and farmers, and she was a mayor's daughter. And a native of the Occupied Zone besides: no reason why she should be remotely like the kind of people he knew.

They came to places that had been almost incomprehensibly transformed by the aliens. There was an abandoned one-street town that looked as though it had been turned to glass, everything eerily translucent – buildings, furniture, plumbing fixtures. If there had been any people still living there you most likely could see right through them too, Demeris supposed. Then came a sandy tract where a row of decayed rusting automobiles had been arranged in an overlapping series, the front of each humped up on the rear end of the one in front of it, like a string of mating horses. Demeris stared at the automobiles as though they were ghosts ready to return to life. He had never actually seen one in use. The whole technology of internal combustion devices had dropped away before he was born, at least in his part of Free Country, though he had heard they still had cars of some sort in certain privileged enclaves of California.

After the row of cars there was a site where old human appliances, sinks and toilets and chairs and fragments of things Demeris wasn't able even to identify, had been fused together to form a dozen perfect pyramids fifty or sixty feet in height. It was like a museum of antiquity. By now Demeris was growing numb to the effects of seeing all this Spook meddling. It was impossible to sustain anger indefinitely when evidence of the alien presence was such a constant impingement.

There were more frequent traces now of the aliens' living presence, too: glows on the horizon, mysterious whizzing sounds far overhead that Jill said were airborne traffic, shining roadways through the desert parallel to the unpaved track they were following. Demeris expected to see Spooks go riding by next, but there was no sign of that. He wondered what they were like. 'Like ghosts,' Bud had said. 'Long shining ghosts, but solid.' That didn't help much.

When they camped that night, Demeris entered the tent with her without hesitation, and waited only a moment or two after lying down to reach for her. Her reaction was noncommittal for the first instant. But then he heard a sort of purring sound and she turned to him, open and ready. There had been nothing remotely like affection between them all afternoon, but now she generated sudden passion out of nothing at all, pulling it up like water from an artesian well; and he rode with her swiftly and expertly toward sweaty, noisy climaxes. He rested a while and went back to her a second time, but she said simply, 'No. Let's sleep now,' and turned her back to him. A very strange woman, he thought. He lay awake for a time, listening to the rhythm of her breathing just to see if she was asleep, thinking he might nuzzle up to her anyway if she was still conscious and seemed at all receptive. He couldn't tell. She was motionless, limp: for all he knew, dead. Her breathing-sounds were virtually imperceptible. After a time Demeris rolled away. He dreamed of a bright sky streaked with crimson fire, and dragons flying in formations out of the south.

Now they were distinctly nearing Spook City. Instead of following along a dusty unpaved trail they had moved onto an actual road, perhaps some old United States of America highway that the aliens had jazzed up by giving it an internal glow, a cool throbbing green luminance rising in eddying waves from a point deep underground. Other travelers joined them here, some riding wagons drawn by alien beasts of burden, a few floating along on silent flatbed vehicles that had no apparent means of propulsion. The travelers all seemed to be human.

'How do Spooks get around?' Demeris asked.

'Any way they like,' said Jill.

A corroded highway sign that looked five thousand years old announced that they had reached a town called Dimmitt. There wasn't any town there, only a sort of checkpoint of light like a benign version of the border barrier: a cheerful shimmering sheen, a dazzling moire pattern dancing in the air. One by one the wagons and flatbeds and carts passed through it and disappeared. 'It's the hunt perimeter,' Jill explained, while they were waiting for their turn to go through. 'Like a big pen around Spook City, miles in diameter, to keep the animals in. They won't cross the line. It scares them.'

He felt no effect at all as they crossed it. On the other side she told him that she had some formalities to take care of, and walked off toward a battered shed a hundred feet from the road. Demeris waited for her beside the elephant-camel.

A grizzled-looking weatherbeaten man of about fifty came limping up and grinned at him.

'Jack Lawson,' he announced. He put out his hand. 'On my way back from my daughter's wedding, Oklahoma City.'

'Nick Demeris.'

'Interesting traveling companion you got, Nick. What's it like, traveling with one of those? I've always wondered about that.'

'One of what?' Demeris said.

Lawson winked. 'Come on, friend. You know what I mean.'

'I don't think I do.'

'Your pal's a Spook, friend. Surely you aren't going to try to make me believe she's anything else.'

'Friend, my ass. And she's as human as you or me.'

'Right.'

'Believe me,' Demeris said flatly. 'I know. I've checked her out at very close range.'

Lawson's eyebrows rose a little. 'That's what I figured. I've heard there are men who go in for that. Some women, too.'

'Shit,' Demeris said, feeling himself beginning to heat up. He didn't have the time or the inclination for a fight, and Lawson looked about twice his age anyway. As calmly as he could he said, 'You're fucking wrong, just the way that Mex kid down south who said she was a Spook was wrong. Neither of you knows shit about her.'

'I know one when I see one.'

'And I know an asshole when I see one,' said Demeris.

'Easy, friend. Easy. I see I'm mistaken, that you simply don't understand what's going on. Okay. A thousand pardons, friend. Ten thousand.' Lawson gave him an oily, smarmy smile, a courtly bow, and started to move away.

'Wait,' Demeris said. 'You really think she's a Spook?'

'Bet your ass I do.'

'Prove it, then.'

'Don't have any proof. Just intuition.'

'Intuition's not worth much where I come from.'

'Sometimes you can just tell. There's something about her. I don't know. I couldn't put it into words.'

'My father used to say that if you can't put something into words, that's on account of you don't know what you're talking about.'

Lawson laughed. It was that same patronizing I-know-better-than-you laugh that the kid in the village had given him. Anger welled up again in Demeris and it was all he could do to keep from swinging on the older man.

But just then Jill returned. She looked human as hell as she came walking up, swinging her hips. Lawson tipped his hat to her with exaggerated courtesy and went sauntering back to his wagon.

'Ready?' Demeris asked her.

'All set.' She glanced at him. 'You okay, Nick?'

'Sure.'

'What was that fellow saying to you?'

'Telling me about his daughter's wedding in Oklahoma.'

He clambered up on the elephant-camel, taking up his position on the middle hump.

His anger over what Lawson had said gradually subsided. They all knew so much, these Occupied Zone people. Or thought they did. Always trying to get one up on the greenhorn from Free Country, giving you their knowledgeable looks, hitting you with their sly insinuations.

Some rational part of him told him that if two people over here had said the same thing about Jill, it might just be true. A fair chance of it, in fact. Well, fuck it. She looked human, she smelled human, she felt human when he ran his hands over her body. That was good enough for him. Let these Spook Land people say what they liked. He intended to go on accepting her as human no matter what anyone might try to tell him. It was too late for him to believe anything else. He had had his mouth to hers; he had been inside her body; he had

251

given himself to her in the most intimate way there was. There was no way he could let himself believe that he had been embracing something from another planet, not now. He absolutely could not permit himself to believe that now.

And then he felt a sudden stab of wild, almost intoxicating temptation: the paradoxical hope that she *was* a Spook after all, that by embracing her he had done something extraordinary and outrageous. A true crossing of borders: his youth restored. He was amazed. It was a stunning moment, a glimpse of what it might be like to step outside the prisons of his soul. But it passed quickly and he was his old sober self again. She is human, he told himself stolidly. Human. Human.

A little closer in, he saw one of the pens where the hunt animals were being kept. It was like a sheet of lightning rising from the ground, but lightning that stayed and stayed and stayed. Behind it Demeris thought he could make out huge dark moving shapes. Nothing was clear, and after a few moments of staring at that fluid rippling wall of light he started to feel the way he had felt when he was first pushing through the border barrier.

'What kind of things do they have in there?' he asked her.

'Everything,' she said. 'Wait and see, when they turn them loose.'

'When is that?'

'Couple of days from now.' She swung around and pointed. 'Look there, Nick. There's Spook City.'

They were at the crest of a little hill. In the valley below lay a fair-sized sprawling town, not as big as he had expected, a mongrel place made up in part of little boxy houses and in part of tall, tapering, flickering constructions that didn't seem to be of material substance at all, ghost-towers, fairy castles, houses fit for Spooks. The sight of them gave him a jolt, the way everything was mixed together, human and non. A low line of the same immaterial stuff ran around the edge of the city like a miniature border barrier, but softer in hue and dancing like little swamp-fires.

'I don't see any Spooks,' he said to her.

'You want to see a Spook? There's a Spook for you.'

An alien fluttered up into view right then and there, as though

252

she had conjured it out of empty air. Demeris, caught unprepared, muttered a whispered curse and his fingers moved with desperate urgency through the patterns of protection-signs that his mother had taught him more than twenty years before and that he had never had occasion to use. The Spook was incorporeal, elegant, almost blindingly beautiful: a sleek cone of translucence, a node of darkness limned by a dancing core of internal light. He had expected them to be frightening, not beautiful: but this one, at least, was frightening in its beauty. Then a second one appeared, and it was nothing like the first, except that it too had no solidity. It was flat below and almost formless higher up, and drifted a little way above the ground atop a pool of its own luminescence. The first one vanished; the second one revolved and seemed to spawn three more, and then it too was gone; the newest three, which had s-shaped curves and shining blue eye-like features at their upper tips, twined themselves together almost coquettishly and coalesced into a single fleshy spheroid crisscrossed by radiant purple lines. The spheroid folded itself across its own equator, taking on a half-moon configuration, and slipped downward into the earth.

Demeris shivered.

Spooks, yes. Well named. Dream-beings. No wonder there had been no way of defeating them. How could you touch them? How could you injure them in any way, when they mutated and melted and vanished while you were looking at them? It wasn't fair, creatures like that coming to the world and taking a big chunk of it the way they had, simply grabbing, not even bothering to explain why, just moving in, knowing that they were too powerful to be opposed. All his ancient hatred of them sprang into new life. And yet they were beautiful, almost godlike. He feared and loathed them but at the same time he found himself fighting back an impulse to drop to his knees.

He and Jill rode into town without speaking. There was a sweet little tingle when they went through the wall of dancing light, and then they were inside.

'Here we are,' Jill said. 'Spook City. I'll show you a place where you can stay.'

The city's streets were unpaved – the Spooks wouldn't need sidewalks

– and most of the human-style buildings had windows of some kind of semi-clear oiled cloth instead of glass. The buildings themselves were of slovenly construction and were set down higgledy-piggledy without much regard for order and logic. Sometimes there was a gap between them out of which a tall Spook structure sprouted like nightmare fungus, but mainly the Spook sectors of the city and the human sectors were separate, however it had seemed when he had been looking down from the hill. All manner of flying creatures that had been gathered for the hunt were in busy circulation overhead: the delta-winged herders, the flying snakes, a whole host of weirdities traversing the air above the city with such demonic intensity that it seemed to sizzle as they passed through it.

Jill conveyed him to a hotel of sorts made out of crudely squared logs held together clumsily by pegs, a gigantic ramshackle three-story cabin that looked as if it had been designed by people who were inventing architecture from scratch, and left him at the door. 'I'll see you later,' she told him, when he had jumped down. 'I've got some business to tend to.'

'Wait,' he said. 'How am I going to find you when –'

Too late. The elephant-camel had already made a massive about-face and was ambling away.

Demeris stood looking after her, feeling puzzled and a little hurt. But he had begun to grow accustomed to her brusqueness and her arbitrary shifts by now. Very likely she'd turn up again in a day or two, he told himself. Meanwhile, though, he was on his own, just when he had started to count on her help in this place.

He shrugged and went inside.

The place had the same jerry-built look within: a long dark entry hall, exposed rafters, crazily leaning walls. To the left, from behind a tattered curtain of red gauze, came the sounds of barroom chatter and clinking glasses. On the right was a cubicle with a pale, owlish-looking heavyset woman peering out of a lopsided opening.

'I need a room,' Demeris told her.

'We just got one left. Busy time, on account of the hunt. It's five labor units a night, room and board and a drink or two.'

'Labor units?'

'We don't take Free Country money here, chumbo. An hour cleaning out the shithouse, that's one labor unit. Two hours swabbing grease in the kitchen, that's one. Don't worry, we'll find things for you to do. You staying the usual thirty days?'

'I'm not on an Entrada,' Demeris said. 'I'm here to find my brother.' Then, with a sudden rush of hope: 'Maybe you've seen him. Looks a lot like me, shorter, around eighteen years old. Tom Demeris.'

'Nobody here by that name,' she said, and shoved a square metal key toward him. 'Second floor on the left, 103. Welcome to Spook City, chumbo.'

The room was small, squalid, dim. Hardly any light came through the oilcloth window. A strangely shaped lamp sat on the crooked table next to the bare cot that would be his bed. It turned on when he touched it and an eerie tapering glow rose from it, like a tiny Spook. He saw now that there were hangings on the wall, coarse cloth bearing cryptic inscriptions in Spook script.

Downstairs, he found four men and a parched-looking woman in the bar. They were having some sort of good-natured argument and gave him only the quickest of glances. Sized him up, wrote him off: he could see that. Free Country written all over his face. His nostrils flared and he clamped his lips.

'Whiskey,' Demeris told the bartender.

'We got Shagback, Billyhow, Donovan, and Thread.'

'Donovan,' he said at random. The bartender poured him a shot from a lumpy-looking blue bottle with a garish yellow label. The stuff was inky-dark, vaguely sour-smelling, strong. Demeris felt it hit bottom like a fishhook. The others were looking at him with more interest now. He took that for an opening and turned to them with a forced smile to tell them what they plainly already knew, which was that he was a stranger here, and to ask them the one thing he wanted to know, which was could they help him discover the whereabouts of a kid named Tom Demeris.

'How do you like the whiskey?' the woman asked him.

'It's different from what I'm accustomed to. But not bad.' He fought back his anger. 'He's my kid brother, that's the thing, and I've come all this way looking for him, because –'

'Tom what?' one of the men said.

'Demeris. We're from Albuquerque.'

They began to laugh. 'Abblecricky,' the woman said.

'Dabblecricky,' said one of the other men, sallow-skinned with a livid scar across his cheek.

Demeris looked coldly from one face to another. 'Albuquerque,' he said with great precision. 'It used to be a big city in New Mexico. That's in Free Country. We still got eight, ten thousand people living there, maybe more. My brother was on his Entrada, only he didn't come back. Been gone since June. I think he's got some idea of settling here, and I want to talk to him about that. Tom Demeris is his name. Not quite as tall as I am, a little heavier set, longer hair than mine.'

But he could see that he had lost their attention. The woman rolled her eyes and shrugged, and one of the men gestured to the bartender for another round of drinks.

'You want one too?' the bartender asked Demeris.

'A different kind this time.'

It wasn't any better. He sipped it morosely. A few moments later the others began to file out of the room. 'Abblekirky,' the woman said, as she went past Demeris, and laughed again.

He spent a troubled night. The room was musty and dank and made him feel claustrophobic. The little bed offered no comfort. Sounds came from outside, grinding noises, screeches, strange honkings. When he turned the lamp off the darkness was absolute and ominous, and when he turned it on the light bothered him. He lay stiffly, waiting watchfully for sleep to take him, and when it failed to arrive he rose and pulled the oilcloth window-cover aside to stare into the night. Attenuated streaks of brightness were floating through the air, ghostly will-o'-the-wisp glowings, and by that faint illumination he saw huge winged things pumping stolidly across the sky, great dragons no more graceful than flying oxen, while in the road below the building three flickering columns of light that surely were Spooks went past, driving a herd of lean little square-headed monsters as though they were so many sheep.

In the morning, after the grudging breakfast of stale bread and some sort of coffee-like beverage with an undertaste of barley that the hotel bar provided, he went out into Spook City to look for Tom. But where was he supposed to begin? He had no idea.

It was a chaotic, incomprehensible town. The unpaved streets went squiggling off in all directions, no two of them parallel. Wagons and flatbeds of the kind he had seen at the perimeter checkpoint, some of them very ornate and bizarre, swept by constantly, stirring up whirlwinds of gray dust. Ethereal shimmering Spooks drifted in and among them, ignoring the perils of the busy traffic as though they were operating on some other plane of existence entirely, which very likely they were. Now and again came a great bleating of horns and everyone moved to the side of the street to allow a parade of menacing-looking beasts to pass through, a dozen green-scaled things like dinosaurs with high-stepping big-taloned feet or a procession of elephant-camels linked trunk to tail or a string of long slithery serpentine creatures moving on scores of powerful stubby legs.

Demeris felt a curious numbness coming over him as one enormity after another presented itself to his eyes. These few days across the border were changing him, creating a kind of dreamy tolerance in him. He had absorbed all the new alien sights and experiences he could and he was overloaded now, no room left for reactions of surprise or fear or even of loathing. The crazy superabundance of strangeness in Spook City was quickly starting to appear normal to him. Albuquerque in all its somnolent ordinariness seemed to him now like a static vision, a mere photograph of a city rather than an actual thriving place. There was still the problem of Tom, though. Demeris walked for hours and found no clue, no starting place: no building marked *Police Station* or *City Hall* or *Questions Answered Here*. What he really hoped to come upon was someone who was recognizably a native of Free Country, someone who could give him an inkling of how to go about tracing his brother through the network of kids making Entradas that must exist on this side. But he saw no one like that either. Where the hell was Jill? She was his only ally, and she had left him to cope with this lunacy all by himself, abandoning him as abruptly as she had picked him up in the first place.

But she, at least, could be located. She was the mayor's daughter, after all.

He entered a dark, squalid little building that seemed to be some sort of shop. A small hunched-looking woman who could have been made of old leather gave him a surly look from behind a warped counter. He met it with the best smile he could manage and said to her, 'I'm new in town and I'm trying to find Jill Gorton, Ben Gorton's daughter. She's a friend of mine.'

'Who?'

'Jill Gorton? Ben Gorton's –'

She shook her head curtly. 'Don't know anybody by that name.'

'Ben Gorton, then. Where can he be found?'

'Wherever he might happen to be,' she said. 'How would I know?' And slammed shut on him like a trapdoor. He peered at her in astonishment. She had turned away from him and was moving things around behind her counter as though no one was there.

'Doesn't he have an office?' Demeris asked. 'Some kind of head-quarters?'

No response. She got up, moving around in the shadows, ignoring him.

'I'm talking to you,' Demeris said.

She might just as well have been deaf. He quivered with frustration. It was midday and he had had practically nothing to eat since yesterday afternoon and he hadn't accomplished anything all this day and it had started to dawn on him that he had no idea how he was going to find his way back to his hotel through the maze of the city – he didn't even know its name or address, and the streets bore no signs anyway – and now this old bitch was pretending he was invisible. Furiously he said, 'Jesus Christ, what's the matter with you people? Haven't you ever heard of common courtesy here? Have the fucking Spooks drained everything that's human out of you all? All I want to know is how to find the goddamned mayor. Can't you tell me that one little thing? Can't you?'

Instead of answering him, she looked back over her shoulder and made a sound in Spook language, a wheezing whistling noise, the kind of sound that Jill might have directed to her elephant-camel.

Almost instantly a tall flat-faced man of about thirty with the same sort of dark leathery skin as hers came out of a back room and gave Demeris a black, threatening stare.

'What the hell you think you're doing yelling at my mother?'

'Look,' Demeris said, 'I just asked her for a little help, that's all.' He was still churning with rage. 'I need to find the mayor. I'm a friend of his daughter Jill's, and she's supposed to help me track down my brother Tom, who came across from Free Country a few months ago, and I don't know one goddamned building from the next in this town, so I stopped in here hoping she could give me some directions and instead –'

'You yelled at her. You cursed at her.'

'Yeah. Maybe so. But if you people don't have any decency why the hell should I? All I want to know –'

'You cursed at my mother.'

'Yeah,' Demeris said. 'Yeah, I did.' It was all too much. He was tired and hungry and far from home and the streets were full of monsters and nobody would give him the time of day here and he was sick of it. He had no idea who moved first, but suddenly they were both on the same side of the counter and swinging at each other, butting heads and pummeling each other's chests and trying to slam each other against the wall. The other man was bigger and heavier, but Demeris was angrier, and he got his hands to the other man's throat and started to squeeze. Dimly he was aware of sounds all around him, doors slamming, rapid footsteps, people shouting, a thick incoherent babble of sound. Then someone's arm was bent around his chin and throat and hands were clamped on his wrists and he was being pulled to the floor, kicking as he went and struggling to reach the knife at his waist. The confusion grew worse after that: he had no idea how many of them there were, but they were sitting on him, they were holding his arms, they were dragging him out into the daylight. He thought he saw a Spook hovering in the air above him, but perhaps he was wrong about that. There was too much light everywhere around. Nothing was clear. 'Listen,' he said, 'The only thing I want is –' and they hit him in the mouth and kicked him in the side, and there was some raucous laughter and he heard them speaking in the Spook language; and then he came to understand that he was in a wagon, a cart, some kind of moving contrivance. His hands and feet were tied. A flushed sweaty face looked down at him, grinning.

'Where are you taking me?' Demeris asked.

'Ben Gorton. That's who you wanted to see, isn't it? Ben Gorton, right?'

He was in a basement room somewhere, windowless, lit by three of the little Spook-lamps. It was the next day, he supposed. Certainly a lot of time had gone by, perhaps a whole night. They had given him a little to eat, some sort of bean mush. He was still bound, but two men were holding him anyway.

'Untie him,' Gorton said.

He had to be Gorton. He was around six feet seven, wide as a slab, with a big bald head and a great beaky nose, and everything about him spoke of power and authority. Demeris rubbed his wrists where the cord had chafed them and said, 'I wasn't interested in a fight. That's not the sort of person I am. But sometimes when it builds up and builds up and builds up, and you can't stand it any more –'

'Right. You damn near killed Bobby Bridger, you know that? His eyes were bugging right out of his head. This is hunt season here, mister. The Spooks will be turning the critters loose any minute now and things are going to get real lively. It's important for everybody to stay civil so things don't get any more complicated than they usually are when the hunt's going on.'

'If Bridger's mother had been a little more civil to me, it would all have been a lot different,' Demeris said.

Gorton gave him a weary look. 'Who are you and what are you doing here, anyway?'

Taking a deep breath, Demeris said, 'My name's Nick Demeris, and I live in Free Country, and I came over here to find my kid brother Tom, who seems to have gotten sidetracked coming back from his Entrada.'

'Tom Demeris,' Gorton said, lifting his eyebrows.

'Yes. Then I met your daughter Jill at some little town near the

border, and she invited me to travel with her. But when we got to
Spook City she dropped me at some hotel and disappeared, so –'

'Wait a second,' said Gorton. His eyebrows went even higher. 'My
daughter Jill?'

'That's right.'

'Shit,' the big man said. 'What daughter? I don't have no fucking
daughter.'

'No daughter,' said Demeris.

'No daughter. None. Must have been some Spook playing games
with you.'

The words fell on Demeris like stones. 'Some Spook,' he repeated
numbly. 'Pretending to be your daughter. You mean that? For Christ's
sake, are you serious, or are you playing games with me too?'

Something in Demeris's agonized tone seemed to register sympa-
thetically on Gorton. He squinted, he blinked, he tugged at the tip of
his great nose. He said in a much softer voice, 'I'm not playing any
games with you. I can't say for sure that she was a Spook but she
sure as hell wasn't my daughter, because I don't have any daughter.
Spooks doing masks will tell you anything they damn please, though.
Chances are, she was a Spook.'

'Doing masks?'

'Spooks going around playing at being human. It's a big thing
with them these days. The latest Spook fad.'

Demeris nodded. *Doing masks*, he thought. He considered it and
it began to sink in, and sink and sink and sink.

Then quietly he said, 'Maybe you can help me find my brother,
at least.'

'No. I can't do that and neither can anybody else. Tom Demeris,
you said his name is?'

'That's right.'

Gorton glanced toward one of his men. 'Mack, how long ago was
it that the Demeris kid took the Spooks' nickel?'

'Middle of July, I think.'

'Right.' To Demeris Gorton said, 'What we call "taking the Spooks'
nickel" means selling yourself to them, do you know what I mean?
You agree to go with them to their home planet. They've got a kind

261

of plush country club for humans there where you live like a grand emperor for the rest of your life, comfort, luxury, women, anything you damn please, but the deal is that in return you belong to them forever, that they get to run psychological experiments on you to see what makes you tick, like a mouse in a cage. At least that's what the Spooks tell us goes on there, and we might as well believe it. Nobody who's sold himself to the Spooks has ever come back. I'm sorry, man. I wish it wasn't so.'

Demeris looked away for a moment. He felt like smashing things, but he held himself perfectly still. My brother, he thought, my baby brother.

'He was just a kid,' he said.

'Well, he must have been a damned unhappy kid. Nobody with his head screwed on right would take the nickel. Hardly anybody ever does.' Something flashed momentarily in Gorton's eyes, and Demeris sensed that to these people selling yourself to the Spooks was the ultimate surrender, the deepest sort of self-betrayal. They had all sold themselves to the Spooks, in a sense, by choosing to live in the Occupied Zone; but even here there were levels of yielding to the alien conqueror, he realized, and in the eyes of Spook City people the thing that Tom had done was the lowest level of all. He felt the weight of Gorton's mingling of contempt for Tom and pity for him, suddenly, and hated it, and tried to throw it back with a furious glare. Gorton watched him quietly, not reacting.

After a little while Demeris said, 'All right. There's nothing I can do, is there? I guess I'd better go back to Albuquerque now.'

'You'd better go back to your hotel and wait until the hunt is over,' said Gorton. 'It isn't safe wandering around in the open while the critters are loose.'

'No,' said Demeris. 'I suppose it isn't.'

'Take him to wherever he's staying, Mack,' Gorton said to his man. He stared for a time at Demeris. The sorrow in his eyes seemed genuine. 'I'm sorry,' Gorton said again. 'I really am.'

Mack had no difficulty recognizing Demeris's hotel from the description he gave, and took him to it in a floating wagon that made the trip in less than fifteen minutes. The streets were practically empty now: no Spooks in sight and hardly any humans, and those who were still out were moving quickly.

'You want to stay indoors while the hunt is going on,' Mack said. 'A lot of dumb idiots don't, but some of them regret it. This is one event that ought to be left strictly to the Spooks.'

'How will I know when it starts?'

'You'll know,' Mack said.

Demeris got out of the wagon. It turned immediately and headed away. He paused a moment in front of the building, breathing deeply, feeling a little light-headed, thinking of Tom on the Spook planet, Tom living in a Spook palace, Tom sleeping on satin Spook sheets.

'Nick? Over here, Nick! It's me!'

'Oh, Christ,' he said. Jill, coming up the street toward him, smiling as blithely as though this were Christmas Eve. He scanned her, searching for traces of some Spook gleam, some alien shimmer. When she reached him she held out her arms to him as though expecting a hug. He stepped back just far enough to avoid her grasp.

In a flat tight voice he said, 'I found out about my brother. He's gone off to the Spook world. Took their nickel.'

'Oh, Nick. Nick!'

'You knew, didn't you? Everybody in this town must have known about the kid who came from Free Country and sold himself to the Spooks.' His tone turned icy. 'It was your father the mayor that told me. He also told me that he doesn't have any daughters.'

Her cheeks blazed with embarrassment. It was so human a reaction that he was cast into fresh confusion: how could a Spook learn to mimic a human even down to a blush? It didn't seem possible. And it gave him new hope. She had lied to him about being Ben Gorton's daughter, yes, God only knew why; but there was still the possibility that she was human, that she had chosen to put on a false identity but the body he saw was really her own. If only it was so, he thought. His anger with her, his disdain, melted away in a flash. He wanted everything to be all right. He was rocked by a powerful rush of eagerness to be assured that the woman he had embraced those two nights on the desert was indeed a woman; and with it, astonishingly, came a new burst of desire for her, of fresh yearning stronger than anything he had felt for her before.

'What he told me about was that you were a Spook,' Demeris said in a guarded tone. He looked at her hopefully, waiting for her to deny it, praying for her to deny it, ready to accept her denial.

'Yes,' she said. 'I am.'

It was like a gate slamming shut in his face.

Serenely she said, 'Humans fascinate me. Their emotions, their reactions, their attitudes toward things. I've been studying them at close range for a hundred of your years and I still don't know as much as I'd like to. And finally I thought, the only way I can make that final leap of understanding is to become one myself.'

'*Doing masks,*' Demeris said in a hollow voice. Looking at her, he imagined he could see something cold and foreign peering out at him from behind her eyes for a moment, and it seemed to him that great chilly winds were sweeping through the empty caverns of his soul. He began to see now that somewhere deep within him he must have been making plans for a future that included this woman, that he had wanted her so much that he had stubbornly refused to accept for long any of the evidence that had been given him that that was unthinkable. And now he had been given the one bit of evidence that was impossible to reject.

'Right,' she said. 'Doing masks.'

He knew he should be feeling fury, or anguish, or something, at this final revelation that he had slept with a Spook. But he hardly felt anything at all. He was like a stone. Perhaps he had already done the anger and pain, on some level below his consciousness. Or else he had somehow transcended it. The Spooks are in charge here.

All right. We are their toys. All right. All right. You could go only so far into despair and then you stopped feeling it, he supposed. Or hatred. Hating the Spooks was useless. It was like hating an avalanche, like hating an earthquake.

'Taking human men as your lovers, too: that's part of doing masks, isn't it?' he asked. 'Was my brother Tom one of them?'

'No. Never. I saw him only once or twice.'

He believed that. He believed everything she was saying, now.

264

She seemed about to say something else. But then suddenly a flare of lightning burst across the sky, a monstrous forking shaft of flame that looked as though it could split the world in two. It was followed not by thunder but by music, an immense alien chord that fell like an avalanche from the air and swelled up around them with oceanic force. The vault of the sky rippled with colors: red, orange, violet, green.

'What's happening?' Demeris asked.

'The hunt is starting,' she said. 'That's the signal.'

Yes. In the wake of the lightning and the rippling colors came swarming throngs of airborne creatures, seeming thousands of them, the delta-winged dragon-like herders and their snake-like pilots, turning the midday sky dark with their numbers, like a swarm of bees overhead, colossal ones whose wings made a terrible droning sound as they beat the air; and then Demeris heard gigantic roaring, bellowing sounds from nearby, as if monsters were approaching. There were no animals in the streets, not yet, but they couldn't be very far away. Above him, Spooks by the dozens flickered in the air. Then he heard footsteps, and a pack of humans came running frantically toward them out of a narrow street, their eyes wild, their faces weirdly rigid. Did the Spooks hunt humans too? Demeris wondered. Or was one of the monsters chasing after them? The runners came sweeping down on him. 'Get out of the way, man!' one of them cried. '*Out of the way!*'

Demeris stepped back, but not fast enough, and the runner on the inside smacked hard into his shoulder, spinning him around a little. For one startling moment Demeris found himself looking straight into the man's eyes, and saw something close to madness there, but no fear at all – only eagerness, impatience, frenzied excitement – and he realized that they must be running not from but to the hunt, that they were on their way to witness the crazy slaughter at close range or even to take part in it themselves, that they lived just as did the Spooks for this annual moment of apocalyptic frenzy.

Jill said, 'It'll be berserk here now for two or three days. You ought to be very careful if you go outdoors.'

'Yes. I will.'

'Listen,' she said, putting an edge on her voice to make it cut through the roaring coming from overhead, 'I've got a proposition for you, now that you know the truth.' She leaned close to him. 'Let's stay together, you and me. Despite all the problems. I like you a lot, Nick.'

He peered at her, utterly astounded.

'I really think we can work something out,' she went on. Another horde of winged things shot by just above them, making raspy tearing sounds as they flailed the air, and a new gush of color stained the sky. 'Seriously, Nick. We can stay in Spook City if you want to, but I don't suppose you do. If you don't I'll go back across the border with you and live with you in Free Country. In my mind I've already crossed over. I don't want just to study you people from the outside. I want to be one of you.'

'Are you crazy?' Demeris asked.

'No. Not in the least, I swear. Can you believe me? Can you?'

'I've got to go inside,' he said. He was trembling. 'It isn't smart to be standing out here while the hunt is going on.'

'What do you say, Nick? Give me an answer.'

'It isn't possible for us to be together. You know it isn't.'

'You want to. Some part of you does.'

'Maybe so,' he said, amazed at what he was saying, but unable to deny it despite himself. 'Just maybe. One little fraction of me. But it isn't possible, all the same. I don't want to live here among the Spooks, and if I take you back with me, some bastard with a sharp nose will sniff you out sooner or later and expose you for what you are, and stand up before the whole community and denounce me for what I am. I'm not going to take that risk. I'm just not, Jill.'

'That's your absolute decision.'

'My absolute decision, yes.'

Something was coming down the street now, some vast hopping thing with a head the size of a cow and teeth like spears. A dozen or so humans ran along beside it, practically within reach of the creature's clashing jaws, and a covey of Spooks hovered over it, bombarding it with flashes of light. Demeris took a step or two toward the door of the hotel. Jill did nothing to hold him back.

He turned when he was in the doorway. She was still standing there. The hunters and their prey sped right past her, but she took no notice. She waved to him.

Sure, he thought. He waved back. Goodbye, Jill.

He went inside. There was a clatter on the stairs, people running down, a woman and some men. He recognized them as the ones who had mocked him in the bar when he had first arrived. Two of the men ran past him and out the door, but the woman halted and caught him by the crook of the arm.

'Hey, Abblecricky!'

Demeris stared at her.

She leaned into his face and grinned. She was flushed and wild-looking, like the ones who had been running through the streets. 'Come on, man! It's the hunt! The hunt, man! You're heading the wrong way. Don't you want to be there?'

He had no answer for that.

She was tugging at him. 'Come on! Live it up! Kill yourself a dragon or two!'

'Ella!' one of the men called after her.

She gave Demeris a wink and ran out the door.

He swayed uncertainly, torn between curiosity about what was going on out there and a profound wish to go upstairs and shut the door behind him. But the street had the stronger pull. He took a step or two after the woman, and then another, and then he was outside again. Jill wasn't there. The scene in the street was wilder than ever: people running back and forth yelling incoherently, colliding with each other in their frenzy, and overhead streams of winged creatures still swarming, and Spooks like beams of pure light moving among them, and in the distance the sounds of bellowing animals and thunderous explosions and high keening cries of what he took to be Spook pleasure. Far off to the south he saw a winged something the size of a small hill circling desperately in the sky, surrounded by implacable flaring pinpoints of Spook-light, and suddenly halting and plummeting like a falling moon toward the ground. He could smell the smell of charred flesh in the air, with a salty underflavor of what he suspected was the blood of alien beasts.

At a sleepwalker's dreamy pace Demeris went to the corner and turned left. Abruptly he found himself confronted with a thing so huge and hideous that it was almost funny – a massive long-snouted frog-shaped thing, sloping upward from a squat base, with a moist-looking greenish-black hide pocked with little red craters and a broad, gaping, yellow-rimmed mouth. It had planted itself in the middle of the street with its shoulders practically touching the buildings at either side and was advancing slowly and clumsily toward the intersection.

Demeris drew his knife. What the hell, he thought. He was here at hunt time, he might as well join the fun. The creature was immense but it didn't have any visible fangs or talons and he figured he could move in at an angle and slash upward through the great baggy throat, and then step back fast before the thing fell on him. And if it turned out to be more dangerous than it looked, he didn't give a damn. Not now.

He moved forward, knife already arcing upward.

'Hey!' someone cried behind him. 'You out of your mind, fel-low?'

Demeris glanced around. The bartender had come out of the hotel and was staring at him.

'That critter's just a big sack of acid,' he said. 'You cut it open, it'll pour all over you.'

The frog-thing made a sound like a burp, or perhaps a sardonic chuckle. Demeris backed away.

'You want to cut something with that,' the bartender said, 'you better know what you're cutting.'

'Yeah.' Demeris said. 'I suppose so.' He put the knife back in its sheath, and headed back across the street, feeling all the craziness of the moment go from him like air ebbing from a balloon. This hunt was no business of his. Let the people who live here get mixed up in it if they liked. But there was no reason why he should. He'd just be buying trouble, and he had never seen any sense in that.

As he reached the hotel entrance he saw Spook-light shimmering in the air at the corner – hunters, hovering above – and then there was a soft sighing sound and a torrent of bluish fluid came rolling out of the side street. It was foaming and hissing as it edged along the gutter.

Demeris shuddered. He went into the building.

Quickly he mounted the stairs and entered his room, and sat for a long while on the edge of the cot, gradually growing calm, letting it all finish sinking in while the din of the hunt went on and on.

Tom was gone, that was the basic thing he had to deal with. Neither dead nor really alive, but certainly gone. Okay. He faced that and grappled with it. It was bitter news, but at least it was a resolution of sorts. He'd mourn for a while and then he'd be all right.

And Jill –

Doing masks. Taking humans as lovers. The whole thing went round and round in his mind, all that he and she had done together, had said, everything that had passed between them. And how he had always felt about Spooks and how – somehow, he had no idea how – his time with Jill had changed that a little.

He remembered what she had said. *I don't just want to study you. I want to be one of you.*

What did that mean? A tourist in the human race? A sightseer across species lines?

They are softening, then. They are starting to whore after strange amusements. And if that's so, he thought, then we are beginning to win. The aliens had infiltrated Earth in the first place; but now Earth was infiltrating them. This yearning to do masks, to look and act like humans, to experience human feelings and human practices and human follies: it meant the end for them. There were too many humans on Earth and not enough Spooks, and the Spooks would eventually be swallowed up. One by one, they would succumb to the temptation of giving up their chilly godliness and trying to imitate the messy, contradictory, troublesome creatures that humans are. And, Demeris thought, over the course of time – five hundred years, a thousand, who could say? – Earth would complete the job of absorbing the invaders and something new would emerge from the mixture of the species. That was an interesting thing to consider.

But then something clicked in his mind and he felt himself being flooded by some strange interior light, a light as weird and intense as the Spook-light in the skies over the city now or the glow of the border barrier, and he realized there was another way of looking at these things altogether. Jill dropped suddenly into a new perspective and instead of thinking of her as a mere sightseer looking for forbidden thrills, he saw her for what she really was – a pioneer, an explorer, a border-jumper, a defiant enemy of boundaries and limitations and rules. The same for Tom. They were two of a kind, those two; and he had been slow to recognize it because he simply wasn't of their sort. Demeris recognized now how little he had understood his youngest brother. To him, Tom was a disturbed kid. To Ben Gorton, he was a contemptible sellout. But the real Tom, Tom's own Tom, might be something entirely different: someone looking not just to make a little thirty-day Entrada but to carry out a real penetration into the alien, to jump deep and far into otherness to find out what it was like. The same with this Jill, this alien, this Spook – she was of that kind too, but coming from the other direction.

And she had wanted his help. She had needed it all along, right from the start. She had missed her chance with Tom, but maybe she thought that Tom's brother might the same sort of person, someone who lived on the edge, who pushed against walls.

Well, well, well. How wrong she was. That was too bad.

For an instant Demeris felt another surge of the strange excitement that had come over him back at the checkpoint, when he had considered the possibility that Jill might be a Spook and had, for a moment, felt exhilarated by the thought. *Could* he take her back with him? *Could* he sneak her into the human community and live happily ever after with her, hiding the astonishing truth like the man in the old story who had married a mermaid? He saw himself, for a moment, lying beside her at night while she told him Spook stories and whispered weird Spook words and showed him sly little Spook shapeshifting tricks as they embraced. It was an astonishing thought. And he began to quiver and sweat as he thought about it.

Then, as it had before, the moment passed.

He couldn't do it. It just wasn't who he was, not really. Tom might have done it, but Tom was gone, and he wasn't Tom or anything like him. Not one of the leapers, one of the soarers, one of the questers. Not one of the adventurous kind at all: just a careful man, a builder, a planner, a preserver, a protector. Nothing wrong with that. But not of any real use to Jill in her quest.

Too bad, he thought. Too damned bad, Jill.

He walked to the window and peered out, past the oilcloth cover. The hunt was reaching some sort of peak. The street was more crowded than ever with frantic monsters. The sky was full of Spooks. Scattered bands of Spook City humans, looking half crazed or more than half, were running back and forth. There was noise everywhere, sharp, percussive, discordant. Jill was nowhere to be seen out there. He let the oilcloth flap drop back in place and lay down on his cot and closed his eyes.

Three days later, when the hunt was over and it was safe to go out again, Demeris set out for home. For the first ten blocks or so a glow that might have been a Spook hovered above him, keeping pace as he walked. He wondered if it was Jill. She had given him a second chance once, he remembered. Maybe she was doing it again.

'Jill?' he called up to it. 'That you?'

No answer came.

'Listen,' he called to the hovering glow. 'Forget it. It isn't going to work out, you and me. I'm sorry, but it isn't. You hear me?'

A little change in the intensity of the flicker overhead, perhaps. Or perhaps not.

He looked upward and said, 'And listen, Jill – if that's you, Jill, I want to tell you: thanks for everything, okay?' It was strange, talking to the sky this way. But he didn't care. '– And good luck. You hear? Good luck, Jill! I hope you get what you want.'

The glow bobbed for a moment, up, down. Then it was gone.

Demeris, shading his eyes, looked upward for a time, but there was nothing up there to see. He felt a sharp little momentary pang, thinking of the possibilities. But what could he have done? She had wanted something from him that he wasn't able to give. If he had been somebody else, things might have been different. But he was who he was. He could go only so far toward becoming someone else, and then he had to pull back and return to being who he really was, and that was all there was to it.

He moved onward, toward the edge of the city.

No one gave him any trouble at all on his way out, and the return trip through the western fringe of the Occupied Zone was just as smooth. Everything was quiet, all was peaceful, clear on to the border.

The border crossing itself was equally uncomplicated. The fizzing lights and the weird hallucinatory effects of the barrier were visible, but they had no impact from this side. Demeris passed through them as though they were so much smoke, and kept on walking. In hardly any time he was across the border and back in Free Country again.

The Red Blaze is the Morning

I didn't write any science-fiction short stories at all in 1992, the first time in many years that was the case, and I wrote only two in 1993 and one in 1994 – a sign, I suspect, of the increasing difficulties I've been experiencing in working in the shorter forms.

The themes of these few-and-far-between latter-day stories may reflect some of that difficulty. Here, written in April, 1993 for Greg Bear's *New Legends* anthology and centering in my long-held passion for archaeology, is a tale of a veteran professional whose career, as it enters its later years, has become much more of a struggle than he ever could have anticipated in his younger days.

> *The Red - Blaze - is the Morning –*
> *The Violet - is Noon –*
> *The Yellow - Day - is falling –*
> *And after that - is none –*
> — Emily Dickinson

Day by blazing day Halvorsen stretches himself across a blistering abyss, patiently searching in recalcitrant rock and hot sand for morsels of the useless past, even though he has begun to doubt the meaning and value of his own work. By chilly night, soaking his damaged and aching leg in a shallow basin of tepid sea-water – in this arid part of Turkey, fresh water is a luxury – he feels seductive fingers tickling the membranes of his mind. Something is trying to get in: perhaps already has. Something keeps nestling down alongside his consciousness and whispering fantastic, tempting things to him, visions of far-off times, mighty civilizations yet unborn. Or so it often seems.

273

What is actually going on, Halvorsen suspects, is that he is beginning to go crazy. The fascination of what's difficult, he thinks, has not merely dried the sap out of his veins, as old Yeats feared it would, but has parched his brain beyond the bounds of sanity. And yet he can still speak six languages, including Turkish and Hebrew and modern Greek, and he can read Latin and classical Greek besides. He can recite the names of the Roman emperors from Augustus to Romulus Augustulus without missing one. Yes, his mind still functions well enough. Something else, something equally intangible and even harder to define, is what has become impaired. And then there is the sore leg, too, which mended inadequately after last summer's accident on the rocky slope and is painful all the time. The leg is really in very bad shape. He ought not to be out here on the summit of the hill with a pick and shovel. He should be sitting in his tent, supervising the work of others. But Halvorsen has always been a hands-on kind of archaeologist: a point of great pride for him.

This is the fifth week of the third season of the dig. It is high summer, when the blue cloudless sky reflects the light of the swollen sun like a hot metal plate, and the *meltem*, the dry, hot, unrelenting wind out of the inland plateau, sends fifty-mile-an-hour blasts of brown dust into your nostrils and eyes and mouth and every cranny of your clothing for four or five days without halting. Halvorsen's site is on a ragged little peninsula in southwest Turkey, overlooking the Mediterranean coast. It is an unimportant place that does not even have a paved road running to it, nor running water or electricity, and yet it has a long history. There is a tiny fishing village here now; before that, there was a Byzantine naval base; before that, Romans; before them, a Greek trading outpost; before that, a Minoan trading outpost; before that, Halvorsen thinks, a proto-Hittite encampment. And before that – ah, nobody knows what was here before that. But Halvorsen has a hypothesis, based on a few scattered and questionable bits of evidence. For three summers, now, he has been trying to find more satisfactory proof to support that hypothesis.

At mid-morning on this blazingly hot day Halvorsen is working alone on high, extending the trench that runs along the proto-Hittite side of the hill. Nobody he knows believes that the Hittites ever lived here, or anywhere else along this coast; and he himself has nothing to go by in that direction except the presence at the highest point of the site of a double line of mud-brick walls, two courses high, that feel more or less Hittite to him. But he is not particularly concerned with the Hittites, anyway: they are a Bronze Age folk, and he is looking for something much more ancient. Still, it would be helpful to prove that the Hittites had passed this way too. And this is his dig. He can call this wall proto-Hittite if he feels like it, at least for the time being.

The site where he is working is a difficult one, steep and precarious. A rainstorm of unprecedented ferocity for this dry coast, six winters back, had carved away half the western face of the hill, laying bare the very finds that had brought Halvorsen here in the first place; but the angle of the lie is practically vertical, the soil crumbles easily, and Halvorsen's budget will not allow him to put proper bridging across the worst of the gaps. So he hobbles around up here, walking lopsided as it is because of his torn-up leg, testing the ground as he goes in order to make sure it will bear his weight, and fearing at every moment that he will hit a weak spot and go tumbling down in a black cloud to land on the fanged rocks below.

He knows that he ought to be letting his Turks extend this trench for him. But he feels that he is on the brink of a major discovery. How would the workmen be able to detect the place where the terrain changes, and the proto-Hittite stratum gives way to an even older one?

'They'll know,' Jane Sparmann says. She's the graduate student from Columbia who has been working with him out here for three years, now. 'They may be illiterate laborers, but they've spent their whole lives digging in these mounds and they have a sixth sense about any kind of shift in the matrix.'

'Even so,' Halvorsen has replied whenever this comes up. 'I want to do this myself. I have a *seventh* sense.'

Sparmann laughs. Halvorsen knows that she thinks he is stubborn to the point of irrationality. Very likely Sparmann believes that too many summers under the Mediterranean sun have addled his brain, grand old figure of the field that he is. Well, so be it: she's probably right. But he intends to do his own digging up here, even so. Moving slowly along the stone base of the mud wall, looking for the precise spot at the end of the proto-Hittite wall where the soil darkens into virginity and then the place just beyond it where, he hopes, the Neolithic occupants of this site had erected their primordial acropolis.

It's a fine place for an acropolis. No enemies can come upon you unaware, if you have watchmen posted up here. The hill runs athwart the peninsula for five hundred meters, a sharp rocky ridge. Look to the west and you see the smooth blue sea. To the east, you have a long view of the baking dusty plain.

Halvorsen pokes with his pick, scrapes, peers, brushes the dirt aside, pokes again. Nothing. It's dull work, but he's used to it. Steady toil, unrelieved boredom, sweat and dust, one clump of dirt and rock after another, poke and sift, move along. He thinks enviously of Schliemann unearthing rooms of golden treasure, Howard Carter shining his flashlight beam into the tomb of Tut-ankh-Amen. But of course they had put in their months and years of dusty boredom too.

'*Mudur Bey!*' calls a loud rasping voice from below. '*Mudur Bey!*' His title: 'Mr Director'. The Turks can't or won't learn to pronounce his name. With difficulty Halvorsen levers himself upright, leaning on his shovel, and peers down the eastern slope of the hill to the place where Sparmann and three of the diggers are working, over at the edge of the Greek settlement. Ibrahim, his foreman, is standing in the trench, triumphantly holding up a crude buff-colored pot.

'What is it?' Halvorsen asks.

Jane Sparmann, at Ibrahim's elbow, cups her hand and calls, 'It's full of coins! Athenian owls, some Corinthians, something from Syracuse.'

'Fine,' Halvorsen says, without enthusiasm. 'Give him his bonus.'

'You don't want to see them?'

'Later,' he says.

They always pay the diggers extra for any easily marketable artifacts, to keep them from taking them on their own behalf. The expense is trivial, a hundred lire per coin. Sparmann is excited by the find – she's still young – but to Halvorsen the coins, and indeed the whole Greek settlement, are merely an irritating distraction. Dozens of Greek coins turn up wherever you put a spade in the ground. As for the stumps of a little temple, the hazy outlines of a marketplace: who cares? The Mediterranean world is full of Greek temples. They bring no news. Halvorsen is looking beneath such things, beyond, behind, searching for the secret from which all this Mediterranean splendor sprang. The unknown progenitor-race, the pivot, the fulcrum on which the magnificence turned as it began the centrifugal outreach of its grandeur.

He returns to his digging.

But almost immediately comes another booming cry from Ibrahim: '*Paydos! Paydos!*' Time to quit for the lunch-break.

Halvorsen would just as soon go on working while the others knock off. That would be bad form, though: you mustn't let your workmen think you're lazy, but it's not good to seem maniacally compulsive, either. He hobbles down the hill and over to the workshed, where the usual meal of olives, eggs, canned tuna fish, and warm beer is being dispensed.

'How'd things go, Dr H?' Sparmann asks. She smiles pleasantly – she's very pretty, actually, though Halvorsen would never dream of laying a hand on her – but her subtext is fundamentally malevolent. She knows damned well how it has gone up there, how it goes all the time. But she is politely maintaining the pretense that he may eventually find something on the hill.

'Starting to look promising,' Halvorsen says. Why not? Hope costs nothing.

This season's dig has four weeks to go. And then? Will he spend the off season, as usual, raising money for next year's work, the grant applications, the lecture series, the endless begging among the well-heeled? Not to mention the interminable business of renewing the digging permit, a hassle that was always complicated in unpredictable ways by the twists and turns of Turkish politics. How much easier it would be simply to give up, retire from field work, write some books, find a soft curatorship or chairmanship somewhere.

But that would be an admission of defeat. It had been a calculated risk to propose his theory as openly as he had; if the notion had come from a forty-year-old, the eventual failure to produce substantiation would be accepted by his colleagues simply as a case of a young man's reach exceeding his grasp, but at Halvorsen's age any such failure would be an irrevocable mark of decline, even senility, a regrettable third act to such a brilliant career. He didn't dare abandon his field work. He was condemned by his own insistent hypothesis to stay out here under this glazed blue sky until he found what he was looking for, or else die trying.

'Beer?' someone asks him.

'Please,' says Halvorsen, taking the bottle, though he knows that it will be weary, stale, flat, unprofitable. No surprises there. It is Efes Pilsen, the terrible Turkish beer. Halvorsen would have preferred a Carlsberg; but Copenhagen is a long way away. So he guzzles it, wincing a little, and even has a second one. Warm and weary, yes. Stale. Flat. And definitely unprofitable.

The nights are always strangely cool here, even in summer, with a sharp autumnal edge on them, as though the sun's intense heat has burned a hole in the atmosphere by day and the place is as airless as the moon after dark. Halvorsen sits apart from the others, reads, broods, sips raki, soaks his sore leg. The archaeologists' compound consists of two whitewashed cinderblock storage buildings, a work-shed, and six little tents down by the sandy beach where they sleep. Most of the Turkish workmen make their camps for the night on the shallow slopes just back of the dig, covering themselves with leafy branches or threadbare blankets, though some go home on donkeyback to their village five or six miles up the road.

Halvorsen's assistants – two women, three men, this year – sit outside their tents, waiting for him to go inside and fall asleep. During the season they have coupled off in various spasmodic patterns, as usual, but they try to hide that from him as though he were some sort of chaperone for them. For most of the summer, Halvorsen is aware, Jane Sparmann has been sharing the tent of Bruce Feld of the University of Pennsylvania, and the Chicago girl, Elaine Harris, has been shifting her affections between Martin Altman of Michigan State and the other boy – Riley, O'Reilly, Halvorsen can never remember which – from that university in Ohio. Let them have their fun, Halvorsen thinks: what they do at night is no business of his. But still they wait for him; and at last, though he isn't sleepy yet, he rises and waves goodnight and limps into his tent.

His body aches, his mind is terribly alert. He stretches out on his cot and prays in the clammy darkness for sleep to take him.

Instead the night-voice, that insinuating, tickling voice in his head that has been so insistently frequent of late, comes to him again and says:

– *Here. I want you to see this. This is the Palace of the Triple Queen.*

Every word is perfectly distinct. He has never heard the voice with such clarity before.

And this time the words are followed by an image. Halvorsen beholds on the screen of his mind the façade of a many-columned three-terraced structure that might almost be Hatshepsut's temple at Deir al-Bahri, except that the colonnades fold back upon themselves in topologically implausible ways, as if they were pivoting into some adjacent dimension, and the glowing bas-reliefs along the pediment are utterly alien in style, a procession of slender angular figures interlocking and bending out of focus in the same incomprehensible twisting way. Behind the columns of the topmost terrace lurks some filmy, shadow-cloaked being, barely perceptible except as huge eyes and a ripple of shimmering light, whose frail silvery form nevertheless emanates immense strength and power.

'Who are you?' Halvorsen asks. 'What do you want with me?'

– *And this, this is the courtyard of the Tribunal of the People in the time of the Second Mandala.*

Halvorsen sees a sort of marble beehive, fifty or sixty hexagonal tanks out of each of which rises the face of a huge-eyed hairless figure, more or less human in general outline. They are submerged from their shoulders down in a radiant luminous fluid. Halvorsen is given to understand that these creatures are a single entity in fifty bodies, that in their own era they exerted some kind of high governmental function, that they spent lifetimes of unimaginable length standing in these six-sided pools of nutrients.

– *And what I show you now,* says the voice, *are the ruins of the*

*building known as the Concord of Worlds, which also is of the time
of the Second Mandala, and above it the outlying precincts of the
City of Brass, constructed thirty cycles later.*

Scenes of confused splendor flood his mind. Marble pillars, shining
metal slabs inscribed in unknown languages, obelisks of chalcedony,
all strewn about as though by a giant's hand; and, overlying them
with a casual disdain, the streets of some rigidly geometrical later
city, gleaming with a cruel metallic sheen.

'This is madness,' Halvorsen mutters. He sits up, gropes in the
darkness for his sleeping-pills. 'Leave me alone, will you? Get out
of my mind.'

– I mean no harm.

'Tell me who you are, then.'

– A friend. A colleague.

'I want to know your name.'

– It would mean nothing to you.

This is a new development, actually to be holding a conversation of
sorts with this phantom: with himself, to be more accurate. It seems
to mark a dismaying advance in his mental deterioration and he finds
it terrifying. Halvorsen begins to tremble.

'What do you want with me?' he demands. Shouting out loud,
now. Careful, he thinks. The others will hear you and come running,
and the secret will be out. Poor old coot has lost his mind. He will
beg them to cover it up, and they will promise, but of course gossip
travels so quickly in academic circles –

– I want to offer you – to offer you –

Sputter. Hiss. Static on the line. Then silence.

'Come on, damn you, finish your sentence!'

Nothing. Nothing. Halvorsen feels like weeping. He finds a pill.
Looks for the water pitcher, finds the raki bottle instead. What the
hell. He washes the pill down with a shot of straight raki. Getting
suicidal now? he asks himself. The Turkish whiskey burns his throat.
Almost at once he feels groggy. He wonders, as the drug and the raki
hit him simultaneously, whether he will live to see morning.

But of course he does. After breakfast everyone assembles, Jane
Sparmann calls the roll of workmen, a new day's toil begins. Sweat,

dust, sunscreen, bug repellent. And the tools of the trade: picks, shovels, sifting screens, brushes, tape-measures, envelopes, tags, dust-goggles, sketch-pads, cameras. Jane continues to work in the Greek-era trench; Bruce and Martin will be photographing the Minoan level, this season's central focus, which now has begun to emerge from its overburden; the other two have projects of their own in the Byzantine strata. And Halvorsen painfully ascends the hill for another attempt at unearthing some trace of his long-sought prehistoric civilization.

Business as usual, yes. Another day under the dazzling sun. That fierce light bleaches all color out of everything. Nor is there much in the way of sound: even the surf makes merely a faint snuffling noise here. Two dark puffs of dust to the east are the only blemishes on the brilliant dome of the sky. A stork appears from somewhere and hovers for a long while, wings scarcely moving, surveying the busy archaeologists skeptically from aloft.

Halvorsen, down on his knees, nose to the ground, reaches the end of the brick wall, jabs a probing-fork into the soil, feels the change in texture. It was around here somewhere that the handful of scraggly, badly eroded artifacts of apparent Neolithic origin that had lured him into this project in the first place had been exposed by the storm: a crude bull's-head in baked clay, a fragment of a double-axe amulet of distinctly un-Minoan style, a painted snippet of what he is convinced was a mother-goddess amulet. Year after year he has cut his way toward this point – delayed for two whole seasons by the discovery of the Hittite wall – and now, almost afraid of the answers he is about to get, he is ready to strike downward into the hill to see what lies five or ten meters beneath the surface. He will need the workmen to do that for him, he realizes. But he will be over them like a hawk, watching every shovelful they lift.

This afternoon – maybe tomorrow –

An unexpected interruption comes just then. From the east, a throbbing sputtering sound, a cloud of dust, a dirt-bike chugging down the rough little road that leads to the site. The workmen wave at him from below, calling out, 'Mudur Bey! Mudur Bey!' A messenger has arrived, bringing him a letter from Ankara. Perturbed, Halvorsen makes his way uneasily down from his hilltop. The envelope, soiled and creased, bears the insignia of the Ministry of Education. His fingers quiver a little as he opens it: the Department of Antiquities of the Ministry of Education has jurisdiction over all archaeological digs. Some change must have occurred; and in Turkey all change involving the bureaucracy is change for the worse.

There's been a change, yes. But perhaps not a problem. Halvorsen scans the letter, purple typescript on manila stock, translating quickly. Hikmet Aytul, the Department of Antiquities official who has charge of all archaeological work in this part of the country – Hikmet Bey, Halvorsen calls him, because he is so vast and self-important – has resigned. The new superintendent of excavations is a certain Selim Erbek, an assistant curator of a provincial museum further north along the coast. He is making the rounds of his new responsibilities and intends to pay a visit to Halvorsen's dig in the next two or three days.

'Trouble?' Bruce Feld asks.

Halvorsen shrugs. 'I'm not sure. Bureaucratic reshuffling. Hikmet Bey's out, somebody named Selim Erbek's in. He'll be dropping in to get acquainted with us later in the week.'

'Should we take any special action?' Jane Sparmann wants to know.

'You mean, hide yesterday's coins?' Halvorsen laughs. 'No, no, we play by the rules here. When Selim Bey gets here, we show him everything we've found. Such as it is.' He has already debated, briefly and silently, whether he ought to get started on his own penetration of the hill before the new man arrives. Significant finds might produce unpredictable reactions; it might be wiser to take a reading on this Selim Erbek before plunging in. But Halvorsen rejects the idea. He is here to dig and, if possible, find. No sense wasting time trying to outguess the inscrutable bureaucrats.

After lunch he picks Ibrahim, Ayhan, and Zeki as his workmen and finally begins peeling back the hill, after years of anticipation. Halvorsen has worked with these three men over many seasons and trusts them totally, though he watches them closely all the same. They dig carefully and well, using their picks with surgical delicacy, running their fingers through the clods of earth in search of tiny overlooked artifacts before letting the wheelbarrow man carry the sifted dirt away. But there is nothing to find. This part of the hill, despite the fact that a few anomalous artifacts had been found in one corner of it after that monster storm, seems in general never to have felt the imprint of human use. Wherever you dig, around this site, you turn up *something*, be it Turkish, Byzantine, Greek, Roman, Minoan, whatever. Except here. Halvorsen has magically located the one corner of the place that nobody in the last ten thousand years has seen fit to occupy. It is the utter opposite of his expectations.

Still, there's always tomorrow.

'*Paydos! Paydos!*' comes the call, finally, at dusk. Another day gone, less than nothing to show for it.

Lying in the darkness of his tent, Halvorsen waits for the voice to come, and soon enough it is with him.

– *I will show you more, if you allow it.*

'Go on. Anything you like.'

Halvorsen strives to be calm. He wants to attain numbness in the face of this absurdity. He knows that he must accept the fact of his own unfolding insanity the way he accepts the fact that his left leg will never function properly again.

– *These are the ruins of Costa Stambool.*

Into Halvorsen's mind springs the horrific sight of vast destruction seen at a great distance, an enormous field of horror, a barren and gritty tumble of dreary gray fragments and drab threadbare shards that would make a trash-midden look like a meadow, and all of it strewn incoherently about in a willy-nilly chaotic way. He has spent his life among ruins, but this one is a ruin among ruins, the omega of omegas. Some terrible catastrophe has taken place here.

But then the focus shifts. He is able to see the zone of devastation at closer range, and suddenly it appears far from hideous. Even at its perimeter, flickers of magic and wonder dance over the porous, limy soil of its surface: sprites and visitations, singing wordlessly to him of Earth's immense history and of futures already past, drift upward from the broken edge-tilted slabs and caper temptingly about him.

A shimmer of delicate golden green iridescence that had not been visible a moment ago rises above everything and surrounds it.

– *This was the City of Cities.*

The broken shards are coming to life. The city of Costa Stambool begins to rise into view like a whale breaching the surface of the sea, or like a missile climbing out of an underground silo, or like a vast subterranean tower emerging from its hiding-place in the bowels of the earth. It is an irresistible force as it heaves itself out of the rubble and climbs with a roaring rush to a height Halvorsen can barely calculate.

It is less a city than a single enormous building, incredibly massive at its base and tapering to a narrow, impossibly lofty summit; and it is skinless, wholly without walls, its exterior peeled away on all sides to reveal the layered intricacies of its teeming core. Halvorsen can see a myriad inhabitants moving about within, following the patterns of their daily lives from level to level, from street to street, from room to room.

Bizarrely, the building seems to be standing on edge, its floors at right angles to the ground. But how can that be? It makes no sense. Then Halvorsen realizes that he is being granted a double perspective: somehow he is able to see the interior of the great structure from the side and top at once, a four-dimensional view, piercing downward and upward and backward and forward through the thousands or perhaps even millions of years of the city's existence. That puts him at ease. He understands how one reads the multifarious layers of a long-occupied site.

The voice in his mind guides him along.

– *The walls you see down there, glowing with scarlet phosphorescence, are the oldest levels. On top of these are the structures of the Second Mandala, and then the Third. Here you will recognize the Concord of Worlds and the City of Brass. This is Glissade, the pleasure-city of the Later Third. Here is the palace of the Triple Queen; here, the courtyard of the Emperor of All; down here, the cells of the Tribunal of the People.*

Everything is as perfect as the day it was built; and yet simultaneously every layer reveals signs of the destruction wrought by builders of later eras, and over everything else are the brutal marks of some climactic onslaught of vandals: the work, Halvorsen is told, of the bestial invaders who at the dawn of the climactic Fourth Mandala brought fire and death to this place.

In awe Halvorsen tours the temples of unknown gods and the palaces of dynasties yet unborn but already forgotten. He stares at a vast marble slab proclaiming some empire's grandeur in an incomprehensible script. He enters the Library of Old Stambool, and sees iron-bound chests overflowing with what he understands to be books, though they look more like rubies and emeralds. The guiding voice never ceases, identifying for him the Market of All Wonders, the Gymnasium, the Field of Combat, the Tower of the Winds.

Halvorsen has never seen anything like it. He has never so much as *imagined* anything like it. It is Rome and Babylon and Byzantium and Thebes all at once, raised to the fiftieth power. In this single crushing vision Halvorson feels that he has experienced an entire great civilization, that he has been buried beneath the totality of its immensity.

Then it is gone. As suddenly as it erupted from the ground, the great building subsides into it again, not with a crash but a sigh, a gentle cadence of descent. It falls like a feather on the wind, shrinking down on itself, and within moments Halvorsen sees nothing but the gray field of rubble again.

After a time he says, 'Very impressive. I didn't know I had such powers of invention.'

– *They are not inventions. They are the reality of our age, which I freely make available to you.*

'And who are you, may I ask?'

– *I will tell you. I am an inhabitant of the Fifth Mandala, which is the last epoch of the world you call Earth, very close to the end of all things.*

Halvorsen shivers. The lunacy deepens and deepens.

'You live in the future and are reaching back across time to talk to me?'

– The very distant future, yes.

Halvorsen contemplates that for a moment.

Then he says, 'Why? What do you want from me?'

– *Simply to give you an opportunity to see my world. And to beg you to allow me to see yours. A trade, my time for your time: your body for mine, our minds to change places. I want that very much. I want it more than life itself.*

By day none of what he has heard or seen in the night seems real. There is only the brown sandy site, and the unrelenting red blaze of the sun, and the blue sea, and the different blue of the sky's rigid vault. From the white tents come his young assistants. The workmen have already breakfasted and are waiting for their assignments. '*Gun aydin,*' they say, grinning, showing big white crooked teeth. 'Good morning.' For them this job is a bonanza, the best pay they will ever see. They love it. '*Gun aydin, gun aydin, gun aydin.*'

The morning's work begins. Sunscreen, bug repellent, sweat, dust. Picks, shovels, brushes, tape-measures.

So the madness seems to overtake him, he thinks, only by night. Halvorsen wonders about that. Perhaps the power of his quest for understanding the buried past, here in the remorseless brightness of the day, drives off these phantoms of the imaginary future. Or perhaps it is that the monkish solitude and close atmosphere of his dark, stifling little tent invite hallucinations, especially to a tired man who tends to drink too much raki when he is alone. Either way, he is grateful to leave it behind, the craziness, as he stomps toward this new day's work.

He believes passionately in archaeology as metaphysics. Without true knowledge of the past, how can one comprehend the present, how can one begin to triangulate the future? Of course *true* true knowledge is impossible, but we can attempt partial truths: we can skin the earth's surface looking for clues, we can sift and sort, we can postulate. Halvorsen has spent most of his life doing this. What has it gained him? He can recognize the varying soils of differing layers of occupation. He can name the Emperors of Rome from Augustus to Romulus Augustulus, remembering even to include Quintillus and Florianus. He has – what? Five years left? Ten? – to master all the rest of it, to solve all the pieces of the riddle that he has arrogated to himself. Then he will be gone. He will join the vastness of the past, and the work will belong to others. But for the moment it is his responsibility. And so the work goes on, today for him, tomorrow for the Jane Sparmanns, the Bruce Felds. Will they see it as he does? Or will it merely be a job for them, a highway toward the comforts of tenure? How can you be an archaeologist at all, except out of love, an insatiable desire for the truth, the willingness to give yourself up to quests that may all too easily become obsessions?

Halvorsen's obsessive notion is that Asia Minor and not Mesopotamia was the cradle of civilization. Fertile, with easy access to the Mediterranean, rich in mineral ores, forests, grasslands for grazing, a reasonably benign climate, the peninsula seems to him to have been an ideal site for the transition from Neolithic life to the splendors of the Bronze Age. The flow of conceptualization could only have been down out of Anatolia's rocky spine, he is convinced: to Sumerian Iraq on one side of the cultural watershed, to proto-Minoan Crete on the other, and onward also to Egypt in the south. But there is no proof. There is no proof. Mere smudges and traces remain, where he needs walls and pillars, inscribed tablets, potsherds, idols, weapons. Time has erased it all here in Anatolia, or at least has erased what he needs to provide a foundation for his bold thesis, leaving only confusion and conjecture.

Still, he is certain that this is where it all began. The Catal Huyuk findings tell him that, the engraved pebbles in the Karain Cave, the rock paintings of Beldibi: this is where the first canto of the great epic was written. But where is the proof? He knows that he is working from *a priori* hypotheses, always a great peril for a scientist. This sort of thing is the antithesis of the scientific method. He has allowed himself to seem to be a fanatic, a nut, a Schliemann, an Evans, obsessed with obfuscatory special pleading in defense of his *idée fixe*. Schliemann and Evans, at least, eventually delivered the goods. But he has nothing to show, and soon they will be laughing at him in the halls of academe, if that has not begun already.

Still, he digs on. What else can he do?

It's a long day. The new trench gets deeper and longer and it's still absolutely virgin. Thinking incorrectly that he has spotted something significant jutting from its side, Halvorsen jumps eagerly down into it and wrenches his bad leg so severely that he almost bursts into tears, though they are tears of rage rather than pain. Halvorsen is a big, strapping man whose physical endurance was legendary in the profession, and now he is little more than a cripple. If he could, he would have the leg cut off and replaced with something made of steel and plastic.

The raki helps a little. But only a little.

Lying on his back and massaging the throbbing leg with his left hand with the raki bottle in his right one, Halvorsen says into the dense clinging darkness, 'How did you find me? And why?' He is somewhat tipsy. More than somewhat, maybe.

There is no answer.

'Come on, speak up! Have you been in touch with others before me? Twenty, fifty, a hundred, a hundred thousand different minds, every era from First Dynasty Egypt to the fortieth century? Looking for someone, anyone, who would go for your deal?'

Silence, still.

'Sure you did. You've got a million-year lifespan, right? All the time in the world to cast your line. This fish, that one, this. And now you have me on the hook. You play me. Trade bodies with me, you say, come see the marvels of the far future. You think I'm tempted, don't you? Don't you? But I'm not. Why should I be? Don't I have enough on my plate right here? You think I want to start over, at my age, learning a whole new archaeology? You suppose I need to worry about identifying the strata that signify the fucking Second Mandala?'

No answer. He knows that he is losing control. He never uses obscenities except under extreme stress.

'Well, go fish somewhere else,' Halvorsen says. 'I reject your deal. I piss on your crazy deal. I stay here, you stay there, the way God intended it to be. I go on digging in the dirt of Turkey until my brains are completely fried and you sit there amidst all your fucking post-historic apocalyptic miracles, okay? Costa Stambool! You can take Costa Stambool and –'

At last the voice out of distant time breaks its silence.

– *Is your refusal a final one?*

And, almost in the same moment, another voice from closer at hand, from just outside his tent, in fact:

'Dr Halvorsen? Are you all right, Dr Halvorsen?'

Bruce Feld's voice.

My God, Halvorsen thinks. I'm bellowing and ranting at the top of my lungs, and now they all finally know that I've gone nuts.

'I'm – fine,' he says. 'Just singing, a little. Am I too loud?'

'If you need anything, Dr Halvorsen –'

'Maybe another bottle of raki, that's all.' He laughs raucously. 'No, no, just joking. I'm fine, really. Sorry if I disturbed you.' Let them think I'm drunk; better than thinking I'm crazy. 'Good night, Bruce. I'll try to keep it down.'

And then, again:

– *Is your refusal final?*

'Yes! No. Wait. I have to consider this thing a little, all right? All right?'

Silence.

'God damn it, I need some time to think! – Hey, are you still there?'

Silence.

Gone, Halvorsen thinks. He has given his answer, and the being from the far end of time has broken off the contact, and that is that. Even at this moment the offer is being made to someone of the thirtieth century A.D., or perhaps the thirtieth century B.C., or any of a million other years along the time-line between prehistory and the Fifth Mandala of Costa Stambool. *A trade, my time for your time: your body for mine, our minds to change places.*

'Listen,' Halvorsen says piteously, 'I'm still thinking it over, do you know what I mean? Although I have to tell you, in all honesty, you'd be getting a bum deal. I'm not in really good physical condition. But I want to discuss this proposition of yours a little further before I give you a definitive answer, anyway.'

Nothing. Nothing. An agony of regret.

But then, suddenly:

– Let us discuss, then. What else would you like to know?

The promised visit of the new superintendent of excavations does not occur on the second day after the receipt of the letter from the Ministry of Education, nor on the third. Halvorsen is unsurprised by that. Time moves differently in different cultures; he lives on the Turkish calendar here.

The work is now going so badly that he actually has begun to regard his nightly bouts of madness as comic relief. His leg has swollen, practically immobilizing him; it is so difficult for him to get around now that he is unable to reach his excavation site at the top of the hill, short of being hoisted up there with a sling and pulley. So he supervises fretfully from below. But that makes no difference, because Ibrahim, Ayhan, and Zeki are still digging through virgin soil. Elsewhere all around the site, nice little things are turning up for the others: Riley and Harris have found some bits of Byzantine mosaic in association with coins of the Emperor Heraclius, Feld and Altman have struck an interesting layer of early Minoan sherds, Jane Sparmann has found a cache of glass and terra-cotta beads that may indicate the presence of a previously unsuspected zone of late Greek occupation. The hilltop work, though, is plainly a bust. Hittites, or somebody who built walls in Hittite style, undoubtedly had had a fortress up there four or maybe five thousand years ago, but what Halvorsen is after is some sign of civilization two or three thousand years older than that – some deposit that will convincingly link this coastal outpost to the known Neolithic settlements far to the east at Catal Huyuk – and he has not had the slightest luck. The three anomalous artifacts that that storm had laid bare remain perplexing enigmas, tantalizing, inexplicable.

He consoles himself with conversations in the darkness. The visions of the Fifth Mandala grow ever more baroquely detailed. Halvorsen, who still believes that he is spinning these fantasies within the walls of his own tortured mind, is bemused by the discovery that he has such lavish qualities of imagination within himself. He has thought of himself all along as a prosaic drudge, a plodding digger in musty, dusty ancient realms. Evidently there is more to him than that, a rich

vein of the fabulist locked away somewhere. The realization makes
him uneasy; it seems to call in question the integrity of his own
scholarly findings.

He wants to know about the inhabitants of the remote eon of which
his informant is a denizen.

– There are very few of us. I may be the only one.

'You aren't sure?'

– Contact is very difficult.

'It's easier for you to speak with someone who lived a million
years in your past than it is to pick up the phone and call someone
who lives around the corner from you?'

Apparently so. There has been a great cataclysm, an invasion of
some sort, a climactic battle: the last and ultimately futile stand of
the human race, or rather the evolved and vastly superior successors
to the human race, against an inexorable enemy so terrible that its
nature seems beyond the abilities of Halvorsen's informant to com-
municate. This, it seems, occurred as the closing act of the epoch
known as the Fourth Mandala, when humanity, after having attained
a supreme, essentially god-like height, was thrust down irreparably
into the dust. Now only a few lurkers remain, scuttling through the
heaped-up ruins of previous glorious civilizations, waiting for their
final hours to arrive. Halvorsen gets the impression that they are not
even creatures of flesh and blood, these last few humans, but some
kind of metallic mechanisms, low spherical beetle-like housings, virtually indestructible, in which the souls of the remaining inhabitants
of Earth have taken refuge.

Some resonant chord in Halvorsen's Nordic soul is struck by the
revelation that there will be a Ragnarok after all, a *Götterdämmerung*:
that all gods must have their twilight, even the supernal beings of
humanity's final epoch. He is saddened and exalted by it all at once.
They were beings of a magnificence and power beyond comprehension, a race of glorious heroes, demigods and more than demigods,
and yet they fell, even they. *Will* fall. It is the myth of myths, the
ultimate saga. Odin and and Thor and Heimdall and Tyr and all the
rest of the Aesir will die in the *Fimbulwinter* of the world, when
Fenrir the Wolf breaks his chains and the Midgard Serpent rises and

the fire-demons of Muspelheim come riding forth upon the world. So it has been, over and over, and so it must and will be, to the end of time, even into the days of the great Mandalas yet to come.

'Why come here, though?' Halvorsen asks. 'We're only smelly primitives, hardly more than apes. We live in ignoble times. Why not just stay where you are, up there in the grand and glorious final act of the human drama, and wait for the curtain to come down?'

– *The curtain has already come down, and it happens that I have lived on beyond it. Where is the nobility in that? I want to close the circle; I want to return to the starting point. Come: take my body. Explore my world, which to you will be full of wonders beyond belief. There will be much for you to study here: our immense past is your immeasurable future. Spend a million years, two million, as long as you like, roaming the ruins of Costa Stambool. And let me take your place in your own era.*

'It won't be a fair trade,' Halvorsen warns again. 'You won't be getting as good as you give.'

– *Let me be the judge of that.*

'No. Listen to me. I need to have you realize what you'd be getting. Not only are we mortal – do you really understand what that means, to be mortal? – but I'm not even an especially good specimen of my race. I'm getting to be old, as old goes among us, and I feel very tired and my leg, if you know what a leg is, was badly damaged in an accident last year and I can barely hobble around. Besides which, I've painted myself into a corner professionally and I'm about to become a laughing stock. You'd be walking into a miserable situation. The way I feel now, even the end of the world would be preferable to the mess I'm in.'

– *Is this a refusal of my offer, or an acceptance?*

Halvorsen is baffled for a moment by that. Then he understands, and he begins to laugh.

But of course he is aware that the game he is playing with himself, out there along the borders of sanity, is a dangerous one; and he is glad when sleep at last frees him of these fantastical colloquies. When morning comes, he knows, he must rid his mind of all such nonsense and turn his full attention to the trench on the hill. And either find in it the things that he hopes will be there, or else abandon this site at last, confess his defeat, and make his choice between letting himself be pensioned off and humbly petitioning the Turks to allow him to hunt for traces of extreme Anatolian antiquity someplace else. But he ought not to go on diverting himself with these wishful and fundamentally unhealthy dreams of an escape to the Fifth Mandala.

And eventually morning comes, bringing the usual blast of dry heat, the usual clouds of little black flies, and the usual breakfast of hard-boiled eggs, processed cheese, canned sardines, and powdered coffee. Morning also brings, a couple of hours later, the Department of Antiquities' new superintendent of excavations for this district, Selim Erbek: Selim Bey, as Halvorsen calls him, since in Turkey it's always a good idea to bestow formal honorific titles on anyone who holds any sort of power over you.

Not that Selim Bey seems particularly intimidating. He is very young, thirty at most, a slender man, almost slight, with sleek black hair. He is clean-shaven except for a narrow mustache and is wearing khaki slacks and a thin green shirt already stained with sweat. And – Halvorsen finds this very strange – Selim Bey's demeanor, right from the start, is extraordinarily diffident, almost withdrawn. His voice is almost inaudible and he can barely bring himself to make contact with Halvorsen. The contrast with Hikmet Pasha, his big-bellied, swaggering predecessor, could not be more marked.

Halvorsen offers him breakfast. Selim Bey shakes him off.

'May we speak?' he asks softly, almost timidly.

What the hell is this? Halvorsen wonders. 'Of course,' he says.

'The two of us, only. Man to man, apart from the others.'

Of his assistants, only Jane Sparmann is within hearing range. Does Selim Bey want privacy, or is he simply uncomfortable around women? Halvorsen shrugs and signals to Jane that she should return to her dig. Selim Bey smiles faintly, a quick crinkling of the corner of his mouth. This is all quite odd, Halvorsen thinks.

He says, 'Shall we begin with a tour of the site?'

'You may show me later. We must have our talk first,' says Selim Bey.

'Yes. Certainly.'

The slender little man gestures from the shoreline to the top of the hill. 'You have not found, I take it, any additional Neolithic artifacts here, is that correct?'

'Not as yet, no. I've only recently begun trenching along the original find site – the proto-Hittite wall up there needed a careful excavation first, you see – and although the work thus far hasn't been especially rewarding, there's every reason to expect that –'

'No,' says Selim Bey. 'There is no reason to expect anything.'

'Sorry. I don't follow what you're saying.'

Selim Bey shifts his weight from one foot to the other. His gaze rests on Halvorsen's left cheekbone. His prominent Adam's apple moves up and down like an adolescent's. He seems about to burst into tears.

He says, after a little while, 'I must tell you that the previous superintendent of excavations, Hikmet Bey, did not in fact resign. Hikmet Bey was dismissed.'

'Ah?'

'There were many reasons for this,' says Selim Bey quietly, digging the tip of his boot into the sand as an embarrassed child might do. 'His behavior toward his superiors on certain occasions – his failure to file certain reports in a timely way – his excessive drinking – even his handling, I am sorry to say, of his official financial responsibilities. It is a very unfortunate story and I regret to be telling you of such deplorable things. He needs help, that man. We must all hope that he finds it.'

'Of course,' says Halvorsen piously. 'The poor man.' He has to choke back laughter. The fat old tyrant, unseated at last! Caught with his hand in the till, no doubt. Pocketing the fees that the tourists pay to get into the museum at Bodrum and pissing the money away on raki and little boys.

'The reason I tell you this,' Selim Bey says, 'is that examination of Hikmet Bey's records, such as they were, brought forth certain revelations that it is necessary to share with you, Dr Halvorsen. They concern the Neolithic artifacts that were found at this site after the great storms of some winters ago.'

'Yes?' Halvorsen says. He feels some pressure in his chest.

'A small clay bull's head, a double-axe amulet, a female figurine, all in the Catal Huyuk style.'

'Yes? Yes?'

'I deeply regret to say, Dr Halvorsen, that it appears that these were authentic Catal Huyuk artifacts, which Hikmet Bey obtained at their proper site many hundreds of kilometers from here through illegitimate channels and planted on this hill so that they would be discovered here by a shepherd boy and eventually brought to your attention.'

Halvorsen makes a husky sound, not quite a word.

Selim Bey rushes onward. 'Hikmet Bey knew of your theories, of course. He thought it would be a proud thing for Turkey if they could be proven to be sound. He is correct about that. And so he sought to entice you to return to our land and carry out researches in his area of supervision. But the method that he used to attract your attention was very wrong. I am extremely sorry to inform you of this, and on behalf of my government I wish to offer our profound apologies for this unfortunate if well-meaning deception, for which no justification can possibly be found that can in any way negate the tremendous injury that has been done to you. Again, my deepest apologies, Dr Halvorsen.'

The young man takes half a step back, as if he expects Halvorsen to strike him. But Halvorsen simply stares. He is without words. His mouth opens and closes.

A hoax. A plant. His head is swimming.

'*Pardonnez-moi,*' he says finally, unable for the moment to remember how to say 'Excuse me' in Turkish. He lurches forward, sending Selim Bey skittering out of his way like a frightened gazelle, and stumbles like a wounded ox down the path that leads to the tent colony along the beach. He moves at a terrible speed, heedless of his injured leg, virtually unaware that he has legs at all: he might have been moving on wheels.

'Dr Halvorsen? Dr Halvorsen?' voices call from behind him.

He enters his tent.

I am extremely sorry to inform . . . I wish to offer our profound

apologies . . . no justification can possibly be found . . . the tremen-
dous injury that has been done to you . . .

Right. Right. Right.

The raki provides a kind of quick palliative. He takes a deep pull straight from the bottle, exhales, takes another, takes one more. Good.

Then he kicks off his boots and stretches out on his cot, facing upward. The day's work is well along, out there on the dig, but he can't bring himself to return to it. There is no way that he can face the others, now, after what he has just learned.

The impact of Selim Bey's words is still sinking in. But there is no escaping the fact of his destruction. His theory is empty; he has wasted his time and expended the last of his professional capital on a foolish quest spurred by fraudulent clues.

As the lunch hour nears and Halvorsen still has not emerged from his tent, Feld and Martin Altman and Jane Sparmann come to him to see if he is all right. Even without knowing what it is that Selim Bey has told him, they evidently have guessed that it was highly upsetting news of some sort.

He tries to bluff it through. 'There were some little questions about our permit application,' he tells them. 'Trivial stuff, nothing to worry about. The usual bureaucratic nonsense.'

'If we can help in any way, sir –'

'No need. No need at all.'

Halvorsen realizes, from the way they are looking at him, that they don't believe a word he has said. They must be able to see the outward manifestations of the shock wave that has coursed through his body, the visible signs of his inner demolition. They can have no doubt now that he has heard something shattering from this morning's visitor and that he is struggling to conceal it from them. There is a look of deep concern on their faces, but also, so it seems to him, sympathy verging on pity.

That is more than he can bear. He will not let them patronize him. Feld makes one more stammering offer of assistance, and Halvorsen replies brusquely that it is not necessary, that everything is all right, that he can handle the problem himself. His tone is so blunt that they are startled, and even a little angered, maybe, at this rejection of their solicitude. But he has left them no choice but to go. Jane Sparmann is the last to leave, hovering at the door of his tent an extra moment, searching for the right words but unable to articulate them. Then she too withdraws.

So, then. He is alone with his anguish. And the central issue remains. His occupation is gone. He has made himself something pitiable in the eyes of his colleagues, and that is intolerable.

Contemplating his options now in the face of this disaster, he sees that he really has none at all. Except one, and that is an even greater foolishness than the one that has brought him to this sorry shipwreck on the Turkish shore.

Nevertheless Halvorsen voices it, more out of rage than conviction.

He stares at the roof of the tent. 'All right,' he says savagely. 'It's daytime here, now, but maybe you can hear me anyway. Are you there? Are you listening? I call your bluff. The offer is accepted. You can take over my life back here, and I'll take over yours. Come and get me, if you can. Get me right now.'

Nothing happens. Of course not, Halvorsen thinks. What madness.

He remains motionless, listening to the wind. He hears voices outside, but no words, only faint, indistinct sounds. Perhaps that's the wind too. He feels the faintest of tremors in the tips of his fingers, and perhaps the twitch of a muscle in his cheek, and a certain mild and quickly passing queasiness in the pit of his stomach. That is the raki, he thinks.

'Well?' he says. 'No deal, eh? No, I didn't really think there would be. You were just a fucking hallucination, weren't you? Weren't you?'

What else could it have been? he wonders. What else but an old man's lunatic fantasies? Thoughts of a dry brain in a dry season, nothing more. It was shameful to have made the attempt, even in bitter jest. And now he must get up and go back outside, and formally accept the apologies that Selim Bey has come here to deliver, and explain to the others what has happened, and then go on to pick up the pieces of his life somehow, after all. Yes. Yes. Somehow. He will have to be strong in the face of the humiliation that will be his, but there is no choice. Up, then.

He rises to go outside.

But he discovers as he sets about the process of rising from the cot that he is no longer lying on it, nor is he in his tent, and that in fact he has been utterly changed: in a moment, in the twinkling of an eye. His aging, aching body is gone, and he is a gleaming metallic sphere that moves in a wondrously frictionless way, as if by magic; and when he emerges into the open air from the airless vaulted place in which he has awakened, he enters into a realm of mighty silence, and it is the apocalyptic glories of the Fifth Mandala that he sees under the thin yellow light of evening, the immense tumbled many-layered ruins of the great City of Cities, Costa Stambool, at the end of time.

Death Do Us Part

My book for 1993-94 was the relatively short novel *The Mountains of Majipoor*, which I finished so early in the rainy season that there was time to do a short story or two afterward before I shut the fiction factory down for its traditional spring recess. So I wrote this one in February 1994 tacking a couple of new twists on the old notion of the quasi-immortal who falls in love with someone of normal lifespan. Ellen Datlow bought it for *Omni*, but it never saw print there, because *Omni*'s owner, some months later, decided to transfer his magazine to the mysterious on-line world of the Internet. I was tardy in exploring that world myself and anything 'published' there might just as well have been published on Mars, so far as I was concerned then. The on-line version of *Omni* did indeed make the story available to its cyberspace following, finally, in December of 1996, and technically that's its first publication. But in my own reactionary way I still consider the print media as the only real place of publication for fiction, and to my outmoded way of thinking 'Death Do Us Part' made its publishing debut in the August, 1997 issue of *Asimov's Science Fiction*. As a concession to the realities of the twenty-first century I've given the *Omni* use of the story priority in the copyright acknowledgments at the front of this book, though.

It was her first, his seventh. She was 32, he was 363: the good old April/September number. They honeymooned in Venice, Nairobi, the Malaysia Pleasure Dome, and one of the posh L-5 resorts, a shimmering glassy sphere with round-the-clock sunlight and waterfalls that tumbled like cascades of diamonds, and then they came home to his lovely sky-house suspended on tremulous guy-wires a thousand meters above the Pacific to begin the everyday part of their life together.

Her friends couldn't get over it. 'He's ten times your age!' they would exclaim. 'How could you possibly want anybody that *old*?' Marilisa admitted that marrying Leo was more of a lark for her than anything else. An impulsive thing; a sudden impetuous leap. Marriages weren't forever, after all – just thirty or forty years and then you moved along. But Leo was sweet and kind and actually quite sexy. And he had wanted *her* so much. He genuinely did seem to love her. Why should his age be an issue? He didn't appear to be any older than 35 or so. These days you could look as young as you liked. Leo did his Process faithfully and punctually, twice each decade, and it kept him as dashing and vigorous as a boy.

There were little drawbacks, of course. Once upon a time, long long ago, he had been a friend of Marilisa's great-grandmother: they might even have been lovers. She wasn't going to ask. Such things sometimes happened and you simply had to work your way around them. And then also he had an ex-wife on the scene, Number Three, Katrin, 247 years old and not looking a day over 30. She was constantly hovering about. Leo still had warm feelings for her. 'A wonderfully dear woman, a good and loyal friend,' he would say. 'When you get to know her you'll be as fond of her as I am.' That one was hard, all right. What was almost as bad, he had children three times Marilisa's age and more. One of them – the next-to-youngest, Fyodor – had an insufferable and presumptuous way of winking and sniggering at her, that hundred-year-old son of a bitch. 'I want you to meet our father's newest toy,' Fyodor said of her, once, when yet another of Leo's centenarian sons, previously unsuspected by Marilisa, turned up. 'We get to play with her when he's tired of her.' Someday Marilisa was going to pay him back for that.

Still and all, she had no serious complaints. Leo was an ideal first husband: wise, warm, loving, attentive, generous. She felt nothing but the greatest tenderness for him. And then too he was so immeasurably experienced in the ways of the world. If being married to him was a little like being married to Abraham Lincoln or Augustus Caesar, well, so be it: they had been great men, and so was Leo. He was endlessly fascinating. He was like seven husbands rolled into one. She had no regrets, none at all, not really.

*   *   *

In the spring of '87 they go to Capri for their first anniversary. Their hotel is a reconstructed Roman villa on the southern slope of Monte Tiberio: alabaster walls frescoed in black and red, a brilliantly colored mosaic of sea-creatures in the marble bathtub, a broad travertine terrace that looks out over the sea. They stand together in the darkness, staring at the awesome sparkle of the stars. A crescent moon slashes across the night. His arm is around her; her head rests against his breast. Though she is a tall woman, Marilisa is barely heart-high to him.

'Tomorrow at sunrise,' he says, 'we'll see the Blue Grotto. And then in the afternoon we'll hike down below here to the Cave of the Mater Magna. I always get a shiver when I'm there. Thinking about the ancient islanders who worshipped their goddess under that cliff, somewhere back in the Pleistocene. Their rites and rituals, the offerings they made to her.'

'Is that when you first came here?' she asks, keeping it light and sly. 'Somewhere back in the Pleistocene?'

'A little later than that, really. The Renaissance, I think it was. Leonardo and I traveled down together from Florence –'

'You and Leonardo, you were just like *that*.'

'Like *that*, yes. But not like *that*, if you take my meaning.'

'And Cosimo di' Medici. Another one from the good old days. Cosimo gave such great parties, right?'

'That was Lorenzo,' he says. 'Lorenzo the Magnificent, Cosimo's grandson. Much more fun than the old man. You would have adored him.'

'I almost think you're serious when you talk like that.'

'I'm always serious. Even when I'm not.' His arm tightens around her. He leans forward and down, and buries a kiss in her thick dark hair. 'I love you,' he whispers.

'I love you,' she says. 'You're the best first husband a girl could want.'

'You're the finest last wife a man could ever desire.'

The words skewer her. *Last* wife? Is he expecting to die in the next ten or twenty or thirty years? He is old – ancient – but nobody has any idea yet where the limits of Process lie. Five hundred years? A thousand? Who can say? No one able to afford the treatments has died a natural death yet, in the four hundred years since Process was invented. Why, then, does he speak so knowingly of her as his last wife? He may live long enough to have seven, ten, fifty wives after her.

Marilisa is silent a long while.

Then she asks him, quietly, uncertainly, 'I don't understand why you said that.'

'Said what?'

'The thing about my being your last wife.'

He hesitates just a moment. 'But why would I ever want another, now that I have you?'

'Am I so utterly perfect?'

'I love you.'

'You loved Tedesca and Thane and Iavilda too,' she says. 'And Miaule and Katrin.' She is counting on her fingers in the darkness. One wife missing from the list. 'And – Syantha. See, I know all their names. You must have loved them but the marriages ended anyway. They *have* to end. No matter how much you love a person, you can't keep a marriage going forever.'

'How do you know that?'

'I just do. Everybody knows it.'

'I would like this marriage never to end,' he tells her. 'I'd like it to go on and on and on. To continue to the end of time. Is that all right? Is such a sentiment permissible, do you think?'

'What a romantic you are, Leo!'

'What else can I be but romantic, tonight? This place; the spring night; the moon, the stars, the sea; the fragrance of the flowers in the air. Our anniversary. I love you. Nothing will ever end for us. Nothing.'

'Can that really be so?' she asks.

'Of course. Forever and ever, as it is this moment.'

She thinks from time to time of the men she will marry after she and Leo have gone their separate ways. For she knows that she will. Perhaps she'll stay with Leo for ten years, perhaps for fifty;

302

but ultimately, despite all his assurances to the contrary, one or the other of them will want to move on. No one stays married forever. Fifteen, twenty years, that's the usual. Sixty or seventy, tops.

She'll marry a great athlete next, she decides. And then a philosopher; and then a political leader; and then stay single for a few decades, just to clear her palate, so to speak, an intermezzo in her life, and when she wearies of that she'll find someone entirely different, a simple rugged man who likes to hunt, to work in the fields with his hands, and then a yachtsman with whom she'll sail the world, and then maybe when she's about 300 she'll marry a boy, an innocent of 18 or 19 who hasn't even had his first Prep yet, and then – then –

A childish game. It always brings her to tears, eventually. The unknown husbands that wait for her in the misty future are vague chilly phantoms, fantasies, frightening, inimical. They are like swords that will inevitably fall between her and Leo, and she hates them for that.

The thought of having the same husband for all the vast expanse of time that is the rest of her life, is a little disturbing – it gives her a sense of walls closing in, and closing and closing and closing – but the thought of leaving Leo is even worse. Or of his leaving her. Maybe she isn't truly in love with him, at any rate not as she imagines love at its deepest to be, but she is happy with him. She wants to stay with him. She can't really envision parting from him and moving on to someone else.

But of course she knows that she will. Everybody does, in the fullness of time.

Everybody.

Leo is a sand-painter. Sand-painting is his fifteenth or twentieth career. He has been an architect, an archaeologist, a space-habitats developer, a professional gambler, an astronomer, and a number of other disparate and dazzling things. He reinvents himself every decade or two. That's as necessary to him as Process itself. Making money is never an issue, since he lives on the compounding interest of investments set aside centuries ago. But the fresh challenge – ah, yes, always the fresh challenge –!

Marilisa hasn't entered on any career path yet. It's much too soon. She is, after all, still in her first life, too young for Process, merely in the Prep stage yet. Just a child, really. She has dabbled in ceramics, written some poetry, composed a little music. Lately she has begun to think about studying economics or perhaps Spanish literature. No doubt her actual choice of a path to follow will be very far from any of these. But there's time to decide. Oh, is there ever time!

Just after the turn of the year she and Leo go to Antibes to attend the unveiling of Leo's newest work, commissioned by Lucien Nicolas, a French industrialist. Leo and Lucien Nicolas were schoolmates, eons ago. At the airport they embrace warmly, almost endlessly, like brothers long separated. They even look a little alike, two full-faced square-jawed dark-haired men with wide-flanged noses and strong, prominent lips.

'My wife Marilisa,' Leo says finally.

'How marvelous,' says Lucien Nicolas. 'How superb.' He kisses the tips of his fingers to her.

Nicolas lives in a lofty villa overlooking the Mediterranean, surrounded by a lush garden in which the red spikes of aloes and the yellow blooms of acacias stand out dazzlingly against a palisade of towering palms. The weather, this January day, is mild and pleasant, with a light drizzle falling. The industrialist has invited a splendid international roster of guests to attend the unveiling of the painting; diplomats and jurists, poets and playwrights, dancers and opera singers, physicists and astronauts and mentalists and sculptors and seers. Leo introduces Marilisa to them all. In the antechamber to the agate dining hall she listens, bemused, to the swirl of conversations in half a dozen languages. The talk ranges across continents, decades, generations. It seems to her that she hears from a distance the names of several of Leo's former wives invoked – Syantha, Tedesca, Katrin? – but possibly she is mistaken.

Dinner is an overindulgent feast of delicacies. Squat animated servitors bring the food on glistening covered trays of some exotic metal that shimmers diffractively. After every third course a cool ray of blue light descends from a ceiling aperture and a secondary red radiance rises from the floor: they meet in the vicinity of the great slab of black diamond that is the table, and a faint whiff of burning carbon trickles into the air, and then the diners are hungry all over again, ready for the next delight.

The meal is a symphony of flavors and textures. The balance is perfect between sweet and tart, warm and cool, spicy and bland. A pink meat is followed by a white one, and then by fruit, then cheese, and meat again, a different kind, and finer cheeses. A dozen wines or more are served. An occasional course is still alive, moving slowly about its plate; Marilisa takes her cue from Leo, conquers any squeamishness, traps and consumes her little wriggling victims with pleasure. Now and then the underlying dish is meant to be eaten along with its contents, as she discovers by lagging just a moment behind the other guests and imitating their behavior.

After dinner comes the unveiling of the painting, in the atrium below the dining-hall. The guests gather along the balcony of the dining-hall and the atrium roof is retracted.

Leo's paintings are huge rectangular constructions made of fine sparkling sand of many colors, laid out within a high border of molten copper. The surfaces of each work are two-dimensional, but the cloudy hint of a third dimension is always visible, and even that is only the tip of an underlying multidimensional manifold that vanishes at mysterious angles into the fabric of the piece. Down in those churning sandy depths lie wells of color with their roots embedded in the hidden mechanisms that control the piece. These wells constantly contribute streams of minute glittering particles to the patterns at the surface, in accordance with the changing signals from below. There is unending alteration; none of Leo's pieces is ever the same two hours running.

A ripple of astonishment breaks forth as the painting is revealed, and then a rising burst of applause. The pattern is one of interlaced spirals in gentle pastels, curvilinear traceries in pink and blue and pale green, with thin black circles surrounding them and frail white lines radiating outward in groups of three to the vivid turquoise borders of the sand. Leo's friends swarm around him to congratulate him. They even congratulate Marilisa. 'He is a master – an absolute master!' She basks in his triumph.

Later in the evening she returns to the balcony to see if she can detect the first changes in the pattern. The changes, usually, are minute and subtle ones, requiring a discriminating eye, but even in her short while with Leo she has learned to discern the tiniest of alterations.

This time, though, no expertise is required. In little more than an hour the lovely surface has been significantly transformed. A thick, jagged black line has abruptly sprung into being, descending like a dark scar from upper right to lower left. Marilisa has never seen such a thing happen before. It is like a wound in the painting: a mutilation. It draws a little involuntary cry of shock from her.

Others gather. 'What does it mean?' they ask. 'What is he saying?'

From someone in African tribal dress, someone who nevertheless is plainly not African, comes an interpretation: 'We see the foretelling of schism, the evocation of a transformation of the era. The dark line moves in brutal strokes through the center of our stability-point. There, do you see, the pink lines and the blue? And then it drops down into the unknown dominion beyond the painting's eastern border, the realm of the mythic, the grand apocalyptic.'

Leo is summoned. He is calm. But Leo is always calm. He shrugs away the urgent questions: the painting, he says, is its own meaning, not subject to literal analysis. It is what it is, nothing more. A stochastic formula governs the changes in his works. All is random. The jagged black line is simply a jagged black line.

Music comes from another room. New servitors appear, creatures with three metal legs and one telescoping arm, offering brandies and liqueurs. The guests murmur and laugh. 'A master,' they tell Marilisa once again. 'An absolute master!'

She likes to ask him about the far-away past – the quaint and remote 23rd century, the brusque and dynamic 24th. He is like some great heroic statue rising up out of the mists of time, embodying in himself first-hand knowledge of eras that are mere legends to her.

'Tell me how people dressed, back then,' she begs him. 'What sorts of things they said, the games they played, where they liked to go on their holidays. And the buildings, the architecture: how did things look? Make me feel what it was like: the sounds, the smells, the whole flavor of the long-ago times.'

He laughs. 'It gets pretty jumbled, you know. The longer you live, the more muddled-up your mind becomes.'

'Oh, I don't believe that at all! I think you remember every bit of it. Tell me about your father and mother.'

'My father and my mother –' He pronounces the words musingly, as though they are newly minted concepts for him. 'My father – he was tall, even taller than I am – a mathematician, he was, or maybe a composer, something abstruse like that –'

'And his eyes? What kind of eyes did he have?'

'His eyes – I don't know, his eyes were unusual, but I can't tell you how – an odd color, or very penetrating, maybe – there was *something* about his eyes –' His voice trails off.

'And your mother?'

'My mother. Yes.' He is staring into the past and it seems as if he sees nothing but haze and smoke there. 'My mother. I just don't know what to tell you. She's dead, you realize. A long time, now. Hundreds of years. They both died before Process. It was all such a long time ago, Marilisa.'

His discomfort is only too apparent.

'All right,' she says. 'We don't have to talk about them. But tell me about the clothing, at least. What you wore when you were a young man. Whether people liked darker colors then. Or the food, the favorite dishes. Anything. The shape of ordinary things. How they were different.'

Obligingly he tries to bring the distant past to life for her. Images come through, though, however blurry, however indistinct. The strangeness, the alien textures of the long ago. Whoever said the past is another country was right; and Leo is a native of that country. He speaks of obsolete vehicles, styles, ideas, flavors. She works hard at comprehending his words, she eagerly snatches concrete meanings from his clusters of hazy impressions. Somehow the past seems as important to her as the future, or even more so. The past is where Leo has lived so very much of his life. His gigantic past stretches before her like an endless pathless plain. She needs to learn her way across it; she needs to find her bearings, the points of her compass, or she will be lost.

It is time for Leo to undergo Process once more. He goes every five years and remains at the clinic for eleven days. She would like to accompany him, but guests are not allowed, not even spouses. The procedures are difficult and delicate. The patients are in a vulnerable state while undergoing treatment.

So off he goes without her to be made young again. Elegant homeostatic techniques of automatic bioenergetic correction will extend his exemption from sagging flesh and spreading waistline and blurry eyesight and graying hair and hardening arteries for another term.

Marilisa has no idea what Process is actually like. She imagines him sitting patiently upright day after day in some bizarre womb-like tank, his body entirely covered in a thick mass of some sort of warm, quivering purplish gel, only his head protruding, while the age-poisons are extracted from him by an elaborate array of intricate pipettes and tubes, and the glorious fluids of new youthfulness are pumped into him. But of course she is only imagining. For all she knows, the whole thing is done with a single injection, like the Prep that she undergoes every couple of years to keep her in good trim until she is old enough for Process.

While Leo is away, his son Fyodor pays her an uninvited visit. Fyodor is the child of Miaule, the fifth wife. The marriage to Miaule was Leo's briefest one, only eight years. Marilisa has never asked why. She knows nothing substantial about Leo's previous marriages and prefers to keep it that way.

'Your father's not here,' she says immediately, when she finds Fyodor's flitter docked to the harbor of their sky-house.

'I'm not here to visit him. I'm here to see you.' He is a compact, blockily built man with a low center of gravity, nothing at all in appearance like his rangy father. His sly sidewise smile is insinuating, possessive, maddening. 'We don't know each other as well as we should, Marilisa. You're my stepmother, after all.'

'What does that have to do with anything? You have half a

dozen stepmothers.' Was that true? Could the wives before Miaule be regarded as his stepmothers, strictly speaking?

'You're the newest one. The most mysterious one.'

'There's nothing mysterious about me at all. I'm terribly uninteresting.'

'Not to my father, apparently.' A vicious sparkle enters Fyodor's eyes. 'Are you and he going to have children?'

The suggestion startles her. She and Leo have never talked about that; she has never so much as given it a thought.

Angrily she says, 'I don't think that that's any of your –'

'He'll want to. He always does.'

'Then we will. Twenty years from now, maybe. Or fifty. Whenever it seems appropriate. Right now we're quite content just with each other.' He has found an entirely new level on which to unsettle her, and Marilisa is infuriated even more with him for that. She turns away from him. 'If you'll excuse me, Fyodor, I have things to –'

'Wait.' His hand darts out, encircles her wrist, seizes it a little too tightly, then relaxes to a gentler, almost affectionate grip. 'You shouldn't be alone at a time like this. Come stay with me for a few days while he's at the clinic.'

She glowers at him. 'Don't be absurd.'

'I'm simply being hospitable, Mother.'

'I'm sure he'd be very amused to hear that.'

'He's always found what I do highly amusing. Come. Pack your things and let's go. Don't you think you owe yourself a little amusement too?'

Not bothering to conceal her anger and loathing, Marilisa says, 'What exactly are you up to, Fyodor? Are you looking for vengeance? Trying to get even with him for something?'

'Vengeance? Vengeance?' Fyodor seems genuinely puzzled. 'Why would I want that? I mean, after all, what is he to me?'

'Your father, for one thing.'

'Well, yes. I'll grant you that much. But what of it? All of that happened such a long time ago.' He laughs. He sounds almost jolly. 'You're such an old-fashioned kind of girl, Marilisa!'

*　　*　　*

A couple of hours after she succeeds in getting rid of Fyodor, she has another unexpected and unwanted visitor: Katrin. At least Katrin has the grace to call while she is still over Nevada to say that she would like to drop in. Marilisa is afraid to refuse. She knows that Leo wants some sort of relationship to develop between them. Quite likely he has instigated this very visit. If she turns Katrin away, Leo will find out, and he will be hurt. The last thing Marilisa would want to do is to hurt Leo.

It is impossible for her to get used to Katrin's beauty: that sublime agelessness, which looks so unreal precisely because it is real. She genuinely seems to be only 30, golden-haired and shining in the first dewy bloom of youth. Katrin was Leo's wife for forty years. Estil and Liss, the two children they had together, are almost 200 years old. The immensity of Katrin's history with Leo looms over her like some great monolithic slab.

'I talked to Leo this morning at the clinic,' Katrin announces. 'He's doing very well.'

'You *talked* to him? But I thought that nobody was allowed –'

'Oh, my dear, I've taken forty turns through that place! I know everybody there only too well. When I call, they put me right through. Leo sends his warmest love.'

'Thank you.'

'He loves you terribly, you know. Perhaps more than is really good for him. You're the great love of his life, Marilisa.'

Marilisa feels a surge of irritation, and allows it to reach the surface. 'Oh, Katrin, be serious with me! How could I ever believe something like that?' And what does she mean, *Perhaps more than is really good for him*?

'You should believe it. You must, in fact. I've had many long talks with him about you. He adores you. He'd do anything for you. It's never been like this for him before. I have absolute proof of that. Not with me, not with Tedesca, not with Thane, not with –'

She recites the whole rest of the list. Syantha, Miaule, Iavilda, while Marilisa ticks each one off in her mind. They could do it together in a kind of choral speaking, the litany of wives' names, but Marilisa remains grimly silent. She is weary of that list of names. She hates the idea that Katrin talks with Leo about her; she hates the idea that Katrin still talks with Leo at all. But she must accept it, apparently. Katrin bustles about the house, admiring this, exclaiming rapturously over that. To celebrate Leo's imminent return she has brought a gift, a tiny artifact, a greenish little bronze sculpture recovered from the sea off Greece, so encrusted by marine growths that it is hard to make out what it represents. A figurine of some sort, an archer, perhaps, holding a bow that has lost its string. Leo is a collector of small antiquities. Tiny fragments of the past are arrayed in elegant cases in every room of their house. Marilisa offers proper appreciation. 'Leo will love it,' she tells Katrin. 'It's perfect for him.'

'Yes. I know.'

Yes. You do.

Marilisa offers drinks. They nibble at sweet dainty cakes and chat. Two pretty young well-to-do women idling away a pleasant afternoon, but one is 200 years older than the other. For Marilisa it is like playing hostess to Cleopatra, or Helen of Troy.

Inevitably the conversation keeps circling back to Leo.

'The kindest man I've ever known,' says Katrin. 'If he has a fault, I think, it's that he's *too* kind. Time and again, he's let himself endure great pain for the sake of avoiding being unkind to some other person. He's utterly incapable of disappointing other people, of letting anyone down in any way, of hurting anyone, regardless of the distress to himself, the damage, the pain. I'm speaking of emotional pain, of course.'

Marilisa doesn't want to hear Katrin talk about Leo's faults, or his virtues, or anything else. But she is a dutiful wife; she sees the visit through to its end, and embraces Katrin with something indistinguishable from warmth, and stands by the port watching Katrin's flitter undock and go zipping off into the northern sky. Then, only then, she permits herself to cry. The conversation, following so soon upon Fyodor's visit, has unnerved her. She sifts through it, seeking clues to the hidden truths that everyone but she seems to know. Leo's alleged vast love for her. Leo's unwillingness to injure others, heedless of the costs to himself. *He loves you terribly, you know. Perhaps more than is really good for him.* And suddenly she has the answer. Leo does love her, yes. Leo always loves his wives. But the marriage was fundamentally a mistake; she is much too young for him, callow, unformed; what he really needs is a woman like Katrin, ancient behind her beauty and infinitely, diabolically wise. The reality, she sees, is that he has grown bored already with his new young wife, he is in fact unhappy in the marriage, but he is far too kindhearted to break the truth to her, and so he inverts it, he talks of a marriage that will endure forever and ever. And confides in Katrin, unburdening himself of his misery to her.

If any of this is true, Marilisa thinks, then I should leave him. I can't ask him to suffer on and on indefinitely with a wife who can't give him what he needs.

She wonders what effect all this crying has had on her face, and activates a mirror in front of her. Her eyes are red and puffy, yes. But what's this? A line, in the corner of her eye? The beginning of age-wrinkles? These doubts and conflicts are suddenly aging her: can it be? And this? A gray hair? She tugs it out and stares at it; but as she holds it at one angle or another it seems just as dark as all the rest. Illusions. An overactive imagination, nothing more. *Damn* Katrin! Damn her!

Even so, she goes for a quick gerontological exam two days before Leo is due to come home from the clinic. It is still six months until the scheduled date of her next Prep injection, but perhaps a few signs of age are beginning to crop up prematurely. Prep will arrest the onset of aging but it won't halt it altogether, the way Process will do; and it is occasionally the case, so she has heard, for people in the immediate pre-Process age group to sprout a few lines on their faces, a few gray hairs, while they are waiting to receive the full treatment that will render them ageless forever.

The doctor is unwilling to accelerate her Prep schedule, but he does confirm that a few little changes are cropping up, and sends her downstairs for some fast cosmetic repairs. 'It won't get any worse, will it?' she asks him, and he laughs and assures her that everything can be fixed, everything, all evidence that she is in fact closer now to her fortieth birthday than she is to her thirtieth swiftly and painlessly and confidentially eradicated. But she hates the idea that she is actually aging, ever so slightly, while all about her are people much older than she – her husband, his many former wives, his swarm of children – whose appearance is frozen forever in perfect unassailable youthfulness. If only she could start Process now and be done with it! But she is still too young. Her somatotype report is unanswerable; the treatment will not only be ineffective at this stage in her cellular development, it might actually be injurious. She will have to wait. And wait and wait and wait.

Then Leo comes back, refreshed, invigorated, revitalized. Marilisa's been around people fresh from Process many times before – her parents, her grandparents, her great-grandparents – and knows what to expect; but even so she finds it hard to keep up with him. He's exhaustingly cheerful, almost frighteningly ardent, full of high talk and ambitious plans. He shows her the schematics for six new paintings, a decade's worth of work conceived all at once. He proposes that they give a party for three hundred people. He suggests that they take a grand tour for their next anniversary – it will be their fifth – to see the wonders of the world, the Pyramids, the Taj Mahal, the floor of the Mindanao Trench. Or a tour of the moon – the asteroid belt –

'Stop!' she cries, feeling breathless. 'You're going too fast!'

'A weekend in Paris, at least,' he says.

'Paris. All right. Paris.'

They will leave next week. Just before they go, she has lunch with a friend from her single days, Loisa, a pre-Process woman like herself who is married to Ted, who is also pre-Process by just a few years. Loisa has had affairs with a couple of older men, men in their nineties and early hundreds, so perhaps she understands the other side of things as well.

'I don't understand why he married me,' Marilisa says. 'I must seem like a child to him. He's forgotten more things than I've ever known, and he still knows plenty. What can he possibly see in me?'

'You give him back his youth,' Loisa says. 'That's what all of them want. They're like vampires, sucking the vitality out of the young.'

313

'That's nonsense and you know it. *Process* gives him back his youth. He doesn't need a young wife to do that for him. I can provide him with the illusion of being young, maybe, but Process gives him the real thing.'

'Process jazzes them up, and then they need confirmation that it's genuine. Which only someone like you can give. They don't want to go to bed with some old hag a thousand years old. She may look gorgeous on the outside but she's corroded within, full of a million memories, loaded with all the hate and poison and vindictiveness that you store up over a life that long, and he can feel it all ticking away inside her and he doesn't want it. Whereas you – all fresh and new –'

'No. No. It isn't like that at all. The older women are the interesting ones. We just seem empty.'

'All right. If that's what you want to believe.'

'And yet he wants me. He tells me he loves me. He tells one of his old ex-wives that I'm the great love of his life. I don't understand it.'

'Well, neither do I,' says Loisa, and they leave it at that.

In the bathroom mirror, after lunch, Marilisa finds new lines in her forehead, new wisps of gray at her temples. She has them taken care of before Paris. Paris is no city to look old in.

In Paris they visit the Louvre and take the boat ride along the Seine and eat at little Latin Quarter bistros and buy ancient *objets d'art* in the galleries of St-Germain-des-Prés. She has never been to Paris before, though of course he has, so often that he has lost count. It is very beautiful but strikes her as somehow fossilized, a museum exhibit rather than a living city, despite all the life she sees going on around her, the animated discussions in the cafes, the bustling restaurants, the crowds in the Metro. Nothing must have changed here in five hundred years. It is all static – frozen – lifeless. As though the entire place has been through Process.

Leo seems to sense her gathering restlessness, and she sees a darkening in his own mood in response. On the third day, in front of one of the rows of ancient bookstalls along the river, he says, 'It's me, isn't it?'

'What is?'

'The reason why you're so glum. It can't be the city, so it has to be me. *Us*. Do you want to leave, Marilisa?'

'Leave Paris? So soon?'

'Leave me, I mean. Perhaps the whole thing has been just a big mistake. I don't want to hold you against your will. If you've started to feel that I'm too old for you, that what you really need is a much younger man, I wouldn't for a moment stand in your way.'

Is this how it happens? Is this how his marriages end, with him sadly, lovingly, putting words in your mouth?

'No,' she says. 'I love you, Leo. Younger men don't interest me. The thought of leaving you has never crossed my mind.'

'I'll survive, you know, if you tell me that you want out.'

'I *don't* want out.'

'I wish I felt completely sure of that.'

She is getting annoyed with him, now. 'I wish you did too. You're being silly, Leo. Leaving you is the last thing in the world I want to do. And Paris is the last place in the world where I would want my marriage to break up. I love you. I want to be your wife forever and ever.'

'Well, then.' He smiles and draws her to him; they embrace; they kiss. She hears a patter of light applause. People are watching them. People have been listening to them and are pleased at the outcome of their negotiations. Paris! Ah, Paris!

When they return home, though, he is called away almost immediately to Barcelona to repair one of his paintings, which has developed some technical problem and is undergoing rapid disagreeable metamorphosis. The work will take three or four days; and Marilisa, unwilling to put herself through the fatigue of a second European trip so soon, tells him to go without her. That seems to be some sort of cue for Fyodor to show up, scarcely hours after Leo's departure. How does he know so unerringly when to find her alone?

His pretense is that he has brought an artifact for Leo's collection, an ugly little idol, squat and frog-faced, covered with lumps of brown oxidation. She takes it from him brusquely and sets it on a randomly chosen shelf, and says, mechanically, 'Thank you very much. Leo will be pleased. I'll tell him you were here.'

'Such charm. Such hospitality.'

'I'm being as polite as I can. I didn't invite you.'

'Come on, Marilisa. Let's get going.'

'Going? Where? What for?'

'We can have plenty of fun together and you damned well know it. Aren't you tired of being such a loyal little wife? Politely sliding through the motions of your preposterous little marriage with your incredibly ancient husband?'

His eyes are shining strangely. His face is flushed.

She says softly, 'You're crazy, aren't you?'

'Oh, no, not crazy at all. Not as nice as my father, maybe, but perfectly sane. I see you rusting away here like one of the artifacts in his collection and I want to give you a little excitement in your life before it's too late. A touch of the wild side, do you know what I mean, Marilisa? Places and things he can't show you, that he can't even imagine. He's old. He doesn't know anything about the world we live in today. Jesus, why do I have to spell it out for you? Just drop everything and come away with me. You won't regret it.' He leans forward, smiling into her face, utterly sure of himself, plainly confident now that his blunt unceasing campaign of bald invitation will at last be crowned with success.

His audacity astounds her. But she is mystified, too.

'Before it's too late, you said. Too late for what?'

'You know.'

'Do I?'

Fyodor seems exasperated by what he takes to be her wilful obtuseness. His mouth opens and closes like a shutting trap; a muscle quivers in his cheek; something seems to be cracking within him, some carefully guarded bastion of self-control. He stares at her in a new way – angrily? Contemptuously? – and says, 'Before it's too late for anybody to want you. Before you get old and saggy and shriveled. Before you get so withered and ancient-looking that nobody would touch you.'

Surely he is out of his mind. Surely. 'Nobody has to get that way any more, Fyodor.'

'Not if they undergo Process, no. But you – you, Marilisa –' He smiles sadly, shakes his head, turns his hands palms upward in a gesture of hopeless regret.

She peers at him, bewildered. 'What can you possibly be talking about?'

For the first time in her memory Fyodor's cool cocky aplomb vanishes. He blinks and gapes. 'So you still haven't found out. He actually did keep you in the dark all this time. You're a null, Marilisa! A short-timer! Process won't work for you! The one-in-ten-thousand shot, that's you, the inherent somatic unreceptivity. Christ, what a bastard he is, to hide it from you like this! You've got eighty, maybe ninety years and that's it. Getting older and older, wrinkled and bent and ugly, and then you'll die, the way everybody in the world used to. So you don't have forever and a day to get your fun, like the rest of us. You have to grab it right now, fast, while you're still young. He made us all swear never to say a word to you, that he was going to be the one to tell you the truth in his own good time, but why should I give a damn about that? We aren't children. You have a right to know what you really are. Fuck him, is what I say. Fuck him!' Fyodor's face is crimson now. His eyes are rigid and eerily bright with a weird fervor. 'You think I'm making this up? Why would I make up something like this?'

It is like being in an earthquake. The floor seems to heave. She has never been so close to the presence of pure evil before. With the tightest control she can manage she says, 'You'd make it up because you're a lying miserable bastard, Fyodor, full of hatred and anger and pus. And if you think – But I don't need to listen to you any more. Just get out of here!'

'It's true. Everybody knows it, the whole family! Ask Katrin! She's the one I heard it from first. Christ, ask Leo! Ask Leo!'

'Out,' she says, flicking her hand at him as though he is vermin. 'Now. Get the hell out. Out.'

*   *   *

She promises herself that she will say nothing to Leo about the monstrous fantastic tale that has come pouring out of his horrid son, or even about his clumsy idiotic attempt at seduction – it's all too shameful, too disgusting, too repulsive, and she wants to spare him the knowledge of Fyodor's various perfidies – but of course it all comes blurting from her within an hour after Leo is back from Barcelona. Fyodor is intolerable, she says. Fyodor's behavior has been too bizarre and outrageous to conceal. Fyodor has come here unasked and spewed a torrent of cruel fantastic nonsense in a grotesque attempt at bludgeoning her into bed.

Leo says gravely, 'What kind of nonsense?' and she tells him in a quick unpunctuated burst and watches his smooth taut face collapse into weary jowls, watches him seem to age a thousand years in the course of half a minute. He stands there looking at her, aghast; and then she understands that it has to be true, every terrible word of what Fyodor has said. She is one of *those*, the miserable statistical few of whom everybody has heard, but only at second or third hand. The treatments will not work on her. She will grow old and then she will die. They have tested her and they know the truth, but the whole bunch of them have conspired to keep it from her, the doctors at the clinic, Leo's sons and daughters and wives, her own family, everyone. All of it Leo's doing. Using his influence all over the place, his enormous accrued power, to shelter her in her ignorance.

'You knew from the start?' she asks, finally. 'All along?'

'Almost. I knew very early. The clinic called me and told me, not long after we got engaged.'

'My God. Why did you marry me, then?'

'Because I loved you.'

'Because you loved me.'

'Yes. Yes. Yes. Yes.'

'I wish I knew what that meant,' she says. 'If you loved me, how could you hide a thing like this from me? How could you let me build my life around a lie?'

Leo says, after a moment, 'I wanted you to have the good years, untainted by what would come later. There was time for you to discover the truth later. But for now – while you were still young

– the clothes, the jewelry, the traveling, all the joy of being beautiful and young – why ruin it for you? Why darken it with the knowledge of what would be coming?'

'So you made everybody go along with the lie? The people at the clinic. Even my own family, for God's sake!'

'Yes.'

'And all the Prep treatments I've been taking – just a stupid pointless charade, right? Accomplishing nothing. Leading nowhere.'

'Yes. Yes.'

She begins to tremble. She understands the true depths of his compassion now, and she is appalled. He has married her out of charity. No man her own age would have wanted her, because the developing signs of bodily deterioration in the years just ahead would surely horrify him; but Leo is beyond all that, he is willing to overlook her unfortunate little somatic defect and give her a few decades of happiness before she has to die. And then he will proceed with the rest of his life, the hundreds or thousands of years yet to come, serene in the knowledge of having allowed the tragically doomed Marilisa the happy illusion of having been a member of the ageless elite for a little while. It is stunning. It is horrifying. There is no way that she can bear it.

'Marilisa –'

He reaches for her, but she turns away. Runs. Flees.

It was three years before he found her. She was living in London, then, a little flat in the Bayswater Road, and in just those three years her face had changed so much, the little erosions of the transition between youth and middle age, that it was impossible for him entirely to conceal his instant reaction. He, of course, had not changed in the slightest way. He stood in the doorway, practically filling it, trying to plaster some sort of facade over his all too visible dismay, trying to show her the familiar Leo smile, trying to make the old Leo-like warmth glow in his eyes. Then after a moment he extended his arms toward her. She stayed where she was.

'You shouldn't have tracked me down,' she says.

319

'I love you,' he tells her. 'Come home with me.'

'It wouldn't be right. It wouldn't be fair to you. My getting old, and you always so young.'

'To hell with that. I want you back, Marilisa. I love you and I always will.'

'You love me?' she says. 'Even though –?'

'Even though. For better, for worse.'

She knows the rest of the passage – for richer for poorer, in sickness and in health – and where it goes from there. But there is nothing more she can say. She wants to smile gently and thank him for all his kindness and close the door, but instead she stands there and stands there and stands there, neither inviting him in nor shutting him out, with a roaring sound in her ears as all the million years of mortal history rise up around her like mountains.

The Martian Invasion
Journals of Henry James

Kevin Anderson and I were having dinner one night late in 1994 – he wanted me to provide him with some technical information about the business aspect of a writing career – and at the end of the meal he asked me, changing the subject completely, whether I'd be interested in doing a story for an anthology he was about to edit. 'I very much doubt it,' I replied, perhaps a trifle coolly. I was still working on my novel *Starborne* and was looking forward to an extended holiday from writing once I finished it. And short-story writing had become such a pain in the neck for me, anyway. Kevin persisted. He mentioned the theme: H.G. Wells's *War Of The Worlds* retold as eye-witness accounts from the viewpoints of other great writers of the era (Kipling, Verne, Tolstoy, Mark Twain). I perked up. He mentioned the fee, a very generous one. *Very* generous. Sometimes even a pain in the neck can be worthwhile. 'Can I have Henry James?' I asked.

I might have asked for Joseph Conrad, I suppose. He was a friend of Wells's and lived nearby at the time Wells was writing *War Of The Worlds*. But I've already done plenty of Conrad-channeling (the novel *Downward To The Earth*, which was a replay of 'Heart of Darkness' set on another world, the novella 'The Secret Sharer' that's loosely based on his story of the same name, and a section of my novel *Hot Sky At Midnight* that tangentially re-explores a theme out of *Lord Jim*). And Wells, at the turn of the century, had another friend and neighbor whose writing, very different from Conrad's in all ways, I also admired greatly. The notion of retelling Wells's tale of Martian invaders as if the invasion had been experienced at first hand by pudgy, timid Henry James was too good to resist.

I didn't resist at all. I've rarely had so much fun writing a story.

Omni purchased magazine rights, but very shortly afterward that publication vanished into cyberspace, where I don't spend much time, and I have no idea whether they used it or not. So far as I know, the story's first appearance was in Kevin Anderson's *The War Of The Worlds: Global Dispatches*, published in June, 1996.

Editor's Note:

Of all the treasures contained in the coffin-shaped wooden sea-chest at Harvard's Widener Library in which those of Henry James's notebooks and journals that survived his death were preserved and in the associated James archive at Harvard, only James's account of his bizarre encounter with the Martian invaders in the summer of 1900 has gone unpublished until now. The rest of the material the box contained – the diaries and datebooks, the notes for unfinished novels, the variant drafts of his late plays, and so forth – has long since been made available to James scholars, first in the form of selections under the editorship of F.O. Matthiessen and Kenneth B. Murdock (*The Notebooks of Henry James*, Oxford University Press, 1947), and then a generation later in the magisterial full text edited by Leon Edel and Lyall H. Powers (*The Complete Notebooks of Henry James*, Oxford University Press, 1987).

Despite the superb latter volume's assertions, in its title and subtitle, of being 'complete', 'authoritative', and 'definitive', one brief text was indeed omitted from it, which was, of course, the invasion journal. Edel and Powers are in no way to be faulted for this, since they could not have been aware of the existence of the Martian papers, which had (apparently accidentally) been sequestered long ago among a group of documents at Harvard associated with the life of James's sister Alice (1848-1892) and had either gone unnoticed by the biographers of Alice James or else, since the diary had obviously been composed some years after her death, had been dismissed by them as irrelevant to their research. It may also be that they found the little notebook simply illegible, for James had suffered severely from writer's cramp from the winter of 1896-97 onward; his handwriting by 1900 had become quite erratic, and many of the (largely pencilled) entries in the Martian notebook are extremely challenging even to a reader experienced in Henry James's hand, set down as they were in great haste under intensely strange circumstances.

The text is contained in a pocket diary book, four and a half inches by six, bound in a green leatherette cover. It appears that James used such books, in those years, in which to jot notes that he would later transcribe into his permanent notebook (*Houghton Journal VI*, 26 October 1896 to 10

February 1909); but this is the only one of its kind that has survived. The first entry is undated, but can be specifically identified as belonging to mid-May of 1900 by its references to James's visit to London in that month. At that time James made his home at Lamb House in the pleasant Sussex town of Rye, about seventy miles southeast of London. After an absence of nearly two years he had made a brief trip to the capital in March, 1900, at which time, he wrote, he was greeted by his friends 'almost as if I had returned from African or Asian exile'. After seventeen days he went home to Lamb House, but he returned to London in May, having suddenly shaven off, a few days before, the beard that he had worn since the 1860s, because it had begun to turn white and offended his vanity. (James was then 57.) From internal evidence, then, we can date the first entry in the Martian journals to the period between May 15 and May 25, 1900.

[Undated] Stepped clean-shaven from the train at Charing Cross. Felt clean and light and eerily young: I could have been forty. A miraculous transformation, so simply achieved! Alas, the sad truth of it is that it will always be I, never any younger even without the beard; but this is a good way to greet the new century nevertheless.

Called on Helena De Kay. Gratifying surprise and expressions of pleasure over my rejuvenated physiognomy. Clemens is there, that is, 'Mark Twain'. He has aged greatly in the three years since our last meeting. 'The twentieth century is a stranger to me,' he sadly declares. His health is bad: has been to Sweden for a cure. Not clear what ails him, physically, at least. He is a dark and troubled soul in any case. His best work is behind him and plainly he knows it. I pray whatever God there be that that is not to be my fate.

To the club in the evening. Tomorrow a full day, the galleries, the booksellers, the customary dismaying conference with the publishers. (The war in South Africa is depressing all trade, publishing particularly badly hit, though I should think people would read more novels at a time of such tension.) Luncheon and dinner engagements, of course, the usual hosts, no doubt the usual guests. And so on and on the next day and the next and the next. I yearn already for little restful, red-roofed, uncomplicated Rye.

June 7, LH [Lamb House, Rye]: Home again at long last. London tires me: that is the truth of things. I have lost the habit of it, *je crois*. How I yearned, all the while I was there, for cabless days and dinnerless nights! And of course there is work to do. *The Sacred Fount* is now finished and ready to go to the agent. A fine flight into the high fantastic, I think – fanciful, fantastic, but very close and sustained. Writing in the first person makes me uneasy – it lends itself so readily to garrulity, to a fluidity of self-revelation – but there is no questioning that such a structure was essential to this tale.

What is to be next? There is of course the great Project, the fine and major thing, which perhaps I mean to call *The Ambassadors*. Am I ready to begin it? It will call for the most supreme effort, though I think the reward will be commensurate. A masterpiece, dare I say? I might do well to set down one more sketch of it before commencing. But not immediately. There is powerful temptation to be dilatory: I find a note here from Wells, who suggests that I bicycle over to Sandgate and indulge in a bit of conversation with him. Indeed it has been a while, and I am terribly fond of him. Wells first, yes, and some serious thought about my ambassadors after that.

June 14, Sandgate. I am at Wells's this fine bright Thursday, very warm even for June. The bicycle ride in such heat across Romney Marsh to this grand new villa of his on the Kentish coast left me quite wilted, but Wells's robust hospitality has quickly restored me.

What a vigorous man Wells is! Not that you would know it to look at him; his health is much improved since his great sickly time two years ago, but he is nonetheless such a flimsy little wisp of a man, with those short legs, that high squeaky voice, his somewhat absurd moustaches. And yet the mind of the man burns like a sun within that frail body! The energy comes forth in that stream of books, the marvelous fantastic tales, the time-machine story and the one about Dr Moreau's bestial monsters and the one that I think is my favorite, the pitiful narrative of the invisible man. Now he wants to write the story of a journey to the Moon, among innumerable other projects, all of which he will probably fulfill. But of course there is much more to Wells than these outlandish if amusing fables: his recent book, *Love and Mr Lewisham*, is not at all a scientific romance but rather quite the searching analysis of matters of love and power.

Even so Wells is not just a novelist (a mere novelist, I came close to saying!); he is a seer, a prophet, he genuinely wishes to transform the world according to his great plan for it. I doubt very much that he will have the chance, but I wish him well. It is a trifle exhausting to listen to him go on and on about the new century and the miracles that it will bring, but it is enthralling as well. And of course behind his scientific optimism lurks a dark vision, quite contradictory, of the inherent nature of mankind. He is a fascinating man, a raw, elemental force. I wish he paid more attention to matters of literary style; but, then, he wishes that I would pay *less*. I dare say each of us is both right and wrong about the other.

We spoke sadly of our poor friend and neighbor, Crane [Stephen Crane, the American novelist], whose untimely death last week we both lament. His short life was chaotic and his disregard for his own health was virtually criminal; but *The Red Badge of Courage*, I believe, will surely long outlive him. I wonder what other magnificent works were still in him when he died.

We talk of paying calls the next day on some of our other literary friends who live nearby, Conrad, perhaps, or young Hueffer, or even Kipling up at Burwash. What a den of novelists these few counties possess!

A fine dinner and splendid talk afterward.

Early to bed for me; Wells, I suppose, will stay awake far into the night, writing, writing, writing.

June 15, Spade House, Sandgate. In mid-morning after a generous late breakfast Wells is just at the point of composing a note to Conrad proposing an impromptu visit – Conrad is still despondently toiling at his interminable *Lord Jim* and no doubt would welcome an interruption, Wells says – when a young fellow whom Wells knows comes riding up, all out of breath, with news that a falling star has been seen crossing the skies in the night, rushing high overhead, inscribing a line of flame visible from Winchester eastward, and that – no doubt as a consequence of that event – something strange has dropped from the heavens and landed in Wells's old town of Woking, over Surrey way. It is a tangible thunderbolt, a meteor, some kind of shaft flung by the hand of Zeus, at any rate.

So, *instanter*, all is up with our visit to Conrad. Wells's scientific curiosity takes full hold of him. He must go to Woking this very moment to inspect this gift of the gods; and, willy-nilly, I am to accompany him. 'You must come, you *must*!' he cries, voice disappearing upward into an octave extraordinary even for him. I ask him why, and he will only say that there will be revelations of an earthshaking kind, of planetary dimensions. 'To what are you fantastically alluding?' I demand, but he will only smile enigmatically. And, shortly afterward, off we go.

June 15, much later, Woking. Utterly extraordinary! We make the lengthy journey over from Sandgate by pony-carriage, Wells and I, two literary gentleman out for an excursion on this bright and extravagantly warm morning in late spring. I am garbed as though for a bicycle journey, my usual knickerbockers and my exiguous jacket of black and white stripes and my peaked cap; I feel ill at ease in these regalia but I have brought nothing else with me suitable for this outing. We arrive at Woking by late afternoon and plunge at once into – what other word can I use? – into madness.

The object from on high, we immediately learn, landed with an evidently violent impact in the common between Woking, Horsell, and Ottershaw, burying itself deep in the ground. The heat and fury of its impact have hurled sand and gravel in every direction and set the surrounding heather ablaze, though the fires were quickly enough extinguished. But what has fallen is no meteorite. The top of an immense metallic cylinder, perhaps thirty yards across, can be seen protruding from the pit.

Early this morning Ogilvy, the astronomer, hastened to inspect the site; and, he tells us now, he was able despite the heat emanating from the cylinder's surface to get close enough to perceive that the top of the thing had begun to rotate – as though, so he declares, there were creatures within attempting to get out!

'What we have here is a visitation from the denizens of Mars, I would hazard,' says Wells without hesitation, in a tone of amazing calmness and assurance.

'Exactly so!' cries Ogilvy. 'Exactly so!'

These are both men of science, and I am but a litterateur. I stare in bewilderment from one to the other. 'How can you be so certain?' I ask them, finally.

To which Wells replies, 'The peculiar bursts of light we have observed on the face of that world in recent years have aroused much curiosity, as I am sure you are aware. And then, some time ago, the sight of jets of flame leaping up night after night from the red planet, as if some great gun were being repeatedly fired – in direct consequence of which, let me propose, there eventually came the streak of light in the sky late last night, which I noticed from my study window – betokening, I would argue, the arrival here of this projectile – why, what else can it all mean, James, other than that travelers from our neighbor world lie embedded here before us on Horsell Common!'

'It can be nothing else,' Ogilvy cries enthusiastically. 'Travelers from Mars! But are they suffering, I wonder? Has their passage through our atmosphere engendered heat too great for them to endure?'

A flush of sorrow and compassion rushes through me at that. It awes and flutters me to think that the red planet holds sentient life, and that an intrepid band of Martians has ventured to cross the great sea of space that separates their world from ours. To have come such an immense and to me unimaginable distance – only to perish in the attempt – ! Can it be, as Ogilvy suggests, that this brave interplanetary venture will end in tragedy for the brave voyagers? I am racked briefly by the deepest concern.

How ironic, I suppose, in view of the dark and violent later events of this day, that I should expend such pity upon our visitors. But we could tell nothing, then, nor for some little while thereafter. Crowds of curiosity-seekers came and went, as they have done all day; workmen with digging tools now began to attempt to excavate the cylinder, which had cooled considerably since the morning; their attempts to complete the unscrewing of the top were wholly unsuccessful. Wells could not take his eyes from the pit. He seemed utterly possessed by a fierce joy that had been kindled in him by the possibility that the cylinder held actual Martians. It was, he told me several times, almost as though one of his own scientific fantasy-books were turning to reality before his eyes; and Wells confessed that he had indeed sketched out the outline of a novel about an invasion from Mars, intending to write it some two or three years hence, but of course now that scheme has been overtaken by actual events and he shall have to abandon it. He evidences little regret at this; he appears wholly delighted, precisely as a small boy might be, that the Martians are here. I dare say that he would have regarded the intrusion of a furious horde of dinosaurs into the Surrey countryside with equal pleasure.

But I must admit that I am somewhat excited as well. Travelers from Mars! How extraordinary! *Quel phénomène!* And what vistas open to the mind of the intrepid seeker after novelty! I have traveled somewhat myself, of course, to the Continent, at least, if not to Africa or China, but I have not ruled such farther journeys completely out, and now the prospect of an even farther one becomes possible. To make the Grand Tour of Mars! To see its great monuments and temples, and perhaps have an audience at the court of the Great Martian Cham! It is a beguiling thought, if not a completely serious one. See, see, I am becoming a fantasist worthy of Wells!

(Later. The hour of sunset.) The cylinder is open. To our immense awe we find ourselves staring at a Martian. Did I expect them to be essentially human in form? Well, then, I was foolish in my expectations. What we see is a bulky ungainly thing; two huge eyes, great as saucers; tentacles of some sort; a strange quivering mouth – yes, yes, an alien being *sènza dùbbio*, preternaturally other.

Wells, unexpectedly, is appalled. 'Disgusting . . .dreadful,' he mutters. 'That oily skin! Those frightful eyes! What a hideous devil it is!' Where has his scientific objectivity gone? For my part I am altogether fascinated. I tell him that I see rare beauty in the Martian's strangeness, not the beauty of a Greek vase or of a ceiling by Tiepolo, of course, but beauty of a distinct kind all the same. In this, I think, my perceptions are the superior of Wells's. There is beauty in the squirming octopus dangling from the hand of some grinning fisherman at the shore of Capri; there is beauty in the *terrifiant* bas-reliefs of winged bulls from the palaces of Nineveh; and there is beauty of a sort, I maintain, in this Martian also.

He laughs heartily. 'You are ever the esthete, eh, James!'

I suppose that I am. But I will not retreat from my appreciation of the strange being who – struggling, it seems, against the unfamiliar conditions of our world – is moving about slowly and clumsily at the edge of its cylinder.

The creature drops back out of sight. The twilight is deepening to darkness. An hour passes, and nothing occurs. Wells suggests we seek dinner, and I heartily agree.

(Later still.) Horror! Just past eight, while Wells and I were dining, a delegation bearing a white flag of peace approached the pit, so we have learned – evidently in the desire to demonstrate to the Martians that we are intelligent and friendly beings. Ogilvy was in the group, and Stent, the Astronomer Royal, and some poor journalist who had arrived to report on the event. There came suddenly a blinding flash of flame from the pit, and another and another, and the whole delegation met with a terrible instant death, forty souls in all. The fiery beam also ignited adjacent trees and brought down a portion of a nearby house; and all those who had survived the massacre fled the scene in the wildest of terror.

'So they are monsters,' Wells ejaculates fiercely, 'and this is war between the worlds!'

'No, no,' I protest, though I too am stunned by the dire news. 'They are far from home – frightened, discomforted – it is a tragic misunderstanding and nothing more.'

Wells gives me a condescending glance. That one withering look places our relationship, otherwise so cordial, in its proper context. He is the hard-headed man of realities who has clawed his way up from poverty and ignorance; I am the moneyed and comfortable and overly gentle literary artist, the connoisseur of the life of the leisured classes. And then too, not for the first time, I have failed to seize the immediate horrific implications of a situation whilst concentrating on peripheral pretty responses. To brusque and self-confident Wells, in his heart of hearts, I surely must appear as something charming but effete.

I think that Wells greatly underestimates the strength of my fibre, but this is no moment to debate the point.

'Shall we pay a call on your unhappy friends from Mars, and see if they receive us more amiably?' he suggests.

I cannot tell whether he is sincere. It is always necessary to allow for Wells's insatiable scientific curiosity.

'By all means, if that is what you wish,' I bravely say, and wait for his response. But in fact he is not serious; he has no desire to share the fate of Ogilvy and Stent; and, since it is too late now to return to Sandgate this night, we take lodgings at an inn he knows here in Woking. Clearly Wells is torn, I see, between his conviction that the Martians are here to do evil and his powerful desire to learn all that a human mind can possibly learn about these beings from an unknown world.

June 16, Woking and points east. Perhaps the most ghastly day of my life.

Just as well we made no attempt last evening to revisit the pit. Those who did – there were some such foolhardy ones – did not return, for the heat-ray was seen to flash more than once in the darkness. Great hammering noises came from the pit all night, and occasional puffs of greenish-white smoke. Devil's work, to be sure. Just after midnight a second falling star could be seen in the northwest sky. The invasion, and there is no doubt now that that is what it is, proceeds apace.

In the morning several companies of soldiers took possession of the entire common and much of the area surrounding it. No one may approach the site and indeed the military have ordered an evacuation of part of Horsell. It is a hot, close day and we have, of course, no changes of clothing with us. Rye and dear old Lamb House seem now to be half a world away. In the night I began to yearn terribly for home, but Wells's determination to remain here and observe the unfolding events was manifest from the time of our awakening. I was unwilling to be rebuked for my timidity, nor could I very well take his pony-carriage and go off with it whilst leaving him behind, and so I resolved to see it all out at his side.

But would there be any unfolding events to observe? The morning and afternoon were dull and wearying. Wells was an endless fount of scientific speculation – he was convinced that the greater gravitational pull of Earth would keep the Martians from moving about freely on our world, and that conceivably they might drown in our thicker atmosphere, et cetera, and that was interesting to me at first and then considerably less so as he went on with it. Unasked, he lectured me interminably on the subject of Mars, its topography, its climate, its seasons, its bleak and forlorn landscape. Wells is an irrepressible lecturer: there is no halting him once he has the bit between his teeth.

In mid-afternoon we heard the sound of distant gunfire to the north: evidently attempts were being made to destroy the second cylinder before it could open. But at Woking all remained in a nervewracking stasis the whole day, until, abruptly, at six in the evening there came an explosion from the common, and gunfire, and a fierce shaking and a crashing that brought into my mind the force of the eruption of Vesuvius as it must have been on the day of the doom of Pompeii. We looked out and saw treetops breaking into flame like struck matches; buildings began to collapse as though the breath of a giant had been angrily expended upon them; and fires sprang up all about. The Martians had begun to destroy Woking.

'Come,' Wells said. He had quickly concluded that it was suicidal folly to remain here any longer, and certainly I would not disagree. We hastened to the pony-carriage; he seized the reins; and off we went to the east, with black smoke rising behind us and the sounds of rifles and machine-guns providing incongruous contrapuntal rhythms as we made our way on this humid spring evening through this most pleasant of green countrysides.

We traveled without incident as far as Leatherhead; all was tranquil; it was next to impossible to believe that behind us lay a dreadful scene of death and destruction. Wells's wife has cousins at Leatherhead, and they, listening gravely and with obvious skepticism to our wild tales of Martians with heat-rays laying waste to Woking, gave us supper and evidently expected that we would be guests for the night, it now being nearly ten; but no, Wells had taken it into his head to drive all night, going on by way of Maidstone or perhaps Tunbridge Wells down into Sussex to deliver me to Rye, and thence homeward for him to Sandgate. It was lunacy, but in the frenzy of the moment I agreed to his plan, wishing at this point quickly to put as much distance between the invaders and myself as could be managed.

And so we took our hasty leave of Leatherhead. Glancing back, we saw a fearsome scarlet glow on the western horizon, and huge clots of black smoke. And, as we drove onward, there came a horrid splash of green light overhead, which we both knew must be the third falling star, bringing with it the next contingent of Martians.

Nevertheless I believed myself to be safe. I have known little if any physical danger in my life and it has a certain unreal quality to me; I cannot ever easily accept it as impinging on my existence. Therefore it came as a great astonishment and a near unhinging of my inner stability when, some time past midnight, with thunder sounding in the distance and the air portending imminent rain, the pony abruptly whinnied and reared in terror, and a moment later we beheld a titanic metal creature, perhaps one hundred feet high, striding through the young forest before us on three great metal legs, smashing aside all that lay in its way.

'Quickly!' Wells cried, and seized me by the wrist in an iron grasp and tumbled me out of the cart, down into the grass by the side of the road, just as the poor pony swung round in its fright and bolted off, cart and all, into the woods. The beast traveled no more than a dozen yards before it became fouled amidst low-lying branches and tumbled over, breaking the cart to splinters and, I am afraid, snapping its own neck in the fall. Wells and I lay huddled beneath a shrub as the colossal three-legged metal engine passed high above us. Then came a second one, following in its track, setting up a monstrous outcry as it strode along. 'Aloo! Aloo!' it called, and from its predecessor came back an acknowledging 'Aloo!'

'The Martians have built war-machines for themselves,' Wells murmured. 'That was the hammering we heard in the pit. And now these two are going to greet the companions who have just arrived aboard the third cylinder.'

How I admired his cool analytical mind just then! For the thunder-storm had reached us, and we suddenly now were being wholly drenched, and muddied as well, and it was late at night and our cart was smashed and our pony was dead, the two of us alone out here in a deserted countryside at the mercy of marauding metal monsters, and even then Wells was capable of so cool an assessment of the events exploding all around us.

I have no idea how long we remained where we were. Perhaps we even dozed a little. No more Martians did we see. A great calmness came over me as the rain went on and on and I came to understand that I could not possibly get any wetter. At length the storm moved away; Wells aroused me and announced that we were not far from Epsom, where perhaps we might find shelter if the Martians had not already devastated it; and so, drenched to the bone, we set out on foot in the darkness. Wells prattled all the while, about the parchedness of Mars and how intensely interested the Martians must be in the phenomenon of water falling from the skies. I replied somewhat curtly that it was not a phenomenon of such great interest to me, the rain now showing signs of returning. In fact I doubted I should survive this soaking. Already I was beginning to feel unwell. But I drew on unsuspected reservoirs of strength and kept pace with the indomitable Wells as we endlessly walked. To me this excursion was like a dream, and not a pleasing one. We tottered on Epsomward all through the dreadful night, arriving with the dawn.

June 20? 21? 22? Epsom.

My doubt as to today's date is trivial in regard to my doubt over everything else. It seems that I have been in a delirium of fever for at least a week, perhaps more, and the world has tottered all about me in that time.

Wells believes that today is Thursday, the 21st of June, 1900. Our innkeeper passionately insists it is a day earlier than that. His daughter thinks we have reached Saturday or even Sunday. If we had today's newspaper we should be able to settle the question easily enough, but there are no newspapers. Nor can we wire Greenwich to learn whether the summer solstice has yet occurred, for the Observatory no doubt has been abandoned, as has all the rest of London. Civilization, it appears, has collapsed utterly in this single week. All days are Sundays now: nothing stirs, there is no edifying life.

I too collapsed utterly within an hour or two of the end of our night's march to Epsom, lost in a dizzying rhapsody of fatigue and exposure. Wells has nursed me devotedly. Apparently I have had nearly all of his meager ration of food. There are five of us here, the innkeeper and his wife and daughter and us, safely barricaded, so we hope, against the Martian killing-machines and the lethal black gas that they have been disseminating. Somehow this town, this inn, this little island within England where we lie concealed, has escaped the general destruction – thus far. But now comes word that our sanctuary may soon be violated; and what shall we do, Wells and I? Proceeding eastward to our homes along the coast is impossible: the Martians have devastated everything in that direction. 'We must to London,' Wells insists. 'The great city stands empty. Only there will we find food enough to continue, and places to hide from them.'

It is a source of wonder and mystery to me that all has fallen apart so swiftly, that – in southern England, at least – the comfortable structures of the society I knew have evaporated entirely, within a week, vanishing with the speed of snowflakes after a spring storm.

What has happened? *This* has happened:

Cylinders laden with Martians have continued daily to arrive from the void. The creatures emerge; they assemble their gigantic transporting-carriages; the mechanical colossi go back and forth upon the land, spreading chaos and death with their heat-rays, their clouds of poisonous black vapor, and any number of other devices of deviltry. Whole towns have been charred; whole regiments have been dropped in their tracks; whole counties have been abandoned. The government, the military, all has disintegrated. Our leaders have vanished in a hundred directions. Her Majesty and the Members of Parliament and the entire authority-wielding apparatus of the state now seem as mythical as the knights of the Round Table. We have been thrown back into a state of nature, every man for himself.

In London, so our hosts have told us, all remained ignorantly calm through Sunday last, until news came to the capital from the south of the terror and destruction there, the giant invulnerable spider-like machines, the fires, the suffocating poisonous gas. Evidently a ring of devastation had been laid down on a great arc south of the Thames from Windsor and Staines over through Reigate, at least, and on past Maidstone to Deal and Broadstairs on the Kentish coast. Surely they were closing the net on London, and on Monday morning the populace of that great city commenced to flee in all directions. A few of those who came this way, hoping to reach friends or kin in Kent or East Sussex – there were many thousands – told Wells and the innkeeper of the furious frantic exodus, the great mobs streaming northward, and those other desperate mobs flooding eastward to the Essex shore, as the methodical Martians advanced on London, exterminating all in their path. The loss of life, in that mad rush, must have been unthinkably great.

'And we have had no Martians here?' I asked Wells.

'On occasion, yes,' he replied casually, as though I had asked him about cricket matches or rainstorms. 'A few of their great machines passed through earlier in the week, bound on deadly business elsewhere, no doubt; we called no attention to ourselves, and they took no notice of us. We have been quite fortunate, James.'

The landlord's daughter, though – a wild boyish girl of fourteen or fifteen – has been out boldly roving these last few days, and reports increasing numbers of Martians going to and fro to the immediate south and east of us. She says that everything is burned and ruined as far as she went in the directions of Banstead and Leatherhead, and some sort of red weed, no doubt of Martian origin, is weirdly spreading across the land. It is only a matter of time, Wells believes, before they come into Epsom again, and this time, like the randomly striking godlike beings that they seem to be, they may take it into their minds to hurl this place into ruin as well. We must be off, he says; we must to London, where we will be invisible in the vastness of the place.

'And should we not make an attempt to reach our homes, instead?' I ask.

'There is no hope of that, none,' says Wells. 'The Martians will have closed the entire coast, to prevent an attack through the Strait of Dover by our maritime forces. Even if we survived the journey to the coast, we should find nothing there, James, nothing but ash and rubble. To London, my friend: that is where we must go, now that you are sturdy again.'

There is no arguing with Wells. It would be like arguing with a typhoon.

* * *

June 23, let us say. En route to London. How strange this once-familiar landscape seems! I feel almost as though I have been transported to Mars and my old familiar life has been left behind on some other star.

We are just outside Wimbledon. Everything is scorched and blackened to our rear; everything seems scorched and blackened ahead of us. We have seen things too terrible to relate, signs of the mass death that must have been inflicted here. Yet all is quiet now. The weather continues fiercely hot and largely dry, and the red Martian weed, doubtless finding conditions similar to those at home, has spread everywhere. It reminds me of the enormous cactus plants one sees in southern Italy, but for its somber brick-red hue and the great luxuriance of its habit of growth: it is red, red, red, as far as the eye can see. A dreamlike transformation, somber and depressing in its morbid implications, and of course terrifying. I am certain I will never see my home again, which saddens me. It seems pure insanity to me to be going on into London, despite all the seemingly cogent reasons Wells expresses.

And yet, and yet! Behind the terror and the sadness, how wonderfully exhilarating all this is, really! Shameful of me to say so, but I confess it only to my notebook: this is the great adventure of my life, the wondrous powerful action in which I have ever longed to be involved. At last I am fully living! My heart weeps for the destruction I see all about me, for the fall of civilization itself, but yet – I will not deny it – I am invigorated far beyond my considerable years by the constant peril, by the demands placed upon my formerly coddled body, above all, by the sheer *strangeness* of everything within my ken. If I survive this journey and live to make my escape to some unblighted land I shall dine out on these events forever.

We are traveling, to my supreme astonishment, by *motor-car*. Wells found one at a house adjacent to the inn, fully stocked with petrol, and he is driving the noisy thing, very slowly but with great perseverance, with all the skill of an expert *chauffeur*. He steers around obstacles capably; he handles sharp and frightening turns in the road with supreme aplomb. It was only after we had been on the road for over an hour that he remarked to me, in an offhand way, 'Do you know,

James, I have never driven one of these machines before. But there's nothing at all to it, really! Nothing!' Wells is extraordinary. He has offered to give me a chance at the wheel; but no, no, I think I shall let him be the driver on this journey.

(Later.) An astonishing incident, somewhere between Wimbledon and London, unforgettably strange.

Wells sees the cupola of a Martian walking-machine rising above the treetops not far ahead of us, and brings the motor-car to a halt while we contemplate the situation. The alien engine stands completely still, minute after minute; perhaps it has no tenant, or possibly even its occupant was destroyed in some rare successful attempt at a counter-attack. Wells proposes daringly but characteristically that we go up to it on foot and take a close look at it, after which, since we are so close to London and ought not to be drawing the Martians' attention to ourselves as we enter a city which presumably they occupy, we should abandon our motorcar and slip into the capital on foot, like the furtive fugitives that we are.

Naturally I think it's rash to go anywhere near the Martian machine. But Wells will not be gainsaid. And so we warily advance, until we are no more than twenty yards from it; whereupon we discover an amazing sight. The Martians ride in a kind of cabin or basket high up above the great legs of their machines. But this one had dismounted and descended somehow to the ground, where it stands fully exposed in a little open space by the side of a small stream just beyond its mechanical carrier, peering reflectively toward the water for all the world as though it were considering passing the next hour with a bit of angling.

The Martian was globular in form, a mere ambulatory head without body – or a body without head, if you will – a yard or more in diameter, limbless, with an array of many whip-like tentacles grouped in two bunches by its mouth. As we breathlessly watched, the creature leaned ponderously forward and dipped a few of these tentacles into the stream, holding them there a long while in evident satisfaction, as though it were a Frenchman and this was a river of the finest claret passing before it, which could somehow be enjoyed and appreciated in this fashion. We could not take our eyes from the spectacle. I saw Wells glance toward a jagged rock of some size lying nearby, as though he had it in mind to attempt some brutal act of heroism against the alien as it stood with its back to us; but I shook my head, more out of an unwillingness to see him take life than out of fear of the consequences of such an attack, and he let the rock be.

How long did this interlude go on? I could not say. We were rooted, fascinated, by our encounter with *the other*. Then the Martian turned – with the greatest difficulty – and trained its huge dark eyes on us. Wells and I exchanged wary glances. Should we finally flee? The Martian seemed to carry no weapons; but who knew what powers of the mind it might bring to bear on us? Yet it simply studied us, dispassionately, as one might study a badger or a mole that has wandered out of the woods. It was a magical moment, of a sort: beings of two disparate worlds face to face (so to speak) and eye to eye, and no hostile action taken on either side.

The Martian then uttered a kind of clicking noise, which we took to be a threat, or a warning. 'Time for us to be going,' Wells said, and we backed hastily out of the clearing. The clicking sound, we saw, had notified the Martian's transport-mechanism that it wished to be re-seated in the cupola, and a kind of cable quickly came down, gathered it up, and raised it to its lofty perch. Now the Martian was in full possession of its armaments again, and I was convinced that my last moments had arrived. But no; no. The thing evinced no interest in murdering us. Perhaps it too had felt the magic of our little encounter; or it may be that we were deemed too insignificant to be worth slaughtering. In any event the great machine lumbered into life and went striding off toward the west, leaving Wells and me gaping slackjawed at each other like two men who had just experienced the company of some basilisk or chimera or banshee and had lived to tell the tale.

The following day, whichever one that may be. We are in London, having entered the metropolis from the south by way of the Vauxhall Bridge after a journey on foot that makes my old trampings in Provence and the Campagna and the one long ago over the Alps into Italy seem like the merest trifling strolls. And yet I feel little weariness, for all my hunger and the extreme physical effort of these days past. It is the strange exhilaration, still, that drives me onward, muddied and tattered though I am, and with my banished beard, alas, re-emerging in all its dread whiteness.

Here in the greatest of cities the full extent of the catastrophe comes home with overwhelming impact. There is no one here. We could not be more alone were we on Crusoe's island. The desolation is magnified by the richness of the amenities all about us, the grand hotels, the splendid town-houses, the rich shops, the theaters. Those still remain: but whom do they serve? We see a few corpses lying about here and there, no doubt those who failed to heed the warning to flee; the murderous black powder, apparently no longer lethal, covers much of the city like a horrid dark snowfall; there is some sign of looting, but not really very much, so quickly did everyone flee. The stillness is profound. It is the stillness of Pompeii, the stillness of Agamemnon's Mycenae. But those are bleached ruins; London has the look of a vibrant city, yet, except that there is no one here.

So far as we can see, Wells and I are the only living things, but for birds, and stray cats and dogs. Not even the Martians are in evidence: they must be extending their conquests elsewhere, meaning to return in leisure when the job is done. We help ourselves to food in the fine shops of Belgravia, whose doors stand mostly open; we even dare to refresh ourselves, guiltlessly, with a bottle of three-guinea Chambertin, after much effort on Wells's part in extracting the cork; and then we plunge onward past Buckingham Palace – empty, empty! – into the strangely bleak precincts of Mayfair and Piccadilly.

Like some revenant wandering through a dream-world I revisit the London I loved. Now it is Wells who feels the outsider, and I who am at home. Here are my first lodgings at Bolton St., in Piccadilly; here are the clubs where I so often dined, pre-eminent among them for me the Reform Club, my dear refuge and sanctuary in the city, where when still young I was to meet Gladstone and Tennyson and Schliemann of Troy. What would Schliemann make of London now? I invite Wells to admire my little *pied-à-terre* at the Reform, but the building is sealed and we move on. The city is ours. Perhaps we will go to Kensington, where I can show him my chaste and secluded flat at De Vere Mansions with its pretty view of the park; but no, no, we turn the other way, through the terrifying silence, the tragic solitude. Wells wishes to ascertain whether the British Museum is open. So it is up Charing Cross Road for us, and into Bloomsbury, and yes, amazingly, the museum door stands ajar. We can, if we wish, help ourselves to the Elgin Marbles and the Rosetta Stone and the Portland Vase. But to what avail? Everything is meaningless now. Wells stations himself before some battered pharaoh in the hall of Egyptian sculpture and cries out, in what I suppose he thinks is a mighty and terrible voice, 'My name is Ozymandias, king of kings! Look on my works, ye mighty, and despair!'

What, I wonder, shall we do? Wander London at will, until the Martians come and slay us as they have slain the others? There is a certain wonderful *frisson* to be had from being the last men in London; but in truth it is terrible, terrible, terrible. What is the worth of having survived, when civilization has perished?

Cold sausages and stale beer in a pub just off Russell Square. The red weed, we see, is encroaching everywhere in London as it is in the countryside. Wells is loquacious; talks of his impoverished youth, his early ambitions, his ferociously self-imposed education, his gradual accretion of achievement and his ultimate great triumph as popular novelist and philosopher. He has a high opinion of his intellect, but there is nothing offensive in the way he voices it, for his self-approbation is well earned. He is a remarkable man. I could have done worse for a companion in this apocalypse. Imagine being here with poor gloomy tormented Conrad, for example!

A terrifying moment toward nightfall. We have drifted down toward Covent Garden; I turn toward Wells, who has been walking a pace or two behind me peering into shop-windows, and suggest that we appropriate lodgings for ourselves at the Savoy or the Ritz. No Wells! He has vanished like his own Invisible Man!

'Wells?' I cry. 'Wells, where are you?'

Silence. *Calma come la tomba*. Has he plunged unsuspecting into some unguarded abyss of the street? Or perhaps been snatched away by some silent machine of the Martians? How am I to survive without him in this dead city? It is Wells who has the knack of breaking into food shops and such, Wells who will meet all the practical challenges of our strange life here: not I.

'*Wells!*' I call again. There is panic in my voice, I fear.

But I am alone. He is utterly gone. What shall I do? Five minutes go by; ten, fifteen. Logic dictates that I remain right on this spot until he reappears, for how else shall we find each other in this huge city? But night is coming; I am suddenly afraid; I am weary and unutterably sad; I see my death looming before me now. I will go to the Savoy. Yes. Yes. I begin to walk, and then to run, as my terror mounts, along Southampton Street.

Then I am at the Strand, at last. There is the hotel; and there is Wells, arms folded, calmly waiting outside it for me.

'I thought you would come here,' he says.

'Where have you been? Is this some prank, Wells?' I hotly demand.

'I called to you to follow me. You must not have heard me. Come: I must show you something, James.'

'Now? For the love of God, Wells, I'm ready to drop!' But he will hear no protests, of course. He has me by the wrist; he drags me away from the hotel, back toward Covent Garden, over to little Henrietta Street. And there, pushed up against the façade of a shabby old building – Number 14, Henrietta Street – is the wreckage of some Martian machine, a kind of low motor-car with metallic tentacles, that has smashed itself in a wild career through the street. A dead Martian is visible through the shattered window of the passenger carriage. We stare a while in awe. 'Do you see?' he asks, as though I could not. 'They are not wholly invulnerable, it seems!' To which I agree, thinking only of finding a place where I can lie down; and then he allows us to withdraw, and we go to the hotel, which stands open to us, and esconce ourselves in the most lavish suites we can find. I sleep as though I have not slept in months.

A day later yet. It is beyond all belief, but the war is over, and we are, miraculously, free of the Martian terror!

Wells and I discovered, in the morning, a second motionless Martian machine standing like a sentinel at the approach to the

Waterloo Bridge. Creeping fearlessly up to it, we saw that its back-most leg was frozen in flexed position, so that the thing was balanced only on two; with one good shove we might have been able to push the whole unstable mechanism over. Of the Martian in its cabin we could see no sign.

All during the day we roamed London, searching out the Martians. I felt strangely tranquil. Perhaps it was only my extreme fatigue; but certainly we were accustomed now to the desolation, to the tangles of the red weed, the packs of newly wild dogs.

Between the Strand and Grosvenor Square we came upon three more Martian machines: dead, dead, all dead. Then we heard a strange sound, emanating from the vicinity of the Marble Arch: 'Ulla, ulla, ulla,' it was, a mysterious sobbing howl. In the general silence that sound had tremendous power. It drew us; instead of fleeing, as sane men should have done, we approached. 'Ulla, ulla!' A short distance down the Bayswater Road we saw a towering Martian fighting-machine looming above Hyde Park: the sound was coming from it. A signal of distress? A call to its distant cohorts, if any yet lived? Hands clapped to our ears – for the cry was deafening – we drew nearer still; and, suddenly, it stopped. There seemed an emphatic permanence to that stoppage. We waited. The sound did not begin anew.

'Dead,' Wells said. 'The last of them, I suspect. Crying a requiem for its race.'

'What do you mean?' I asked.

'What our guns could not do, the lowly germs of Earth have achieved – I'll wager a year's earnings on that! Do you think, James, that the Martians had any way of defending themselves against our microbes? I have been waiting for this! I knew it would happen!'

Did he? He had never said a word.

July 7, Lamb House. How sweet to be home!

And so it has ended, the long nightmare of the interplanetary war. Wells and I found, all over London, the wrecked and useless vehicles of the Martians, with their dead occupants trapped within. Dead, all dead, every invader. And as we walked about, other human beings came forth from hiding places, and we embraced one another in wild congratulation.

Wells's hypothesis was correct, as we all have learned by now. The Martians have perished in mid-conquest, victims of our terrestrial bacteria. No one has seen a living one anywhere in the past two weeks. We fugitive humans have returned to our homes; the wheels of civilization have begun to turn once more.

We are safe, yes – and yet we are not. Whether the Martians will return, fortified now against our microorganisms and ready to bend us once more to their wishes, we cannot say. But it is clear now to me that the little sense of security that we of Earth feel, most especially we inhabitants of England in the sixty-third year of the reign of Her Majesty Queen Victoria, is a pathetic illusion. Our world is no impregnable fortress. We stand open to the unpredictable sky. If Martians can come one day, Venusians may come another, or Jovians, or warlike beings from some wholly unknown star. The events of these weeks have been marvelous and terrible, and without shame I admit having derived great rewards even from my fear and my exertions; but we must all be aware now that we are at great risk of a reprise of these dark happenings. We have learned, now, that we are far from being the masters of the cosmos, as we like to suppose. It is a bitter lesson to be given at the outset of this glorious new century.

I discussed these points with Wells when he called here yesterday. He was in complete agreement.

And, as he was taking his leave, I went on, somewhat hesitantly, to express to him the other thought that had been forming in my mind all this past week. 'You said once,' I began, 'that you had had some scheme in mind, even before the coming of the Martians, for writing a novel of interplanetary invasion. Is that still your intent now that fantasy has become fact, Wells?'

He allowed that it was.

'But it would not now be,' I said, 'your usual kind of fantastic fiction, would it? It would be more in the line of *reportage*, would you not say? An account of the responses of certain persons to the true and actual extreme event?'

'Of course it would, of necessity,' he said. I smiled expressively and said nothing. And then, quickly divining my meaning, he added: 'But of course I would yield, *cher maître*, if it were your intention to –'

'It is,' I said serenely.

He was quite graceful about it, all in all. And so I will set to work tomorrow. *The Ambassadors* may perhaps be the grandest and finest of my novels, but it will have to wait another year or two, I suppose, for there is something much more urgent that must be written first.*

* [James's notebooks indicate that he did not actually begin work on his classic novel of interplanetary conflict, *The War of the Worlds*, until the 28th of July, 1900. The book was finished by the 17th of November, unusually quickly for James, and after serialization in *The Atlantic Monthly* (August-December, 1901) was published in England by Macmillan and Company in March, 1902 and in the United States by Harper & Brothers one month later. It has remained his most popular book ever since and has on three occasions been adapted for motion pictures. Wells never did write an account of his experiences during the Martian invasion, though those experiences did, of course, have a profound influence on his life and work thereafter. – The Editor.]

Crossing into the Empire

An odd history involved with this one. I had just finished the Henry James story; and here it was still only January of 1995, my rainy-season novel well behind me, the weather bad, time on my hands. Another short story seemed like a good idea, and, as is usual at such times, my thoughts turned to *Playboy*. I came up with a really lovely alternate-history background, a city that is not quite Byzantine Constantinople but has some resonances with it, and, since *Playboy* is published in Chicago, I interwove Chicago background into it. And sent it off to Alice Turner, who accepted it with pleasing promptitude.

It's always gratifying to sell a story to Alice; but at the very time that she was saying yes to this one, I heard from Janet Berliner, whom I had known years before as Janet Gluckman when she lived in California. She was working with the magician David Copperfield on an anthology of stories of miracles and wonders: did I care to participate? And it struck me that I had just written the perfect David Copperfield story. He is famous, after all, for astonishing disappearance illusions – he will disappear an entire jet airplane, for example, or even the complete Statue of Liberty. Pretty impressive, but what about a whole *city*? That might be beyond even his skills. But not mine: I had just caused the mighty capital of a great empire to vanish from its moorings and reappear in modern-day Chicago. I wanted that story to be in his book.

But I had just sold it to *Playboy*, which has always been my favorite story market. Withdrawing a story that Alice Turner has accepted is, well, one of the two most disagreeable kinds of withdrawal I can imagine. While I was pondering what to do, though, a second story leaped unbidden into my mind – the story with which this book closes, as a matter of fact. And in an astonishingly few number of days it was written. 'Listen,' I told Alice, 'I've just had another story come out of nowhere, and I see another place where I think "Crossing into the Empire" would fit. Suppose I send you the new story and if you like it

345

you can buy that one in place of "Crossing" and send "Crossing" back to me, okay?'

It was a strange way for a writer to do business, but Alice and I have never had a very orthodox editor-writer relationship. I sent her 'The Second Shield,' she liked it well enough to buy it, and I was free to offer 'Crossing into the Empire' for the Copperfield book, *Beyond Imagination*, where it duly appeared in December, 1996. If you had told me, forty years ago, that I would sell two stories to *Playboy* the same week and then would pull one of them back to offer to someone else I would have had a very hard time believing you. But, then, there's a lot that has happened to me over the past forty years that my younger self would have difficulty believing.

Mulreany is still asleep when the Empire makes its mid-year reappearance, a bit ahead of schedule. It was due to show up in Chicago on the afternoon of June 24, somewhere between five and six o'clock, and here it is only eight goddamned o'clock in the morning on the 23rd and the phone is squalling and it's Anderson on the line to say, 'Well, I can't exactly tell you why, boss, but it's back here already, over on the Near West Side. The eastern border runs along Blue Island Avenue, and up as far north as the Eisenhower Expressway, practically. Duplessis says that this time it's going to be a 52-hour visitation, plus or minus 90 minutes.'

Dazzling summer sunlight floods Mulreany's bedroom, high up above the lake. He hates being awake at this hour. Blinking, grimacing, he says, 'If Duplessis missed the time of arrival by a day and a half, how the hell can he be so sure about the visitation length? Sometimes I think Duplessis is full of shit. – Which Empire is it, anyway? What are the towers in the Forum like?'

'The big square pointy-topped pink one is there, with two slender ones flanking it, dark stone, golden domes,' Anderson says.

'Basil III, most likely.'

'You're the man who'd know, boss. How soon do we go across?'

'It's eight in the morning, Stu.'

'Jesus, we've only got the 52 hours, and then there won't be another chance until Christmas. Fifty-one and a half, by now. Everything's packed and ready to go whenever you are.'

'Come get me at half past nine.'

'What about nine sharp?' Anderson says hopefully.

'I need some time to shower and get my costume on, if that's all right with you,' Mulreany says. 'Half past nine.'

It's the Empire of Basil III this time, no question about that. What has arrived is the capital city from the waterfront all the way back to the Walls of Artabanus and even a little strip of the Byzantine Quarter beyond – the entire magnificent metropolis, that great antique city of a hundred palaces and five hundred temples and mosques, green parks and leafy promenades, shining stone obelisks and eye-dazzling colonnades. The Caspian Sea side of the city lines up precisely along South Blue Island Avenue, with the wharves and piers of the city harbor high and dry, jutting from the eastern side of the street. The longest piers reach a couple of blocks beyond Blue Island where it crosses Polk, stretching almost to the southbound lanes of the Dan Ryan Expressway, which seems to be the absolute boundary of the materialization zone. A bunch of fishing boats and what looks like an imperial barge have been taken along for the ride this time, and sit forlornly beached right at the zone's flickering edge, cut neatly in half, their sterns visible here in Chicago but their bows still back in the twelfth century. The whole interface line is bright with the customary shimmering glow. You could walk around the outside edge of the interface and find yourself in the Near West Side, which has been intruded upon but not harmed. Or you could go straight ahead into that glowing field of light and step across the boundary into the capital of the Empire.

One glance and Mulreany has no doubt that the version of the capital that has arrived on this trip is the twelfth-century one. The two golden-domed towers of black basalt that Basil III erected to mark the twentieth anniversary of his accession are visible high above the Forum on either side of the pink marble Tower of Nicholas IX, but there's no sign of the gigantic hexagonal Cathedral of All the Gods that Basil's nephew and successor, Simeon II, will eventually build on what is presently the site of the camel market. So Mulreany can date the manifestation of the Empire that he is looking at now

347

very precisely to the period between 1150 and 1185. Which is good news, not only because that was one of the richest periods of the Empire's long history, making today's trading possibilities especially promising, but also because the Empire of the time of Basil III turns up here more often than that of any other era, and Mulreany knows his way around Basil's capital almost like a native. Considering the risks involved, he prefers to be in familiar territory when he's doing business over there,

The usual enormous crowd is lined up along the interface, gawking goggle-eyed at the medieval city across the way. 'You'd think the dopey bastards had never seen the Empire get here before,' Mulreany mutters, as he and Anderson clamber out of the limo and head for the police barricade. The usual murmuring goes up from the onlookers at the sight of them in their working clothes.

Mulreany, as the front man in this enterprise, has outfitted himself elegantly in a tight-sleeved, close-fitting knee-length tunic of green silk piped with scarlet brocade, turquoise hose, and soft leather boots in the Persian style. On his head he wears a stiff and lofty pyramid-shaped hat of Turkish design, on his left hip a long curving dagger in an elaborately chased silver sheath.

Anderson, as befits his lesser status, is more simply garbed in an old-fashioned flowing tunic of pale muslin, baggy blue trousers, and sandals; his headgear is a white bonnet tied by a red ribbon. These are the clothes of a merchant of late imperial times and his amanuensis, nothing unusual over there, but pretty gaudy stuff to see on a Chicago street, and they draw plenty of attention.

Duplessis, Schmidt, and Kulikowski wait by the barricade, gabbing with a couple of the cops. Schmidt has a short woollen tunic on, like the porter he is supposed to be; he is toting the trading merchandise, two bulging burlap bags. Neither Duplessis nor Kulikowski is in costume. They won't be going across. They're antiquities dealers; what they do is peddle the goodies that Mulreany and his two assistants bring back from their ventures into the Empire. They don't ever put their own necks on the line over there.

Duplessis is fidgeting around, the way he always does, looking at his watch every ten seconds or so. 'About time you got here, Mike,' he tells Mulreany. 'The clock is ticking-ticking-ticking.'

'Ticking so fast the Empire showed up a day and a half early, didn't it?' Mulreany says sourly. 'You screwed up the calculation a little, eh?'

'Christ, man! It's never all that precise and you know it. We've got a lot of complicated factors to take into account. The equinoctial precession – the whole sidereal element – the problem of topological displacement – listen, Mike, I do my best. It gets here every six months, give or take a couple of days, that's all we can figure. There's no way I can tell you to the split second when it's going to –'

'What about the calculation of when it leaves again? Suppose you miss that one by a factor of a couple of days too?'

'No,' Duplessis says. 'No chance. The math's perfectly clear: this is a two-day visitation. Look, stop worrying, Mike. You sneak across, you do your business, you come back late tomorrow afternoon. You're just grouchy because you don't like getting up this early.'

'And you ought to start moving,' Kulikowski tells him. 'Waxman and Gross went across an hour ago. There's Davidson about to cross over down by Roosevelt, and here comes McNeill.'

Mulreany nods. Competitors, yes, moving in on all sides. The Empire's already been in for a couple of hours; most of the licensed crossers are probably there by now. But what the hell: there's plenty for everybody. 'You got the coins?' he asks.

Kulikowski hands Mulreany a jingling velvet purse: some walking-around money. He shakes a few of the coins out into his palm. The Emperor Basil's broad big-nosed face looks up at him from the shiny obverse of a gold nomisma. There are a couple of little silver argentei from the time of Casimir and a few thick, impressive copper sesterces showing the hooded profile of Empress Juliana.

Impatiently Kulikowski says, 'What do you think, Mike, I'd give you the wrong ones? Nothing there's later than Basil III. Nothing earlier than the Peloponnesian Dynasty.' Passing false money, or obsolete money that has been withdrawn from circulation by imperial decree, is a serious mercantile crime over there, punishable by mutilation for the first offense, by death for the second. There are no decrees about passing money of emperors yet to be born, naturally. But that would be stupid as well as dangerous.

'Come on, Mike,' Duplessis says. 'Time's wasting. Go on in.'

'How long did you say can I stay?'

'Like I told you. Almost until sundown tomorrow.'

'That long? You sure?'

'You think it does me any good if you get stranded over there?' Duplessis says. 'Trust me. I tell you you've got until sundown, you've got until sundown. Go on, now. Will you get going, for Christ's sake?'

There's no need for Mulreany to show his transit license. The police know all the licensed border-crossers. Only about two dozen people have the right combination of skills – the knowledge of the Empire's language and customs, the knack of doing business in a medieval country, the willingness to take the risks involved in making the crossing. The risks are big, and crossers don't always come back. The Empire's official attitude toward the merchants who come over from Chicago is that they are sorcerers of some kind, and the penalty for sorcery is public beheading, so you have to keep a low profile as you do your business. Then, too, there's the chance of catching some archaic disease that's unknown and incurable in the modern era, or simply screwing up your timing and getting stuck over there in the Empire when it pops back to its own period of history. There are other odd little one-in-a-thousand glitch possibilities also. You have to have the intellectual equipment of a college professor plus the gall of a bank robber to make a successful living as a crosser.

The easiest place to enter today, according to Kulikowski, is the corner of Blue Island and Taylor. The imperial city is only about four feet above Chicago street level there, and Kulikowski has brought along a plank that he sets up as a little bridge to carry them up the slight grade. Mulreany leads the way; Anderson follows, and Schmidt brings up the rear, toting the two bags of trade goods. As they pass through the eerie yellow glow of the interface Mulreany glances back at Duplessis and Kulikowski, who are beginning to fade from view. He grins, winks, gives them the upturned thumb.

Another couple of steps and Chicago disappears altogether, nothing visible now to the rear except the golden flicker, opaque when seen from this side, that marks the border of the materialization zone. They are in the Empire, now. Halfway across the planet and nine centuries ago in time, waltzing once more into the glittering capital city of the powerful realm that was the great rival of the Byzantines and the Turks for the domination of the medieval world.

Can of corn, he tells himself.

In today, out tomorrow, another ten or twenty million bucks' worth of highly desirable and readily salable treasures in the bag.

The imperial barge – its back half, anyway – is just on their left as they come up the ramp. Its hull bears the royal crest and part of an inscription testifying to the greatness of the Emperor. Lounging alongside it with their backs to the interface glow are half a dozen rough-looking members of the Bulgarian Guard, the Emperor's crack private militia. Bad news right at the outset. They give Mulreany and his companions black menacing glances.

'Nasty bastards,' Anderson murmurs. 'They going to be difficult, you think?'

'Nah. Just practicing looking tough,' says Mulreany. 'We stay cool and we'll be okay.' Staying cool means telling yourself that you are simply an innocent merchant from a distant land who happens to be here at this unusual time purely by coincidence, and never showing a smidgeon of uneasiness. 'But keep close to your gun, all the same.'

'Right.' Anderson slips his hand under his tunic. Both he and Schmidt are armed. Mulreany isn't. He never is.

He figures they'll get past the guardsmen okay. The Bulgars are a wild and unpredictable bunch, but Mulreany knows that nobody over here wants to go out of his way to find trouble at a time when the weird golden light in the sky is shining, not even the Bulgars, because when the light appears and everything surrounding the capital disappears from the view of its inhabitants it means that the powers of sorcery are at work again. Events like this have been going on for 800 years in this city, and everyone understands by now that during one of the sorcery-times there's a fair possibility that some stranger you try to hassle may come right back at you and hit you with very mighty mojo indeed. It's been known to happen.

This is something like Mulreany's 25th crossing – he doesn't keep count, but he doesn't miss an Empire appearance and he's been a licensed crosser for about a dozen years – and he knows his way around town as well as anybody in the trade. The big boulevard that runs along the shore parallel to the wharves is the Street of the Eastern Sun, which leads to the Plaza of the Customs-Brokers, from which five long streets radiate into different parts of the city: the Street of Persians, the Street of Turks, the Street of Romans, the Street of Jews, and the Street of Thieves. There are no Jews to be found on the Street of Jews or anywhere else in the capital, not since the Edict of Thyarodes VII, but most of the best metal-workers and jewelers and ivory-carvers have shops in the quadrant between the Street of Jews and the Street of Thieves, so it's in that section that Mulreany will make his headquarters while he's here.

Plenty of citizens are milling around in the Plaza of the Customs-Brokers, which is one of the city's big gathering-places. Mulreany hears them chattering in a whole bouillabaise of languages. Greek is the Empire's official tongue, but Mulreany can also make out Latin, Persian, Turkish, Arabic, a Slavic dialect, and something that sounds a little like Swedish. Nobody is very upset by what has happened to the city. They've all had experience with this sort of thing before, and all of them are aware that it's just a temporary thing: when the sky turns golden and the capital goes flying off into the land of sorcery, the thing to do is sit tight and wait for everything to get back to normal again, which it eventually will do.

He and Anderson and Schmidt slide smoothly into the crowd, trying to seem inconspicuous without conspicuously seeming to be trying to seem inconspicuous, and leave the plaza on the far side by way of the Street of Jews. There was a decent hotel seven or eight blocks up that way the last time he was here in the reign of Basil III, and though he doesn't know whether the date of that visit, in Empire time, was five years ago or five years yet to come, he figures there's a good chance the hotel will be there today. Things don't change really fast in the medieval world, except when some invading horde comes in and rearranges the real estate, and that isn't due to happen in this city for another couple of centuries.

The hotel is exactly where he remembers it. It's not quite in a class with the Drake or the Ritz-Carlton: more like a big barn, in fact, since the ground floor is entirely given over to straw-strewn stables for the horses and camels and donkeys of the guests, and the actual guest rooms are upstairs, a series of small square chambers with stiff clammy mattresses placed right on the stone floors, and tiny windows that have actual glass in them, almost clear enough to see through. Nothing lavish, not even really very comfortable, but the place is reasonably clean, at least, with respectable lavatory facilities on every floor and a relatively insignificant population of bugs and ticks. A pleasant smell of spices from the bazaar next door, ginger and aniseed and nutmeg and cinnamon, maybe a little opium and hashish too, drifts in and conceals other less savory aromas that might be wandering through the building. The place is okay. It'll do for one night, anyway.

The innkeeper is a different one from last time, a gap-toothed red-haired Greek with only one eye, who gives Mulreany a leering smirk and says, 'In town for the sorcery-trading, are you?'

'The what?' Mulreany asks, all innocence.

'Don't pretend you don't know, brother. What do you think that ring of witch-fire is, all around the city? Where do you think the Eastern Sea has gone, and the Genoese Quarter, and Persian Town, and everything else that lies just outside the city walls? It's sorcery-time here again, my friend!'

'Is it, now?' Mulreany says, making no great show of interest. 'I wouldn't know. My cousins and I are here to deal in pots and pans, and perhaps do a little business in daggers and swords.' He colors his Greek with a broad, braying yokel accent, by way of emphasizing that he's much too dumb to be a sorcerer.

But the innkeeper is annoyingly persistent. 'Merely let me have one of those metal tubes that bring near what is far off,' he says, with a little wheedling movement of his big shoulders, 'and my best rooms are yours for three weeks, and all your meals besides.'

He must mean a spyglass. Binoculars aren't likely to do him much good. Even more broadly Mulreany says, 'Pots, yes, my good brother. Pans, yes. But miraculous metal tubes, I must say ye nay. Such things are not our commodities, brother.'

The lone eye, ice-blue and bloodshot, bores nastily in on him. 'Would a knife of many blades be among your commodities, then? A metal box of fire? A flask of the devil's brandy?'

'I tell you, we be not sorcerers,' says Mulreany stolidly, letting just a bit of annoyance show. He shifts his weight slowly from leg to leg, a ponderous hayseed gesture. 'We are but decent simple merchants in search of lodging in return for good coin, and if we cannot find it here, brother, we fain must seek it elsewhere.'

He starts to swing about to leave. The innkeeper hastily backs off from his wheedling, and Mulreany is able to strike a straightforward deal for a night's lodging, three rooms for a couple of heavy copper sesterces, with tomorrow's breakfast of rough bread, preserved lamb, and beer thrown in.

Wistfully the innkeeper says, 'I was sure at last I had some sorcerers before me, who would favor me with some of the wondrous things that the high dukes possess.'

'You have sorcerers on the brain,' Mulreany tells him, as they start upstairs. 'We are but simple folk, with none of the devil's goods in our bags.'

Does the innkeeper believe him? Who knows? They all covet the illicit stuff the sorcerers bring, but only the very richest can afford it. Skepticism and greed still glitter in that single eye.

Well, Mulreany has told nothing but God's truth: he is no sorcerer, just a merchant from a far land. But real sorcerers must have been at work here at some time in the past. What else could it have been but black magic, Mulreany figures, that set the city floating in time in the first place? The capital, he knows, has been adrift for most of its lengthy history. He himself, on various crossings, has entered versions of the city as early as that of the reign of Miklos, who was fourth century A.D., and as late as the somber time of Kartouf the Hapless, right at the end, just before the Mongol conquest in 1412. For Chicagoans, the periodic comings and goings of the city are just an interesting novelty, but for these people it must be a real nuisance to find themselves constantly floating around in time and space. Mulreany imagines that one of the imperial wizards must have accidentally put the hex on the place, long ago, some kind of wizardy experiment that misfired and set up a time-travel effect that won't stop.

'Half past ten,' Mulreany announces. It's more like noon, actually – the sun's practically straight overhead, glinting behind the spooky light of the interface effects – but he'll stay on Chicago time throughout the crossing. It's simpler that way. If Duplessis is right the city is due to disappear back into its own era about eleven o'clock Thursday morning. Mulreany likes a 12-to-14 hour safety margin, which means heading back into Chicago by seven o'clock or so Wednesday night. 'Let's get to work,' he says.

The first stop is a jeweler's shop three blocks east of the Street of Jews that belongs to a Turkish family named Suleimanyi. Mulreany has been doing satisfactory business with the Suleimanyis, on and off, for something like a century Empire time, beginning with Mehmet Suleimanyi early in Basil III's reign and continuing with his grandfather Ahmet, who ran the shop fifty years earlier in the time of the Emperor Polifemas, and then with Mehmet's son Ali, and with Ali's grandson, also named Mehmet, during the reign of Simeon II. He does his best to conceal from the various Suleimanyis that he's been coming to them out of chronological order, but he doubts that they would care anyway. What they care about is the profit they can turn on the highly desirable foreign goods he brings them. It's a real meeting of common interests, every time.

Mulreany gets a blank look of nonrecognition from the man who opens the slitted door of the familiar shop for him. The Suleimanyis all look more or less alike – slender, swarthy hawk-nosed men with impressive curling mustachios – and Mulreany isn't sure, as he enters, which one he's encountering today. This one has the standard Suleimanyi features and appears to be about thirty. Mulreany assumes, pending further information, that it's Mehmet the First or his son Ali, the main Suleimanyis of Basil's reign, but perhaps he has showed up on this trip some point in time at which neither of them has met him before. So for all intents and purposes he is facing an absolute stranger. You get a lot of mismatches of this sort when you move back and forth across the time interface.

A tricky business. He has to decide whether to identify himself for what he really is or to fold his cards and try someplace else that seems safer. It calls for an act of faith: there's always the chance that the man he approaches may figure that there's more profit to be had in selling him out to the police as a sorcerer than in doing business with him. But the Suleimanyis have always been on the up and up and Mulreany has no reason to mistrust this one. So he takes a deep breath and offers a sweeping salaam and says, in classier Greek than he had used with the innkeeper, 'I am Mulreany of Chicago, who once more returns bringing treasure from afar to offer my friend the inestimable master Suleimanyi.'

This is the moment of maximum danger. He searches Suleimanyi's face for hints of incipient treachery.

But what he sees is a quick warm smile with nothing more sinister than balance-sheet calculations behind it: a flash of genuine mercantile pleasure. The jeweler eagerly beckons him into the shop, which is dark and musty, lit only by two immense wax tapers. Anderson and Schmidt come in behind him, Schmidt taking care to bolt the door. Suleimanyi snaps his fingers, and a small solemn boy of about ten appears out of the shadows, bearing an ornate flask and four shallow crystal bowls. The jeweler pours some sort of yellowish-green brandy for them. 'My late father often spoke of you, O Mulreany, and his father before him. It gives me great joy that you have returned to us. I am Selim, son of Ali.'

If Ali is dead, this must be very late in the long reign of Basil III. The little boy is probably Mehmet the Second, whom Mulreany will meet twenty or thirty years down the line in the time of Emperor Simeon. It makes him a little edgy to discover that he has landed here in the great Emperor Basil's final years, because the Emperor apparently went a little crazy when he was very old, turning into something of a despot, and a lot of peculiar things were known to have occurred. But what the hell: they don't plan to be dropping in for tea at the imperial palace.

Before any transactions can take place an elaborate ritual of sipping the fiery brandy and exchanging bland snippets of conversation must occur. Selim Suleimanyi politely inquires after the health of the monarch of Mulreany's country and asks if it has been the case that unruly barbarians have been causing problems for them lately along their borders. Mulreany assures him that all is well in and around Chicago and that the Mayor is fine. He expresses the hope that the Empire's far-flung armies are meeting with success in the distant lands where they currently campaign. This goes on and on, an interminable spinning of trivial talk. Mulreany has learned to be patient. There is no hurrying these bazaar guys. But finally Suleimanyi says, 'Perhaps now you will show me the things you have brought with you.'

Mulreany has his own ritual for this. Schmidt opens one of the big burlap bags and holds it stolidly out; Mulreany gives instructions in English to Anderson; Anderson pulls items out of the bag and lays them out for Suleimanyi's inspection.

Five Swiss Army knives come forth first. Then two nice pairs of Bausch & Lomb binoculars, and three cans of Coca-Cola.

'All right,' Mulreany orders. 'Hold it there.'

He waits. Suleimanyi opens a chest beneath the table and draws out a beautiful ivory hunting horn encircled by three intricately engraved silver bands showing dogs, stags, and hunters. He rests it expectantly on his open palm and smiles.

'A couple of more Cokes,' Mulreany says. 'And three bottles of Giorgio.'

Suleimanyi's smile grows broader. But still he doesn't hand over the hunting horn.

'Plus two of the cigarette lighters,' says Mulreany.

Even that doesn't seem to be enough. There is a long tense pause. 'Take away one of the Swiss Army knives and pull out six ball point pens.'

The subtraction of the knife is intended as a signal to Suleimanyi that Mulreany is starting to reach the limits of his price. Suleimanyi understands. He picks up one of the binoculars, twiddles with its focus, peers through it. Binoculars have long been one of the most popular trading items for Mulreany, the magical tubes that bring far things close. 'Another of these?' Suleimanyi says.

'In place of two knives, yes.'

'Done,' says Suleimanyi.

Now it's the Turk's turn. He produces an exquisite pendant of gold filigree inlaid with cloisonné enamel and hands it to Mulreany to be admired. Mulreany tells Anderson to bring out the Chanel Number Five, a bottle of Chivas, two more pairs of binoculars, and a packet of sewing needles. Suleimanyi appears pleased, but not pleased enough. 'Give him a compass,' Mulreany orders.

Obviously Suleimanyi has never seen a compass before. He fingers the shiny steel case and says, 'What is this?'

Mulreany indicates the needle. 'This points north. Now turn toward the door. Do you see? The needle still points north.'

The jeweler grasps the principle, and its commercial value in a maritime nation, instantly. His eyes light up and he says, 'One more of these and we have a deal.'

'Alas,' says Mulreany. 'Compasses are great rarities. I can spare only one.' He signals Anderson to begin putting things away.

But Suleimanyi, grinning, pulls back his hand when Mulreany reaches for the compass. 'It is sufficient, then, the one,' he says. 'The pendant is yours.' He leans close. 'This is witchcraft, this north-pointing device?'

'Not at all. A simple natural law at work.'

'Ah. Of course. You will bring me more of these?'

'On my very next visit,' Mulreany promises.

They move along, after Suleimanyi has treated them to the spicy tea that concludes every business transaction in the Empire. Mulreany doesn't like to do all his trading at a single shop. He goes looking now for a place he remembers near the intersection of Baghdad Way and the Street of Thieves, a dealer in precious stones, but it isn't there; what he finds instead, though, is even better, a Persian goldsmith's place where – after more brandy, more chitchat – he warily lets it be known that he has unusual merchandise from far-off lands for sale, meets with a reassuring response, and exchanges some Swiss Army knives, binoculars, various sorts of perfume, a bottle of Jack Daniel, and a pair of roller skates for a fantastic necklace of interwoven gold chains studded with pearls, amethysts, and emeralds. Even at that the Persian evidently feels guilty about the one-sidedness of the deal, and while they are sipping the inevitable wrapping-up tea he presses a pair of exquisite earrings set with gaudy rubies on Mulreany as an unsolicited sweetener. 'You will come back to me the next time,' he declares intensely. 'I will have even finer things for you – you will see!'

'And we'll have some gorgeous pruning shears for you,' Mulreany tells him. 'Maybe even a sewing machine or two.'

'I await them with extraordinary zeal,' declares the Persian ebulliently, just as though he understands what Mulreany is talking about. 'Such miraculous things have long been desired by me!'

The sincerity of his greed is obvious and comforting. Mulreany always counts on the cheerful self-interest of the bazaar dealers – and the covetousness of the local aristocrats to whom the bazaaaris sell the merchandise that they buy from the sorcerers from Chicago – to preserve his neck. Sorcery is a capital offense here, sure, but the allure of big profits for the bazaaris and the insatiable hunger among the wealthy for exotic toys like Swiss Army knives and cigarette lighters causes everybody to wink at the laws. *Almost* everybody, anyway.

As they emerge from the Persian's shop Schmidt says, 'Hey, isn't that our innkeeper down the block?'

'That son of a bitch,' Mulreany mutters. 'Let's hope not.' He follows Schmidt's pointing finger and sees a burly red-haired man heading off in the opposite direction. The last thing he needs is for the innkeeper to spot the purported dealers in pots and pans doing business in the jewelry bazaar. But red hair isn't all that uncommon in this city and in all likelihood the innkeeper is busy banging one of the chambermaids at this very moment. He's glad Schmidt is on his toes, anyway.

They go onward now down the Street of Thieves and back past the Baths of Amozyas and the Obelisk of Suplicides into a district thick with astrologers and fortune-tellers, where they pause at a kebab stand for a late lunch of sausages and beer, and then, as the afternoon winds down, they go back into the bazaar quarter. Mulreany succeeds in locating, after following a couple of false trails, the shop of a bookseller he remembers, where a staff of shaven-headed Byzantine scribes produces illuminated manuscripts for sale to the nobility. The place doesn't normally do off-the-shelf business, but Mulreany has been able on previous trips to persuade them to sell books that were awaiting pickup by the duke or prince who had commissioned them, and he turns the trick again this time too. He comes away with a gloriously illustrated vellum codex of the *Iliad*, with an astonishing binding of tooled ebony inlaid with gold and three rows of rubies, in exchange for some of their remaining knives, Coca-Cola, cigarette lighters, sunglasses, and whiskey, and another of the little pocket-compasses. This is shaping up into one of the best buying trips in years.

'We ought to have brought a lot more compasses,' Anderson says, when they're outside and looking around for their last deal of the day before heading back to the inn. 'They don't take up much space in the bag and they really turn everybody on.'

'Next trip,' says Mulreany. 'I agree: they're a natural.'

'I still can't get over this entire business,' Schmidt says wonderingly. This is only his third time across. 'That they're willing to swap fabulous museum masterpieces like these for pocketknives and cans of Coke. And they'd go out of their minds over potato chips too, I bet.'

'But those things *aren't* fabulous museum masterpieces to them,' Mulreany says. They're just routine luxury goods that it's their everyday business to make and sell. Look at it from their point of view. We come in here with a sackful of miracles that they couldn't duplicate in a hundred years. *Five* hundred. They can always take some more gold and some more emeralds and whack out another dozen necklaces. But where the hell are they going to get a pair of binoculars except from us? And Coke probably tastes like ambrosia to them. So it's just as sweet a deal for them as it is for us, and – Hello, look who's here!'

A stocky bearded man with coarse froggy features is waving at them from the other side of the street. He's wearing a brocaded crimson robe worthy of an archbishop and a spectacular green tiara of stunning princely style, but the flat gap-toothed face looking out at them is pure Milwaukee. A taller man dressed in a porter's simple costume stands behind him with a bag of merchandise slung over his shoulder. 'Hey, Leo!' Mulreany calls. 'How's it going?' To Schmidt he explains, 'That's Leo Waxman. Used to carry the merchandise bags for me, five, six years ago. Now he's a trader on his own account.' And, loudly, again, 'Come on over, say hello, Leo! Meet the boys!'

Waxman, as he crosses the street, puts one finger to his lips. 'Ixnay on the English, Mike,' he says, keeping his voice low. 'Let's stick to the Grik, okay, man? And not so much yelling.' He casts a shifty look down toward the end of the block, where a couple of the ubiquitous Bulgarian Guardsmen are lolling against the wall of a mosque.

'Something wrong?' Mulreany asks.

'Plenty. Don't you know? The word is out that the Emperor has ordered a crackdown. He's just told the imperial gendarmerie to pull in anybody caught dealing in sorcery-goods.'

'You sure about that? Why would he want to rock the boat?'

'Well, the old man's crazy, isn't he? Maybe he woke up this morning and decided it was time finally to enforce his own goddamned laws. All I know is that I've done a very nice day's business and I'm going to call it a trip right here and now.'

'Sure,' Mulreany says. 'If that's what you want. But not me. The Emperor can issue any cockeyed order he likes, but that doesn't mean anyone will pay attention. Too many people in this town get big benefits out of the trade we bring.'

'You're going to stay?'

'Right. Till sundown tomorrow. There's business to do here.'

'You're welcome to it,' Waxman says. 'I wish you a lot of joy of it. Me, I'm for dinner at Charlie Trotter's tonight, and to hell with turning any more tricks here just now, thank you. Not if there's a chance I'll miss the last bus back to the Loop.' Waxman blows Mulreany a kiss, beckons to his porter, and starts off up the street.

'We really going to stay?' Schmidt asks, when Waxman has moved along.

Mulreany gives him a scornful look. 'We've still got almost a bag and a half of goods to trade, don't we?'

'But if this Waxman thinks that –'

'He was always a chickenshit wimp,' Mulreany says. 'Look, if they were really serious about their sorcery laws here, they'd have ways of reaching out and picking us up just like that. Go into the bazaar, ask the dealers who they got their Swiss Army knives from, and give them the old bamboo on the soles of the feet until they cough up our full descriptions. But that doesn't happen. Nobody in his right mind would want to cut off the supply of magical nifties that we bring to town.'

'This Emperor isn't in his right mind,' Anderson points out.

'But everybody else is. Let Waxman panic if he wants to. We finish our business and we clear out tomorrow afternoon as scheduled. You want to go home now, either of you, then go home, but if you do, this'll be the last trip across you ever make.' It's a point of pride for Mulreany to max out his trading opportunities, even if it means running along the edge occasionally. He has long since become a rich man just on the twelve and a half percent he gets from Duplessis and Kulikowski's placements of the artifacts he supplies them with, but nevertheless he isn't going to abort the trip simply because Leo Waxman has picked up some goofy rumor. He detests Waxman's cowardice. The risks haven't changed at all, so far as he can see. This job was always dangerous. But the merchants will protect him. It's in their own best interest not to sell the golden geese to the imperial cops.

When they get back to the hotel, the innkeeper grins smarmily at them out of his cubicle next to the stable. 'You sell a lot of pots and pans today?'

'Pretty good business, yes,' Mulreany allows.

An avid gleam shines in the lone eye. 'Look, you sell me something, hear? I give you a dozen girls, I give you a barrel of fine wine, I give you any damn thing you want, but you let me have one of the magic things, you know what I mean?'

'Gods be my witness, we are but ordinary merchants and let there be an end on this foolishness!' Mulreany says testily, thickening his yokel accent almost to the point of incoherence. 'Why do you plague us this way? Would you raise a false charge of sorcery down on innocent men?' The innkeeper raises his hands placatingly, but Mulreany sails right on: 'By the gods, I will bring action against you for defaming us, do you not stop this! I will take you to the courts for these slanders! I will say that you knowingly give lodging to men you think are sorcerers, hoping to gain evil goods from them! I will – I will –'

He halts, huffing and puffing. The innkeeper, retreating fast, begs Mulreany's forgiveness and vows never to suggest again that they are anything but what they claim to be. Would the good merchants care for some pleasant entertainment in their room tonight, very reasonable price? Yes, the good merchants would, as a matter of fact. For a single silver argenteus the size of a dime Mulreany is able to arrange a feast of apples and figs and melons, grilled fish, roasted lamb stuffed with minced doves and artichokes, and tangy resinated wine from Crete, along with a trio of Circassian dancing girls to serve them during the meal and service them afterward. It's very late by the time he finally gets to sleep, and very early when half a dozen huge shaggy Bulgarian Guardsmen come bashing into his room and pounce on him.

The bastard has sold him to the Emperor, it seems. That must have been him in the bazaar at lunchtime, then, watching them go in and out of the fancy shops. Thwarted in his dreams of wangling a nice Swiss Army knife for himself, or at least a fifth of Courvoisier, he has whistled up the constables by way of getting even.

There's no sign of Anderson and Schmidt. They must have wriggled through their windows at the first sound of intruders and scrambled down the drainpipe and at this moment are hightailing it for the interface, Chicago-bound. But for Mulreany there's a cell waiting in the dungeon of the imperial palace.

He doesn't get a very good look at the palace, just one awesome glimpse in the moment of his arrival: white marble walls inlaid with medallions of onyx and porphyry, delicate many-windowed towers of dizzying height, two vast courtyards lined by strips of immaculately tended shrubbery stretching off to left and right, with crystalline reflecting pools, narrow as daggers, running down their middles.

Then a thick smelly hood is pulled down over his head and for a long while he sees nothing further. They pick him up and haul him away down some long corridor. Eventually he hears the sound of a great door being swung back; and then he feels the bruising impact of being dropped like a sack of potatoes onto a stone floor.

Mulreany remains weirdly calm. He's furious, of course, but what good is getting into a lather? He's too upset to let himself get upset. He's a gone goose and he knows it, and it pisses him off immensely, but there isn't a damned thing he can do to save himself. Maybe they'll burn him or maybe, if he's lucky, he'll be beheaded, but either way they can only do it to him once. And there's no lawyer in town who can get him off and no court of appeals to complain to. His only salvation now is a miracle. But he doesn't believe in miracles. The main thing he regrets is that a schmuck like Waxman is home free in Chicago right now and he's not.

He lies there for what feels like hours. They took his watch away when they tied his wrists together, and in any case he wouldn't be able to see it with this hood on, but he knows that the day is moving along and in a matter of hours the interface between the Empire and Chicago is going to close. So even if they don't behead him he's going to be stranded here, the dumbest fate a crosser can experience. The ropes that encircle his wrists start to chafe his skin, and he feels nauseated by the increasingly stale, moist air within the hood covering his face.

Eventually he dozes: sleeps, even. Then he wakes suddenly, muddle-headed, not knowing where he is at first, feeling a little feverish, and starving, besides; he's been cooped up in here, he figures, twelve or eighteen hours, or even longer than that. The interface certainly has closed by now. Stranded. Stranded. You goddamned idiot, he thinks.

Footsteps, finally. People coming. A lot of them.

They pull him to his feet, yank the hood off, untie his wrists. He sees that he's in a big square stone room with a high ceiling and no windows. On all sides of him stand guardsmen in terrific Arabian Nights uniforms: golden turbans, baggy scarlet pantaloons, purple silk sashes, blousy green tunics with great flaring shoulder-pads. Each of them carries a scimitar big enough to cut an ox in half at a single stroke. Right before him is a trio of cold-eyed older men in the crimson robes of court officials.

They've brought him a hard crust of bread and some peppery gruel. He gobbles it as if it's five-star-quality stuff. Then the chilliest-looking of the officials pokes him in the belly with an ornate wooden staff and says, 'Where are you from?'

'Ireland,' Mulreany says, improvising quickly. Ireland's a long way away. They probably don't know much more about it here than they do about Mars.

The interrogator is unfazed. 'Speak to me in the language of your country, then,' he says calmly.

Mulreany is utterly innocent of Gaelic. But he suspects that they are too. 'Erin go bragh!' he says. 'Sean connery! Eamon de valera! Up the rebels, macushlah!'

There are frowns, and then a lengthy whispered conference among the three officials. Mulreany is unable to catch a single word of it. Then the hood is roughly pulled down over his head and everybody leaves, and once more he is left alone for a long hungry time that feels like about a day and a half. Finally he hears footsteps again, and the same bunch returns, but this time they have with them a huge wild-eyed man with long, flowing yellow hair who is wearing rawhide leggings and a bulky woolen cloak fastened across the breast by a big metal brooch made of interlocked flaring loops. He looks very foreign indeed.

'Here is a countryman of yours,' the chilly-faced court official informs Mulreany. 'Speak with him. Tell him where in Ireland you are from, and name your lineage.'

Mulreany, frowning, ponders what to do. After a time the newcomer unleashes a string of crackling gibberish, utterly incomprehensible to Mulreany, and folds his arms and waits for a reply.

'Shannon yer shillelagh, me leprechaun,' Mulreany offers earnestly, appealing to the Irishman with his eyes for mercy and understanding. 'God bless Saint Paddy! Faith and begorrah, is it known t'ye where they'd be selling the Guinness in this town?'

Looking not at all amused, the other says in thick-tongued Greek, 'This man is no Irishman,' and goes stalking out.

They threaten him with torture if he won't tell them where he really comes from. He's cooked either way, it seems. Tell the truth and go to the block, or keep his mouth shut and have it opened for him by methods he'd rather not think about. But he knows his imperial law. The Emperor in person is the final court of appeal for all high crimes. Mulreany demands then and there to be taken before His Majesty for judgment.

'We will do that,' says the frosty-faced one. 'As soon as you admit that you're from Chicago.'

'What if I don't?'

He makes disagreeable racking gestures.

'But you'll take me to him if I do?'

'Most certainly we will. But only if you swear you are from Chicago. If you are not from Chicago, you die.'

If you are *not* from Chicago you die? It doesn't make any sense. But what does he have to lose? One way they'll rack him for sure, the other there's at least a chance. It's worth the gamble.

'I am from Chicago, yes,' Mulreany says.

They let him wash himself up and give him some more bread and gruel, and then they take him to the throne room, which is about nine miles long and six miles high, with dozens of the ferocious Arabian Nights guardsmen everywhere and cloth-of-gold on the walls and thick red carpeting on the floor. Two of the guardsmen shove him forward to the middle of the great room, and there, studying him with an intent frown as though he is looking at the Ambassador from Mars, is the Emperor Basil III.

Mulreany has never seen an emperor before. Or wanted to. He comes over twice a year, does his business, goes back where he came from. It's merchants and craftsmen he comes here to see, not emperors. But there's no doubt in his mind that this is His Nibs. The emperor is a trim, compact little man who looks to be about 99 years old; his skin has the texture of fine vellum, and his expression is mild and benign, except for his eyes, which are dark and glossy and burn with the sort of fire that it takes to maintain yourself as absolute tyrant of a great empire for forty or fifty years. He is dressed surprisingly simply, in a white silk tunic and flaring green trousers, but there is a golden circlet on his brow and he wears on his chest a many-sided gold pendant, suspended from a heavy chain of the same metal, that bears the unmistakable crossed-thunderbolt symbol of the imperial dynasty inlaid upon it in lapis lazuli. Standing just to his right is a burly florid-looking man of about forty, imposing and almost regal of presence, garbed in an absurdly splendid black robe trimmed with ermine. Dangling from his hand, as casually as if it were a tennis racquet, is the great scepter of the realm, a thick rod of jade bound in gold, which, as Mulreany is aware, marks this man as the High Thekanotis of the Empire, that is to say, the prime minister, the grand vizier, the second-in-command.

There is a long, long, *long* silence. Then finally the Emperor says, in a thin, faint voice that seems to come from ten thousand miles away, 'Well, are you a sorcerer or aren't you?'

Mulreany draws a deep breath. 'Not at all, your majesty. A merchant is what I am, nothing but a merchant.'

'Would you put your right hand on the holy altar and say that?'

'Absolutely, your majesty.'

'He denies that he is a sorcerer,' the Emperor says pleasantly to the High Thekanotis. 'Make note of that.' There is another great silence. Then the Emperor gives Mulreany a quick lopsided smile and says, 'Why does the sorcery-fire come so often and take the city away?'

'I don't know,' Mulreany says. 'It just does.'

'And when it does, people like you step through the sorceryfires and move among us bringing the magical things to sell.'

'Yes, your majesty. That's so.' Why pretend otherwise?

'Where do you come from?'

'Chicago,' Mulreany says. 'Chicago, Illinois.'

'Chicago,' the Emperor repeats. 'What do you know of this place?'

he asks the High Thekanotis. The High Thekanotis scowls. Shrugs. It's obvious that he finds this whole event irritating and is already eager to ship Mulreany off to the executioner. But the Emperor's curiosity must be satisfied. 'Tell me about your Chicago. Is it a great city?'

'Yes, your majesty.'

'In what part of the world is it to be found?'

'America,' says Mulreany. 'In northern Illinois.' What the hell, he has nothing to lose. 'On the shore of Lake Michigan. We have Wisconsin to the north of us and Indiana to the east.'

'Ah,' the Emperor says, smiling as if that makes everything much clearer. 'And what is this Chicago like? Describe it for me.'

'Well,' Mulreany says, 'it has, oh, two or three million people. Maybe even more.' The Emperor blinks in surprise and the High Thekanotis glares with such ferocity that Mulreany wonders whether he has made a slip of the tongue and used the word for billion instead. But three million would be amazing enough, he decides. The imperial capital is one of the biggest cities of this era and its population is probably around half a million, tops. 'We have some of the tallest buildings in the world, like the Sears Tower, which I think is 110 stories high, and the Marina Towers, which are pretty big too, and some others. We have great restaurants, any kind of food you might want. The Art Institute is a really fine museum and the Museum of Science and Industry is pretty special too.'

He pauses, wondering what else to say. As long as he keeps talking they aren't going to cut his head off. Does the Emperor want to hear about the dinosaurs at the Field Museum? The Aquarium? The Planetarium? He might be impressed by some statistics about O'Hare Airport, but Mulreany isn't sure he has the vocabulary for that. Then he notices that the Emperor is starting to look a little strange – turning pale, rocking weirdly back and forth on the balls of his feet. His eyes have taken on a really odd look, a mixture of profound cunning and utter whackiness.

'You must take me there,' the Emperor says, whispering fiercely. 'When you return to your city, take me with you and show me everything. Everything.'

The High Thekanotis makes a choking sound and his florid face turns an even brighter red. Mulreany is aghast, too. No imperial citizen has ever come across into Chicago, not even one. They are all terrified of the sorcery-fire, and they have no way of seeing beyond the interface anyway to know that there's another city out there.

But is the old man serious? The old man is crazy, Mulreany reminds himself.

'It would be an honor and a privilege, your majesty,' he says grandly, 'to show you Chicago some day. I would greatly enjoy the opportunity.'

'Not some day,' says the Emperor Basil III. 'Now.'

'Now,' Mulreany echoes. An unexpected twist. The Emperor doesn't want to chop off the heads of the sorcerers he has sent his police to round up; the Emperor just wants one to give him a guided tour of Chicago. This afternoon, say. Mulreany smiles and bows. 'Certainly, your majesty. Whatever your majesty wishes.' He wonders how the old Emperor would react to his first glimpse of the downtown skyscrapers. He wonders what sort of greeting Chicago would give the Emperor. The whole thing is nutty, of course. But for him it's a plausible way out. He continues to smile. 'We can leave immediately, if you desire, your majesty.'

The High Thekanotis seems about to have a stroke. His chest heaves, his face puffs up furiously, he brandishes the jade scepter like a battle-axe.

But it's the Emperor who keels over instead. The excitement of the prospect of his trip across the line has done him in. He turns very pale and puts his hands to his chest and utters a little dry rasping sound, and his eyes roll up in his head, and he pitches forward head first so rapidly that two of the guardsmen are just barely able to catch him before he hits the stone floor.

The room goes berserk. The guardsmen start moaning and chanting; court officials come running in from all directions; the Emperor, who seems to be in the grip of some sort of seizure, arches his back, slaps his hands against the floor, stamps his feet, babbles wild nonsensical syllables.

Mulreany, watching in astonishment, feels the High Thekanotis's powerful hand encircling his forearm.

'Go,' the grand vizier tells him. 'Get yourself out of here, and never come back. Out now, before the Emperor returns to consciousness and sees you again. Now.' The vizier shakes his head. 'Chicago! He would visit Chicago! Madness! Madness!'

Mulreany doesn't need a second invitation. A couple of guardsmen grab him under the arms and hustle him from the room and down the hall and through the palace's endless hallways and, at long last, out through an immense arch into the broad plaza in front of the building.

It's the middle of the day. The 52-hour visitation is long over; the gateway between the eras is shut.

Go, the High Thekanotis said. But where? Afghanistan?

And then, to his amazement, Mulreany sees the interface still glowing in the sky down at the eastern end of town. So there must have been another match-up with Chicago while he was in the imperial hoosegow. He can get across after all, back to good old Chi. The Loop, the Bears, the Water Tower, Charlie Trotter's, everything. Sprinting as if six demons are on his tail, he rushes toward the waterfront, jostling people out of his way. He'll be coming back empty-handed this trip, but at least he'll be coming back.

He reaches the Street of the the Eastern Sun. Rushes out onto one of the wharves, plunges joyously into the golden light of the interface.

And comes out in a lovely green forest, the biggest trees he's ever seen this side of California. Everything is wonderfully silent. He hears the chirping of birds, the twittering of insects.

Oh, shit, he thinks. Where the hell is Chicago?

He looks back, bewildered. The interface line is gone, and so is the imperial capital. There's nothing here but trees. Nothing. Nothing. He walks for half an hour, heading east into the sun, and still he sees only this tremendous virgin forest, until at last he stumbles forward out of the woods and discovers himself to be at the shore of a gigantic lake, and then the awful truth strikes him with the impact of a tidal wave.

Of course. It's an era mismatch.

The interface must have closed right on schedule, and opened again a little while afterward, but this time the Empire had lined itself up against some other sector of the time-stream very distant from his own. Just as the Empire that arrives in his Chicago is the one of Basil III sometimes and sometimes the one of Miklos and sometimes the one of Kartouf the Hapless, so too does the Empire of Basil's time line itself up sometimes with Chicago-1990, and sometimes Chicago-1996, and sometimes Chicago-2013 –

And sometimes, probably, the one of 1400 A.D. Or of 1400 B.C., not that it makes much difference. Before 1833, there wasn't any city at all here beside Lake Michigan.

A mismatch, then. He has heard rumors of such things occurring. One of those little thousand-to-one glitches that hardly ever actually happen, and that you assume never will happen to you. But this one has. He's known a few crossers who didn't come back. Schmucks, he always figured. Now it's his turn to be the schmuck. Mulreany wonders what it's going to be like living on nuts and berries, and trying to kill a deer if he feels like having a little protein. It's goddamned embarrassing, is what it is.

But he's an optimist at heart. There's cause for hope, right? Right? Sooner or later, he tells himself, the golden light will glow in the sky again behind him, and the Empire will return, and he'll go through the interface to the glorious city beyond, and eventually, after skulking around in it for a while, waiting for the right Chicago to come along, he'll go back across and find his way home.

Sooner or later, yes.

Or maybe not.

The Second Shield

And this is the story that wandered up out of my unruly imagination while I was trying to puzzle my way out of the Copperfield-*Playboy* dilemma in February of 1995. I wrote it with a swiftness that surprised me in the early days of that month, Alice Turner bought it in her usual lightning-fast way, and it appeared in *Playboy*'s December 1995 issue.

It is, of course, full of all sorts of metaphorical stuff about the artist's anguished struggles with his public and with himself, and I'm afraid that there are some distinctly autobiographical passages scattered here and there in it. If I were a literary critic, I would point to those passages here and analyze them closely. But I don't have to do that. I wrote the story. Let somebody else look after the analysis.

In the night, despite the unsettling trouble that was brewing with the client from Miami, the blustering and the importuning and the implied or even outright threats, Beckerman managed to dream satisfactorily after all. He dreamed a little free-standing staircase of alabaster and malachite that pivoted in the middle and went back down itself through some other dimension like something out of an Escher print; he dreamed an attenuated one-legged bronze statuette with three skinny arms and a funny spiral topknot, Giacometti meets Dr Seuss, so to speak; he dreamed a squat, puckery-skinned cast-iron froggy thing with bulging ivory eyeballs that periodically opened its huge mouth and emitted little soprano squeaks. Everything a bit on the bizarre side, even for Beckerman; but he did have a tendency to go over the edge a little when things got tense. The three pieces were arrayed in a neat row by the side of his bed when he woke, just before noon. It was, he thought, a damned fine batch of work.

But he didn't take the time just yet for a close inspection of the latest products. His shower came first; and then the usual breakfast, a grapefruit and half of another one, nearly a dozen sausages, a platter of scrambled eggs, half a loaf of bread, a couple of bottles of beer. He was drenched with sweat, as he always was on these mornings: stinking acrid sweat, clammy and thick, the sweat of an artisan who has been going at it full throttle for many hours. Beckerman's work took a lot out of him. He worked every bit as hard as any sculptor who hammered away at marble slabs or one who wrestled with heavy iron struts, except that he worked lying down with his eyes closed, and there was no actual physical labor involved.

It felt that way, though. Good productive dreams like these could burn up five or six pounds' worth of energy in a single night. It was all that Beckerman could do to keep his weight up, despite a constantly ravenous appetite. At best he was a slender man, but a busy season of work would reduce him to skin and bones, his clothes hanging from his gaunt limbs like rags flapping in the wind: the Auschwitz look. There was no way around that. It was the necessary cost of his art.

After he was washed and dressed and had some breakfast in him, he checked out the new items, poking and prodding them, looking for blemishes and flaws, areas of insubstantiality, indications of early dissolution. None of Beckerman's work was permanent – he was careful to point that out to potential buyers, *very* careful, which was why this Miami thing was so maddening and disturbing – but he made it a matter of professional pride never to offer anything for sale that was likely to last for less than a year. It wasn't always possible for him to predict a piece's probable life-span accurately – he always pointed *that* out to them, too – but he could usually pinpoint it within a range of plus or minus three months. Some exceptionally evanescent items were gone within hours; some survived for years; most lasted thirty to forty months. The record thus far was eleven years, five months, for a Daliesque melted watch made of copper inlaid with precious stones, set in a silver basin filled with mercury, one of his very finest pieces.

This group looked promising. The Escheresque staircase had a nice solid feel when he tapped it with his knuckle, and there were no soft places anywhere. Beckerman gave it three to five years. The goofy

Giacometti, a lean, stripped-down thing of impressive tangibility and compaction, was a cinch for six or seven. Even the weakest of the three, the froggish thing, which had a hollow interior and some porous places on its surface, and therefore would eventually begin to suffer molecular flyaway beginning from the inside out, looked good for at least two and a half years, maybe three.

His mind began running through the roster of possible purchasers. The frog would go to Michaelson, the cellular phone tycoon, at about thirty grand: Michaelson loved strange-looking things that made weird sounds, and the relatively short life-span, the fact that the artifact would vanish into the air in a couple of years, wasn't an issue to an art collector who had made his fortune out of something as transient as telephone calls. Michaelson had even said once that he was willing to buy six-month items, and even shorter-lived ones than that, if only Beckerman would put them on the market, which he steadfastly refused to do.

Yes, Michaelson for the frog. The staircase, most likely, he would offer to Buddy Talbert, the leveraged-takeover man, who had a weakness for anything with mathematical trickery about it, dimensional twists, mind-dazzling stuff like that. And as for the Giacometti/Seuss, well –

The telephone rang.

Not many people had Beckerman's home number. 'Yes?'

'Alvarez,' a quiet voice said.

Again. Beckerman began taking deep breaths. 'Look, there's no sense you calling me. I told you I would phone just as soon as I had anything good to report.'

'You haven't phoned, though.'

'I'm still coming up short on the new shield.'

'Try harder, Beckerman.'

'You don't seem willing to realize that these things aren't subject to conscious control. They're dreams, remember. Can you predetermine your dreams? Of course not. So why do you think I can?'

'The things I dream about aren't sitting on the floor next to my bed when I wake up, either,' Alvarez said. 'The way I dream has nothing to do with the way you dream. Mr Apostolides is getting very impatient for his shield.'

'I'm doing my best to produce it.'

'Give me an estimate. Two weeks? Three?'

'How can I say? I try every night. I set my mind to it, last thing before I close my eyes, shield shield shield shield. But I end up with different things instead. I can't help it.'

'Focus your attention better, then.'

Beckerman's forehead began to throb. 'I've told you and I've told you. I could focus for a million years and I still wouldn't be able to dream anything to order. Especially a complicated thing like that. The dream products are *accidents*, won't you understand that? Random creations of my subconscious mind.'

'Tell your subconscious mind to be less random. Mr Apostolides paid a fortune for that shield, and he loved it very much, he was tremendously proud of possessing it, and he was extremely disappointed when it faded away.'

'It lasted sixteen months. I told you right at the outset it wasn't good for more than a couple of years.'

'Sixteen months isn't a couple of years. He feels very cheated.'

'The estimates that I give people are never one hundred percent accurate. They know that up front. And I've offered to refund –'

'He doesn't want a refund. This isn't a question of the money. What he can't deal with is not having the shield on his wall. The patriotic pride, the sheer joy of possession: money can't replace that. He wants it back. A new one, just like the old. He feels very strongly about that. Very *very* strongly. You have caused him great personal grief by giving him such a frustrating experience.'

'I'm sorry,' Beckerman said. 'I want only to please my clients. He can have his pick of anything else that I –'

'The shield,' said Alvarez ominously. 'The shield and nothing but the shield.'

'When and if I can.'

'Two weeks, Beckerman.'

'I simply can't promise that.'

'Two weeks. You have given Mr Apostolides deep emotional pain,

Beckerman, and he can be extremely unpleasant to people who create anguish for him. Believe me, he can.'

'What are you telling me?' Beckerman demanded.

But he was talking to a dead phone.

The shield that Beckerman had made for Apostolides, had dreamed for him one humid spring night three years ago, was one of his supreme masterpieces, his two or three finest works ever, and he regretted its evaporation even more, perhaps, than Apostolides did. But he couldn't simply whip up another one, just like that, to replace it. He could only trust to luck, the random scoop of his dreaming mind, as with all of his pieces. And meanwhile here was Alvarez hounding him constantly, chivvying, bullying, fulminating, disturbing his peace of mind in a hundred different ways. Couldn't he see that he was only making things worse?

Apostolides was a shipping magnate – Greek, of course, and he was mixed up in a lot of things besides shipping – with his name on the Forbes list of international billionaires and his fingers in all sorts of pies around the world. His main residence, the one where he had so proudly displayed Beckerman's wondrous shield, was on a private island in Biscayne Bay, back of Miami, but there were homes in London and Majorca and South Africa and Thailand and Caracas too, and business offices in Geneva, the Cayman Islands, Budapest, Kuwait, Singapore, and one or two other places. Beckerman had never actually met or spoken to him. Not many people ever did, apparently. The artist's dealings with Apostolides had been conducted entirely through the medium of Alvarez, who was some sort of agent for him.

Alvarez had tracked Beckerman down on the beach at the Hotel Halekulani in Waikiki, where he had gone for a week or two of tropical sunshine during one of San Diego's rare spells of cool, wet winter weather. He was quietly sipping a daiquiri when Alvarez, a small smooth-faced man with rumpled sandy hair and a thin graying goatee through which you could easily see his chin, came up to him and greeted him by name.

Warily Beckerman admitted that he was who he was.

'I have a commission for you,' Alvarez said.

Beckerman disliked and distrusted him instantly. The little man's eyes were troublesomely shifty and hard, and there was something weirdly incongruous, here on this sunny beach in 80-degree weather, about the fact that he was dressed in an elegant, closely cut Armani suit of some glossy gray-green fabric – jacket and tie, no less, probably the only necktie being worn anywhere in Hawaii that day. It made him look not only out of place but in some way menacing. But Beckerman made it a rule never to turn down the prospect of new business out of hand. After all these years of making money by pulling works of art literally out of thin air, he remained perversely afraid that all that prosperity would vanish some day, fading back to its mysterious source just as his sculptures inevitably did.

'I represent one of the world's wealthiest men and greatest connoisseurs of art,' Alvarez said. 'You would recognize his name immediately if I told it to you,' which he proceeded almost immediately to do. Beckerman did indeed recognize the name of Pericles Apostolides and he suddenly began to pay considerably more attention to Alvarez's words. 'Mr Apostolides,' said Alvarez, 'is, as perhaps you are aware, a student in the most intensely scholarly way of the heroic age of Greece, that is, the Mycenean period, the time of the Trojan War. You may have heard of the Homeric theme park that he is constructing outside Nauplia, with the full-scale replica of Agamemnon's Mycenae, and life-size virtual-reality reenactments of the great moments of the *Iliad* and *Odyssey*, particularly the holographic simulations of Scylla and Charybdis and the blinding of Polyphemus, et cetera, et cetera.'

Beckerman had heard of the project. He thought it was nauseatingly tacky. But he went on listening.

Alvarez said, 'Mr Apostolides is aware of the quality of your work and has admired your splendid art in the collections of many of his friends. In recent months he was particularly keenly taken by the remarkable figure of a centaur in the possession of the Earl of Dorset and by the extraordinary Medusa that is owned by the Comte de Bourgogne. Mr Apostolides has sent me here to inquire of you whether you would be willing to create something of a Homeric nature for him – not for the park, you understand, but for his personal and private gallery.'

'Mr Apostolides must understand,' said Beckerman, 'that I'm unable to work specifically to order – that is, that he can't simply design a piece and expect me to execute it literally. My medium is dreams, dreams made tangible, and dreams are by their very nature unpredictable things. I can attempt to create what he wants, and perhaps it will approximate what he has in mind, but I can make no guarantees of specific pieces.'

'Understood.'

'Furthermore, Mr Apostolides should realize that my work is quite costly.'

'That would hardly be a problem, Mr Beckerman.'

'And finally, is Mr Apostolides aware that the things I make are inherently impermanent? They will last a year or two, perhaps five or six in some cases, but almost never any longer than that. A man with his appreciation of ancient history may be unhappy to find that he has commissioned something that has hardly any more substance than – well, than a dream.'

Furrows appeared in Alvarez's smooth forehead.

'Is there no exception to this? No kind of preservative that can be applied to particularly choice pieces?'

'None whatever.'

'Mr Apostolides is a powerfully retentive man. He is a builder, a keeper. He does not sell the securities he invests in, he does not deaccession the works of art that he collects.'

'In that case perhaps he should give this commission some further thought,' Beckerman said.

'He very much wants a piece of yours comparable to those that he saw in the collections of the Earl of Dorset and the Comte de Bourgogne.'

'I would be extremely pleased to provide one. But the limitations on the durability of my work are not, I'm afraid, within my power to control.'

'I will explain this to him,' said Alvarez, and turned swiftly and walked away.

He reappeared two nights later, while Beckerman was enjoying a peaceful solitary dinner at the Halekulani's elegant second-story open-air French restaurant, looking out over the moonlit Pacific. Taking a seat opposite Beckerman without being asked, Alvarez said, 'How soon can you deliver?'

Beckerman had had an unusually productive autumn, to the point where by late November he had thought he might need to be hospitalized for exhaustion and general debilitation. By now he had recovered most of his loss of weight and was beginning to feel healthy again, but it had not been his plan to go back to work until the summer.

'July?' he said.

'Sooner,' said Alvarez.

'I can't. I simply can't.'

Alvarez named a price.

Beckerman, concealing his astonishment with some effort, said, 'That would be quite adequate. But even so: my work is very demanding – *physically* demanding, is what I mean, with effects on my health – and I'm not ready just now to produce anything new, especially of the quality that Mr Apostolides is undoubtedly expecting.'

Alvarez raised the offer by half.

'I could manage something by May, perhaps,' said Beckerman. 'No earlier.'

'If the difficulty is that prior commissions are in the way, would some additional financial consideration persuade you to make changes in your working schedule?'

'I have no other work waiting. The issue is entirely one of needing time to build up my strength.'

'March?'

'April 15 at the earliest,' said Beckerman.

'We will expect it at that time.'

'Mr Apostolides is fully aware of the conditions?'

'Fully. It is his hope that you will produce something unusually long-lived for him.'

'I'll certainly try.'

'Will there be preliminary sketches for him to see?'

Beckerman felt the tiniest tweak of uneasiness. 'You just told me that Mr Apostolides is fully aware of the conditions. One of the conditions, as I attempted to make clear before, is that I have no *a priori* ability to control the shape of the work that emerges, none at all. If he's dissatisfied with what I produce, he will, of course, be under no obligation to purchase it. But I can't give him anything like sketches.'

'I see,' said Alvarez thoughtfully.

'If he doesn't entirely realize that at this point, please see to it that it is made totally clear to him?'

'Of course,' said Alvarez.

Which was the last that Beckerman heard or saw of Alvarez for some months. He spent ten more days in Honolulu, until he felt fit and rested; and then, tanned and relaxed and almost back up to normal weight on the rich island cuisine, he returned to his studio in La Jolla and set about preparing himself for the Apostolides project.

Something Homeric, the man had said. Very well. Beckerman steeped himself in Homer: the *Iliad*, the *Odyssey*, the *Iliad* again, reading this translation and that one, returning to the poems again and again until the wrath of Achilles and the homeward journey of Odysseus seemed more real to him than anything that was going on in the world he actually inhabited. He made no attempt at purposeful selection of design, no effort at directing his subliminal consciousness; that would be pointless, useless, even counterproductive.

After a while the dreams began.

Not his special kind, not yet. Just ordinary dreams, anybody's kind of dreams, but they were rooted, nearly all of them, in his Homeric readings. Images out of the two poems floated nightly through his mind, the faces of Agamemnon and Menelaus and Hector and Achilles, the loveliness of Helen and the tenderness of Andromache, the monsters and princesses encountered by Odysseus as he made his long way home, the slaughter of Penelope's suitors. Before long Beckerman knew that he was at the threshold of readiness to work. He could feel it building up in him, the sense of apprehension, the tingling in his fingertips and the tightness along his shoulders, an almost sexual tension that could find its release only in a tumultuous night of wild outpouring of artistic force. Beckerman pumped up his strength in anticipation of that night by doubling his intake of food, loading himself with milkshakes, ice cream, steak, mountains of pasta in heavy sauces, bread, potatoes, anything calorific that might give him some reserve of energy against the coming ordeal.

And then he knew, getting into bed one night in the first week of April, that the time was at hand.

In the morning, after some of the most turbulent effort he had ever put forth, the shield was next to his bed, a great gleaming half-dome of metal that seemed to be aglow with the fire of its own inner light.

Beckerman recognized it instantly for what it was. There is no mistaking the shield of Achilles: Homer devotes many pages to a description of it, the five sturdy layers, the shining triple rim of dazzling metal, the splendid silver baldric, above all the extraordinary intricacy of the designs that the god Hephaestus had engraved upon its face when he fashioned that astonishing shield for the foremost of the Greek warriors.

Not that Beckerman's version of the shield was a literal rendition of the one so lovingly depicted by Homer. He never could have duplicated every one of the myriad details. A poet might be able to describe in words what a god had forged in his smithy, but Beckerman was constrained by the finite limitations of the medium in which he worked, and the best he could do was something that approached in general outline the vast and complex thing that Homer had imagined.

Still, it was a remarkable job, a top-level piece, perhaps his best one ever. The earth, the sea, and the sky were there in the center of the shield's face, and the sun and the moon, and more than a suggestion of the major constellations. In the next ring were images of bustling cities, with tiny but carefully sketched figures acting out the events of municipal life, weddings and public meetings and a battle between armies whose generals were robed in gold; and outside that was a scene of farmers in their fields, and one of a king and his attendants at a feast, and a vineyard, and herds of golden cattle with horns of tin. Around everything, at the very rim, ran the mighty stream of the all-encompassing ocean.

He hadn't shown everything Homer that had said was on the shield, but he had done plenty. Beckerman stared at the shield in awe and wonder, marveling that such a thing could have burst forth from his own sleeping mind in a single night. Surely it was the perfect thing for the Apostolides collection, well worth the staggering price and more, a masterpiece beyond even the billionaire's own high expectations.

He called Alvarez in Miami. 'I've got it,' he said. 'The shield of Achilles. Book XVIII, the *Iliad*.'

'How does it look?'

'Terrific. Fantastic. If I say so myself.'

'Mr Apostolides is very involved emotionally with Achilles, you know. I might even put it that he thinks of himself as a kind of modern-day Achilles, the invincible warrior, the all-conquering hero.'

'He'll love it, then,' said Beckerman. 'I guarantee it.'

Indeed he did. Apostolides paid Beckerman an unsolicited five-figure bonus, and gave the shield pride of place in what was apparently one of the finest private museums in the world, and flew his billionaire friends in from Majorca and the Grenadines and the Azores and Lanai to stand before it and admire it. He cherished that shield as though it were the Mona Lisa and the Apollo Belvedere and the David of Michelangelo all rolled into one.

Which was the problem. Because in less than a year and a half it began to melt and sag, and then it was gone altogether, and suddenly Alvarez was on the phone to say, 'He wants another one. He doesn't care how much it costs, but he wants another shield just like that one.'

The days went by. Had Alvarez been serious about that two-week deadline, or was it simply a bluff, a way of stampeding Beckerman into producing a second shield? In either case, there was nothing Beckerman could do about it. He had been telling Alvarez the simple truth when he said that he had no conscious control over the form of the dream-objects that he produced. He could give himself little hints at bedtime, yes, and that was often helpful in guiding the basic direction in which his dreaming mind would go; but that was about as much control as he had. Dreaming up a specific object was something he had never succeeded in doing.

He tried to put Apostolides and Alvarez out of his mind altogether and go about the normal routines of his business. He set up appointments with the collectors to whom he intended to offer the three new pieces; he made arrangements to be interviewed by an important art magazine that had wanted for months to do a feature on his work; he met with his broker for the regular semi-annual review of his stock portfolio.

'I could retire,' he told the broker, after he had gone over the portfolio and been apprised of the surprisingly strong gains it had made in the past six months. 'I could sell all these stocks and put the money into municipal bonds and never do a night's work again in my life.'

'Why would you want to do that?' the broker asked. 'It isn't as if the work takes up a lot of your time. Didn't you once tell me that you actually produce your entire output in just six or seven nights a year?'

'Six or seven very strenuous and difficult nights, yes.'

'But you're a great artist. Great artists don't retire, no matter how wealthy they are. Did Picasso retire? Did Matisse? Monet was practically blind, and even richer than you are now, and he went on painting anyway, right to the end.'

'I am not Monet,' said Beckerman. 'I am certainly not Picasso. I am Max Beckerman and I find my work increasingly demanding, too demanding, and it is becoming a great temptation to give it up altogether.'

'You don't mean that, Max. You've just been working too hard lately, that's all. Go to Hawaii again. Go to Majorca. You'll feel better in a week or two.'

'*Majorca*,' Beckerman said bitterly. 'Yes, sure, absolutely. I could go to Majorca.' He said it as if the broker had recommended a holiday in one of the suburbs of Hell. Apostolides had a house on Majorca, didn't he? Everywhere he turned, something reminded him of Apostolides.

He knew what was behind this sudden talk of retiring. It wasn't fatigue. The broker was right: he really did work only six or seven nights a year, and, arduous as those nights were, he recovered quickly enough from each ordeal, and there were new masterpieces to show for it. If he gave up work entirely, his entire oeuvre would fade away in a few years, and then there would be nothing left to indicate that he had ever lived at all. He would be utterly forgotten, a wealthy nobody who once had been a great artist, a rich old man sitting quietly on some tropical beach waiting for the eventual end to arrive. The museums were full of Matisses, Picassos, Monets, and always would be; but the moment Max Beckerman stopped working, that was the moment he would begin his slide into oblivion. He couldn't face that prospect.

No, it was *fear* that had him thinking of retiring, of disappearing to some quiet and luxurious place where nobody would ever be able to find him again. Fear of Apostolides – of Alvarez, rather, because Apostolides was just a name to him, and Alvarez was a threatening voice on the telephone. The very rich, Beckerman knew, were utterly ruthless when they were thwarted. Run. Hide. Disappear. That was what he had to do. A villa in Monaco; an apartment in Zurich; a plantation in the Seychelles Islands. He could afford to go anywhere.

Beckerman went nowhere. He was surprised to find himself unexpectedly gliding into work mode again, much too soon after the last episode of creativity. He dreamed a small dinosaur-shaped animal the size of a large cat, a perpetual motion machine that energetically moved a complex arrangements of pistons through an elaborate pattern without pause even though it had no power source, and something that even he couldn't identify, an abstract bunch of metallic squiggles, which to his relief melted away within a couple of hours. Good work, lots of it. But not the shield, no. Not the shield.

And then the two weeks were up.

'Beckerman?'

Alvarez, right on schedule. Beckerman hung up.

The phone rang again.

'Don't do that,' Alvarez said. 'Listen to me.'

'I'm listening.'

'What about the shield?'

'Nothing. Nothing. I'm very sorry.'

'You'll be sorrier,' said Alvarez. 'The client is getting extremely displeased now, *extremely*. Holding my feet to the fire, as a matter of fact. I was the one who brought you to his attention. Now he requires me to obtain a second shield from you for him. Dream him another shield, Beckerman. The shield of Achilles, just like the last one.'

'I'm trying to. Believe me, I'm trying. The Iliad is the last thing I read every night before I close my eyes. I fill my head with Homer. Heroes, swords, shields. But what comes out? Little dinosaurs come out. Perpetual motion machines come out. You see the problem?'

'I see the problem,' Alvarez said. 'Do you?'

'Tell Mr Apostolides that if he likes he can have my entire output for the next three years, free of charge, every single thing I produce. Only he must leave me alone on this thing of the shield.'

'What he wants is the shield, Beckerman.'

'I can't give it to him.'

'Nobody tells things like that to Pericles Apostolides.'

'One day the Angel of Death is going to come for Mr Apostolides, just like he comes for everybody else, and the angel is going to say, "All right, Pericles, come along with me". Is he going to look the Angel in the eye and say that nobody tells things like that to Pericles Apostolides?'

'That's not my problem, Beckerman. My problem is the shield. Your problem is the shield.'

'I'm doing the best I can. I can't do better than that.'

'Two more weeks,' Alvarez said.

'And then?'

'Don't ask. Just produce. Sweet dreams, Beckerman.'

He tried desperately to generate the shield. He lay rigid in his bed with his eyes closed, envisioning the shield as though hoping it would spring fully formed from his forehead while he was still awake. But it didn't. Eventually he would drop off to sleep, and when he awoke in the middle of the following morning he could tell at once from the way he was trembling and the ferocious hunger he felt and the stink of sweat in the bedroom that he had worked during the night, and he would look eagerly at the floor beside his bed, and there would be something there, yes, a grinning ebony face with Picasso eyes, or a five-sided pyramid with a brilliant point of ruby light at its summit, or a formidable Wagnerian horned helmet that might very well have belonged to Wotan himself; but the shield of Achilles, no, no, never that.

He was exhausting himself in the effort, dreaming every night as though his life depended on it, which quite possibly it did, and accomplishing nothing. Beckerman was feverish all the time, now, wild-eyed with weariness and fear. The effects of the energy drain were horrifyingly apparent, the Auschwitz look again, Buchenwald, Dachau, a walking skeleton. He tried every remedy he knew to keep his strength up. Steroids; glucose injections; four meals a day, five; round-the-clock pizza delivery. Nothing worked for long. He was wasting away.

The telephone. Alvarez.

'Well, Beckerman?'

'Nothing.'

'I'm going to have to visit you in person, right?'

'What do you mean, visit me?'

'What do you think I mean?'

'Sit next to me while I sleep, and *make* me generate the shield?'

'That isn't what I mean, no.'

'Don't threaten me, Alvarez!'

'Who's threatening? I just said I would come visiting.'

'Don't even think of it. There was a contract that said the object I delivered was of its inherent nature impermanent, and that I could not be held responsible for its disappearance after a stipulated period of time. The stipulated minimum was twelve months. It's in the contract, Alvarez. Which, as you know, Mr Apostolides quite willingly signed.'

'You fulfilled that contract, yes. Mr Apostolides now wants to enter into a second contract with you for a similar work of art. I'll be coming soon to get your signature on it.'

'I never sign contracts that stipulate the design of a particular work.'

'You will this time.'

'Keep away from me, Alvarez!'

'Unfortunately, I can't. I'll be seeing you soon. And don't try to run away. I'll find you wherever you may be, Beckerman. You know that I will.'

Time was running out. Alvarez would be coming. The bell ringing downstairs; the voice on the intercom; and then the cold-eyed little man in the tight-fitting Armani suit, standing unsmilingly in the doorway, sadly shaking his head. And there would be no shield for Mr Apostolides. Beckerman thought of a thousand different things he could do to protect himself, each one more implausible than the one before, and finally he thought of the thousand-and-first, which was not merely implausible but apparently impossible, and that was the one he resolved to try.

Never in his life had he been able to dream something to order. But that was what he intended to try now, one last wild attempt born of desperation. Not the shield, no: plainly that was beyond his power. Not only was he trying to dream something at somebody else's command, but he was trying to dream a piece that he had already created once, and apparently his mind was unwilling to go back over a track that it had already traversed. Everything he had ever made had been one-of-a-kind.

But perhaps, *perhaps*, he could indeed by deliberate intent dream something to his *own* specifications that he had never dreamed before, something which would rescue him from the dilemma in which he found himself. It was worth a try, anyway.

That night he ate until he thought he would burst. Then he slept, and then he dreamed; and even as he dreamed he felt a flood of sudden strange optimism; and what he found beside his bed the next morning exceeded all his expectations. It was crude, it was badly proportioned, it was almost laughable; it would never fool Alvarez even for a moment. But it was a rough approximation of what he had set out to dream, and that was new, that was unique in his entire experience of the phenomenon about which he had built his life.

He tried again the next night, and the next, ordering his dreaming mind to work with the material at hand and shape it toward perfection. The first night's work brought no visible improvement over what he already had, but to his amazement and delight there was a distinct transformation a night later, and when he awoke after one more night of work he realized that he had – in the final paroxysm of despair over his dire predicament – produced precisely what he needed.

If only I could have managed to do the second shield this way, he thought. Then I could have managed to keep my life intact.

But this, at least, would give him a way of sidestepping the wrath of Apostolides and the vindictiveness of Alvarez.

He looked down at the pale, haggard figure lying on the floor next to his bed and said, 'Stand up.'

It shambled unsteadily to its feet.

'Stand straight,' Beckerman said. 'Hold yourself like a man, will you?'

The figure attempted to improve its posture. It was, Beckerman saw, slightly lopsided, the left shoulder too narrow, the right leg a little short. Still, he was impressed with his own skill.

'Can you speak?' he asked.

'Yes. I can speak.'

It sounded rusty, and the voice seemed too high. But the faint European accent was a familiar one.

'Do you know who I am?'

'You are the artist Max Beckerman.'

'Yes. And who are you?'

A moment of silence.

'I am the artist Max Beckerman,' it said.

'Good. Good. We are both the artist Max Beckerman. Keep that in mind. Go to the closet, now. Find yourself some clothes, get yourself dressed.'

'I am hungry. I am in need of a shower.'

'Never mind that. Obey me. Get yourself dressed. Cover your body. Christ, you're nothing but a skeleton with skin! I can't stand looking at those ribs of yours. Cover yourself. Cover yourself!'

'What shall I wear?'

'Anything you like,' Beckerman said. 'Whatever strikes your fancy.'

He went into the bathroom and took a quick shower. Then, ravenous, he grabbed up a loaf of bread and began to gnaw at it. The other Beckerman was dressed when he returned to the bedroom. It had chosen gray gabardine slacks, one of the good London shirts, and Beckerman's favorite black shoes, the John Lobbs. Too bad about the shoes, he thought. But he could always have another pair run up for him.

What time was it right now, he wondered, in Zurich? Eight hours later, was it? Nine? Early evening, he figured. He picked up the phone and dialed Elise's number.

Another miracle! She was there!

'*Wer spricht, bitte?*'

'It's me, Max. Listen, I'll be coming to stay with you for a little while, is that all right?'

'Max? Where are you, Max?'

'California, still. But I'll be getting the next plane out. I'll be there in twenty-four hours, maybe less. Can you manage that, Elise?'

'Of course! But – why –?'

'I'll explain everything when I get there. Listen, I'll phone you again from the airport in an hour or two, when I know which flight I'm on. You can meet me when I land, can't you?'

'*Natürlich, liebchen, natürlich!* It's just that – it's all such a surprise –'

'I know,' he said. 'I love you, Elise.' He blew her a kiss and hung up. He called the airport next; and then phoned his usual taxi service to arrange for a cab in thirty minutes.

The other Beckerman was still standing next to the bed.

'I am very hungry,' it said.

Beckerman gestured impatiently. 'Go, then. Eat. Eat all you like. You know where to find it.' He began to shovel things into his suitcase, a couple of shirts, some slacks, his shaver, a pair of shoes, a few pairs of socks, underwear, three neckties.

The telephone rang. Beckerman went on packing. After eight or nine rings the phone fell silent; and then, in another moment, it began to ring again.

He closed his suitcase. Took a last look around. He probably would never be coming back here, he knew.

The telephone was still ringing.

'Should I answer it?' the other Beckerman asked.

'No,' Beckerman said. 'Just let it ring.' He picked up the suitcase and walked toward the door. The cab would be here in another five or ten minutes. He would wait for it downstairs.

He paused at the door. The dream-Beckerman, dull-eyed, simpering, lopsided, but his twin in all essential respects, gazed stupidly at him.

'I'm expecting a visit shortly from a Mr Alvarez,' Beckerman said. The other Beckerman nodded. 'He'll ring the bell downstairs. You press this buzzer to let him in. You got that?'

'Yes. I have that.'

'Good. Well, so long, my friend,' said Beckerman. 'The place is yours now. Good luck.'

And be sure to tell Alvarez to give Mr Apostolides my regards, he thought, as he headed downstairs to the waiting cab.

WIN A TRIP TO NASA

worth over £2,000 with *Voyager*Direct

The book you're holding now is just one of the many fantastic titles you could be getting direct to your door. What's more, order our new catalogue today and you could be heading for Florida.

Exclusive offers, big savings, signed copies and free books!
*Voyager*Direct – A whole new world direct to your door

Yes! Send me a *Voyager*Direct catalogue today

Name ....

Address ....

....

....

Postcode ....

Send to Jeremy Millington, *Voyager*Direct, 77–85 Fulham Palace Road, Hammersmith, London W6 8JB.

Membership is free and there is no obligation to buy at any time.

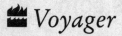 *Voyager*

www.voyager-books.com